Peripheries

Peripheries

Helene Littmann

CORMORANT BOOKS

The publisher gratefully acknowledges the support of
The Canada Council for the Arts
and the Ontario Arts Council for its publishing program.

Cover design by Bill Douglas @ The Bang

Author photo by Elaine Littmann.

Printed and bound in Canada.

Cormorant Books Inc.
RR 1
Dunvegan, Ontario
Canada K0C 1J0

Canadian Cataloguing in Publication Data

Littmann, Helene, 1960-

Peripheries : three novellas

ISBN 0-896951-08-2

1. Title.

PS8573.I87P47 1998   C813'.54   C98-900012-5
PR9199.3.L557P47 1998

CONTENTS

GROUND ZERO

GROUND ZERO

"These are the pictures the children drew at Lord Granville Elementary," said Claire. "After I gave my little talk last week. Aren't they wonderful?"

Poster paint on newsprint, blunt brushes; Stephanie, interested, shuffled pointed houses, balloon trees, cats bristled as spiders, stick dads and the mushroom cloud, the foul fungus variously black or red or — curiously — a livid purple.

"Don't they just, I don't know, tear your heart out? Sort of?" said Claire.

"When I was that age I used to get so frustrated," said Stephanie. "I wanted things to look real. I'd get furious when the grown-ups went on about how cute my drawings were."

"Look at this one," said Claire. "See, at the bottom she's written: I don't want nuclear war because I love my mommy, my daddy and my baby sister. Doesn't that just say it all, Stephanie?"

Linda came into the back office carrying a fresh cup of coffee. "Are those the kids' pictures?" she said, leaning over Stephanie's shoulder. "Oh, super excellent. We've got to do something with these. Use one for the poster."

"See this one, Linda?" said Claire. "It's a bit detailed for that. But he's put in everything, you know, that would, you know, blow up. See? My baseball mitt. My yellow stone from Yellowstone Park. All labelled. So much work."

"You must really have made an impression," said Stephanie.

"Well, I hope so," said Claire. When she smiled the skin around her mouth and eyes broke into fine wrinkles. "I try to be very clear and direct in these talks. To really concretize what's at stake."

"It's so wonderful that kids that age are getting politicized," said Linda. "They have such a gut-level grasp of issues."

"Exactly," said Claire. "They don't have any of the defence mechanisms of adults."

"Do you actually discuss politics with them?" said Stephanie, curious. "How much can they follow?"

"That's something we have to be very careful with," said Claire. "I mean, we're in the schools. We can't be seen to be partisan. All we can do is discuss the general issue. What nuclear war would mean on a personal level."

"The personal level is where you *get* people," said Linda. "The personal is where you *organize* from."

"Look at this one," said Claire. "She's written: I had a dream that the bomb went off and every one was gone, and I woke up crying but it was only a dream."

"I used to have nightmares about lightning and floods when I was a kid," said Stephanie. "Before I had heard about the bomb."

"See, that's because you probably knew subliminally about it," said Linda. "We're doing such a disservice to kids, telling them their fears are stupid. When we should be levelling with them so they can take action. Because kids *know* these things."

"Yeah," said Stephanie.

"Like my parents," said Linda. " They've got this wipe-smooth surface and nothing ever makes a dent in it. They just wanted to keep me in this bubble. When I went to university I was such an airhead. They hate it that I've started to think."

"We've always been very straight with Crystal," said Claire. "Like when we were getting divorced. We've always tried to make her realize she has to make all her own decisions."

"How is Crystal?" said Linda.

Claire sighed; her face sagged. "It's the age," she said. "Everyone keeps telling me not to worry. But I find the hostility very hard to take. Here is a child who has been brought up with complete permission. Nobody has ever thwarted her or misled her. And here she is tossing it all away. It's very hard to stand by and watch."

"How old is she?" said Stephanie.

"Fourteen. Fifteen this summer."

"I remember being fourteen," said Linda. "I'm sure you don't have to worry."

"I hope you're right, Linda," said Claire. "But I really want to shake her sometimes. She makes me so frustrated."

Claire and Linda went back into the front office. Stephanie lit a cigarette and riffled through the drawings.

Outside, rain was falling steadily, leisurely: confident rain, rain that would go the distance. It wasn't about to give up and blow away today or tomorrow, or this week or the next.

Inside, cold light strained through plastic panels, plastic light without depth or shadow. It fell flatly on plastic surfaces, the botched beige Dacron carpet, the woodgrain table chipped to reveal its heart of pressed fibre. A room scrounged on the cheap, temporary and urgent as the back rooms of all political campaigns. On the false table under false light, Stephanie spread the paintings.

Trees did not grow like green balloons, here on the coast amid the spindle of second-growth fir and weed alder. Likewise, roofs were not tipped and tilted in the flatness of ranch-house suburbia; mothers invariably had noses. Stephanie thought about learning, in college, to draw from life, the constant command to observe. But did drawing actually begin somewhere else, in notation of the idea rather than visible reality? In the magic of cave painting? The baseball mitt, the stone from Yellowstone, and the Labrador retriever named Killer: all roughly the same size, and the same shape.

The cloud itself, the unthinkable: it made its appearance in every size from fairy-ring toadstool to Niagara Falls, blending oddly, in a few cases, into forests of mushroom trees.

With such similarity of content, thought Stephanie, her task would be to pick the most graphically effective to illustrate the Teachpeace Teachers' Kit. Strong, simple lines that would reproduce well.

Families, trees, cats, babies. One exception. At the bottom of the pile, no colour, hard and obsessive pencil — rocketships blocked in with a straight-edge. And, Stephanie saw in a moment, a narrative of sorts: bubble dialogue and cartoon captions. *Z-Man is escaping the enemy ships. He let off a BOMB. The world was dead. Z-Man laughs hahaha,* a plume of smoke as the rocket shoots to Pluto.

She read it through, and then she giggled. She laughed. It

wasn't so much the content, as how he was thumbing his nose. If it was even that, and not a deep dreaming obsession turning every opportunity its own way. Of course she couldn't use it. But still, it raised a giggle.

Stephanie stubbed out her cigarette, picked up the paper and went into the front office. Claire, leaning over her desk, shiny bob discreetly tinted; Linda, wide hips by the photocopier.

"Did you see this one?" Stephanie said.

Claire looked up, squinted; her mouth fell. "They're quite concerned about that boy," she said. "It's rather sad. He's very much on his own planet."

Linda came over and took the page. She sighed. "You'll get this sometimes when you're organizing men," she said. "Identifying with the aggressor. It's one of the defence mechanisms. A way of being in denial."

"I can't help thinking that a boy like that has an awful lot of anger," said Claire. "It's so sad, what's been done to him, how he could draw that after everything I said to the class. It's a real slap in the face. I almost cried when I saw that picture."

"Oh," said Stephanie. She wanted to rescind her giggles. "He must read a lot of comics."

"Exactly," said Linda. "You said it exactly. We are raising little boys to identify with aggression. We are feeding them this crap."

"I know I felt almost physically sick when I saw that," said Claire. "It makes you think, are you getting through at all? Is anyone giving you any respect?"

"He might have meant it as a joke," said Stephanie.

"This is no joke," said Linda. "This is where the men who do violence come from."

"Well, I won't include it in the Teachpeace package," said Stephanie.

Claire and Linda stared at her.

"I was kidding," said Stephanie. "I wouldn't. Ha ha."

"Actually, we should have a section on denial," said Linda. "What to do when someone like this tells you nuclear war can't happen."

"That's an excellent idea, Linda," said Claire.

Stephanie poured herself a cup of coffee and went back into her office. She dropped the rocket-ship boy on top of the pile of paintings, nuclear plumes brash as hothouse flowers.

Outside, behind or above the curtain of rain, the afternoon tilted towards dusk.

Stephanie was not in denial. Stephanie had no defences up. The bomb, ground zero, incineration, all this merely confirmed something she had known her whole life. Only, as a child, it had been apolitical and idiosyncratic: the personalized lightning bolt, midnight burglars, the moaning maw of the furnace. And even if the bomb didn't go off, the world, Earth, was a failing system: economic collapse, ecological catastrophe, the simple algebraic calculation that said we would, sooner rather than later, just run out of space. You would have to wipe it all out and start fresh, reorganize. Or wait until it imploded, and build in the ashes. Of course, that wasn't possible with nuclear war.

Stephanie kept her eye firmly fixed on the worst in order to act against it. This also kept the fear at bay, the stab of fear deep in the bowels, like waking from first sleep, two a.m., thinking frantically *I don't want to die.* Punching the pillow to kill the thought. It could come up like that, the fear. If you didn't acknowledge it every minute. If you weren't always expecting the worst.

She lit another cigarette, she sipped her coffee, the rain kept falling.

The control room at the community radio station smelled of mice and dust. Stephanie flattened herself against the back wall. Joel was leaning over the mixing board, nudging down the faders. Tash, studio director, stood at his elbow wearing headphones, her eyes locked with Duncan's through the glass. She raised her finger, held it, let it fall as the music slid under and out. Joel pushed a switch; the monitor speakers snapped on.

"...representative of the federal government employees' union," Duncan was saying, "here to talk about the escalating conflict in the current round of contract talks. Good evening."

Duncan behind glass, sitting up straight so he could talk deeply, from his diaphragm. Using his intent look that Stephanie loved even when it wasn't directed at her, training it right now on a brown beard and hiking jacket saying seriously: "...refused to bargain in good faith. The membership had no choice but to go for a strike vote."

Joel flicked off the speakers to cue a record, whomp and

whomp as he spun the turntable. Duncan's lips moved silently, he glanced at his notes, leaned towards the microphone.

When Stephanie had met Duncan, her first thought had been that he was handsome, her second, oddly enough, that he wasn't; the clarity of his profile melted too closely into the ordinary, a point where blond became beige. And very shortly after, it had not mattered at all, because, desired, he became luminously himself, beyond judgement. Tonight, nearly two years later — two years in the spring — he was merely and totally himself: *Duncan*.

From the back of the control room Stephanie watched through the soundproof glass and thought, as she often had that fall and winter: *I love him*. She had not yet said this aloud. Why? For one thing, the knowledge lit her life so brightly that the words were almost redundant. Surely this, at the least, Duncan could tell, surely he felt the same. For another, declarations didn't suit, yet, the tone of their camaraderie. It was not yet time to speak.

Stephanie was leaning against the wall. The speakers sputtered on. Joel was pushing up the music under the voices. "Union hall," said the beard through the hiss of maracas. "Picket line. Benefit dance."

In a minute Duncan would be here beside her, edgy and excited as he always was after a broadcast, brushing his hair out of his eyes, asking Joel about dead air or a miscued tape at a quarter past the hour. Then they'd be out the door, all of them, down the stairs and into the night, hissing rain and vertiginous pools of neon.

In a minute he would be beside her. For now Stephanie leaned against the wall, watched the tilt of his head through the glass and waited.

The pub had special beer, brewed locally, and potato skins with melted cheese. Tash, Stephanie and Duncan stepped out at closing time into the rain's lull: damp air, drops sparse as tears.

"I know Linda," said Tash. "I went on the Peace Caravan with her."

"I think the job will be fun," said Stephanie. "I have to design a package for teachers."

"It's a rip-off they make you use up your unemployment benefits, though," said Duncan.

"I was getting so little UI from the job at Bookends," said

Stephanie. "I couldn't have lived on it much longer." A good job, she thought, and friends, and all the complex pockets of her day: the radio station, the pub with its pink walls and brass rails. *I've done it,* she thought. *I've put all the pieces together. I have a life.* She was mildly drunk.

"These cobblestone sidewalks are so fake," she said happily. "They just put them in ten years ago."

"The steam clock, too," said Duncan. "It went up in 1972."

"No way," said Tash, cheerfully ready to be scandalized. "It says on the plaque. It's the first steam clock."

"The only one," said Duncan.

"These lampposts are fake too," said Stephanie. "Everything down here is fake."

"Even the tourists," said Tash, getting into the mood.

"Especially the tourists," said Stephanie. "They come from a special tourist factory."

"It's in Wisconsin," said Duncan. He had lived there for a year as a child. "They have a big assembly line. One worker puts on the white shorts. The next one paints on the stunned expression."

"Another one slaps on the beer bellies," said Stephanie.

"You guys," said Tash.

"It's true. I've seen it," said Duncan.

"He's going to do a documentary," said Stephanie.

"Investigative journalism," said Duncan. "Ralph Nader is getting them recalled for factory defects. It's a terrible secret."

"Yeah," said Stephanie. "Some of them are trying to think for themselves."

"Running amok," said Duncan. "Leaving the tour group. Going slumming."

"You *guys,*" said Tash.

They had passed out of the renovated quarter while they were talking, and turned south towards Hastings Street, where the buses ran. Brick paving gave way to ordinary concrete. From the doorways of beer parlours, a stale fug of cigarettes and beer, alleys soaked in urine.

The girl was bare-headed, bare-armed, standing under the beer parlour awning. The man was ten feet away, coming towards her.

"You bitch. You fucking going to give it to me," he said.

She was walking backwards, listing slightly. "Fuck off, bastard," she said. "Fuck off and leave me alone."

Tash, Stephanie and Duncan slowed. The five of them were the only people on the street. Cars skinned by up on Hastings, tin music rattled through the walls of the beer parlour.

The man was five feet away from the girl. "You fucking bastard. Fucking go away," she said.

Tash, Stephanie and Duncan stopped.

The man grabbed the girl by the arm. They scuffled; she stumbled back against the building.

"Stupid bitch," he said. "You fucking going to pay."

Tash looked at Stephanie and they stepped forward, came up beside the girl. Duncan followed them. The man let go of the girl's arm and stepped back, looking deeply puzzled. He was not so old, younger than them, early twenties at most. But his face was staved in, thwarted, ruined. He concentrated hard, searching for his words. "Fucking bitch stole my lighter," he said finally.

"Fuck you," said the girl, rubbing her arm. "Fuck you."

"Come on," said Tash. "We'll walk you down the block."

"I want my fucking lighter," said the man. The girl stepped out from under the awning between Tash and Stephanie.

"Do you have his lighter?" said Duncan, speaking very clearly.

The girl giggled. "I took his bloody lighter," she said. "He's fucking flipping."

The man was standing under the awning. Tash and the girl, Stephanie and Duncan, were about ten feet away. The girl stopped.

"Come and get it," she shouted. "Come and get your fucking lighter. I got protection now."

The man stepped out from under the awning.

"Come on," said Tash. "Let's get you out of here."

"I got protection," said the girl. "You fucking try anything, we'll beat the shit out of you. You want to fight?"

"You bitch," said the man. "You going to pay."

"Let's get out of here," Tash said to the girl.

"Just try it," said the girl, and walked up to the man. He caught her arm and twisted it. "Bitch," he said. "Bastard," she said.

Tash hadn't moved. "Leave her alone, asshole," she said.

"Let's get out of here," said Duncan.

"We have to do something," said Tash. "He's going to kill her."

"Not tonight he won't," said Duncan. The girl was leaning against the brick wall, sobbing.

"There's got to be somebody we can call," said Tash. "Not the cops." The rain was starting up again. "There must be somebody that takes *care* of this kind of stuff."

"We're going to get soaked," said Stephanie. They walked down the block past the doorway of the radio station, and sat in the bus shelter.

"It's the blues show tonight," said Duncan, looking up at the lit window of the third-floor studio.

Tash sat huddled up, shaking on the bench. The night had shattered, irrevocably altered, become horrible and intimate. And also, Stephanie thought after a moment, that much more interesting.

"It makes me so sick," Tash said. "It makes me want to kill men like that."

"I know," said Stephanie. Neon bled down the pavement, the night was terrible and complex. But she hadn't been scared. It had been too sordid, too dramatic, for fear; it had been like television. Obviously this wasn't the right reaction. "She seemed to want to go back to him."

"That's blaming the victim," said Tash. "She's been brainwashed into thinking you need a man. Any man."

"Yeah," said Stephanie.

"She doesn't have a choice," said Tash.

The Victoria Drive bus glided to the curb.

"Our place or yours? It's really raining hard," Stephanie said to Duncan.

"I should have gone with Joel to that public meeting," said Duncan. "It was probably really important."

Stephanie's room was in the attic at the front of the house. Rain on the roof, on the black window, on the fire escape. She shivered as she stripped off her wet jeans and slid into bed beside Duncan.

"Cold hands," he said.

"Sorry," she said, and tucked them into her armpits. This late at night the sheets always felt twice as chilled, as if the damp came in after dark like dew. She switched off the bedside lamp. In the streetlight cracking through bamboo blinds, Duncan lay on his back, in profile: his beautiful profile. She kissed his cheek. He didn't roll over and kiss her back. She ran her newly warmed hand lightly down his body, letting her wrist casually brush his penis. Soft and sleeping.

"It's awfully late, isn't it," she said. "I'm pretty tired. Are you tired?"

"There wasn't anything we could do for that girl," said Duncan.

"No, there wasn't, was there," said Stephanie. "They need a crisis shelter down there. Like Tash was saying."

"There really wasn't. Not if she still wanted to go back to that guy."

"Yeah. She doesn't have a choice, yet."

"I mean I could have hit him or something," said Duncan. "Maybe I should have done something like that."

"Oh, shit," said Stephanie. "He probably had a knife. Besides, that's not really your scene. Your style."

"I could have done something like that."

"No. There wasn't anything you could do."

"Tash was really upset, wasn't she?"

"She's hanging out with those women from the rape crisis centre," said Stephanie. "She hears about this stuff all the time."

"The thing is," said Duncan after a minute, "it's really no different than in the suburbs. Only down on skid road it's all out in public. It just looks worse because everyone can see what's going on."

His parents had divorced, Stephanie knew. They had screamed and drunk and then divorced, and a year later his father, a lawyer, had died of a heart attack in another city.

"That's what Tash says," said Stephanie. "She says violence against women is everywhere."

"Yeah," said Duncan. He lay on his back with his eyes closed. Stephanie lay on her side, her hand resting on his flat belly. She was watching for his next word, but after a few minutes his breathing shifted, became deeper and slower, and broke into what was almost, very nearly, a snore.

Smudged white glare in the Portuguese coffee bar: walls and floor, and the little tin tables. Outside the plate-glass windows the afternoon fell hard and grey, hit the sidewalk, ran under parked cars and into the culverts of Commercial Drive.

Stephanie put her bag of vegetables on the floor and hung her leather jacket to drip on an empty chair.

"We need to bring all the issues together," said Tash. She had cut her hair very short except for a few thin braids here and there on her skull. "See, nuclear war and violence against women, at root it's the same issue. It's about power and attitude."

"Male aggression," said Stephanie.

"Exactly," said Tash. "Also things like the environment, poverty, all that. People think of them as separate issues. Then they get overwhelmed and feel powerless. But if they saw they were all one thing, they'd find it easier to act."

The owner of the coffee bar came out from behind the counter with their drinks. He was stocky and dark, middle-aged and glum.

"What did you order?" said Stephanie.

"A steamed milk," said Tash. "I'm trying to quit caffeine."

"I know it isn't very good for you," said Stephanie. She sprinkled sugar on the crest of her cappuccino.

"Actually I shouldn't be doing dairy either," said Tash. "It makes mucus. Like when you get a cold. You shouldn't drink milk."

"Oh really?" said Stephanie. She leaned across the table. "Joel said the owner here is a fascist. He said the photo behind the cash register is of some old general." They glanced towards the counter. The owner was lost in the hiss of the espresso machine.

"It's true he never smiles," said Tash. "Maybe we should boycott the place."

"But they make the best coffee."

"Actually I find the smoke in this place is starting to get to me," said Tash. "No, no. Go ahead and finish it. It's not too bad today. Just move your ashtray. Thanks."

"You were saying about the women and peace group," said Stephanie.

"We could do a bunch of stuff," said Tash. "Education work and leafleting. Maybe even a newsletter."

"A radio program."

"Do some actions."

"Go in the peace march."

They drained their cups, pulled on wet jackets, picked up groceries and went out the glass doors into the rain.

The Victoria bus hissed past, raising a fine cold spray. Down its length was plastered a bikini woman, odalisque.

"Shit," said Tash. "That crap makes me so angry. What does she have to do with orange juice, anyway?"

"I think the idea is, if you drink orange juice, you'll look like her," said Stephanie.

"This business of using women's bodies. Rape imagery," said Tash. "It's the same as pornography. It's there to keep us in our place."

"But it's everywhere, isn't it," said Stephanie.

"We're numb to it, for sure," said Tash. "That's one of the things we need to make people see."

They were walking downhill, cutting left away from the blocks of old houses, and into the zone of warehouses and light industry.

Their house was the last left on the block, boxed in by a body shop and an importer of jokes and novelties: seasonal balloons, squirt rings, exploding soap. The house itself tilted against the rain clouds, gabled and gaunt as the opening shot of a cheap horror movie. The rent was low; it looked abandoned. Stephanie loved all of this. Unwanted, the house was safely theirs; real security lay in surviving on the minimum. Driving past, you would never guess they lived there, never guess what they thought or what they did.

This made them less a target.

Today the image in Stephanie's mind was of cars, smoked windows and loud engines coursing through the dusk. The nonchalant smashed beer bottle, the hurled insult. At the close of a Sunday afternoon with Tash, fear definitely took the shape of men, random and faceless.

Stephanie and Tash went through the front door and dropped their groceries in the kitchen.

Bare floors, stripped and sanded but never varnished, high ceilings, wainscotting, shadowed corners. All this beauty cheap because out of fashion.

The walls shut out, to an extent, larger fears as well: the fireball, total collapse. The house itself was proof of resistance. The house refused to collaborate. It contained, by design, only what was strictly necessary: a big sofa from the Salvation Army, Joel's stereo and records, posters of the peace march and of Latin

American guerrillas, old handbills for concerts — the Normals, Stund — taped to the fridge, stark black and white.

Tash slumped at the kitchen table. "I'm thrashed," she said. "I'm going to crash out before supper."

"Good idea," said Stephanie. She climbed the stairs to her own room, changed into a dry pair of sweat pants and crawled under the blankets to warm up. With the lamp shining the room floated high above the wet street, the night. This early in the year, it was already dark.

Outside the rain fell over miles and miles of wet roofs, empty streets, and beyond that the gap and absence of forest and mountains, of nothing, going straight back to the Pole.

Stephanie concentrated on the light. Cozy. Secure. She was warming up. The rain was outside. It was the light that mattered.

She slept.

Claire took off Monday morning in lieu of a speech she'd made one evening the week before. Linda was at the library. Stephanie let herself into the office at nine a.m., and made a pot of coffee. She proofread a chapter of the Teachers' Kit, and corrected some typing errors. She pencilled a sketch of a little girl hard at work on *Alternatives to Aggression: A Check List*, and inked her in; then she drew two little boys peacefully sharing a baseball bat. But there wasn't much point doing illustrations this early, before she knew the amount of space available.

She poured another cup of coffee and tidied her desk. The hands on the clock barely moved. She took the two morning newspapers and flipped through them for clippings related to peace, nuclear war, nonviolence, cruise missiles and protest marches. Then she read the rest of the articles. Then she read the Lost Pets and Business sections, and the advice column. She filed the clippings. The rain came down. So dark outside that she could see her reflection in the window, as at dusk.

Eleven a.m.

She skimmed through a couple of reference books that lay on Claire's desk. These were the details, dry as high school history class, which she could never retain for long: megatons and treaties, the concentric circles of destruction, the feints and jabs of dead presidents. It was important to know all this, of course, if you wanted to give talks or write articles. Or if you wanted to convince a skeptic. But Stephanie never met any skeptics, except her parents, Christmas dinner three weeks ago in Victoria.

"I'm sure the generals don't want to blow themselves up, dear," her mother had said. "Is the turkey cooked all the way through? Are you sure? Don't take that pink piece. You'll get salmonella. Here, let me serve you."

Stephanie had been unable to marshal any arguments, had felt about nine years old, tongue-tied and irrelevant, a little girl rattling away over the adventures of her dolls and her cat.

Today in the office, she thought that, after all, these facts would convince no one, dry and unbelievable as textbooks. It took someone like Claire to make you feel the danger. And really, if you didn't feel a cause, how much support would you ever give it?

The books irritated Stephanie. Even faced with an exam, she wouldn't have been able to buckle down and memorize them. Their reasonable surface was an insult to what she already knew in her bones.

Eleven forty-five. She could take an early lunch. Surely someone would be back before she returned.

The office was east along Hastings, almost to the Burnaby boundary. Though the sidewalks were lined with little shops, there were fewer places to eat lunch than Stephanie had expected. She walked a bit, then settled for Noodle with Beef Brisket and Shrimp Flavour at the Guangdong Pearl, a big box of a place done up in pink and grey, a tank of sleepy lobster by the door.

Linda was at her desk when Stephanie returned.

"Gosh," said Linda. "I don't know what you can do. Claire might have something. She should be in soon."

Stephanie went into the back office. Out the window she could see a bare tree, and the blank stucco rear of an apartment block, small functional windows. An old woman came up to one of these, peered out at the ground, then drew the curtains. The rain kept falling. Stephanie watched a while. There was no further movement in the apartment. She opened the newspaper to the crossword puzzle but all the clues were for TV actors and sports stars.

Claire came in at two, dripping rain. She hung up her coat and propped her umbrella in the corner.

"I've just been to the Secretary of State office," she said. "This is so frustrating. I am so frustrated."

"What is it?" said Linda.

"I am so frustrated I can barely see straight. Pour me a cup of coffee, can you? I'm frozen. Thank you, Linda. So I wanted to get the next quarter of the Sec State grant into our account before they go on strike. Do you think they would? It can't come through until the first. Do you think our landlord here is going to say, Fine the government employees are on strike, you don't have to pay rent this month?"

"Shit," said Linda.

"They could be out tomorrow," said Claire. "What it is, is they don't seem to realize that we are actually working. It's like they think we're volunteers. Do-gooders. You start to wonder if you're getting through at all."

"When are they walking out?" said Stephanie.

"Nobody knows. And you, Stephanie. You're getting paid by Employment Canada. Your cheques will stop completely. You'll get them later, of course. How will you manage?"

"I should be okay for a bit," said Stephanie. This job had tripled her benefit cheque, and doubled what she'd made last year at the bookstore. She had already opened a savings account.

"Because you're making almost nothing as it is," said Claire. "I don't see how you can survive on it."

"My rent's pretty low," said Stephanie.

"I am barely making it from paycheque to paycheque," said Claire. "I have Visa bills from Christmas. Stan pays for Crystal's orthodontist, thank God. But we'll be out on the street if I don't get paid next month. Sec State want results, they want those monthly reports, but do they give us any respect? Are they paying any attention?"

"Bureaucrats," said Stephanie.

"Exactly," said Linda. There was a companionable pause.

"These drawings you did are adorable," Claire said after a minute. "We'll definitely have to use them somewhere."

"Is there anything else I could do?" said Stephanie.

"You have proofreading. And the clipping file?"

"Oh, I did that this morning."

"Aren't you efficient," said Claire. "That's just wonderful."

"Do you have anything else for me to do?"

"Oh, goodness," said Claire. "I can't think of anything. We really have to come up with some little project for you. Don't we?"

Boredom could hurt. It was possible to actually ache with boredom. Stephanie phoned Duncan at five.

"I'm just leaving work," she said. "Want to go eat?"

"I don't know," he said. "I'm supposed to finish some stuff for the newspaper." He worked three days a week for the *Collingwood Shopper-Advocate,* writing headlines, taking and printing photos, and rewriting the press releases that formed the bulk of the news copy. *Spring Craft Fair at Unitarian Church. Pepsi-Cola to Donate $5000 to Adventure Playground. Broadway Business Owners Press for Lighting, Security, Lower Taxes.* He had found the job six months ago, and had felt fortunate to get it, then. "I'm also trying to start that freelance piece," he added.

"The one about who on city council owns what in the city?"

"Yeah. Only I can't really come up with an angle. And I'm not sure if I should be slanting it at a big newspaper or a magazine."

"Shit," said Stephanie. "Come out and have dinner with me. That'll give you a break."

The pizza restaurant had flocked wallpaper and dim lighting. Stephanie arrived first, ordered a beer, read the menu and then the placemats. Blue ruins, the sea. Fluted columns out of first year Art History, truncated goddesses packed full of cultural meaning she would never grasp. Only here they were advertising cheap charter flights to the Mediterranean.

She had been eating in this restaurant for several years, she had played spot-the-typo on the placemats: *all fights guaranteed. Your homo away from home.* But tonight, for the first time, it occurred to her: you could go there. All you had to do was take your money, walk down the block to Odyssey Travel, buy a ticket, and there you would be.

In the Parthenon.

It still exists.

You could just go there and walk around. Inside history.

The thought seemed enormously audacious. It had never occurred to her before that the things and places she had studied still existed. That she could go and see them.

On the other hand, she had never been able to afford it. But now, by the end of the job, six months if she kept saving. Yes.

Of course, thought Stephanie, she couldn't walk away from the politics, or from Duncan. It was strange to be thinking of leaving right now when everything was finally coming together. But it was an idea. Yes.

Duncan came in through the door of the restaurant. He was shining. The whole grey day fell away. Stephanie was so happy she said, "Darn it, Harvey, I can't make heads nor tails of this damn menu. What the dickens are these anchovy things?"

"Let me see, Martha. They're like them vegetables, I reckon. Like them tall green vegetables. Shit, I'm tired," said Duncan, rubbing his eyes. "I've written pages and pages on this city hall piece, trying to set up the background, but I can't get it in focus. Yeah, a beer," he said to the waitress. "What do you want? The usual? Medium vegetarian?"

"Double cheese," said Stephanie.

"Medium vegetarian, double cheese," said Duncan.

"Work was pretty slow today, too," said Stephanie.

"I wish the paper was slow," said Duncan. "It's starting to eat up all my time."

"But you still have lots of time to do the radio and freelance."

"Theoretically. I should be able to. If I just got organized. I should be out there doing investigative reporting. Talking to editors. Except no one will touch the kind of stories I want to write. Obviously. I could blow the lid off this town, what I already know."

"You could do it on the radio."

"They aren't radio pieces. I see something with more analysis. A series. Tying it all together. Because what's at the root of it all is power and connections. If you could map all that out, basically you could explain and predict everything that goes down at city hall. People see things as separate issues. A freeway here, a zoning change, a building permit, a park, whatever. But it all goes back to who owns what. Who owns who. It's all basically one issue."

"You could do something so great," said Stephanie.

"I see it all laid out," said Duncan. "But it's hard getting it down on paper."

He sipped his beer. After a minute he said, "What it is, is we're all just wasting our time. Spinning our wheels."

"What?" said Stephanie.

"Like I'm doing this shit for this advertising rag. I should be putting my time into magazine work. Or writing a novel."

"You want to write a novel?" said Stephanie. "What about?"

"I don't know," said Duncan. "Stuff. Life. That's not important. I mean I can't even think about it now. Or I should go back and finish my BA."

"You're almost done, aren't you?" said Stephanie.

"But there's no time. No money. Like you. What do you want to do?"

"When?" said Stephanie. The question jarred her. When she thought about the future, she saw a grey wall. Or else smoking ruins. "What do you mean?" she said, playing for time.

"Like what do you want out of life?" said Duncan. "All this time, you've never said."

"What do I want?" said Stephanie. She lit a cigarette. "I don't know. Life is pretty much okay." The job, and Duncan, and the house. Politics. The hope that disaster foretold would hold off in the near future, at any rate: she would see Stund play on the weekend, and buy that pair of army boots.

You could not have that much hope for the *distant* future.

"I'm having an okay time," she said. Understatement. At fifteen she'd imagined adulthood as a series of grey boxes, the office typewriter, the high-rise bachelor suite. Fussy duty: sponging spotted skirts, dusting crumbs, dabbing correction fluid, the tedious skid and slip of shiny carbon paper, previsioned by grade nine typing class. And ten years later, life was nothing like that.

Ten years later, in fact, life was much more like the adolescence she had never had.

"I'm having fun," she added.

"Fun," said Duncan. "That's exactly it. We're all having fun. Doing nothing. You should be painting. Really you're an artist. Not using up your UI weeks on this make-work project. I should be writing a novel."

"But I don't want to paint," said Stephanie, alarmed. "Not right now. I don't have any ideas." She suspected now that she had never had any, her college admission portfolio a teenage pastiche of pencil portraits, dreamy unicorns and landscapes in careful perspective. The portfolio of a good girl. None of this had translated to the concepts and installations of the moment, clearly unconcerned with pleasing.

"None of us have any ideas," said Duncan. "That's just it."

"Working for the peace group is really important," said Stephanie. Her voice cracked; she was more upset than she had believed. "Don't you think it's important?"

"Oh, of course I do," said Duncan. "I think it's great you got that job. Only you're still selling yourself short."

"But what else could I be doing?"

"I don't know," said Duncan. "I just don't know."

After dinner, Duncan did not go home to work on his stories. Instead, they walked down the block and over to Stephanie's house. In the damp, the empty faces of the warehouses reared up stagelit by streetlamps. At the far end, in diminishing perspective, hung the lights of the office towers in the city centre, away west. Stephanie thought briefly that she could paint this. She loved these blank façades, absence of artifice or false beauty, that now signified home.

A moment later she knew she lacked the skill to balance all these slanting lines. And if she could, what then? The more realistic it turned out, the cornier it would be, verging on the genre of picture most often seen on the cover of rock albums.

She wouldn't try.

Tash was out, but Joel was in the kitchen.

"Haven't seen you in ages," said Stephanie.

"How's it going?" said Duncan.

"Wild," said Joel. "Sit down. Have a beer. It's really heating up. We're going to shut down the university."

"How so?" said Stephanie.

"Us student society staff are in the government employees' union. When they walk, we go out in sympathy. Throw up a picket line. There's only one road up the hill onto campus. It's so easy to cut it off. The support staff union won't cross."

"Wow," said Stephanie.

"Of course the university will get an injunction against us. That will take a day. Meanwhile we shut the campus down. Five of us can do that."

"Great," said Duncan. "Do you know when you're going out?"

"No one knows yet. Have to be ready any minute. Phone trees. Picket signs. The day we get called, have to be out there before seven a.m. Too bad it's not midterms or final exams. That would really piss them off."

"That's so cool," said Stephanie. "My boss at Teachpeace was freaking because if they strike, we don't get our next part of the grant. She's really straight. She used to be a kindergarten teacher."

"Yeah, shit," said Joel. "The peace movement is full of these small-L liberals now. No sense of politics. I hate them."

"She's got this teenage daughter," said Stephanie. "She's freaking because the kid's starting to hang out, and mouth off at her, and maybe smoke. It's so weird hearing it from the mom's point of view. I don't know what to say."

"Kid sounds really cool," said Joel.

"Yeah, I know," said Stephanie.

"Shit, when I was that age," said Joel. "This was in a mining town in Nova Scotia. Big union place, right? When there were strikes me and my buddies used to go tip over management's cars. Once we phoned in a bomb threat to the company office."

"Excellent," said Stephanie.

"Wild town," said Joel. "We used to get shitfaced every weekend in high school."

"High school," said Duncan. "We used to drop acid down in the empty container trucks by the railroad tracks. Go around and smash out the streetlights. Teenage wasteland all right. There wasn't any sense of politics in North Vancouver."

"Except, see, that kind of violence," said Joel. "It's about alienation. One step away from consciousness. You knew the whole set-up in the suburbs sucked."

"Yes," said Duncan. "We knew that for sure."

"You guys were so lucky," said Stephanie.

"Really?" said Joel. "What sort of shit did you get up to?"

"Nothing," said Stephanie. "I was a goof. A girl goof. A nice girl."

"No way," said Joel.

"It's hard to believe, isn't it?" said Duncan.

"No really," said Stephanie. "There was a bunch of us. We ate lunch in the French classroom on the top floor. The popular kids ate in the courtyard and the greasers hung out in the bushes and smoked. Nobody ever came up to our floor. It was really boring."

"So why didn't you go smoke in the bushes?" said Joel.

"You couldn't. Your personality got set in grade eight and after that you weren't allowed to change. All that was wrong with us was just we were kind of immature. We'd sit up there and giggle about popular boys we never talked to."

"Weren't there any boys that matched you?" said Duncan.

"Yeah. They ate in the biology lab. They played chess and tossed around cows' eyeballs. We wouldn't have been caught dead with them."

"You lacked class solidarity," said Joel. "You could have gotten together and overturned that place."

Stephanie laughed. "It wouldn't have worked."

"I bet it would have," said Joel.

"Nice idea," said Stephanie. But when she thought about those hazy lunch hours — spring sunshine, or closed in by the drone of rain — she knew revolt had always been out of the question. It would have been unsustainable. One kind word from a popular girl, one sneer from a tough one, and any of them would have defected immediately. On their own they could create nothing they valued, nothing lasting; they did not even much like each other.

A few girls had made it out, one to the drama club, another, unexpectedly, to the bushes. Fragile migrations fraught with policy and planning. Stephanie had not been able to imagine such a transformation for herself; she had waited it out.

It had not been so bad. Nothing had been expected of her. She had survived without damage, she now felt. Nobody had beaten her up; her name had never been written on the washroom walls. That was not such a bad thing.

She could not tell this to Joel, in fact could barely articulate it to herself. Instead she said, "The funny thing about being quote unquote intelligent wasn't that it was uncool, necessarily. It was more that it was something you were by default. If you weren't pretty or athletic or popular or tough, if you were just kind of a blank, then people decided you must be smart. Teachers too."

"Well, but weren't you?" said Duncan.

"That says something about our education system," said Joel.

"Yes, but," said Stephanie, "you got marks for neat handwriting. Not for having an analysis."

"And university is the same," said Joel.

"Not exactly the same," said Duncan.

"Essentially."

"Oh, essentially, sure. But there's pockets. There's good profs."

"There's a few," said Joel. "Hey. It's time for the news. The protest will be on."

Regional news: landslips and floods, contract talks continue between the government and its employees aimed at preventing a walkout that could take place with forty-eight hours' notice.

Hair shellacked, and face too. Younger than Claire, just a knife-edge line at each corner of the glossy mouth. Which pursed a bit in distaste as it said: "An unexpected welcome for the premier when he arrived on campus for the dedication ceremony today."

"Hey cool," said Joel. "This is it."

Hubbub and commotion, the camera panning wide. Stephanie saw faces she recognized. Caught in the eye of the news, they looked angry and confident. *Freeze tuition. Social Credit is discredit. They say cutback, we say fightback.* She wanted immediately to have been there, at the heart of the world, where something had happened: action. At the same time she knew that, in the crowd, she'd be most aware of a certain stagy artificiality. Taken aback of course by the audacity of stepping out of line, a little node of self-consciousness she knew she had to overcome. But also, the sense of performance. She wondered if anyone else ever felt that, and if she could read it in their faces through the time lapse of video.

A girl she knew by sight stepped up to the camera, or perhaps the camera zoomed in on her. The lens tipped and distorted her face, her mouth opened wide. "They're destroying our education," she shouted, breathless rush. "They're taking it all away."

Shellacked hair filled the screen. "A three-car collision early this morning is being blamed on poor weather conditions and lack of visibility according to Surrey RCMP."

"Is that all?" said Joel.

"I saw you in back with the banner," said Stephanie.

"They sure didn't get into the issues, did they?" said Duncan.

"This car accident gets more time," said Joel.

Stephanie and Duncan drained their beer bottles and climbed the stairs to her room in the attic. They stripped, crawled under the covers and turned to hold each other. Stephanie felt him begin to shift and harden against her thigh; she kissed his throat, the silky place below his ear.

Duncan pulled back. He still lay facing her, hand on her waist, but the length of their bodies no longer touched and clung.

"That was such bullshit, what I was telling Joel," he said. "About being cool in high school."

"You mean you never did acid?" said Stephanie. "That's hardly missing a major life experience. I wouldn't worry." She slid her hand along his side — dry and smooth — the bone of his hip. He felt delicious. She wanted to touch, to taste, to gobble him up.

"Oh, I did acid," said Duncan. "That part's true. And drank and smoked a lot of dope. But what I mean is, it wasn't cool. It wasn't fun. This was right after my dad was gone and we had to move into the apartment. I just had to get the fuck out of there at night."

"Yeah," said Stephanie.

"The thing was, my friends weren't really cool. They were just scummy. They set fire to cats. They sniffed glue. They were younger than me."

Duncan paused.

"Yeah, well," said Stephanie. "It's all gone now."

"It was just really gross and sordid. I don't think they even wanted me around, only they were always too stoned to care."

"Teenage wasteland," said Stephanie. "Like you were saying." His thigh was taut, muscled. Her hand fell to the cool cap of his knee and started inching upwards.

"I really hated it. Hated myself for hating it. At school I was more like those guys you were describing. Chess and cows' eyeballs. Actually, we were tossing around bits of pickled fetal pigs."

"Yeah. Well, *we* used to sit around ordering bubble bath from an Avon catalogue. I thought life would never begin."

"You would have hated me if you'd met me then."

"I bet I wouldn't have," said Stephanie. Right at his upper thigh, inner thigh, that slight bulge of muscle, the hair seemed to stop, skin polished as a hand. And then, a few inches upwards, the different crisp of pubes, the sideways slump of testicles, surprisingly cold, surprisingly heavy. How would it feel to always have to make do with all that flopping around down there? How could you ever ride a bike? She let her hand brush back up to belly. Semi-hard, she noted in passing.

"You would have hated me," said Duncan.

"I don't know," said Stephanie. Hard little nipples, hint of ribs. Honesty compelled her to add: "Well, maybe. Probably, I just wouldn't have noticed. You would have hated me, too. You would have said: Who is this boring girl? I bet you were checking out all the greaser chicks with the tube tops and the high-heeled clogs."

"I never met anyone like that. They weren't smoking up in the container trucks."

"It's a good thing we're grown up," said Stephanie. "It's a good thing we like each other now."

"Do you, though?"

"Dun*can*," said Stephanie, and kissed him hard, with a bit of tongue.

"Well, I'm just never completely sure," he said.

"How about when I do this?" she said. "Does this convince you? Mm? How about this?"

"That's nice," he said. He was completely hard in her hand. Stephanie pulled his body against her, slim and taut under her fingers, his hair silky fine under her lips, her skin awake and shining.

Linda was at the kitchen table with a cup of camomile tea. Stephanie was sitting in a straight-backed chair with a towel tucked around her collar. Tash took a snip, and another snip.

"It looks excellent," said Linda. "Really cool."

Stephanie put her hand to the back of her neck. She could feel the sharp angle, and below, the brushcut nape, so short it bristled under her fingers like the old-fashioned plush velour on the living-room sofa.

"It feels really neat," she said.

"Everyone's going to want to come rub your neck now," said Tash.

Stephanie unwound the towel and went through the pantry to the bathroom, built into the old back porch. She tilted into the mirror, delighted. Her hair, thick and straight, held the shape well. This cut was more extreme than you'd ever get in a beauty salon: shaved short on one side, on the other a heavy chunk to her chin. It marked her, this hair, it pushed her over one of the boundaries.

She shook the towel into the toilet and brushed away the snippets that clung to the seat.

"I think I'll dye it black," she said, sitting down at the table and pouring a cup of tea.

"That would look excellent," said Linda. "You could get away with it, too."

"I was in that corner store down the block," said Tash. "A couple of days ago. Have you ever looked at the magazines in there?"

"Are they really awful?" said Linda.

"I can't believe I've been going in there a year and I never noticed."

"It's amazing what you start to see when you pay attention," said Linda.

"I just felt all that aggression coming off those magazines," said Tash. "They really are advertisements for rape, like they were saying at the crisis centre. If I saw a guy buying one, I'd want to kick his head in."

"I won't go in places that carry stuff like that," said Linda.

"I'm not going in there again," said Tash. "I feel so sick now when I just go past it. Yesterday I went around the block on my way home."

"But all the little stores are like that," said Stephanie. The conversation excited her: direct and honest, uncompromising. She could not yet summon this much rage. The last time she had looked at a skin magazine, she'd been so young her only reaction was curiosity. Obviously she needed to work on her analysis, Stephanie thought.

"I know," said Linda. "That's why we need to start a clean-up campaign."

"Isn't that kind of like censorship?" said Stephanie.

"No. Not at all," said Linda. "Censorship is when the government stops something the people want. It's not censorship when it's grassroots. When it's about community standards."

"Just knowing they are there right now feels like an attack," said Tash. "It's like my neighbourhood isn't safe."

"It isn't," said Linda. "You're right. It should be. But it isn't."

"It's all this male aggression," said Tash. "I'm getting so sick of it. I'd just like to go in there and burn them all. You know?"

"Here's something you can do," said Claire. "This is the most up-to-date union directory we have. It's three years old. We need to start on a mailing list. Call the local ones and check we have the right addresses. Then you can type them onto labels."

Stephanie took the heavy book into the back office and set her coffee-cup and cigarettes beside the telephone. Ten a.m., and the rain sluicing down in ropes and cords, tangling on the windows, tying up the culverts.

After three days of doing nothing, it was hard to rouse herself to a set task. The phone still made her nervous, her own voice, thin and childish, stammering requests to polished receptionists. An hour later, Stephanie had confirmed five addresses and found three numbers out of service. For the rest, the phone had rung emptily into space, or wheezed and croaked into an answering machine. This was a relatively new invention, to which Stephanie was still unused. She found herself stuttering into a void, unable to end in the absence of a human voice cutting her off brightly with promises to pass on the message.

Stephanie put the sheet of labels into the electric typewriter and typed the five verified addresses. When she snapped the sheet from the machine, three labels wrapped and glued themselves, round and round, to the platen roller.

"Fucking shit," said Stephanie, and began scraping with the tip of a pencil. The lead snapped; she used her fingers, feeling the nailbeds pull back and tear under pressure.

When the roller was clean, Stephanie opened the book to the out-of-town unions. She wondered how to choose. After reading through the list, she went into the front office.

"Gee, I don't know," said Linda. "Claire's gone over to Sec State. I don't think she's coming back today. Why don't you go to lunch early? I have to wait for a phone call."

"The director was nearly arrested by the military," said Duncan. "This was during the 1970s. The whole film is about that coup."

"Shit," said Stephanie. "I never knew about all that. This is our stop, isn't it? I never thought a lot about that part of the world."

"The same junta is still in power," said Duncan. "Actually the Americans support them."

They hopped off the bus. Dusk, rain scudding down Granville, the pedestrian corridor closed to all but buses and taxis. This was right downtown, glass towers and art deco sandstone façades. But the shops at street level were cramped and faded: brass hook-ahs, Indian cottons, a newsagent selling expensive cocktail cigarettes, black and pink and silver. The new boutiques were all underground, in the mall.

Stephanie and Duncan walked down the street towards the movie theatre.

"We're kind of early," she said. They were passing the block-long bulk of the Hudson's Bay department store, windows shimmering with resort wear, white and navy, straw hats.

"Actually, I was thinking about getting a new razor," said Duncan.

"That could be kind of hilarious, going in," said Stephanie.

An expanse of marble, a breath of ersatz spring, brass sparkling, the discreet charm of music. Ranks and ranks of glass counters, behind which stood women of painstaking perfection, priestesses of beauty, each robed according to the colours of her order. A dozen different perfumes, chemical sweet, and a hundred promises, or prayers.

It was not hilarious. It was something else altogether, this knot in her stomach. Stephanie had set her back to all this years ago, had made herself into the antithesis of the wasteful traps of femininity: her chopped hair and leather jacket, her army boots. Antimatter to the material world. Surely, according to the laws of science, or science fiction, her presence here ought to cause a jolt, a puff, the disappearance of this delusion or illusion, ephemeral and false.

But that did not seem to be happening. If anything, it was Stephanie who was slowly fading amid the powdered noses and lacquered hair, revealed as neither outrageous nor daring, merely dull and ugly.

She never came into places like this any more.

That was just it. She used to. The knot in her stomach, she dimly sensed, was also about the years of back-to-school sales, September kilts in Children's Wear, her mother and the clerk of the moment tugging and poking, fingers down collars and up skirts, the humiliating spin in the green depths of triple mirrors. Obscure difficulties and shame: *Will it wash? Does she look like a little old lady? Is it marked down?* Shading as the years passed into muted tussles over neck and hemlines, muted because Stephanie had not yet begun to exert herself. Muted also because there was no point trying. By the terms of the store, and of her mother, she failed in advance, could not be revived by lipstick or the new colours.

She had failed, but at something meretricious; now she set herself to destroying it.

Still, the knot in her stomach worried her. It suggested she was not yet free. Of course if she were truly free, she would not be in here. The truly free did not buy electric shavers.

"This is amazing," said Stephanie. "It's like walking into the heart of consumerism. See how they make everything fake luxurious? That's so you think you're getting something really valuable. Ten cents' worth of grease for thirty dollars."

"They do all kinds of psychological studies," said Duncan. "I think the elevators are this way."

They waited by the water fountains; the minutes ticked by. They were joined by a bald spot in a grey suit, a younger brown suit and a woman in a cheap tailored skirt: secretary rather than lady executive. The woman tapped her toe, the grey suit checked his watch. The elevator didn't arrive.

"Caroline," said Duncan. His voice was grave, portentous and highly audible. "I have something to tell you."

"What, Fernando?" said Stephanie shrilly. "Oh, God. Not. Not."

The elevator pinged. The five of them got on. Stephanie and Duncan had a view of backs.

"Yes, Caroline," said Duncan. The elevator bumped and glided. "I'm sorry it's come to this. But I'm leaving you."

There was silence in the elevator.

"Oh my God, Fernando," said Stephanie. "How will I support little Bobby?"

"You won't have to," said Duncan. "Little Bobby goes with me."

"You can't," said Stephanie.

"I'm sure the courts will agree," said Duncan. "Once they find out about your drinking. Your drugs. Your orgies."

"Fernando," said Stephanie. "I didn't want to tell you this. But little Bobby is — is — is not your son!"

"He isn't?" said Duncan.

The elevator door slid open at Personal Appliances and Small

Housewares.

"Excuse me," said Stephanie. They stepped past three impassive backs.

"You must tell me who!" cried Duncan.

The door snicked shut behind them.

"His father is your half-brother Reginald," said Stephanie.

"Oh my God," said Duncan. "This way," he added in his normal voice. "Ma'am," he said with a country drawl, eager and servile, "do you want a Cuisinart with sixteen attachments? Stirfreezebakeboildice? Can I interest you in a home espresso centre? Surely you need a bread-making machine, a little lady like you?"

"A bread-making machine?" said Stephanie. "Shit, you made that up. Oh shit. There it is. Make your own Wonderbread at home. I don't believe it."

"May I help you?" said a clerk, rather icily, appearing at her elbow.

"Perhaps," said Duncan, very dignified. "I hope so, anyways."

Stephanie and Duncan came in the street-level door and up the stairs to the Oddfellows' Hall. They could hear the bass beat through the walls, and Stephanie took the steps two at a time, thinking the band had started. But when they reached the top, paid and had their hands stamped, she saw it was only the sound system, cranked up.

"Great turnout," said Joel, leaning towards her and shouting. "This will really help the legal defence fund."

"Hi," said Tash. "How was the movie?"

"All right," said Stephanie.

"Excellent," said Duncan. "You have to see it."

"I've never been here before," said Linda. "It's kind of interesting. The music's pretty loud, though."

"It gets louder," said Stephanie.

"Oh, no," said Linda.

"Actually the smoke is really starting to bug me," said Tash.

"It's time I got up there," said Joel.

"We got to go watch him," said Linda.

They pushed their way to the stage, through the crowd: short hair, men and women both, jeans, T-shirts.

"Profits tonight," Joel was saying into the microphone, "are going to help the students arrested for trespassing at last year's sit-in."

Cheers and applause.

"Trumped-up charges. But we won't be intimidated. The legal defence committee will meet all the costs. Make this a test case. Free speech."

"He sounds really, really good, doesn't he?" said Linda. "Yay, Joel!" She clapped her hands.

"The first band tonight," said Joel. "X-Site. From Vancouver."

Hard chords and a blur of drums. The lyrics were drowned, a snarl of rage. The lead singer bounced stiff-legged, overbalanced, grabbed the microphone stand, teetered backwards, as if the music buffeted him like rain. He wore a plain T-shirt, old pants, cheap sneakers. His hair was cut brutally short, bringing out a perverse beauty like old photos of young soldiers or prisoners. The crowd in front of the stage was starting to move in imitation, a zero degree of dancing, sprung grace.

Yes, thought Stephanie. The night swooped to a point, gelled, took shape. She had seen this band before; they were not the best. But, playing live, they were enough to pick her up, make her yearn to be the one on stage, capable of opening her mouth in a line of rage.

X-Site crashed to a halt. The crowd up front started stomping for an encore. Duncan was talking to Joel. Stephanie pushed her way back through to the washrooms.

Linda and Tash were sunk deep in the broken sofa in the anteroom to the ladies' toilet.

"Did you like that band?" said Linda.

"They're okay," said Stephanie. "Stund are way better. They're on next."

"I don't know," said Linda. "I think I'm just going to go home."

"You can't," said Stephanie. "Stund are excellent."

"It's too loud," said Linda. "I've got a headache. And I don't like being up in the crowd like that. Everyone pushing."

"You can stand at the back."

"You can't see there. I think I'll just take off. Sorry, guys."

"I'll come with you," said Tash.

"You're going to miss Stund!" said Stephanie.

"I've seen them lots," said Tash. "Actually, I'm getting kind of sick of this scene. You know?"

"We got to say goodbye to Joel, though," said Linda. "Where's Joel, Stephanie? Did you see Joel out there?"

When Stephanie came back out of the washroom, Linda and Tash were gone. She bought another beer and found Duncan.

Stund came out on stage. Unlike the first band, they didn't launch into a fast song, three chords and three minutes. They stood completely still. Only the guitarist's fingers moved. The melody he was playing, over and over, was harsh and angry, slow and heavy anger, building.

The hall went silent. Nobody chatted near the ticket table, or laughed by the hatch where the beer was being sold. The band had everybody, had their undivided attention. The slow heavy guitar said despair and rage were the only logical response to the world. After a while the bassist began moving his fingers, and the drummer picked up his sticks. Then the lead singer took the microphone from the stand.

Stephanie knew the lyrics. There was not much to remember. *You cannot tell me no. And you can not. Tell me no. And you cannot tell me. No.* Just that. It worked. They had something, intensity or insanity. Stephanie did not want to be them or know them, certainly not to sleep with them. They looked damaged in ways she found too familiar: gawky and lost, unable to dissemble failure. But the music went past all that. It went right past it.

Out on the wet sidewalk at one a.m., Stephanie's ears were ringing, and her skin too, as the wet air hit. She walked down the street with Duncan, past tall wooden houses, Edwardian gingerbread.

Tucked in at the end of the block, a police cruiser, lights doused. Bulked shadowed shoulders inside.

"They've got us staked out," said Stephanie.

"Of course," said Duncan. "They were around earlier insisting on seeing the liquor licence. Wanting to shut things down. Joel said."

Stephanie and Duncan walked east into a net of short streets laid without plan when the farms were broken up at the turn of the century. Duncan lived in the basement of a huge house, a double mansion, long gone into the half-life of apartments.

They went in a side door past the dimness of furnace and water tank, concrete tubs, the white geometry of washer and dryer, and behind that a chill mystery of beached lawn chairs, summer's mowers, flammable paint tins, lethal rakes and hoes, ex-tenants' trunks never sent for, a threat of spiders and mice.

His room had been built into the basement, Gyproc walls and the carpet laid over a raised plywood floor.

In his narrow bed, they made love that was practised and efficient, love based in the pleasures of the night: the music, the film, even the gilded non sequitur of the department store. But it was also love diluted and filtered by all this. Then they curled up and slept.

When Stephanie woke the next morning, the room was deep in twilight. Duncan slept on, toppled by fatigue. Stephanie pulled on T-shirt and panties and shivered out the door across damp concrete to the toilet. She washed her face, then used finger and cold water to rub her furred teeth.

She crawled back into bed. The clock radio brightly blinked 10:07. In the dusk, bulk of desk and typewriter, armchair, bookcase, skids of paper, magazines, crumpled clothes. There was not enough light to think about reading. She snuggled against the curve of Duncan's back and slept.

When they both awoke it was half-past eleven, Stephanie sodden now with too much sleep, and hungry, drawn out like the day. It was no lighter in the room. Duncan switched on the lamp, and went out the door. Stephanie could hear the tin rattle of the shower, on and on. She dipped on the floor for an old news magazine, read mechanically, retaining only an impression of crisis and urgency. Her stomach hollowed out, caved in; she smoked a cigarette. This early in the day, it tasted filthy, and her throat hurt. Duncan came in, freshly shaved, bathrobe and two cups of instant coffee.

"There's no milk," he said. "We'll have to go out for breakfast." He leaned over to the clock radio and switched on the noon news. Wash-outs and walkouts threatening locally, on an international level talks continue aimed at reducing Soviet arms stockpiles, the Vancouver Stock Exchange calling for an inquiry into allegations surrounding conflict of interest in the Goldstar Mines affair. A three-alarm fire. A foiled hold-up.

"Oh shit," said Stephanie. "That's Uncle Freddy."

"The armed robber?" said Duncan.

"No, I'm sure it was Goldstar he was promoting last year. I'm sure it was. He's not really my uncle. He's Dad's cousin or something."

"I thought your father worked for the provincial government."

"Yeah, he does. Energy and Resources."

"And his cousin is selling mining shares?"

"He does what they call venture capital. They sell shares in new mines to get the money to open them up."

"Isn't that all a big scam, though?" said Duncan. "Half the time, isn't there nothing in the ground? The stocks go up and up and crash, and then the last buyers are left bankrupt?"

"Oh, there's usually something in the ground," said Stephanie. "They have to get geologists' reports for the prospectus. But yeah, a lot of the time, in the end, it's not worthwhile to dig it up. Only that's after."

"After what?"

"After Dad and Uncle Freddy have sold their shares."

"Stephan*ie*," said Duncan. "Your father buys and sells shares in mining stocks?"

"Yeah. Real capitalist, eh?"

"It's *illegal*," said Duncan. "Your father works for the Ministry of Mines. They regulate this stuff. He can't buy shares in it."

"He doesn't regulate. He's in the finance department."

"Still," said Duncan. "I never knew you were up on all this."

"I'm not, really," said Stephanie. "I used to like looking at the geology maps when I was a kid. Granite, shale, schist."

"If what you're saying is true, it's totally illegal."

"Maybe I've got it wrong, then. Mom was always saying Dad and Uncle Freddy weren't doing anything wrong, and besides everyone knew about it."

"Still."

"They're so straight. They're such fuss-budgets. You'd know what I mean if you met them. They don't even know I smoke."

Stephanie and Duncan dressed and headed out past looming appliances. Her jeans were still damp; she shivered in the chill afternoon. They leaned into driving rain and walked to the cash machine on Hastings Street, then along, nearly two p.m., to a dusty diner serving all-day breakfasts.

After eggs and sausages, toast and jam, and three cups of coffee, Stephanie felt better. Rain snaked down the windows, the afternoon already sliding backwards into night.

"I was going to get an early start. Do some work," said Duncan.

"Guess you blew it," said Stephanie.

"I should be home right now," he said. He didn't move. The rain hit the window behind him in a gust. The waitress topped up their coffee-cups. "This newspaper crap is taking up all my time. I hate it."

"Yeah," said Stephanie. She was finally warm for the first time since leaving the Oddfellows' Hall last night. In no hurry to plough back out into the downpour. "Well, go if you want," she said, fairly confident he wouldn't.

"I should," he said. "I really should. Right now." He popped a cream into his coffee, stirred and sipped, elbows on the table. Fatigue and sadness made him look young and vulnerable and touching. Watching him in the grey wash of light, holding onto him a few minutes longer, knowing he wouldn't leave until she did, Stephanie felt entirely at peace, suffused, pleasantly exhausted.

They had not made love that morning. Now, after eating, she felt her skin and blood start to rise. Was there much chance of following him home, or of extending the day to dinner and bed?

"I have so much work to do," said Duncan. "I shouldn't even be here."

Silver morning. With coffee-cup and sewing shears, Stephanie pored over the morning papers. Headlines: *Stalemate in Soviet Stockpile Talks*, snip snip, as well as AP afterthoughts cowering in crevices of back-page advertising: *Women Form Human Chain Round British Air Base.*

She laid aside the gutted, fluttering news section. Business: look for arms deals, nuclear plants, the international sales of high-tech bomber jets.

Regulators on the VSE will decide this week whether to proceed with an inquiry into possible conflict of interest between the provincial government and several publicly listed mining companies, particularly volatile Goldstar Resources Ltd., whose crash last week set off reverberations throughout the industry.

"Shit," said Stephanie. She scanned the article. First page, top story, of the business section. No names mentioned. *A prominent stock promoter.* Was Uncle Freddy prominent? *Sources close to the premier.*

The door to the front office clicked open. Stephanie flipped the business section face down, displaying its dull rump of classified ads.

"You're still doing that stuff?" said Linda. "Do you have time for lunch?"

"This can wait," said Stephanie. On her first day, Claire had taken them out for pizza. Since then, Stephanie had eaten alone, Linda and Claire absent or busy.

Lunching with Linda, someone to chat with in the epicentre of this grey day, felt almost festive. The gaiety increased with the wide scarlet umbrella Linda flared at street level. The frantic rain scrabbled harmlessly as they walked shoulder to shoulder towards an Italian restaurant.

Stephanie broke her garlic bread, sipped coffee, sprinkled soapy Parmesan.

"Joel made a really good speech the other night, didn't he?" said Linda. "He's super-involved with the student society, isn't he?"

"Yeah. They're getting really militant," said Stephanie.

"He seems like a super-nice guy."

"Joel? Oh, yeah." Stephanie had no cause to think Joel not a nice guy. She had never paid that much attention to him. And, even though they were sharing the house, his attention seemed elsewhere, too. "He's not home a lot," Stephanie added.

"Tash knows him really well, though."

"Oh, yes," said Stephanie. "They used to go out."

"But that's been over a long time."

"Oh, yes. At least a year. But they're still really good friends. It's not a problem them living together."

"That's so wonderful," said Linda. "I think it says super-good things about a guy when he can do that."

"All this about big break-ups and broken hearts," said Stephanie. "It's so old-fashioned."

"Totally," said Linda. "Tash was saying Joel's involved in that union coalition. It's kind of impressive."

Stephanie waited until the long-distance rates dropped at eleven p.m., and shut the door to the living room.

"Well, what a surprise," said her mother. "Is everything all right?" Strained through cable and sea-bed, her mother's voice sounded just that: strained and washed out. "Is something wrong, dear?"

"No," said Stephanie. "I was just calling. I'm still working and everything."

"Isn't that nice. You're just calling. And the job's fine. Money okay."

"Yes," said Stephanie. "How are you?"

"Oh, we're fine. Yes. The daffodils are almost out. We're fine. Nothing's happening."

"Mom. Um. What was the name of the mining company Uncle Freddy was selling?"

"Mining company?" Her mother's voice raised and frayed an extra notch. Her little laugh was thin as water. "I don't pay any attention to your father's family. What they do. I wash my hands of it."

Stephanie ignored this. "Wasn't it Goldstar?"

"Oh." Her mother's voice dropped five notches to somewhere near its normal register. "You've been reading the papers."

"Uh-huh."

"I want you not to worry about this," her mother said firmly. "Don't let it disturb you in the least."

"I wasn't worrying." This was true; Stephanie took for granted her parents' imperviousness and power.

"Good. You keep on that way. Nothing's going to get linked to anybody. Not that anyone did anything wrong. It's only what everyone has been doing all along."

"That's what I figured."

"Good girl. Don't worry about it. The premier has been very nice, very gracious. He personally phoned your father at home. He was very, very kind. Your father appreciated it very much."

"Gosh."

"You have to remember that your father has friends. Your father is a well-liked man."

"What about Uncle Freddy?"

"Your Uncle Fred can take care of himself. Don't you worry about him."

"Oh, I wasn't."

"Good. The main thing I'm praying now is that it stays out of the media. The last thing I need is TV cameras camped under my magnolias."

"There weren't any names in the paper today."

"Hopefully there won't be, at all. We're taking care of that on this end. Now, listen. You're going to need some new clothes for this job. You need to look smart. When this little mess sorts itself out, come over for the weekend on the ferry. We'll go shopping. Smarten you up."

"Oh, I'm fine with what I have." This was what alarmed Stephanie, the difficult diplomacy of steering her disappointed mother from blazers and silk blouses towards necessary T-shirts, woollen socks, cotton panties.

"Money's not a problem, if that's what you're thinking. You looked so shabby at Christmas. I didn't want to say anything. But as soon as this little mess sorts itself out. I wouldn't want you turning up in the middle of anything unpleasant."

"But what's really going on?"

"Absolutely nothing at all. Business as usual. Actually our lawyer has suggested we not get into details on the phone. You probably think I'm being paranoid."

"Not at all. Joel, he's one of my room-mates, he's always saying the cops tap phones all the time."

"He sounds like a very clever young man. Now I want you not to think about this. And come over as soon as it's sorted out. You understand?"

Two a.m., rain thinned to fine mist. Stephanie, Tash and Linda went down the porch stairs. The streetlamps lit the block flat and yellow: bare of trees, flat-faced as stage set or museum diorama. Nothing moved besides the surface of puddles minimally disturbed by the drizzle. In the distance, the hum and grind of the city, the plaint of shunting trains. Up close, nothing, a hush. A car ripped by on the through street two blocks over, and out of earshot.

They walked to the end of the block. Linda took up position on the corner, Stephanie at the other side of the little grocery store. Tash was wearing an old raincoat, a man's coat, oversized and deep-pocketed. From this she pulled a spray can and walked up to the shop front. *PORN KILLS*, across glass and stucco in hasty big letters. Stephanie caught the hiss of propellant, whiff of fumes. The coast remained entirely clear.

Her heart was pounding, she was trembling, and not from

fear: she felt more or less invincible. This was elation, and release, too, after the long hours drinking peppermint tea and watching the kitchen clock lurch round. The release of battle, a sharp
sweet hum.

Tash stepped back and put the can in her pocket. They took
ten seconds to gaze proudly, then set off down the block.

"That looks so great," said Linda.

"Where next?" said Tash. "How about this wall?"

Linda and Stephanie took their places as lookouts. Tash's
finger pointed, hissed and wrote: *PORN IS THE THEORY, RAPE IS
THE PRACTICE.*

"That's so true," said Linda in her stage whisper. They walked
on to Commercial Drive, shoebox little shops locked down for
the night. The road sloped away empty.

Point and hiss, blank walls and shop fronts. *RESIST VIOLENCE.
KILL RAPISTS. TAKE BACK THE NIGHT. STAMP OUT VIOLENCE
AGAINST WOMEN.*

The street slept on, not innocent or trusting but oblivious,
deep in its own dreams. Butchers and bakers, and beeswax can-
dlesticks in the health-food store. There were shops Stephanie
patronized: the Portuguese coffee bar, the health-food and greengrocers', the little diner serving cheap breakfasts, the second-
hand bookstore. These glowed for her like the lightbulbs set into
the huge relief map of the province, down Hastings Street at the
Exhibition grounds. Ping, and ping; one by one the lonely towns
of the Interior lit up, hopelessly sundered by ridge on ridge of
plaster mountain, dull green paint signifying forest.

Likewise, dull green was the colour of the shops Stephanie
never entered, never considered as to interest or viability. Snaky
high heels, Italian leather, very expensive. Odyssey Travel, tonight advertising charter flights to Hawaii and a portable life-size
hula girl — *THIS EXPLOITS WOMEN* across the glass behind which
she tilted, smiling her paper smile at the sidewalk. The butcher's:
MEAT IS DEATH. A tailor's vivisected suit jacket, amputated arm-
hole plump with manly layers of felt and lining. A furniture store
guarded by a pack of life-size porcelain Dalmatians. The billiard
hall that pocketed local teenagers rather than university students.

The co-ordinates of Stephanie's neighbourhood were imposed
on all this, or underlay it, or were perhaps a parallel universe. It
was only tonight, while it slept, that she could raise her eyes from

the pavement and look straight at it.

Their mission helped. The thrill went deeper than shivers of mischief. It lodged in the knowledge that they were, quite literally, making their mark. No one could ignore the trail of red letters up the Drive.

WOMEN ARE EVERYWHERE, Tash sprayed in three-foot letters on a blank wall. "It's probably enough," she said. "For now."

Stephanie could have kept going for ever, wild and wired. But walking home discreetly, through sidestreets of old houses, the tension eased; she was soon tired and cold.

"We'll need that mailing list by Friday," said Claire. "Don't bother checking the addresses. They're mostly probably all right."

If you pressed too hard, the typewriter went into spasms, sputtering staccato up to the carriage return. This was a new development. Stephanie's spine drooped with exhaustion.

She saw, with approval, that she was losing her taste for the slow grind, remote control, of this kind of politics. Mailing lists for press release, generating perhaps speaking engagements, generating perhaps donations for further publicity. No doubt it would all add up to something in the end. If the end didn't come first. But didn't Joel's picket line get the message across faster? Not to mention Tash's spray paint?

But you couldn't get government grants for spray painting. You couldn't get a *job* doing graffiti. That was all this was, she thought. A job.

Stephanie finished a sheet of labels and went into the front office for a fresh cup of coffee.

Claire was leaning back in her chair, somersaulting a pencil against her desk blotter: lead, eraser, lead. Eraser. Linda was sitting on the edge of her own desk, feet swinging.

"Crystal picks them just to bother me," Claire said. "She comes up the back stairs with a new boy and this kind of smirking, calculating look on her face. Kind of, what's Mom going to say about this one, eh?"

"Shit," said Linda. Stephanie came up and sat behind her, in the desk chair.

"She can't possibly like them. They look like little criminals," said Claire. "Little punk rockers. She's doing it to get at me. She's jealous of me and Ali. She can't stand it that I'm seeing someone finally after all these years."

"It would really change things between you, for sure," said Linda.

"That's what she can't accept, of course. That I'm able to go out and have a life too, at my age. And that he's younger than me. And she can't accept the difference in, you know, culture. Ali is always a perfect gentleman to her. She acts like he's something I'm doing to her personally. She acts like he just wants to use me to stay in the country. Which is ridiculous because, like I tell everyone, he's already a landed immigrant."

"Yeah."

"You really hope you haven't raised a child with, you know, those sort of values. Someone who just makes snap decisions based on how people look. It's so difficult."

"Well, it is a big change for her."

"I know. I keep trying to see it her way. To understand that she's just jealous, and vindictive, and a bit immature, and that she needs to turn everything to do with boys into a battleground. I keep trying to accept this and rise above it. Hello, Stephanie. How are you making out with the labels?"

"Oh, fine. I just came in for coffee."

"Oh, no problem. Take your time. When you're finished, I'll give you the list of school boards."

"This tea is very good for women," said Tash, filling her cup. "It purifies the blood. It gets rid of toxins."

"Excellent," said Linda, pouring for herself.

Stephanie sipped. Fresh-cut lawn with acrid, lawnmower undertones. She reached across the table for the jar of honey.

"White sugar is incredibly bad for you," said Tash. "It actually strips the body of nutrients and stuff. That's because it's so re-fined."

"I super want to find out more about herbs," said Linda.

"Go talk to them at the health-food store," said Tash. "Read the labels. It's easy to educate yourself."

"My mother used to just pop Aspirins into us whenever we had the sniffles," said Linda.

"That's so bad for you," said Tash. "When you get a cold, it's actually the toxins coming out of your system."

"She was one of those people who believed everything she

heard. She just wanted us to be perfect. It was so disgusting."

"Shit," said Stephanie, adding more honey to her tea.

"But, see, I really went along with it," said Linda. "I was a cheerleader. I was on the volleyball team. When I was in grade eight I was going out with this wrestler in grade eleven."

"A jock," said Stephanie. "Were you a real snob?"

"I don't know about snob. I just wanted to do everything right. I let guys have so much control over me. Then when I got to university and got involved in politics I was so mad at all the time I'd wasted. I could see all the guys thought I was really stupid."

"It wasn't your fault," said Tash. "You were programmed into it."

"Oh, totally," said Linda. "I totally know that now."

"I ran away when I was sixteen," said Tash. "For a couple of months. I lived with these hippies down by the beach."

"That's so cool, you did that," said Linda.

"My parents were giving me so much shit all the time. My dad would just scream his fucking head off. My mom freaked if I brought guys over. I went back and finished school, though. Then they were real shits about it when I went to university. Always like, what do you need money for that for?"

"God, yeah," said Linda. "When I came down to Vancouver mine would only let me live in residence. They thought I'd go wild otherwise. Then I had to convince them there was so much partying going on, I couldn't study. I mean, it was true."

"I've heard about the residences," said Tash.

"There were rapes there," said Linda. "This is mixed res, guys and girls on the same floor. A lot of drinking. Girls would pass out. Or there'd be a group of guys. It happened a lot. Well, not a lot. But I knew of a couple of cases in just one semester. Ones that I knew for sure, for myself, that happened."

"Didn't anyone call the cops?" said Stephanie. She was fascinated, appalled and somewhat out of her depth.

"Well, they couldn't," said Linda. "These were guys they knew. Or they were drinking under age. Their parents would kill them. It was the same back in the town I came from, in high school. You knew about it but you never said."

"There was nothing like that in my school," said Stephanie. "Or else I never heard." Life, she thought. All that had been going on down below, out in the bushes or behind the courtyard.

"In my school everyone was too laid back to rape," said Tash. "We smoked up all the time. It was the end of the hippies. You slept with whoever. If you held out, you were uptight. Frigid."

"That's a drag too," said Linda. "In my school you had to be going steady. Or else you got called a slut."

"Any time you don't really want to, that's actually rape," said Tash.

"You're right," said Linda. "You can feel like you've been raped even if you didn't say no."

"If you felt like you couldn't say no."

"Lots of times women can't say no. They're too freaked out or embarrassed."

"It's all about conquest for the guy. He's not going to stop and ask how you feel," said Tash.

"It's such an ego thing for them."

"If most women can't say no, it makes you wonder. Most sex is then actually rape. It really is," said Tash.

"It was totally different for me," said Stephanie, wanting to make a contribution. "I went through high school wanting a boyfriend and never having one." She now thought she would have preferred experience, any experience, and hence the right to be so richly derisive, so positive, so engaged.

"You didn't miss a thing," said Tash. "I don't know how many guys I've slept with. I lost count. I think now I just need to not be around men for a while. You know?"

Stephanie walked up the short street through the rain, and into the basement of the old mansion, past the mumbling furnace.

Duncan was slumped on his bed watching the late news, papers and magazines shifting between the sheets.

"Hi," said Stephanie. "It's pissing down out there." She hung her wet jacket on a chair. "I thought you were going to be writing this evening."

"Yeah," said Duncan. He had his knees to his chin, pillow between back and wall.

"Did you get anything done?"

"Not really."

"Shove over a bit," she said. He moved fractionally. "Were you watching TV again all night?"

"There was a documentary on Nicaragua. Wait a minute. This is kind of interesting."

"...*implications of insider trading that could reach the upper echelons of the provincial government in Victoria.*"

"Remember? What I was saying about my uncle?" said Stephanie, acting on a resolution she'd made after her phone call to her mother.

"What was that?"

"I thought he was mixed up in all this. I was wrong," Stephanie said quickly. "It wasn't him. Nothing to do with him. Or my dad."

"Oh, that. No, I was pretty sure you'd got it wrong."

"Totally. I bet the government is pretty corrupt, though," said Stephanie, not sure herself if she was offering this as atonement for her blatant but necessary lie, or playing with fire.

"Not as corrupt as you were saying."

"No. Of course not." The untruth came so easily that she did not even pause to wonder. She had after all kept from her parents the harder edges of her real life; this then was only a reversal. "Did you get much work done?" she added.

"Piss all. I have to do this advertising supplement for the paper. Puff pieces on local business. Total bullshit."

"Yeah."

"Journalism is shit," said Duncan. "It really is pointless."

"What would you do, then?"

"I don't know. I should have gone into law."

"Like your dad."

"Not like him. Totally different. He got sucked into working for corporations. That's what killed him."

Duncan leaned over to the foot of the bed, and flicked channels. "This was a good movie," he said. White men in black suits walking through a grey park. Duncan crawled back against the wall. Stephanie was sitting cross-legged beside him on the bed.

"After he left I used to imagine getting together and having a really good talk," said Duncan. "Now that the divorce and all the fighting were over. I kept meaning to write him or call him long distance. But I kept putting it off. And then he was dead."

"Shit."

"I kept imagining this bachelor apartment he had in Edmonton. I never saw it. I guess I put it together out of *Playboy* and *Penthouse*. You know, black leather sofa, white carpets, stereo, high-rise view. He died crawling across the carpet trying to reach the phone. That's what my mother said."

"You read *Playboy?* And *Penthouse?"*

"When I was a kid. My father got them sometimes."

"But that's pornography. Didn't it make you see women as total objects?"

"Women as total objects?" said Duncan, a bit blankly. "Did I see them as total objects? I don't know. I didn't know any women. Or girls. I don't know what I would have done if I'd met one close up."

"Would you have wanted to attack them?"

"I probably would have run away."

"It's sick your dad bought them. And let you read them."

"I snuck them from him. And yeah, that was one of the things they fought about. I don't think it was the main problem. The main problem was that they just didn't get along."

"You don't still read them. Of course not."

"No," said Duncan. "Of course it's not something men like to admit to."

"Yeah. They're so sexist. They're all about aggression."

"They're all about jacking off."

"Oh, gross," said Stephanie, embarrassed.

The grey men had inexplicably begun to run through cobbled streets, to the sound of speeded-up jazz. One of them tripped and fell, eyes rolling, clutching his side. One of them went up and up a curving metal staircase. A third did a triple somersault over the hood of a Rolls-Royce.

"The whole bunch of us are just sitting on our asses here," said Duncan suddenly.

"You were saying that the other night," said Stephanie. "But you have your radio show. That's important."

"Like us," said Duncan. "Like what are we doing together? Where the fuck are we going?"

Stephanie felt the ground start to drop away. Blood to ice. "What do you mean, where are we going?" she said. "Where should we be going?"

"I have no idea. Where do *you* think we should be going?"

There was a formula somewhere, and other women no doubt knew the right words that would unsay all this, shift the parameters or the mood: Duncan hunched on the bed, eyes fixed on the television, where the surviving men earnestly conferenced. A wall map, floor plans. The movie appeared to be unravelling with the jump cuts, the sophisticated unreality that said Europe, early 1960s. Stephanie had completely lost the thread.

"I'm pretty happy where we are," she said carefully.

"Pretty happy," said Duncan. "But what do you want out of this?"

"What do I want?" said Stephanie. "I want to go on. We have fun." The panic was like waking at midnight in a smoke-filled house, racing against time, moving by touch from bed to dresser, closet to window. When she reached glass, she'd smash through, crawl out on the porch roof, drop to the shrubbery.

But what if the porch was already ablaze? The windows barred? What if this was a skyscraper, thirty storeys down?

"Don't you think we have fun?" said Stephanie, groping.

"Yeah. We have fun. We go to concerts. We joke around. That's all. We're never really serious."

"Do you want me to be serious? How so? I mean, I can try."

"I don't want you to be anything. I just want to know what you want out of me."

"I don't want anything," said Stephanie. "Nothing special." She was on the verge of tears, icy cold. Missing, she could see, the correct response. The safety exit. What could you want from someone who was already half your soul, and more than half your life?

This was not the time to say *love*. That fit another scenario altogether, one that had never yet materialized. Gentle nudgings and oozings towards diffused warmth, a mild light, a springtime of the emotions in which her soul could unfold its damp petals. Her soul: at times Stephanie felt it brimming with untested generosity and benevolence, quite apart from anything ever called for in quotidian life. But to coax and force that shy flower wasn't possible on a winter night of rain. Duncan, stormcloud.

"You must want something," he said.

"Just to go on." She was crying now, big messy tears, ugly sobs. Duncan kept watching the television. She got up, found a roll of toilet paper on the desk, blew her nose and sat down again on the bed. Duncan put his arm around her.

"You don't have to get upset," he said. "I didn't mean it in a bad way." Across the screen a line of dancing cats demanded their favourite gourmet dinner, a dinner that mimicked the expensive little cans, caviar or salmon, of the human, adult world. One of the bulbs in the kitchen ceiling was dead. The remaining light managed to be, at the same time, both harsh and dim. It threw shadows under noses, and around the crumbs on the table; it highlighted the whitish footprints of cups and saucers.

Stephanie did not have the energy tonight for Tash and Linda, but neither did she want to climb the steep stairs to her room. She was hollowed out and empty. More than that. Emptied and filled, emptied and filled, shaken and dumped out, like a dirty jar. Like the peanut-butter jar on the counter, which needed, before it hardened past redemption, to be scrubbed clean for brown rice or barley. Stephanie looked blankly at the jar and wondered if she would ever have energy again to wash a cup or spoon. Whether cups or spoons, in the wider scheme of things, mattered at all.

She had spent the night, and all day Sunday, with Duncan. He had said, several times, that he didn't mean to upset her, and they had gallantly gone on to talk of books, movies, gossip. But the conversation kept looping round, like a warped record, to — what? To the Thing, the big new queasy lump that squatted between them on the bed. Some kind of anti-incubus, for it killed pleasure dead.

During those twenty-two hours, she'd felt they were circuitously but diligently, with painful honesty, slowly working towards some denser, opaque truth. But now, home, she could not say what that truth was, or upon what they had finally agreed.

She could not even say what exactly they had discussed. The Thing remained shadowy, a kind of nightmare panic. It was not possible to describe it to Tash or Linda, did not fit any conversation she had yet had with them. Besides, she was drained hollow. There was nothing more to say; the thought of recounting this long wrangle to a third party left her nauseated with fatigue.

"I'm quitting dairy and all wheat products," said Tash.

"Oh, super," said Linda.

"That's because of the gluten. Most people in North America are allergic to dairy and gluten. That's because we eat so much of it."

"Totally."

"They cause all kinds of mucus. I can feel my digestion

clearing up already."

"I didn't know you had digestion problems," said Stephanie. The topic did not interest her; she was only conscious of her own stomach after six or seven beers. But she had become overwhelmingly aware of her silence since sitting down. It suddenly seemed necessary to keep up the façade of participation.

"I have terrible problems," said Tash. "Gas. I feel sick almost every time I eat. There's almost nothing I can eat."

"I never knew that," said Stephanie.

"It's been like that all my life. It's getting worse."

They lapsed into silence. As the minutes ticked by, it felt to Stephanie more and more impossible to speak. There was her own exhaustion, and the damping effect of the crippled lightbulb. Beyond that, though, they seemed to have reached a point in the conversation, the culmination of weeks, past which they could not move. Linda sat sipping herb tea, broad-cheeked, placid and extremely plain under the overhead light. Tash sat hard and stolid, immovable.

Joel came in the front door, down the hall and into the kitchen.

"Hi, all," he said, getting a beer from the fridge.

"They use wheat in that," said Tash. "I can't drink it any more." Her voice had a truculence that Joel didn't seem to notice. "You'd feel way better if you quit drinking it."

Linda was still sitting at the table, but she seemed to have faded right out, absented herself. Joel leaned against the kitchen counter. He brought with him a whiff of night air and rain, and, Stephanie thought, something clear and energetic. Fundamentally uncomplicated. This simplicity kept her from being especially interested in him. But tonight it was an enormous relief.

"How's it going?" said Stephanie.

"Excellent," he said. "We're ready to walk out whenever. And this insider trading scam's amazing, eh? Everything we've said about the government is true."

"Yes," said Stephanie. Linda was gazing dreamily into her teacup; Tash had a package of rice cakes, little compact patties of puffed cereal. She was crumbling and nibbling. Joel was talking across their heads at Stephanie.

"You said your father works for the government. I bet he'd have all sorts of information."

"He might," said Stephanie blandly. "But he's not really

connected to those people. He's just an accountant."

"Too bad. We could get incredible mileage out of a few names. We could bring down the government. But Victoria seems to have hushed up the press. We figure the premier is up to his eyeballs in this shit. Obviously."

"I'm sure," said Stephanie.

"See, everything's connected anyhow. The government gets campaign contributions from the mining companies. And the defence contractors. And the CIA, too. The whole province, the whole country, is being run for corporate interests. We always look at it as separate issues. But really it's all tied together. Union busting, missile testing, the rise of the New Right. We need to develop that analysis so it's clear what we're up against."

"For sure," said Stephanie. Neither Tash nor Linda spoke. Stephanie wondered briefly what hidden messages she was missing. Was she detaining Joel too long, letting him diffuse the feminine camaraderie of the kitchen? But Joel was both house-mate and friend; she could not snub him. Besides, just to the extent that she was not obliged to enter into his enthusiasm, it washed over her, soothed her.

"The rise of fascism is the real threat over the next decade," said Joel. "The workers won't take it. They'll be out in the streets. Riots."

"Yes," said Stephanie. What he was saying was reasonable enough. Surely life could not continue like this, temporary, cramped, contingent. Surely the day was coming, and soon, when it would be necessary to make decisions, to take a stand, to act.

"The far right is already doing paramilitary training out in the Fraser Valley. That's the scary part. They're going to be ready. We won't." Joel drained his bottle. "Well, I'm off to bed. Night all."

"Night," said Tash. Linda tilted her teacup.

"Good-night," said Stephanie. Joel went down the hall and up the stairs.

Tash licked her finger and began sponging up crumbs of rice cake. Refreshed or distracted, Stephanie realized she was hungry. She opened the refrigerator.

"I think I'll heat up that lasagna Joel made yesterday," she said.

"Excuse me a minute," said Linda, and went out into the hall, leaving her teacup on the table.

"Do you want some?" said Stephanie.

"I can't eat that stuff," said Tash. "It's all gluten and dairy. I can't eat anything with wheat."

"Right," said Stephanie. "Shit. That must be difficult."

"Doing anything healthy is difficult," said Tash. "We live in a diseased society."

"Linda," said Stephanie, "do you want some lasagna?"

Linda didn't answer. Stephanie went down the hall and looked in the living room. The bathroom was on the back porch, and Linda hadn't gone that direction.

"She didn't leave, did she?" said Stephanie. "Her shoes are still here. She's not in the can, is she?"

"Joel," said Tash. She was powdering a rice cake.

"Joel?" said Stephanie. "Oh, really? Oh, cool." Linda and Joel: the idea hadn't occurred to her. But now it seemed to fit perfectly. A tidy synchronicity, doubling the ties binding them together. Community, she thought.

"I'm not upset," said Tash. "I don't mind at all."

"Of course not," said Stephanie. "Why would you?"

"I think it's really great for Joel," said Tash emphatically. "He only relates to women. He's very dependent on them. He can't talk to other guys."

"That's too bad," said Stephanie, levering a serving of lasagna into a pan.

"Most guys can't talk to other guys. Not like women can. They can't be honest."

"I guess not," said Stephanie. The gas puffed and caught, blue.

"I'm really really happy for them," said Tash. She had reduced a rice cake to a pyramid of crumbs which she was dribbling between her fingers. "It's perfect."

"It is, isn't it?" Stephanie peered under the lid to watch dinner's progress. "Did you eat tonight? Sure you don't want some?"

"I wasn't hungry. Actually I'm getting very sensitive to the smell of animal by-products. They even smell dirty. You know?"

"Uh-huh," said Stephanie, poking the bleeding red edge of the pasta.

"That stuff smells like puke," said Tash. "I don't know what Joel put into it. I'm going to have to go sit in the living room."

"Whatever," said Stephanie. "Sorry." She tilted the pasta onto a plate and sat at the table, across from the empty teacup and the ruined rice cake. The heart of the lasagna was cold and hard, but she ate greedily and put the dish in the sink.

On the way upstairs she looked into the living room. Tash was lying on the sofa wearing the stereo headphones.

On the second-floor landing, where Tash and Joel had their bedrooms side by side, all was silent. Stephanie climbed the last flight to her room and toppled into bed.

"I had a very nice talk with the school board," said Claire. "They're very interested in the nonviolence workshops."

"Super," said Linda.

"This is the *Alternatives to Aggression* package we were talking about marketing before. Conflict resolution. Anger management."

Claire paused. Linda and Stephanie nodded. "I'm going to have to present this very carefully to *our* board of directors," she continued. "I know it's a little controversial."

"How so?"

"Exactly, Stephanie," said Claire. "That's exactly what I want to say to them. *How so?* It's the old-line peace activists. The ones who think we should be basically saying, Ban the Bomb. And that's it."

"Oh," said Stephanie. "I see."

"Of *course* we don't stop saying that," said Claire. "Of course we don't for a *minute* forget our *mandate*. Our mandate is implicit in everything we do. Only it's a matter of broadening our base."

"For sure," said Linda.

"It's also a matter of going with what our participating organizations see as a priority need. And frankly the school board is very interested in an integrated nonviolence component at both the elementary and secondary levels."

"What does it involve?" said Stephanie.

"Ideally I envision thirty hours of participatory workshops, question-and-answer sharing sessions and role play. All around diffusing aggression and anger."

"Does it talk about the peace movement?"

"Well, that's certainly implicit, Stephanie. If any group wanted to discuss it, that would be wonderful. We ideally would see this as very participant-driven."

"That sounds excellent."

"I really appreciate your support, Linda. Because I'm afraid I'm going to have a time convincing our old-time board members. This all gets so *political.*" Claire's nose wrinkled in distaste. "So many little turfs and boundaries to protect. When what they don't see is that family violence, conflict resolution and international conflict all boil down to a question of *attitude.* If we start with children, educating them to negotiate, we attack the problem at its *root.* It's a slower process, but it's one that will work."

"Super."

"It's not like this isn't controversial too. There was a fundamentalist parents' group out in the Fraser Valley that managed to get a high school stress management workshop shut down because it was using creative visualization. Where you imagine what you want. The parents said this was witchcraft."

"This friend of mine says they're super-fascist out there," said Linda.

"Exactly," said Claire. "So you can see that what we are doing is certainly controversial in its own right. I only hope our board sees it that way."

Stephanie waited until midweek before calling Duncan. Sunday night, exhausted, she'd decided to wait for him to call. But as the grey week dragged on, this seemed more and more pointless.

His silence was not necessarily a problem. They had had absences of this length in the past. Or perhaps not.

"Hello," said Duncan. "Actually, I was just about to call you."

In the past, Stephanie would have responded, *Synchronicity!* or *Great minds think alike,* or even *Well, I'll hang up and let you call me back, if you insist.* But tonight she was blank of all levity.

"How you doing?" she said.

"All right. Pretty good. I got quite a bit of work done."

"Excellent." The silence between them was as wide as rain. "We doing anything this weekend?" she said finally.

"I guess we should," said Duncan. "If you want to."

"Oh, of course I do."

"Then we should get together. If you really feel like it."

Joel heaved the casserole dish out of the oven between two

wadded dish towels, and dropped it heavily on the kitchen table. The open oven puffed hot air.

"Nutty Brocci Ringarici," said Linda, and giggled. "The recipes in that vegetarian cookbook all have silly names."

"It's a good recipe, though," said Joel. He lifted the fragrant lid. "Dig in."

"I'm not hungry," said Tash. "I'll just have my rice cakes and peanut butter."

"It's totally gluten-free and dairy-free," said Linda. "We chose the recipe on purpose."

"I don't feel like eating anything these days," said Tash. "I might start a fast."

"I could never do that," said Stephanie, spooning casserole.

"You lose your hunger after a day or two," said Tash. "Then you can go on indefinitely. It's really important for cleansing the body of toxins."

The curtains on the window of the Szechuan Treasure were of plastic lace; beyond them the street lay empty under rain and lamp. Stephanie had chosen the restaurant anticipating warmth and crowd. But tonight it was empty.

"The chicken with peanuts is good," said Stephanie.

"And we can get a sizzling hotpot," said Duncan. "That is, if you want one."

"And we should get rice."

"Oh, yes. Rice."

The Thing had not come in with them, was not squatting on the plastic tablecloth between the teapot and cups. But it was waiting nearby, that was certain: out on the wet sidewalk, leashed to a parking meter, or under the bedsheets back home.

"We should definitely get steamed rice," said Stephanie. They were being elaborately careful with each other, careful and gentle: exhaustion, fear, sorrow. But this gentleness weighed. It was like trying to swim fully clothed.

Rested, braver, they would confront the Thing. Or perhaps not.

Fed, bill paid, tip left, they walked towards the movie theatre. This was a through street, a major road, Commercial Drive, a thick line on the grid of the city map. But tonight, seven p.m. on a Saturday, the sidewalks were blank. Three or four cars sliced by, invisible drivers, separate long swish and rip of tires and engine. Above the bolted shops, apartments showed lit windows, blocks of light. Behind those, there must be people. Still, no one was visible, the city sucked clean: plague, neutron bomb, evacuated pending disaster.

You could not discuss anything in such an obvious void, a world of such enormous chill lack. You wanted only to be inside again, warm, somehow occupied, attention diverted.

The next morning, making love, Stephanie was ambushed by a tenderness terrible and wonderful, to the point of tears. It came out of nothing that had been said or even felt; she was not particularly aroused, knew she wouldn't climax. But the tenderness superseded all that. It was unbearable.

Afterwards they lay without talking, drifting back towards sleep, the day that would never quite congeal dripping down past the window.

Stephanie did not know if Duncan felt the same, and did not know how to ask. A week ago she would have assumed he shared it. But today his body rested so lightly in her arms that all she could imagine was his absence.

"Well, I was quite surprised by the reaction of our board last night. Very pleasantly surprised," said Claire. "I'm not sure of course if it's real support. I'm not sure that they really understand. Of course it's great we got the go-ahead for *Alternatives to Aggression*. But I'm not sure how I feel about that."

Stephanie went out alone looking for lunch. The mountains across the harbour had been blotted out for weeks, but today a breeze was fraying the clouds, showing glimpses of dark shoulders and haunch. But by the time she reached the Saigon Palace, with its half-dozen arborite tables, the clouds had rolled shut again.

She ate her salad rolls and brochette, staring out at a blank parking lot, and the nothingness of the east end of East Hastings. Trolley wires held back the sky, the shop fronts sagged in the rain. She felt, at the same time, both washed empty and hemmed in, vaguely irritated.

"I've been fasting for three days," said Tash. "I feel so good. I feel weightless. You should try it."

"It's an idea," said Stephanie. It wasn't; the thought appalled her. Any effort, even the consideration of any effort past the bare minimum required, made her want to run upstairs and shove her head under the blankets. However, she also lacked the energy to contradict Tash, who was speaking with certitude and emphasis. Besides, Stephanie believed Tash was likely right. In that case, it was herself who lacked rigour, dedication, a clear view of the world. She turned up the gas and poured a dollop of oil into the pan.

"Where are Linda and Joel?" she asked, to change the subject.

"They went to hear the British strikers speak," said Tash. "There's amazing build-ups in the intestines. Fasting clears out all the garbage. The anger, the tension."

"They're getting on well." Stephanie snapped shell against rim.

"Some issues are starting to come up. Not surprising, with Joel. He actually has a lot of sexism he isn't confronting. After a few days just the sight of food is nauseating. You start to think about what it turns into inside you."

"Linda's really easygoing, though. I bet they work it out. I hope so, anyways." The tilted pan whitened.

"The smell of those eggs is making me sick," said Tash. "I'm going upstairs."

"I think what we need to do is talk about the relationship calmly and honestly," said Duncan. "We don't need to get upset about it."

"No, of course not," said Stephanie. To emphasize the seriousness of the evening, they were sitting at his little kitchen table, older than either of them: speckled blue arborite, corners rounded with aluminum stripping, suburban breakfast nook on a robin's-egg morning in the sun-dappled, mysterious 1950s. Tonight, thirty years later, it looked merely shabby and artificial. "I'm not going to get upset," Stephanie said.

"I hope not," said Duncan. "I don't really know what I'm supposed to do when you get like that."

Hold me, take it all back, tell me everything will be all right. Make me believe that. "I don't know that you're supposed to *do* anything in particular," said Stephanie.

"Well, yeah," said Duncan. He took the salt and pepper shakers — cheap glass, as in a café — and began shifting one around the other, two-step on a blue dance floor. "I think we're getting into a rut. We're starting to take each other for granted."

"I don't take you for granted," said Stephanie.

"We just have this formless time together. We never plan it."

"But you like spending time together," said Stephanie. "Don't you."

"Well, yeah. But it's just assumed that I have to spend every weekend with you."

"No, it isn't," said Stephanie. "If you take time off to work or something I don't complain."

"But I never take time off."

"But you could."

"What would you do? Sit home alone?"

"I'd go out with Tash, or Linda and Joel. That wouldn't be a problem." Linda and Joel giggling up the stairs to his bedroom, Tash sulking in the kitchen. The temperature of the house had dropped twenty degrees over the last few weeks. "I'd have fun with them," Stephanie lied.

"Still, I feel like you expect it of me."

"Well, you feel wrong."

Duncan slid the shakers together and stared down at them. After a minute he said, "What we need to do is get organized. If we get together it should be for something special. Not just flake out and watch TV."

"But we only watch TV over here," said Stephanie. "I hardly ever watch it at home. You always have it on."

"And why is that?"

"For the news? Documentaries?"

"We should be able to just turn it off and go out," said Duncan. "Do something fun like normal couples."

"I don't have a problem with that," said Stephanie.

"But you never suggest anything. You just sit down and flake out. You never turn the TV off."

"I wouldn't turn it off when you're in the middle of watching something. But what is it you want to go out and do?"

"It isn't that I want to *do* anything," said Duncan. "I mean, what do other couples do? What are you supposed to do? Dinner, drinks, a movie? Not just this shapeless killing time together."

"I don't feel like I'm killing time with you." *The opposite, really. It's the rest of the week that grinds past. With you, I'm bringing time back to life.* This did not seem like something she could say. "We eat out a lot anyways."

"That's just because we can't be bothered to cook," said Duncan. "It's not anything special."

"But see, I don't mind if you're really wiped and just want to relax. I don't need to do anything."

"That's what I mean about taking the whole thing for granted."

"But I don't take you for granted. I like being with you."

Duncan was balancing the shakers, pepper on salt, hands cupped around the teetering tower. "That's kind of hard to believe," he said.

"Well, it's true."

"But we never do anything."

"We can do things if you want."

"You have to want them too."

"I do, though."

"Yeah," said Duncan. He slid the shakers back into the corner of the table, behind a stack of magazines. After a minute he stretched, yawned and went out to the fridge in the basement. Stephanie flipped a magazine from the pile. *Total Global Collapse,* said the cover. *Five Ecologists' Dire Warnings.* The toilet flushed and Duncan came in uncapping two bottles of beer. He put one in front of Stephanie and flopped down on the bed.

"That's an interesting story," he said. "They think the earth is starting to warm up."

"Yeah?" said Stephanie. She took her beer, left the magazine and came to sit beside him on the bed.

"You can borrow the magazine," he said. "They say it's on account of car exhaust. The world will become uninhabitable."

"The bomb will probably go off first," said Stephanie.

"It does seem more likely," said Duncan. "The Americans have been pretty stupid in the peace talks."

"Yeah," said Stephanie. She reached across the miles between them and put her hand on his chest. The rise of breastbone through sweater and T-shirt, the promise of skin shining beneath, and the ease with which her hand could slide and rise again, nudging under his loose clothes.

"I should really watch the late news," said Duncan.

"I thought you said no TV."

"This isn't really TV," he said. "I have to keep up for work. Unless you really don't want it on."

"I was just joking. Because of what you said."

Duncan sat up to turn the knob, and her hand fell to the blankets. Noise, static, urgent voices, the electronic world catapulted into the room, emptying and then shattering it.

Duncan leaned back against the wall.

"...*succeeded in tracking the registration of controversial Goldstar Resources Ltd. to this offshore investment haven.*" Blow-dried hair and a serious little moustache, behind him unrolling stock footage of a Caribbean beach. *"The premier's office is denying all knowledge."*

"Now that's a story," said Duncan. "I ought to be working on something like that. Something that matters."

"Yeah," said Stephanie.

"I bet your father could find out if you asked him."

"He doesn't really know about that stuff. He's been out of it for ever." This was a lie so necessary it was no longer a lie, no more than smoking her cigarettes out of sight down the lane during Christmas in Victoria. A lie unavoidable as *I'm fine, thank you* and *No, it's no trouble at all.* You lived two lives, at the least, sometimes more; you lived divided loyalties. Stephanie wanted the government to fall, which it would in any case, but not at the expense of her parents. She wanted Duncan to find a story, a scoop, as he sometimes called it, which he would in any case; he did not need this one. Should she be more torn? Stephanie wondered. Was there something missing from her analysis?

"...*a last-minute agreement between the federal government and its employees has averted the walkout scheduled for Monday.*"

"What would you have done if you found out your father was involved in some big scandal?" Stephanie said.

"What would I have done?" Duncan paused. The television pranced and jiggled through a minute of hectic commercials. "I don't actually think it would have come up. It's true he worked for the oil companies. By definition, they're corrupt. They destroy the environment, they leach money out to U.S. multinationals. But within that context my father was completely honest."

"That's what my mom says about my dad," said Stephanie.

"He would never have gotten himself mixed up in anything wrong," said Duncan. "I've always known that. If he were alive, that's how I'd have to explain my position to him. That I have an analysis of the industry within which he's structurally implicated but that he is then free to move within. I think about it a lot, how I'd lay it all out for him."

"So he never did anything wrong, personally?"

"No. It was more a matter of what they call false consciousness. Of believing that what he did was right. That's what killed him, more than the drinking. I know he was drinking a lot before the divorce, and after, in Edmonton, too. But I think it was probably the political contradictions rather than the alcohol that finished him off. If someone had been around to point that out to him, if I'd been able to point it out to him, he'd still be alive."

"Yeah."

"You drink like that because you *know* you're in a false position," said Duncan. "And the rest of it, what my mother was saying back then about the call girls and all that, she was pretty angry. She was probably exaggerating."

"Sounds like he went pretty wild."

"But that's his personal life. He went through a lot of shit with my mother. I don't believe at all what she was saying about the cocaine. How would she know? Anyhow, it doesn't mean he did anything wrong at work."

"No, of course not."

"If he was still alive we could go and talk about it. Move forward from all this."

"I can't talk about anything yet with my parents," said Stephanie.

"When he died he was fourteen years older than I am now," said Duncan. "That's not very old."

Stephanie counted on her fingers. "Claire's age, I guess. She's *middle-aged*, definitely. She has to dye her hair."

"Under forty," said Duncan. "That's young for a man, still. That's young to die."

Fourteen years, thought Stephanie. By then the bomb would have dropped. And if it hadn't, if by some chance they won? Peace worldwide, as Claire said, and all the money for defence diverted to social services, culture, job creation. Between now and then, now and middle age: surely there lay a gap. If life was not to be the tedious grey boxes she'd feared ten years ago, and Stephanie was determined it would not, and if it was not smoking ruins, then something had to happen. Something that would lift her from drab contingency to clear-sighted adulthood, to levels of clarity, unity, omnipotence. Most easily imaginable in the context of a clean, new, brave world. Not, in fact, imaginable at all from this one.

"I guess it's young to *die*," said Stephanie.

Onscreen a wooden house tilted above swollen brown water, against a backdrop of second-growth fir. The camera jolted breathlessly, vicariously; the frame filled with yellow slickers. Below, the sodden soil shivered, raw and oozing in the raw light.

"I *know*," said Linda. "But Joel just doesn't see it as a *problem*."

"You need to call him on it," said Tash. "You can't let him get away with it."

They were at the kitchen table eating plates of grain and vegetables. "Hi," said Stephanie. "Hello."

"Hi," said Linda.

"You just *can't*," said Tash.

"Is there food?" said Stephanie. "I'm starved."

"Help yourself," said Linda. "Millet stir-fry. I've tried bringing it up but it's so hard to define."

Stephanie scooped a plate and sat down. Green peppers, eggplant, shredded kelp, black mushrooms, half cold: a dark damp pile.

"He's always been like that," said Tash. "Really unaware of what he's doing."

The millet tasted like birdseed. More precisely, the clogged floor of the cage after her childhood budgerigar had died of old age and neglect. Stephanie carefully chewed.

"It's so hard," said Linda. "It's so frustrating."

"Are you and Joel having problems?" said Stephanie.

"Kind of," said Linda. "I don't know. Things."

"It's all this stuff he refused to deal with, with me," said Tash. "Now he's with Linda, he's got to. She has to make him. But of course he still doesn't want to."

"So should I be starting to design the pages for the Teacher's Guide?" said Stephanie. "Have you decided if we can get it typeset somewhere?"

"I think we better hold off on that for a bit," said Claire. "Until we know exactly where we're going with *Alternatives to Aggression*. Until we're really focused."

"Linda has it pretty much all researched and written. It wouldn't take much to pull it together."

"No. So we can let it ride just a bit. Until we really know that our board is on-side. Also I have some meetings with the school board next week. We might want to substantially revise in the face of that."

"Oh," said Stephanie. "Of course. That makes perfect sense."

"I've been past here lots but I'd never gone in," said Stephanie. This Italian restaurant had white tablecloths, real fabric, and white bud vases, in each of which teetered one hothouse rose.

"It's not all that more expensive," said Duncan. "Yes," he said to the waiter. "A litre of house red. The salads to start."

The walls were brick; plastic grapevines twined the trellis above the bar. In the dim light they looked real enough.

"It's supposed to be quite good," said Duncan. "It got a write-up in the paper."

"The buns are good," said Stephanie, tearing and buttering the last one. Outside, dusk oozed down. So the days were already longer, behind the gloom of rain. An old woman wrapped in garbage bags trudged past the wide window, humped back, head down, pushing a shopping cart vaguely full of wet blankets. Inside the restaurant there were other couples, adults, nylon stockings, shirts and ties. Stephanie sank back into the warmth of faint classical music.

Her salad arrived, multicoloured and unexpectedly complex, some tangy mystery of herbs.

"Before my parents started fighting, they'd take me out to places like the Bayshore Inn," said Duncan. "We'd have things like mahi-mahi fish from Hawaii."

"Mine never went out that much," said Stephanie. "Mom would do these awful dinner parties for people from Dad's job." Awful — how? She was thinking of the stolidness, the fuss and disarray, getting heavy coats, sweetish musty fur collars and sober gabardine, into the guest room, getting heavy bottoms into chairs and sofas, the house invaded upside-down, her mother's tense smile.

Then the general air of falsity relaxing after a few drinks, into a queasy bonhomie. In which she was somehow shamefully implicated, circulating obediently with her plates of walnut balls, shrimp toast, sausage rolls.

"They were incredibly boring," said Stephanie. She had not been bored at the time. Rather, caught fascinated and repulsed as the large faces flushed and opened. *I can't believe you were standing there simpering while Mr. Gromley was saying things like that,* her mother backing Stephanie, age eleven, up against the dishwasher, blocking escape with a platter of devilled eggs. *What possessed you to put on that sweater. It's much too tight. We're going downtown tomorrow morning and getting a bra for you. That's exactly what we're going to do. And in front of his wife. I wanted to crawl under the sofa. Here, take these.* Stephanie, eyes now on the carpet, noting only the toes of shoes, holding the platter high, hoping it hid the tremulous new chest that until now she had only considered with detached curiosity.

"Such a lot of bother," she said. "Extra forks for the salads. I could never manage all that."

"They're nice sometimes, if you have the money," said Duncan.

The pasta descended. Stephanie twirled and ate. Silence descended. She was not particularly intimidated by the tableware, less extensive and far less expensive than her mother's best. She was not intimidated by the food or even the service, both recognizable from cheaper restaurants. The silence seemed more the effect of the invocation to pleasure and elegance. The last few weeks had in fact reduced considerably the scope of allowable conversation.

She would not, could not, refused to, revert back to the Relationship, which was spelled like that now, capital R in her head. This night, after all, was part of the solution; it stood outside discussion.

Stephanie topped up her third glass of wine. She could not mention work. That led back, on Duncan's part, to gloom. And she had lost the heart for joking, quite apart from his complaint that they were never serious. Serious? She was still not quite sure what that meant, but she had certainly lost lightness.

Watching Duncan chew his fettucine, Stephanie could not read his mood. Bored or pleased, lost in thought or worried? She had never watched him like this before, with this twinge of anxiety, unable to muster the right word. She had never watched him before with this fear, this dry cold knowledge that, more likely than not, she wasn't pleasing him, didn't in fact know how.

Well, she wasn't taking him for granted. That much was true.

"What are you thinking?" she asked after a while.

"What was I thinking?" Duncan raised vague eyes. "Not much. How they make the pasta. How they squeeze it out of machines into different shapes."

Dessert eventually arrived, espresso and hard little balls of ice cream rolled in chocolate powder. By this point Stephanie desperately wanted movement, action, to be up and out. But on the sidewalk she felt aimless. They could not top this elegant meal with a formless pitcher of draught at the beer parlour down by the waterfront. They had seen the local movie, and had no time to get downtown on the bus for the cinemas there. Commercial Drive was locked down, deserted, swept by dark gusts of rain.

There was nowhere, besides the violent neon of skid road, dense enough to wander and loiter, no street of cafés or bars or clubs. You chose a destination and you went there through sodden streets, and that was your evening.

Stephanie had not yet travelled to any city different from this, so the shapeless need she felt tonight for life, action, colour, was not based in real nostalgia for Paris or New York, Montreal or Hong Kong. She did not know what was missing, only that it was not enough, not tonight.

They trudged up the street into the teeth of the rain, past the blazing windows of the Portuguese coffee bar. The air inside looked used up and smoky, bleak and overlit; Stephanie and Duncan did not feel like playing pool. They turned east and walked under weeping bare trees to the low doorway, the cold floor and the faintly damp sheets of Duncan's basement suite.

"You have to confront him," said Tash. "You have to put down your foot."

"I know," said Linda. "But I told you what he said when I tried."

"You just tell him what I told you to say," said Tash. "I know Joel. I know how he's manipulating you. Go up and talk to him now."

"I'll try," said Linda.

"Come back and tell me what he says."

Linda went out the door of the living room and up the stairs. Stephanie was curled in a corner of the sofa with a stack of news magazines borrowed from Duncan. Tash got up abruptly from her armchair and rifled through the records, didn't put anything on the turntable, went back to the chair and flopped down, legs spread.

Death squads trained by the CIA have been responsible for the murders of thousands of men and women, Stephanie read. *Bodies of opposition leaders were uncovered in a shallow grave last month.*

Tash sighed. Stephanie kept her eyes on the page. She was too tired to take the hint and open conversation, but too tired also for the solitude of her room, so early in the evening.

"He's being such a jerk," said Tash. "Just like he was with me."

"Joel," said Stephanie. *They had been tortured with cattle prods and cigarette burns.*

"We all three have to let him know it's not okay," said Tash. "She can't do it alone."

Some had been decapitated. "Duncan and I have been kind of trying to work through some stuff too," said Stephanie. "Things."

"Oh, yeah?" said Tash. "I hope he's not being too much of a jerk for her."

Linda came thumping down the stairs, and peeked in through the living-room door. "Tash. Tash," she said. "I got to talk to you." Her voice was charged, tears or laughter or perhaps just emotion, poised to go either way.

Tash went out into the hallway. Stephanie heard their voices, muffled and urgent, through the door. Then feet on stairs, up and down, slamming doors, and the air continuing to vibrate long after silence had officially fallen. *The state department denies all knowledge.* A photo of dead nuns in a pool of blood. The house shook under a gust of rain.

"I think we really need to look at where we're going," said Duncan.

"We've been doing that. Haven't we?" said Stephanie.

They were at the back of the beer parlour, up against the wall mural of twenty-foot Hawaiians: classic, Italian profiles and

1950s quiffs. The carpet was black with pink hibiscus the size of beer trays.

"We need to assess things," said Duncan.

"Yes," said Stephanie. Her glass of draught was flat and sour.

"I think we need to put it on hold for a while."

"We need to what?" said Stephanie.

"Maybe take a break. See how that goes. Don't you think that would be best?"

"No," said Stephanie. The panic was coming in like race tide, cold flood, the ground tilting below her.

"A break might help us find out where we stand. Help us stop taking each other for granted," said Duncan.

"I don't take you for granted," said Stephanie, hearing her voice rise and crack. "I like being with you. I really really like you."

"You've said. I mean, I like you too," said Duncan. "That doesn't mean we're good for each other."

"How aren't we good for each other?"

"We've been through this before. We fall into ruts. We aren't ever serious. We get bored."

"I'm not bored," said Stephanie. Her mind was racing back and forth, end to end of the cage. There were people she knew three tables over. She took a breath and forced herself to match Duncan's level logic. "I'm not bored with you and I can try to be serious," she said.

"This isn't something we can try," said Duncan. "We either work, or it's a waste of time."

"But it isn't a waste of time." Her voice was growing dangerously petulant; if she lost her grip she would drop hard onto rocks a hundred feet down. "I mean, I really do like you."

"That's what makes it so difficult," said Duncan.

"I love you," Stephanie said. She held her breath and waited for the words to hit the earth and shatter.

"But it doesn't really feel like you do," said Duncan. "It's never really felt like you cared about me."

"But I do," said Stephanie. She had her head bent; splashy tears were running down her cheeks. If she breathed steadily she wouldn't break and sob, wouldn't cause a scene.

Duncan either didn't notice the tears, or chose to ignore them.

"But it just doesn't feel like you do," he said.

Stephanie dumped her dirty clothes into an old duffel bag, hooked the straps over her shoulders like a backpack and walked through the rain to the laundromat.

Saturday afternoon, and the air inside steamy, used up, thick with detergent and wet wool. At the hatch at the back, the manager handed over quarters and soap, without smiling or speaking or indeed looking at Stephanie.

Her clothes toppled into an empty washer. Shot cotton panties, faded T-shirts, pilled socks; the overhead lights were merciless. The shabbiness did not embarrass her, the opposite rather. Like faded jeans, old clothes spoke of serious dedication, time taken to let the body alter and create what covered it, rubbing and wearing, staining and fading. New clothes were unassimilated, impersonal, without value.

But today the tumble of limp clothes saddened Stephanie. They were so very nearly at death's door, these clothes, approaching the point at which elastic would snap and toes poke through to chafe on leather. They would not last many more washings. And as for herself, Stephanie was not sure she would last even this one. The row of chairs was full; she sat on the floor, back to wall, exhausted.

Today the laundromat was full of mothers, young moms younger than her, with heavy thighs, brassy hair, smoky laughter, and older ones, grandmothers perhaps, wrinkled up with cigarettes, talking in carrying voices. No one looked like Stephanie. This was the other world, the neighbourhood around and under which she survived. Or rather, this was part of the world which she, from asymmetric hair to steel-toed boots, was constructed to oppose. And if she hated and rejected this world to this extent, surely it must feel the same about her.

Only today she lacked the energy to stare it down. She sat on the floor and studied her own knees. Between the soporific froth and churn, scraps of conversation tumbled past. *Cody, cut that out I'm going to wallop you, I really am. I said to her, I can get it two times cheaper out in the Valley, I really can. Leave her and take the kids. I warned you, Cody, just you wait.*

There were not enough dryers to handle the volume of the washers. When Stephanie stood up with her wet basket, she saw that while nobody was quite elbowing anyone aside, there was a tense dance in progress. Eyes on the floor, she had missed details of precedence and protocol. Now she wavered, physically afraid, as women stepped briskly past, commandeering dryers. In the set of eyes and mouths, strained through cigarette smoke, she thought she read tension, the tough girls of high school, the effortless presence of hair-trigger violence, poorly repressed.

The afternoon was already dimming when Stephanie hoisted her duffel bag, thoroughly heated now, and walked down Commercial Drive. She did not particularly want to go home, but could think of no alternative. Duncan and she were not over, they were not finished, which in fact was unthinkable. This was breathing space, merely an experiment, time to get the rest of their lives in order. But, walking up the front steps and into the dark front hall, she missed him, body and heart and mind.

Tash and Linda were murmuring at one end of the kitchen table, leaning into each other, almost touching. They didn't look up when Stephanie stood a moment in the doorway. She climbed to her room and let the duffel bag fall. It radiated body heat, or a few degrees higher: a benign and cozy fever. She would have liked to crawl inside amid the matched socks and toasty T-shirts, and fold herself up. Instead she fell on the bed, staring up at the bare bulb in the ceiling. The evening stretched away impossibly long and empty.

"Well, what a nice surprise," said her mother. "Is everything all right?"

"Oh, yes," said Stephanie. "I'm just calling."

"Isn't that nice. Are you all right? You sound a bit quiet."

"Kind of tired. That's all. I was reading the papers. It seems like it's all blowing over."

"What is? Our little problems over here? I thought I told you not to think about that."

"They've wrapped up the investigation, I read. They didn't find any wrongdoing."

"That's because there was none," said her mother. "We do think we're out of the woods now. The last time you phoned, I didn't want to say. But it was rather tense. The police had been here that morning."

"Sheese."

"They spent two hours in your father's den. Of course they didn't find anything. He's not that stupid."

"I'm glad."

"You're glad. I'm relieved. That's what I am. So how are things? How are you doing?"

"All right. I don't know. Remember that guy I was telling you about?"

"How would I remember that?" Her mother's voice rose. "I don't pry into your life. I don't pay any attention to what you say."

"You remember. Duncan."

"Oh, right. The one whose father was a corporate lawyer for Texaco. The boy you met at university. The journalist."

"Right. I don't know. We're not getting on."

"What's he doing to you? Is he criticizing? Is he being like your father? Don't let him take advantage of you."

"It's not that. It's just that we're trying to talk about the relationship."

"You're trying to talk? I know it's the fashion nowadays. But I can't see what good talking is ever going to do."

"No," said Stephanie. "Sometimes I can't either."

"Exactly. I'm glad you agree with me. Because you have to learn to stand up for yourself. Once they start complaining like that."

"He's not complaining."

"Is there someone else? Usually they won't leave one woman until they have another one all lined up. I hate to tell you this but that's how the world is."

"That's not what's happening."

"As long as you've checked it out."

"Yes."

"The important thing is not to let him bring you down. You aren't letting him do that, are you?"

"Oh, no."

"Because you can do better. You can do much, much better. You'd be quite attractive if you just fixed yourself up a bit. When are we going shopping?"

"I don't know."

"Come over at Easter. It's not that far away. All this mess should be settled by then."

"All right."

"And don't let this fellow get to you. You don't need him at all."

"I don't think an organization like Teachpeace is being very reasonable in expecting people to work on grant-funded contracts," said Claire. "On very temporary and uncertain contracts."

"I guess not," said Stephanie.

"When, just for instance, the school board hires specialists in very similar fields and pays at least twice as much. With extended health care, too."

With effort, Stephanie pulled herself into the conversation. "I guess they figure we have a political commitment to the peace movement," she said.

"And we do, Stephanie. And we do. Only that doesn't obscure the fact that we have to make a living. Like you, Stephanie. What are you going to do when this ends?"

"I don't know," said Stephanie. The horizon was socked in, visibility down to zero. She couldn't even imagine disaster, today. "Do you want me to start the design?"

"Soon, Stephanie," said Claire. "We'll find something for you to do soon."

Stephanie went into the back office. The children's drawings lay where she had piled them in January, dull paper warping under paint. Today more than most days, she thought she wanted something to keep her busy, distracted. But at the same time, inertia and fatigue seized her as soon as the door clicked shut.

She laid her head on her arms on the desk. A mistake. The minute she relaxed, the tears began to flow, copious and unwanted, until her sleeves were as damp as the earth outside.

Tripe was the stomach lining of cows, and there was tripe in the broth of Five Flavour Noodles. Tripe was not generally a problem, but tonight, under beefy steam, Stephanie caught a grassy whiff, the odour of half-digested hay, the odour in fact of cow patties. Warm soup on the way home, to freshen and invigorate. Her own stomach clamped tight.

Under the strip lighting, the bright tables of the Guangdong Pearl glowed and quivered. Strands of algae in the tank by the door, where the manacled lobsters were only technically alive, bruised antennae fluttering in the churn from the filtration tube.

The tea tasted peculiar; the hot glass, frosted dull with wear, felt dirty in her hand. The walk home lay ahead like a journey around the world, but she could no longer linger in the dead odours of grease and meat. She got up, paid and headed out into the empty rain.

That night she woke and made it down the two flights of stairs to the chilly toilet, where she vomited first her lunch-time spaghetti, then nothing, stomach clenching on itself, then the glass of water she drank immediately afterwards in the kitchen.

She woke to her alarm clock feeling impossibly lethargic and lazy. By the time she got down to the kitchen, she was shivering from deep in her spine, in the small of her back, and her arms and legs ached.

Stephanie dialled Claire at home.

"Isn't that too bad," said Claire. "Keep warm. Are you taking lots of vitamin C?"

"I don't have any."

"You should go get some now. Before it gets worse."

Stephanie finished the orange juice, poured a glass of water and went back upstairs. As she crawled into bed the thought skittered past that perhaps it was just this comfort she had been seeking, the comfort of collapse.

The chills broke into fever in the afternoon, soaking the back of her T-shirt. The day dimmed as she lay under the blankets. After dark she made it downstairs again, clinging to the bannister, her head spinning. She used up the last of the milk on some muesli; cooking was out of the question.

The next morning she woke thinking the fever had broken, but by the time she got downstairs she was sweating. She phoned Claire and ate dry muesli with a spoon. Then upstairs, rest, get dressed, go to the store on the corner. But when she sat again on the edge of the bed, she lacked the energy to bend for her socks on the floor. She lay down to catch her breath and watched the day lighten towards pearly noon, then slide back to dusk. The house lay below her, deserted.

She went down and cooked some eggs, leaning heavily on the stove, and left a shopping list for Tash or Joel, with a ten-dollar bill under it.

The list was still there the next morning. Dry muesli. Tash tapped on her bedroom door at dusk.

"I got your stuff," she said from the bright doorway. "Yeah, Linda said you weren't at work. I just came back to get some clothes. I'm staying over at her place for a bit."

"Yeah?" said Stephanie.

"It's this male aggression Joel's been putting out since she broke up with him. He isn't doing anything. It's just that we can't stand to be around him. And Linda needs someone with her. You know?"

"Joel hasn't been here much," said Stephanie. Her throat hurt: a new development.

"I don't even want to see his stuff," said Tash.

"Thanks for the food."

"No problem. Actually if you're sick you shouldn't eat at all. It's all the toxins coming out. You should go on a cleansing fast."

"Yeah."

"I got to take off. We're going to the Women and Peace symposium. I'll be back on the weekend sometime probably, to pick up more of my stuff."

"Oh," said Stephanie. "See you."

"You should go down to the health-food store and check out the herbs," said Tash.

She teetered downstairs after Tash had left, and made a meal from the paper bag on the table. Childhood foods, comfort foods, smoothly soothing, a suburban sluice pond of chemicals and additives: canned mushroom soup, crackers, instant chocolate pudding. She was too sick to feel hungry, but once she began eating she couldn't stop.

It was not getting worse; perhaps it was getting better. The days lightened and darkened, lightened and darkened. She ate crackers from the box beside her bed. If Tash returned on the weekend, it must have been while Stephanie dozed; she heard no one.

On Monday she pulled a sweater on over the T-shirt and track pants in which she slept, and shuffled down the sidewalk to the corner store. Midday, weekday; the street was teeming with its other life. Up in her room she'd been distantly aware, through the mist of fever, of clanging and shouting, motors and horns. Now she walked through the workaday world, body-shop doors hoisted open, levered cars, backing and beeping delivery vans, men swearing.

She kept her head down, feeling impossibly worn and soiled, and made it to the store, where she bought dusty cans and paper boxes with dubious expiry dates. She made it home hot and exhausted, considered a bath, but the ringed tub and cold porch discouraged her.

By the middle of the week she was considerably better, except for enormous exhaustion and a racking cough. She knelt and scrubbed the tub, managed to bathe, thinking she would walk up Commercial Drive to the greengrocer's and also to the bank machine; she was out of cash. But after she was dressed in clean clothes, she fell onto the sofa and slept.

The next day she went out. The rain had stopped, a sharp March wind had shattered the clouds. Minus that ceiling, the world was unnaturally airy, oversized, unstable. All the mountains across the harbour rose dark against a watery blue sky.

The wind sliced flesh from her bones, then froze her through leather and denim. She had lost weight, she felt weightless, in a minute the wind would blow her fragments out to sea. As she walked, invisible between the loitering vans and incurious workmen, she felt less herself than ever. The pale sun stung her eyes like the harsh chlorine of swimming pools. She waded against the wind to a cheap café where, exhausted, she ate eggs and toast. The waitress didn't look at her.

Back out on the street each step hurt as she climbed the shallow grade towards the grocery store. Once in, she could not remember what she wanted to buy: oranges? apples? yogurt? She sat on the bus-stop bench outside the laundromat, coughing until her lungs ached, and then trudged the six blocks back home.

"Has it really been three weeks?" said Duncan. "I can't believe it's been three weeks since we saw each other."

"More than that," said Stephanie. They were walking along the service road on the waterfront; between the tin siding on the canneries and the container trucks, the mountains loomed unnaturally close across the harbour. Dark blue for the fir slopes, slate blue for the water, bright hard sapphire for the wind-washed sky, ice blue for the sea breeze itself, cleaving right through her body.

"Time flies," said Duncan.

"I guess," said Stephanie. The wind blew her empty as last summer's weeds rattling between the railroad tracks. Her skin was gone, and her bones and her soul.

They cut down behind some container trucks and squatted

on the edge of the harbour. Rank grass, and below that a tumble of broken rock, landfill, and then the water: up close, both dark and clear, heaving over strands of kelp.

"I've been very busy. Very productive," said Duncan.

"Have you," said Stephanie. The water bothered her. It was not sentient, not even alive, but it rose and fell with a sleeper's slow breathing. Sucked and slurped.

"Very," said Duncan. A seaplane droned between them into the silence of Sunday afternoon.

"That's good," said Stephanie. She thought that if he touched her, if he even said something kind — *It was a terrible mistake, I missed you a lot* — her blood would thaw, the cold tin sea would dance into spring.

"Yeah," said Duncan.

"I missed you," said Stephanie. She thought that her voice shook.

"Well, yeah. I missed you too," said Duncan. "Some things, anyway. But don't you think it's better this way?"

"No," said Stephanie. The tears were unbidden as floodwater, and just when she most wanted to present her case reasonably. Her throat filled.

"But we've been through this before," said Duncan.

"We were just talking about a break—!" Stephanie wailed. She did not plan on wailing, but the sobs were rising from deep in her chest, her body flooding and washing out to sea. She was hunched over now, big gulps, craven.

"But it's better this way," said Duncan. "I've got to figure out where I'm going. Oh, come *on*," he said, hugging her. "It's not that bad. It's not worth getting that upset over."

His arms around her didn't help. She could smell him now: clean cotton, soap, his fairly neutral aftershave. Close enough to taste, and impossibly far away. She opened her mouth to speak and choked: big, messy, complicated sobs.

"I," she managed to blurt, "I, I'm going to miss you."

"Oh, Christ, Stephanie," said Duncan. He pulled back a little to look at her and she saw there were tears standing in his eyes too. "Of course I'm going to miss you, too. But we can't go on like this."

"Why," she heaved out. "Why not?"

"With you getting upset like this all the time."

"I'm not *upset*," said Stephanie, holding onto him as if the bank were sliding away under her, into the cold and waiting sea.

The flat rear wall of the apartment building across the alley blocked the sunlight but, even so, the air in the back office was sharper and clearer. The new light showed the film of grit on the windowpane, the grey path from swivel chair to doorway, the sag and clutter of paper.

There were no windows in the front office. Claire's desk was so tidy it looked empty.

"She didn't really have a choice," said Linda. "The school board offered her twice as much money on a two-year contract to do basically the same thing as *Alternatives to Aggression*."

"She quit?" said Stephanie. The coffee tasted stale; perhaps her sense of taste had not yet returned. "What will we do?"

"I don't know. I was talking to the chair of the Teachpeace board. I guess they're kind of pissed off at her. I guess they figured she should have left all the materials here."

"I bet they're pissed."

"But she explained it all to me. It made sense, what she said."

"Will they hire someone else?"

"They don't know yet. The project funding only goes another few months. The big thing is that Secretary of State doesn't find out. Not until they send us the last quarter of the grant."

"So you and Joel broke up," said Stephanie.

"He was being such a jerk. Like he knew everything all the time."

"I can imagine."

"I don't know what I would have done without Tash. She was so supportive. Always pointing out what he was doing to me."

"I haven't seen him around."

"He went to that union conference in Ottawa. He should be home by now."

"So Tash has been staying with you?"

"Oh, yeah. We're moving into this really cool house. It's going to be this totally woman-only space. We've been over there a lot. We're painting the kitchen lavender and purple."

"She didn't say."

"It's such a cool space."

"Uh. Actually Duncan and I have pretty much broken up too."

"Oh yeah? Now you can really get into the women's scene. Get out from under all that male energy. It's super-important for women to make a safe place for healing and trust."

"So you and Linda broke up," said Stephanie.

"Never really got off the ground," said Joel. His beer was on the kitchen table, his backpack by the door. Outside, the rainless night was silent. Not the velvet silence of real spring but the sour silence of the vacant time before leafbud and songbirds.

"That's too bad," said Stephanie. "What went wrong?"

"Nothing particular. Her and Tash are together now. That's more what she wanted."

"*Together* together?"

"Yeah. Together. They're moving into this women-only house up on Seventh."

"I heard. How do you feel?"

"Feel? It's cool. It's where they're at. It's just as well we didn't really get going. When I was at the conference I got offered a job at union headquarters in Ottawa. I got to go back in two weeks."

"Shit. Oh. Well, that's great."

"Everett or Dick might want to take my room. You know them?"

"No."

"Everett really needs a place. They're getting evicted from that warehouse practice space. It's getting renovated into condos."

"Shit. Well, Duncan and I have called it quits too."

"Yeah? You guys were together for ages. Hey, I saw him yesterday. So he's lost his job?"

"He never said."

"That paper, the *Shopper*, got sold to this chain of suburban weeklies. So they'll do it all from their main office out in Douglas Ridge. Kind of a drag, eh?"

"Sorry I missed Easter," said Stephanie. "I had a bit of a cold."

"Oh, I wasn't expecting you," said her mother. "I'm not trying to run your life. It would have been nice, though."

"I didn't feel up to it."

"You're better now. You're eating right. You're keeping warm. You still have that nice coat with the fur collar."

"Oh, yes."

"It was very quiet here. Your father has gone down to the Bahamas."

"On vacation?"

"You could say that. I didn't really want to go. The women that go down there every winter look like leather. They look used."

"Still. It sounds like fun."

"He and your uncle are just going to sit around the pool and booze it up."

"Oh. Uncle Freddy is down there?"

"It seemed like the best thing at the time. Better than having him loose up here."

"So this is a business trip."

"You could say that. Really, I don't ask. Not about your life, and not about your father's."

"So the trouble is over."

"There never was any trouble. The media blew it out of proportion. The journalists are socialists at heart, they gang up on the government. I don't mean your friend, of course. The one whose father was a lawyer."

"Oh, we're not going out any more."

"You're not? I'm sure that's all for the best. I'm sure you told him where he could put his complaining."

"Yes. Sure I did."

"So when are you coming over? Soon?"

"Yes. Sure. Soon."

Bare trees, the sun surprisingly hot, the streets dusty and worn, attic or windowless room.

Under her leather jacket, a bloom of sweat; perhaps the fever lingered.

In Odyssey Travel, the woman behind the desk had long nails, patently false, probably new; she curled back her fingers so only the pads touched paper, pencil, keyboard. Stephanie had read in fashion magazines about this trick, meant to save chips and cracks.

"Open-ended return," the woman said. "You can come back

any time you like within a year. Let's see if it's cheaper via London, or direct to Athens."

On the walls, high-gloss colour posters: ruins and beaches, domed cities, hill-tribe children, and the familiar coast rainforest, here bracketed and made marvellous through top-quality photography: motes, mist, the aspiring tips of cedar and spruce.

"That sounds all right," said Stephanie. The price the travel agent quoted was less than she'd expected. "Can you do it any cheaper?"

"Let me check the charter flights to Amsterdam. If you can leave before the high season?"

"I can leave any time," said Stephanie.

She walked up Commercial Drive slowly, past the Italian restaurant with the paper place mats, and the other one with the white tablecloths. Overnight, someone had filled the planters outside with forced pansies, velvet blue against fresh-turned earth.

She walked past the second-hand bookstore, past the Portuguese coffee bar, where a few customers were already sitting outside, on chairs carried to the sidewalk. She kept walking, past the snaky shoes and the amputated suit jacket, past the little butcher.

If she walked slowly it was all right. She didn't cough, she didn't grow hot and flushed.

At the corner by the empty lot, a woman was busy with a bucket of paint. She was a middle-aged woman, she looked tired and cranky, as if this task were the last impossibility of a difficult life. Old polyester trousers, spattered and ruined, a scarf over her head. She was painting out Tash's graffiti, letter by letter: *WOMEN ARE EVERYWHERE*.

The wall was cream, off-white, and so was the paint, but the match was not exact. The wall was sooted, the fresh paint shone, the ghost of the letters still hovered white on white.

Stephanie kept walking up past the greengrocers'.

To forget all this, to forget Duncan, would be like taking a knife to her own stomach. She had not yet even started. It terrified her, this knowledge in advance of how lonely she was going to be, again and again, on and on.

In order to forget, she would have to become someone else. There was no other way. She would have to become a different person, and right at the moment she didn't have any idea how that would happen, or who she wanted to be.

MIDSUMMER

MIDSUMMER

The thrift shop filled the hull of a dead supermarket, ten aisles stretching away under high arched roof: *Ladies' Blouses, Ladies' Pant Suits, Costumes, Men's Jackets, Bedding* read small placards. The floor was stripped to concrete, air heavy as an old closet: musty cotton, stale shoes, whiff of naphthalene.

Kelly and Madeline were working their way, gleaning, row by row. Madeline pushed the shopping cart, nearly full; Kelly walked in front.

"This is cool," said Kelly. She turned over the price tag. "This is kind of hilarious."

"Purple suede miniskirt, side lacing, matching long-line vest," said Madeline. "For the go-go girl about town. Swinging sixties. Is it ridiculous?"

"Five ninety-nine," said Kelly.

"Toss it in," said Madeline. "Tania can move that for thirty." Then she bit her tongue and looked over her shoulder. But the clerk was down at the end of the row, sorting *Ladies' Sleeveless Sweaters*. She hadn't heard.

"More summery stuff, Tania wanted, too," Madeline said.

"It's all this kind of yuck," said Kelly. "Sundresses with stretchy tops. From two years back."

Walking in front, Kelly saw the dress first, a glimpse of cotton sateen sliding across her arm, scalloped neckline, fitted bodice, full full skirt a dream of garden parties at dusk, mauve and green.

"Dior New Look, 1947," murmured Madeline. "Cloth rationing just ended." She turned back the neckline: yellowed but clean, label a long-dead Toronto tailor, sturdy layers of interface and lining and stitching.

"It's fucking gorgeous," said Kelly, draping it over the buggy.

"We've got enough for the fitting rooms," said Madeline. They tried on everything during these trips, even when it wasn't their size, checking for odd waistlines, sags, stains, splits.

Madeline was wearing her working uniform: bike shorts, loose T-shirt, denim jacket, sandals she could kick off and on. She wanted to whip in and out of her clothes. And more: she wanted to look anonymous. If the big suburban thrift stores thought city girls were coming out chasing vintage clothes — worse, re-selling them downtown — they'd double the prices like they'd already done on Hastings Street.

Kelly hadn't taken Madeline's hint. Kelly was less anonymous, all right; she definitely had a harder time going undercover. Cerise hair was hard to hide. Right now she was in the booth next door, unlacing eight-holed boots, unzipping, unpeeling cut-offs, vest and shirt, bangles clinking against the wall.

Madeline slid into the mauve dress. It fit like skin: skin from another lifetime, one of discipline and restraint. You couldn't slouch in a dress like this, you couldn't lie on the floor with your head between the speakers, you couldn't kneel vomiting drunk in the herbaceous border at three a.m., you probably couldn't even eat. Madeline twirled in the flecked mirror and thought *big hat, tiny shoes, white gloves.* In the gap between the discipline of the dress and the terms of her own life lay a discordance that excited her. She saw herself zipped up inviolate for one night, pirouetting through the darkness of a big party — warehouse loft, cavernous old house, live band — everything dark, feral, leather. Profaning everything the dress stood for, splitting seams, spilling drinks, twisting and jiving and slam dancing until her sweat made the colours stink and run.

She could buy the dress, of course, put down her own money, leave the bag under the seat when Tania helped them unload at Styx and Stoned. But Madeline needed the thirty per cent commission Tania gave her on big items (Kelly got cashier's hours to come along for the ride). What would a dress like this go for, pristine and perverse? Well, thirty per cent of anything would help, right now.

And she didn't need the dress. She didn't really *need* it.

Madeline and Kelly drove back to the city along the river road. The Fraser was cresting fast and silent, brown silt and broken trees. The car windows were down, the air rushed forward, musky cottonwood, all those perfumed shiny Valentines, the heart-shaped leaves, unrolling in the sun.

"This new one, then," said Madeline. "Since I've been out of town. You said he's not behaving."

"Shit," said Kelly. "Matthew. He's gorgeous. But he's one of these guys that needs space. You know?"

"Tell him to eat it," said Madeline cheerfully. "Tell him to shove it up his ass. His space."

"I didn't mean it like that," said Kelly. "He's not messing me around. Not on purpose. He told me right away at the start how his life is. We talked."

"You talked."

"Yeah."

"But you don't sound too happy."

"Happy. Shit, yeah. You know. Whatever that's all about."

Styx and Stoned had three violet snakes entwining on the front window, and bruised walls sponged black and purple. A single stick of incense burned behind the counter. Under sandalwood, though, the air held the same settled mustiness as the thrift shop.

When Madeline and Kelly came in, Tania looked at her watch and then locked the front door. She opened the first bag.

"Mm," she said. "Oh, now this is very nice. Black lace practically sells itself."

A woman rattled the door, pressed herself against the glass. Tania looked up, shook her head, smiled. Her smile was wide, warm, deeply personal, regretful. Then she turned back to the clothes, and her face went blank.

"A little red dressmaker suit. Size 14. Adorable. This can go in the window, it's light enough for summer."

Kelly was skewed round in the cashier's chair, drumming her fingers on the counter and reading the handbills on the wall.

"Hey, shit," she said. "Cryptic Neon's playing this Saturday. They're super excellent."

"This bag is keepers," said Tania. She looked up at Madeline and gave her a rationed smile, not the full blaze reserved for customers. Meanwhile her hands — small, thin, dry — were working away, folding, aligning, precisely, with love and care. Focus, thought Madeline, who was already mildly bored. She knows what's bringing in the cash.

"Shit, I got wasted at their last gig," said Kelly. "Matthew knows the bass player. You guys going?"

The mauve dress had a bag to itself.

"What's this?" said Tania mildly. "Oh. Goodness. Look at that." She held it to her throat. The garden spilled over her lap.

"Yes," said Madeline. "Isn't it?"

"You could actually *wear* a dress like this," said Tania. "You could go out in the daytime. You've done really well this time, Madeline. You've got a great eye."

"I was right out of control that night," said Kelly. "Matthew had to drag me out of there."

"Thank you," said Madeline, putting simple sincerity into her voice. She was not yet sure about Tania's praise, not yet sure of anything about her. Tania was old enough to have a history; one look told you she did, but Madeline had never been privileged to hear it.

Tania had the long tawny hair, the tough little body, the weathered skin, of another generation altogether. Madeline didn't think *summer of love* when she looked at Tania. She thought of something else, of what came after: *summer of death,* perhaps. Tania made her think of sleeping on the beach, and dealing speed, *one pill makes you smaller,* psychotic marijuana farmers on the Gulf Islands, shotguns rigged over their driveways, *Hotel California.* All that.

Tania didn't look dated, or out of fashion. She wore silver spiders in her ears, she looked timeless. Timeless and possibly dangerous, Madeline thought. Everything that could happen to her had already happened. Nothing now would be a risk.

Today Tania seemed completely sincere. "Lovely," she said, and draped the mauve dress across a chair, fanning out the long skirt. "This goes in the window. Scuse," she said to Kelly, and hit the cash register. "Madeline, for the boots and Jackie Kennedy suit that went yesterday. And your hours today. And Kelly, for today."

Madeline tucked the wad of bills into her pocket and walked into a wave of May sunshine. Late afternoon, and the light pouring down, and a clean little breeze — blue, blue, blue, above the flat dusty shops, the snagged cables.

Everett walked out of the book shop next door.

"Long time no see," he said, which was just gauche enough that Madeline thought he must be registering something, surprise or even pleasure.

"At least a year," said Madeline. "I've been away."

"Oh have you?" he said. She couldn't tell a thing from his profile, the cut of nose and chin, except that it was beautiful. Drawn, though, tight, fraying a bit around the eyes.

"Yes," said Madeline. "Europe. London and Berlin mostly, Italy too." She hadn't known him well enough last year to make a point of saying goodbye. If he'd been curious, wondered at her absence — well, he could have asked around.

"I think I heard something like that," Everett said.

Bingo! Madeline said to herself. *Maybe.* Aloud she said, "There are no secrets in this city, I'm afraid."

"I'd love to hear about it but I've got to run," said Everett. Then he added, so fast Madeline nearly missed her cue, "We should get together some night and you can tell me all about it. Do you have a number?"

"I'm at Kelly's for a few weeks until my place is ready," said Madeline.

"I don't think I know her."

Everett didn't scrawl on the cover of *Mother Jones* or *The New Statesman*. He tucked the magazines under his arm and pulled a datebook from his hip pocket, copied her down in block letters under the correct letter of the alphabet.

Well, thought Madeline. That was almost too easy. Let's see if he uses it.

"Catch you later," said Everett.

"Bye," said Madeline.

She put the key in the driver's door of her little white Chevette and the lock jammed. Chevette: the cheapest item in the *Auto Trader,* an unfortunate American attempt to go Japanese, at the end of the last decade. Datsun and Toyota hadn't depreciated half as fast.

The right lock had been broken when she bought the car three years ago; when Madeline had passengers, she reached across the seat. So today there was nothing else to do. Madeline went round to the hatch back, opened the trunk and crawled forward over the spare tire, an emergency blanket, a case of empty beer bottles, jumper cables, parking brake and the backs of the front seats. Then she opened the driver's door from the inside, stepped out, went around to slam the hatch, settled into the seat and turned the ignition.

The car started.

If she put her foot to the floor, really booted it on the freeway, she could do fifty miles an hour, though not uphill. But tonight was stop-and-go as she picked her way through rush-hour traffic across town towards the beach.

Carl lived in a white stucco box, three-storey walk-up. He followed Madeline onto the balcony with beer and tumblers. The dark glass sweated, the foam crested. Madeline licked the side of her thumb.

"Cheers," she said.

"Welcome back," said Carl.

"I love your view," said Madeline. "Straight across at the mountains and out to sea."

"If you hold your glass like so, you can cut out the bottom half," said Carl. "All these roofs and telephone wires and the neighbour's washing down there."

"I like that, too," said Madeline. "No, honestly. I surprised myself. It was what I missed in Europe. Even though I never come out this far west except to visit you."

"Funny what you miss when you travel, isn't it?"

"What did you miss the year you were in Thailand?"

"What did I miss?" said Carl. "Let me see. I don't know what I missed. I missed some people, a bit. But I was pretty much happy wherever I was."

"Oh, I was happy," said Madeline. "But I didn't think I'd miss the beach and the view. It's so much the tourist thing."

"Tourists know a good thing," said Carl. "Listen. What we should do for supper is get some chicken and sit on the beach and watch the sun go down. If you want chicken, that is. You can get pizza next door. Do you want pizza? Would that be better than chicken?"

"Chicken's fine," said Madeline. "Chicken would be great."

Holding foil bags, Madeline and Carl followed lawns unrolling down the point of land towards the museum. Behind perched the span of an art deco bridge, behind that the city's clustered towers, shooting back sunlight, and behind that the mountains, side-lit, hyper-visible: too much beauty, too many layers, too much to register. Close up, in the wind, fighter kites dipped and hissed: bats, hawks, angry insects. Madeline and Carl stopped to watch. The strings led earthwards to the hands not of children but of men, men in early middle age, each on his own knoll, serious, preoccupied and solitary.

"They must be practising for a contest. War of the giant kites," said Madeline. "They don't look like the kind of guys who would do useless things just for fun."

"No doubt," said Carl. "There's clubs for everything. They're really quite amazing, aren't they? See, lookit, there are two strings, they tilt that bar, the wind does all the work. There's a lot of skill. I wonder if you could make one, how hard that would be, getting the balance."

"You probably buy a kit," said Madeline.

"That would be no fun," said Carl.

They sat on a pocket beach, and unpacked roast chicken and potatoes, coleslaw, hot coffee. Carl was methodical, tidy: a good country boy, Ottawa Valley. Years ago, without discussion, they had ruled out becoming lovers. No fumbled kisses, awkward nights or strained silences hovered behind them.

Madeline had always assumed, without much reflection, that the decision, the abstinence, was hers. And why? Carl was a bit younger, but not enough to matter. He had a nice body, carpenter's shoulders, he looked good in a swimsuit, very good. And yet, dressed, for some reason, he was often diminished. His clothes rarely fit, or they didn't flatter. Perhaps he had the wrong muscles, the wrong body, built on the job and not in a gym. Tonight he was wearing a plain black T-shirt, tonight he looked good, but it was entirely accidental. Madeline knew that.

It was not that clothes in themselves mattered. They didn't matter at all. Only, in this case, they signposted something else.

Insufficiently examined self. Insufficiently examined world. Too much tolerance. You couldn't just pick the world up off the closet floor every morning and walk out into it smiling, Madeline thought. You just couldn't.

There were other people for both of them.

"Is Beth coming back for the summer?" said Madeline idly.

"Maybe later on," said Carl. "She might come out in August. She's got a summer job for a professor right now."

"Good for her," said Madeline. Of course she liked Beth. She didn't dislike her. Beth didn't matter one way or the other. But when she was in town, Carl had less time. More than that: Beth was always underfoot, with her bowl-cut hair and her tense silences, her inescapable Bethness. How could boring little women take up so much space and energy?

"She wants me to come out there," Carl said.

"To Toronto?"

"She says there's lots of work. She says I should finish my degree."

Madeline put down her roasted thigh. "Are you going to go?"

"She wants me to think about it."

Trust Beth, thought Madeline. What an idiotic idea. A Beth idea, all right. Madeline was however aware that she had no objective arguments to support this opinion. She picked up her chicken, took a bite and chewed. Madeline had always chosen to go easy on Beth around Carl: diplomacy, friendship. Going easy on Beth meant mentioning her as little as possible. This was not a bad habit. Right now it came in quite useful. It helped her hold her tongue. What a truly dumb idea, Madeline thought again, and swallowed. Aloud she said, "Are you thinking about it?"

"Yes. I am," said Carl. "It might be time for a change."

Little bitch, thought Madeline, and stabbed a potato with her plastic fork.

The tines snapped. She picked up the potato with her fingers, popped it in her mouth and sat chewing as the neon sun flattened itself on the horizon.

The next morning, light streaming through tall windows, Madeline sat high on a stool in a borrowed studio. Over the drawing table lay a black leather jacket, commission job. Across the back she was painting looped lizards, a sinuous green nest.

When she finished this jacket, she'd do a second one for the lead guitarist, co-ordinating but not identical. When she was finished both, that would be two hundred dollars. And when people saw those lizards go backstage, there'd be more jackets on her table, no doubt about that.

The sun climbed up the sky while Madeline sat painting tiny red eyes. Time did one of its circus tricks, one of its little routines. While she worked, time stopped dead in its tracks. After a while she quit thinking about money, she quit thinking about anything at all. The lizards bent and clung to the leather, rounded yellow bellies and embryonic toes. Then Madeline sat up, stretched, laid down her brush, and the clock spun round. The off-key fog-horn downtown blew the first bar of the national anthem. Noon.

Money isn't the problem, Madeline thought all of a sudden. It isn't the real problem. Not any more.

She went looking for a souvlaki stand she'd liked, but it was closed, windows whitewashed; the building, with its gargoyles and parapets, seemed to be awaiting demolition. She hadn't expected much to change in a year, and it hadn't. But these little things added up, small dislocations.

Madeline walked too far, down into the tourist zone by the cruise-ship docks, fake cobblestones and renovated warehouses full of souvenir shops. Fat white people in white shorts. They squinted up at the steam clock with their mouths open, they peered uncertainly down side alleys, stood blocking the sidewalk.

I did not look like that in Europe, Madeline thought. I always knew where I was going. She was hungry, and dizzy from paint, and getting cranky. Today made three weeks back, euphoria of arrival wearing off fast. This itch was a new feeling, everything choppy, insubstantial, unfocused. And money wasn't the problem. She couldn't blame that.

The pasta she finally ate was limp and overpriced. Tourist food. The café didn't worry about keeping customers; three hundred more stepped off the cruise ships every afternoon. All the past year she'd avoided this, the bad food, surly service, lumpen coach tours of assembly-line travel. And here she was, a tourist in her own town. Today she was dressed in black, narrow pants and tight leotard, her hair a dark cloud to her waist. But it didn't matter. In the pink mirrors lining the walls — double your visual space, an old trick — she was sprouting baby blue Bermuda shorts, a maple leaf T-shirt and a bleached perm.

She'd fled them through Europe and now they'd caught her, where she hadn't expected it. Here, the place in the world where, secretly and to her shame, she fundamentally least belonged.

"One thing I saw in London was, you take the top of an old pair of jeans, the waist and hips," said Madeline. "You chop it off and sew on a bit of cloth. Something with a good print. Or brocade. Make a miniskirt."

"It's an idea," said Tania. She was writing cheques in the stock room, the curtain over the doorway tied back. Madeline was turned round on the cashier's stool. Styx and Stoned was empty, mid-afternoon's lull and dip.

"It would work if you could get the jeans cheap enough," said Madeline. This wasn't necessarily something she wanted to do herself. It was Tania she was watching, Tania's interest she was fishing for.

"Mm," said Tania.

"See, it's hardly any work," said Madeline. "I figured this out today, doing those jackets. It's never going to be worth making something from scratch. No one's ever going to pay you enough for your time. It's better to get something thrown out and make it hip, somehow."

"I was into dressmaking for a while," said Tania. "You're right. It didn't pay."

"Really?" said Madeline, interested. "When was this?"

"A while back."

Ting went the bell over the door, and two women walked in. Tania dropped the curtain.

"Good afternoon," said Madeline, smiling her widest smile of the day. "Can I help you or just browsing?"

Madeline walked out at closing time into the wall of May sunshine. No one stepped out of the book shop next door. She kept walking, past the Portuguese coffee bar with the big windows. Yesterday, according to Tania, the city had arrived to fine the owner for putting tables on the sidewalk. Today the customers were back, sitting outside on plastic milk crates, leaning against the wall so the sun caught their faces. The boys had rolled their jeans, the women hiked their skirts: black skirts, powdery white thighs, dirty hair, pierced ears and noses.

Madeline saw no one she knew. All these people she could, she might, she should know, her type, her city. In one year? Did the population of the east end roll over that fast? She kept walking.

It was all smaller here than she remembered, smaller and flatter and wider, stucco and lath, ephemeral. This street had never had a heyday, she could see that now. Right at the beginning it had been built on the cheap for the poor, flat and functional — no cornices, pediments, turrets, no excess. Into the spaces left by fading butchers and barbers was seeping a new layer, used bookstores and vegetarian cafés, trinkets from Peru and Bali. There were fewer old women and families, fewer dark-haired men talking loudly on the sidewalk, caffeine hyped. Madeline went into the greengrocer's and absentmindedly bought a cantaloup, plain yogurt, tricoloured pasta.

The sun kept blazing away as she turned down the side street to Kelly's house. Candelabra of chestnut blossom, pink flames, melting light. In the cracks of the sidewalks, buckled by roots, blades of grass shot up three, four feet overnight, heavy-headed as oats. Derelict front gardens spilled runaway bearded iris and bleeding heart, snapdragons and foxglove. Mock orange collapsed over picket fences, the last rhododendrons trumpeted in the shadows.

Kelly and Sue had the main floor of an old wooden house, standard 1910 blueprint: front hall, living room, dining room, kitchen, pantry. The archway from living to dining room was nailed shut, and that made Kelly's bedroom. Dim light filtered through a square of stained glass high in the wall, and the air was drowsy with patchouli. The back pantry was Sue's room, futon on the floor. Sue was tree planting in Terrace, and Madeline was sub-letting.

Kelly wasn't in. Madeline used yesterday's sauce on the pasta, opened a beer, found one of Kelly's cigarettes and put one of Kelly's tapes on the stereo. Hard-driving ska, Caribbean reggae bounce mixed with British punk. Dance music from five years back. *Enjoy yourself, it's later than you think.* Bad idea. With that music, you couldn't help but think about everything that was gone, all the parties and the people and the bars, all the kisses and the late nights.

And here she was, after all that. Opening her eyes after a year, here in the city where she was supposed to know everyone, fit right in. Friday night. Outside, that perfect tender afternoon blazed into evening, and she was wasting it, losing it, bored, bored.

"First you have to cook the pasta," said Kelly. "Then you sauté the garlic and mushrooms and add the ricotta. Then you make the tomato sauce. Then you layer the pasta."

"A lot of work, eh," said Madeline. "It smells great, though."

The kitchen door was wide open. Madeline was sitting on the porch drinking wine and watching her legs pinken in the sun. A cacophony of purple finches on the clothesline, lawnmower down the block — and in the other ear Kelly, hot butter hissing. From the living room, cranked up, hard-core three-chord thrash. Saturday afternoon.

"Top me up," said Madeline. "I'm too lazy." She fell backwards into the kitchen, pushing her glass towards the stove. Kelly leaned over, poured.

"This must be what it looks like to a cat," said Madeline. "Or a little kid." She turned her cheek against the tiles and considered the cabinet doors: white paint lumped over old chips. Brown dribbles, coffee or tomato sauce. The ceiling was miles up, shadowy, yellowed. From the waist down Madeline was still in sunshine. She stretched, pointed her toes. "Meow," she said.

"You're shit-faced," said Kelly, and giggled. "You're getting plastered."

"No I'm not." Madeline sat up to prove it. "It's just nice on the floor."

"It hasn't been washed since Sue left," Kelly said, and giggled again. She licked the mixing spoon. "There's all kinds of stuff down there."

"Yeah, right," said Madeline. "So when's this Matthew turning up?"

"For dinner for sure. For the gig. Earlier if he gets done."

"So won't this cheese thing be toast?"

"No, no. It's all together now and then when he turns up it goes in the oven."

"So you're done?"

"Just about. Seen the grater?"

"So why don't we go do something? Walk down to the Drive? It's gorgeous out there."

"Oh, I *can't*. Matthew might turn up."

He knocked on the front door well after dark. Madeline was in her room, Sue's room, getting dressed. Pared down, indestructible: the black leotard, high-top sneakers, narrow jeans she'd tapered by hand with tiny stitches. Wallet and keys in one hip pocket, comb and lipstick in the other. She tied her hair off her neck and went into the living room.

Matthew, eh, thought Madeline. Bad news. Matthew was slumped, legs splayed, staring straight ahead. He had the look of a suffering husband, the look that says: what on earth am I doing here, and who dragged me along?

Kelly was sitting beside him on the sofa, curled up so the brim of her skirt skimmed the brim of her panties. Turned to face him, she actually had a finger under his collar.

"You guys know each other, right?" Kelly said. "Madeline's just come back from Europe. She works in Styx and Stoned with me. I got to check the stove. Can she have one of your beers?"

"Over there," said Matthew. Kelly uncoiled herself and went into the kitchen. Madeline pulled a bottle out of the case by the door. The sofa was the only furniture in the room; Madeline sat cross-legged on the carpet.

"Working today?" she said.

"Shit yeah. I'm thrashed," said Matthew. He said this with finality, he said this as if daring her to continue the conversation, or as if she should know — if she were anyone at all, she'd know — exactly what he'd been doing, every movement.

"So what were you doing?" said Madeline. I'd forgotten this, she thought. I never met a British guy like this, or a European. I'm not ready for America yet. The itch was coming back, the irritation. Fuck you, she thought. I'm going to make conversation. I'm going to be gauche and chirpy and entirely uncool. "You must have been working awfully hard."

"Yeah," said Matthew after a minute. "Moving shit."

"Like what?" said Madeline. "Furniture? Fridges?"

"Nah. No way. This is for these guys in this band."

"Oh," said Madeline. "Heavy amps and things. I can imagine." That wasn't what she was meant to say. By the rules of the game she was meant to say: *Oh really? What band?* But she didn't.

"For this band. I know the guys really well," said Matthew.

"Mmm," said Madeline, and sipped her beer. She was beginning to enjoy herself.

"I help them out a lot," Matthew said. "All the time."

"Uh-huh."

"Rod and Dick and Randy. They're in Cryptic Neon."

"We'll see them play tonight," said Madeline. She didn't add: I'm painting jackets for Dick and Randy.

"They're excellent," said Matthew. "They're going to get a label deal any time now."

Kelly came back into the living room and sat beside Matthew. "Hi, you guys," she said. "We can eat soon. Shit I'm drunk. What do you think of my boots?" She pointed her toes. "Matthew. What do you think of my boots? I just got them."

"They're all right," he said.

"Not from Styx and Stoned. Shit. We go out and get crap from Value Village in Surrey and sell it for five times what we paid. People walk in, I just want to shit myself laughing, they pay that."

"It's fair," said Madeline. "They don't want to find it themselves."

"It's a ripoff," said Kelly. "I don't care, it's a job. But Tania's making a killing. I'd never buy anything there."

"Wouldn't let Tania hear you," said Madeline. Beer on top of wine; pinpoints of pain in her skull. The bare bulb in the ceiling lit everything flat.

"I wouldn't say it to her," said Kelly. "Matthew. Wakey wakey. How you doing?"

"All right," he said.

Kelly ladled lasagna onto plates, and passed the salad bowl. "I think I got all the mud and slugs off," she said. "Hope so anyways."

"This guy," said Matthew suddenly. "This one we were talking about. He says next week is okay."

"Oh excellent," said Kelly.

"We call him Monday."

"That's super great," said Kelly.

Madeline ate a spinach leaf and a mouthful of pasta. It was too rich, she was too drunk; the resilient mozzarella didn't diminish as she chewed. She thought, unwillingly, about erasers.

Matthew. Matthew and Kelly. He was good-looking enough, Madeline thought. Low forehead, shoulder-length hair, blunt cut; he kept tossing it off his face. Stocky body. Cuter now that he was waking up a little.

Kelly put the plates on the counter, and her fingers down the back of Matthew's army pants. They stood up, and Madeline followed them out the door, down the block and up the flight of stairs to the hall where the band was playing.

Madeline woke at eleven a.m., humming ears. It was like that, music. For five hours she'd been at the dark centre of the world. Then the sun came up. Life went on.

Matthew and Kelly slept on silently behind the dining-room door. Madeline ate cold lasagna from the pan on the stove. The sink was stacked with plates, beer bottles and ashtrays on the table, nubbins of scorched popcorn. Twenty minutes brisk work it would take, with the door flung open to the spring air. Suds, hot water, gleam-clean chrome. Instead, Madeline licked her fingers, put her wallet in her pocket and went down the back steps.

Wooden houses, steep gables, gingerbread trim, sagging porches and green green green. All the birds were going, and none of the cars. Sunday morning.

Space. There was certainly space here, breeze snapping off the harbour, waste lots and parking lots and corner lots, front gardens and parking lanes. For a year Madeline had grown used to stone walls, alleys, compression, age. This city was wide open, run flat into sea and mountains. Grass split the sidewalks, and young trees, too: broadleaf maple saplings, dinner-plate leaves on twig trunks.

Madeline had come home because it was home, a clear enough decision two months ago, time finally blurring with night trains, squats, youth hostels and foreign currency. Back then, at a distance, home brimmed over with specific and obvious meanings: order, possibility, belonging.

Coming back was easy: job, housing, all that. But the way this wind was chasing its tail through the gaps and spaces, nothing would stand still.

Madeline went into the coffee bar, ordered cappuccino and opened a newspaper. She had no trouble picking up the thread of the headlines. None of the big stories had moved much in a year: the trial, the political scandal, the trade war, government funding cuts.

Maybe she had never been away. She had dreamed Europe,

as distant and impossible as last night, as far away as dancing.

Kelly and Matthew were on the couch when Madeline came in the front door. A thread of breeze blew past her, circled and died in the shadows. She could smell bacon and eggs, stale beer, marijuana.

"Great gig, eh," said Matthew.

"You got a phone call," said Kelly. "I wrote it down over there somewhere. Everett?"

"Oh really?" said Madeline.

"Shit I'm fucked," said Matthew. "I didn't know you knew those guys. Dick and Randy."

Wednesday evening, Madeline parked her Chevette down on the waterfront across from a flat-faced warehouse. Up three dim flights of stairs she stepped past Everett into a shock of white plaster and varnished pine. A wall of windows framed red gantries and silver sheds, flooded light, the view distinct and abstract as art.

"Nice place," she said.

"It's all right," said Everett. "Until they raise the rent. Look, you can see Coal Harbour and the bridge." He stood in profile to her, a slim man, perfectly cut shirt falling into black jeans. Fashionable little glasses, brown skin and hair, short back and sides.

"Cypress and Grouse," Madeline said to the mountains. "And Hollyburn."

"I can see the cruise ships come in over there." He stood with one hand on the cord of the blind, a careless hand, maybe, but not a lazy one. Nothing about him was lazy, nothing wasted, a tautness that did not translate exactly to nerves.

"It's gorgeous," said Madeline. There was a balancing act in this conversation, there always was. Praise the view, praise the apartment, obviously. But as a topic of conversation it was going to bore them both very shortly.

Everett's face was still closed. He had, however, invited her. He wanted her here.

"That's the tallest building in town," he said. "That tower."

He was standing a foot away, maybe a little more. Twelve inches of air, only that. Madeline moved imperceptibly, seeking the edge of his heat radius, the point at which his body would begin to fill her senses. But he was still banked down, the fire doors shut. Besides, it was too early for that, far too early. All her advances must be verbal, she sensed.

"How's work?" she said.

"The editor is a prick," said Everett. "What would you like, wine or beer or gin and tonic?"

"Oh, gin," said Madeline. "That would be great. If you have it."

They took their drinks to the roof, overlooking a flatness of other roofs, asphalt like the roads and alleys. Beyond, the inlet, the mountains, smudged white at the crests of the ski runs. After-hours hush, that emptiness. Madeline sat lightly on a pile of bricks, letting her skirt flare out and fall. A new fashion, limp print cut on the bias and tied back to show off her waist. Underneath, she was acutely aware of the grip of her best underwear, the purple lace bra boned and wired, her breasts cupped, tilted, proffered. Between her legs, the tug of silk.

"Now that I'm back, there doesn't seem to be much to tell about Europe," she was saying. "You can talk about the tourist sites, which is boring," she added, beginning to grope for words. "Or else what you did every day, which doesn't make a lot of sense if no one knows the people. Shopping, walking around, gossip."

"Yes, exactly," said Everett. "It's like that whenever you do something someone else hasn't. Basically they don't want to listen."

"Were you over there?"

"A long time ago. After high school. I should pack up and go somewhere again. You get into a rut."

"You could afford that. You must be doing all right at the newspaper."

"Yeah. But you can't turn your back on that place. There's ten years' worth of journalism school grads out there that are younger than me and have more experience."

"I thought you had a union."

"They can't fire me. But all this about who gets the best stories, who gets a byline, that crap. You have to be there when it's getting handed out. If I took time off, all that would dry up."

"It sounds like you should wait, for sure."

"I know. But the thing about this city is, it's really limited.

Anyone tries to get good at something, everyone jumps on them and brings them down. Only failure is taken seriously. If you do too well, you must be a fake."

"I've felt that! I've started to feel that! Since I've been back. Everything looks so much smaller and shabbier. There just isn't anything happening."

"This is very simple," said Everett, coming away from his kitchen island: granite grey, bare counters, track lighting. "Some fresh fettucine tossed with cream and Parmesan. Shitake mushrooms. There's balsamic vinegar for the raddichio. Do you like the jazz tape?"

"It's lovely," said Madeline. "Everything's lovely."

"I'll do something better the next time you come around."

"But this is wonderful," said Madeline. The gin was hitting, lovely lazy disembodied, clearer somehow than beer: a colourless drunk. Next time, she thought, and smiled at her plate. The sax solo uncoiled from fairly expensive speakers; night fell like black drapes behind the wall of windows.

"This is my new discovery," she said. "You can actually slow time down if you play the right music."

"You mean get bored?"

"I mean in a good way. Like this music. You just slow down and you eat and you drink and you eat a bit more."

"What would speed time up?"

"Oh. You know. Punk. Thrash. Kelly's got it cranked all the time. It's all right. But you don't stop and notice things."

"You don't relax."

"This is nice." Over Everett's shoulder, down at the end of the room, the loft redoubled in the glass wall. And at the end of that second room, crowned with candles, floated another table, other diners. The girl had a blur of face, a cloud of hair, a print dress; the man had a back. Their glasses rose languidly in time to the music, the girl leaned forward in her chair, leaned back, rested one elbow delicately on the table.

They were at the heart of the world, that mirror couple, or pretty damn close to it. And if they were that close to it, Madeline herself would be there soon enough. Maybe not tonight, but soon, she thought, as they proceeded to mango sorbet, espresso, the long sculpted sofa.

They sat at opposite ends of the sofa, but they sat comfortably, feet tucked and curled. The food and the drink had done it, Madeline decided, opened things. They wandered through work, Europe, music, mutual acquaintances. She let him talk most; that was never a mistake. But when she spoke, she liked the seriousness with which he listened, the way he gave her his full attention. It felt like a responsibility, this; it made her choose her words with more care. Altogether, she felt herself subtly altering, to better fit the hour and the sparse elegance of the long room. Expanding, no doubt, though for a minute she wondered if she was contracting, becoming less herself. No. This was definitely her best self: poised, quiet, beautiful.

Still, Everett was an age away from her, tucked up at the end of the huge sofa: genuine 1950s, beautifully reupholstered. When she finally stood up to go, he walked her downstairs and across the empty street to her car.

She wasn't expecting the urgency of his kiss, the flicker of tongue, his body tilting her back against the driver's door. Her own body rising, points of lace through the thin material of her dress, the sugary rush in her veins — all that she had known beforehand. But she hadn't expected the emotion in him, not yet. Still, he pulled back first.

"That was nice," said Madeline. "Very nice."

"Wasn't it?" said Everett. "I'll give you a call about the weekend." He didn't take his hands from her waist. A few minutes later he pulled back again.

"We can't stand out here necking all night," he said. "This is getting ridiculous." He was smiling at her, grinning even.

"I guess," said Madeline. "You give me a call then."

The little car flew itself home along empty streets. The spring night was tickles and giggles, cottonwood musk blowing over the harbour. Madeline took the front steps two at a time, and found Kelly slumped alone on the sofa. The lugubrious stereo darkly droning, a flood wrack of beer bottles under the bare bulb, telephone on the floor.

"Fucking asshole," said Kelly. "I have had it with that asshole. He is such an asshole."

"You had a fight with Matthew," said Madeline. The room was blear with cigarette smoke, close after the velvet night. She wanted to spin giggling on the carpet, run hugging herself to her bedroom. Instead, she sat down beside Kelly and took a cigarette from the pack on the floor. "It sounds like you had a fight with Matthew," she repeated, reaching way back in her memory for the words, for what it was like to be unhappy.

"We're supposed to do something tonight. Hang out together. Just us. Then he calls up and cancels and I give him shit and then he says I'm being a bitch." Kelly wasn't sobbing; her words were coming fast and hard, spat out.

"Shit," said Madeline, putting sympathy into her voice. All around the house the night was pressing, full of so much possibility she could barely sit still. And coming home to this, to Kelly hunched up and trembling? Well, actually that wasn't so bad. It was part of it all, part of life filling up and up and over. She just had to remember how to speak, what to do.

"What I said to him was just that he promised and we never get any time together. It's just always at bars or with his friends. Which is okay, but. You know?"

"You guys need time alone for sure," said Madeline.

"That's what I told him. See? I was right. Then he says I'm a bitch. Like I'm always after him to do stuff."

"I don't know," said Madeline. "If he's not treating you with affection and respect, maybe it's time to dump him."

"I should. I really should. That would show him. Then he'd really come crawling, wouldn't he. But that's it. Like what you said. He should be treating me with affection and respect. Right? But when do I ever get that out of him? You said it perfect."

"I got to take a piss," said Madeline.

Kelly tapped on the bathroom door while Madeline was flossing her teeth.

"Hey," she said. "I'm going to go down there. I know where he is. It's not that late, it's not last call."

Madeline opened the door. "Is that such a good idea?" she said.

"I can't sit here. I'm just going crazy. I got to talk to him now."

"Well, good luck," said Madeline.

The front door slammed behind Kelly. Madeline went into her room, and flung open the window: sap and blossom and new grass. Between the cool sheets her body felt smooth and utterly desirable. Her breasts tilted heavily against her arm. After a while she fell asleep.

Madeline had the morning shift at Styx and Stoned. The sun was up, hot already, chattering birds, shops open to the day, when she slid her key into the front door at nine-thirty. The mauve dress floated in the window below the manic, impervious smile of an old-fashioned plaster mannequin.

Outside with the sandwich board, *Vintage Clothes and Attic Attitude.* She took the float from the safe, pinged the cash register and propped open the front door. Sunshine floated in, and customers, and every customer was beautiful: the cut of hair, swing of hips, a graceful wrist held appraisingly above a black velvet dress. Beautiful, and more beautiful because, in every case, there was something deliberate mocking that beauty: a streak of blue hair, white lipstick, heavy work boots at the end of long slim legs. She couldn't get enough of it.

Kelly turned up an hour late for the afternoon shift, still in yesterday's clothes, the boots and cut-offs. Her hair was scrunched up and spiky, bleached and dyed and gelled and slept on, and not washed for a while.

"I'm just wiped," she said. "I'm so exhausted." She sounded pleased.

"So things went all right last night?" said Madeline.

"Oh yeah. I'll tell you some time."

Madeline went downtown to the borrowed studio, had a last look at the lizard jackets and drove them over to a house off Fraser Street where Randy's wife or girlfriend counted out ten new twenty-dollar bills.

This was South Vancouver, well into the East Indian area. Madeline stopped for curried spinach in a silent restaurant deep in the lull between lunch and dinner. As she drove home, paid and fed, the day felt rounded and brimming.

Curdled sky, the sun going down in a tangle of fleece to the north-west. After dark the clouds were still visible, lit from below by the city. Dinner had been sushi in a booth hung with straw mats, exquisite mouthfuls of sea and salt.

"We could go check out a band," said Everett at the door of the restaurant. "Or go to a bar."

"We might as well go back to your place," said Madeline. "Make some coffee. Think what to do."

"Sounds good," said Everett. They stepped out into the neon and the blood, the sirens and broken faces, the Saturday-night carnival of Hastings Street. A minute later they turned the corner towards the warehouse and silence lapped up against them.

Everett was continuing a topic begun over dinner: the difficulties faced by young bands, the treacheries of record companies, the fates of his friends from ten years back, the earliest punks. Madeline was walking quietly beside him, not quite touching, nodding and murmuring her assent. She was trying to feel her way to the next step, the next possibility. Supper had divided them, with the low table, the multiplying dishes of fish, pickle, radish, the bowls of tea. Still, he had already kissed her three times that night, once when she arrived at his apartment, once walking to the restaurant, and once, just now, at the foot of the restaurant stairs before they stepped onto Hastings.

Each time he kissed her it was with the same surprising ardency, but there was something cool, even exploratory, about it. A giving and a holding back. Her body would flush and loosen and rise towards him, and then he would pull away, look at her almost quizzically. Not without affection. The last time, though, at the door of the restaurant, it was Madeline herself who pulled back first: descending footsteps on the stairs, and the quick thought that an act of discretion would please him.

Now they were walking through the old heart of the city, blank brick walls, whiffs of urine, rotting vegetables, the night closed in, no longer fragrant.

"Nobody's willing to take any risks on a new band, on anything different," Everett was saying. "People feel they have to water down their sound in order to get anywhere."

"Yes, it's terrible," said Madeline. She could not imagine how they could possibly get from here to love.

In the end it proved very simple. They did not make coffee or open a bottle of wine or go up on the roof with gin and tonic. Everett closed the door of the apartment behind them, and kissed her there, in the vestibule, with only the arc lights from the docks flooding in through the glass wall. He took it slowly, very slowly, working down her cheek and throat and collarbone.

On the bed their clothes came off all at once. Naked, Everett was slim but muscled, wiry, nearly hairless. Powdery skin, very soft; she wanted it all over her, that skin, embracing him with the insides of her arms, her belly, her knees. When he knelt above her and bent to her nipples, his tongue raised bursts of sugar, little bursts of sweetness everywhere. He was so hard his erection curved upwards, dark against his body. She reached out and touched him there, weighed him in her hand, the corded vein and the smooth tip, already wet. But even that was almost too much effort. She was moving with the slowness of dreams, of swimmers, melting and sliding, past volition.

It was over too fast. Everett was inside her, hard and hot and all of that, and very shortly gasping and moaning. Madeline was still grinding against his pubis, but without much hope, when he propped himself up on an elbow and said, "Sorry." A smile in his voice, the old Everett, camaraderie and nothing more. "I guess our timing was off."

Madeline was already falling back towards reality. "Next time," she said, matching his mood with an effort. "We'll just have to do it again."

"It's a deal," he said. She could feel him sliding out of her, a slippery fish between her legs. He reached over her shoulder for a Kleenex.

In the middle of the night she woke up, not at all disoriented: she knew exactly where she was, and why, curled up against Everett's back. Another gust of wind and rain hit the wall of glass; the bed trembled. Outside, the arc lights lit the low clouds like fire.

When Madeline woke again, the room was brimming with grey coast light, white air. Low cloud blotted out the mountains, driving rain spat against the windows, blurred the gantries and the black haunch of Stanley Park. She was alone in the bed, which daylight revealed as a queen-size futon with green sheets. Through the wall she could hear the shower running hard spray playing across the different densities of flesh and tile.

She lay quietly, taking in the light, the spatter of rain, gulls wheeling and crying. Everett came out of the bathroom in a towel, went over to the kitchen island and then sat down on the bed with a tray of coffee and toast. He leaned over and kissed her:

soap and shampoo and toothpaste, a leafy whiff of aftershave. Cool lips, body hot from the shower.

"Sleep all right?" he said.

"Just fine," said Madeline. "Come on, get in beside me, you'll freeze. Watch the tray."

"You do have a nice body," he said. "Really nice."

"I like yours too," she said. "Smooth here and here. Very nice to touch."

"I like touching you here. Down here too. You like that?"

"Mmm."

"Mmmm? That's not an answer."

It was morning lovemaking, partaking of the clarity of the light and the sense of the hours lying open ahead: pragmatic. "Put your hand there," said Madeline. "Yes. Yes." In daylight there was no drowning, no loss of self. She came quickly and intensely, Everett immediately after. They sat up and finished breakfast.

She could have lain for hours watching the rain break on the glass, but something about the width and height of the apartment discouraged this. The sweep of floor, pristine pine, made her want to rise, dress, tidy the bed, erase all markers of her presence. Perhaps Everett was similarly affected. He leaned over and scrabbled in his jeans for his datebook, looked into it, frowning marginally.

Time to be going, Madeline saw.

Everett watched her dress, untangling the riot of black underwear on the floor, tiny bra and tinier panties. She rolled up her long stockings, thigh-high stay-ups with rubber tops, came back to the bed for another kiss and then slid into last night's dress, a sky-blue linen sheath, fitted and tucked.

Everett walked her only as far as the door; he wasn't dressed. Down the stairs she felt the slip of bare skin, that handspan, right at her stocking tops, and more. She felt Everett all over her body, not just kisses but everywhere, imprinted on belly and breasts and hips, silvery and weightless as she stepped into the rain.

Back home she showered, pulled on sweat pants and heavy sweater, then fried eggs and made coffee. Kelly came out of her room and sat heavily at the kitchen table.

"I thought you were out," said Madeline. "There's some coffee hot."

"Thanks," said Kelly. "Okay. It's over. I did it. I can't take this shit."

"You broke up with Matthew."

"We had this really big fight."

"Does he know it's over?"

"He damn well better."

Madeline got up and opened the back door. The rain was pattering and trickling down the old shed, the dead apple tree, the dented garbage cans, the lane.

"The thing is, the thing really is," Kelly was saying, "is he's so self-centred. Everything rises and sets with Matthew."

Madeline leaned on the door-frame. The house was too small and dim, too stale, to contain her humming body. Caught like this between elation and fatigue, what did she need to hold her heart, what palace, what Taj Mahal?

"All Matthew cares about is what's going on with Matthew," said Kelly.

Carl phoned after dark, the house closed in by rain, the singing eaves.

He wanted to talk about work, about refitting a yacht dry-docked out in Delta.

"We're making the cabinets out of teak," he said. "You have to use an oily wood. You have to use something dense that doesn't rot. You have to use brass fixtures that don't rust."

"Uh-huh," said Madeline. She was weightless with fatigue, but at the same time everything was speeded up, intense. Love is a drug, she thought.

"You have to be very careful in a boat. You have to plan everything out just right. You have to make maximum use of space."

"I can imagine," said Madeline. In fact she couldn't, not at all. She couldn't slow herself down to Carl's pace, not tonight.

"The new owner plans to go right around the world. He's going to take a couple of years. He's going to cross over to Asia first."

"Wow," Madeline said, and scratched under the waistband of her sweat pants. "He must be rich."

"He sold off a software company. He's only forty-five. Now he's going to spend the rest of his life doing what he wants. He's always wanted to go around the world."

"Lucky guy." Madeline swallowed a yawn, and opened her eyes very wide.

"He might take us out one weekend on his other boat. We might go out to the Gulf Islands. We might do that one day if it's nice."

"That would be fun, wouldn't it."

"Are you doing anything next weekend? I was wondering if you were doing anything next weekend."

Everett. But Madeline was suddenly shy of naming him to Carl. Why? No reason, reticence. This was her life. It was none of Carl's business, perhaps. "I don't know," she said. She would be floating in the white loft, everything slow and elegant, she would be lost in desire, disembodied.

"If you weren't busy, you might like to come out on the boat with us. If it's nice we'll maybe go Saturday. Or Sunday. Whatever's best for you."

"I'll get back to you," she said.

"Don't worry if it's not a good time for you. Call me if you want to come. Don't worry otherwise. There'll be lots of room."

"If I can I will," she said. But I absolutely won't.

After Madeline hung up and was tilting into sleep between fresh sheets, she thought: I never asked about Beth. I should have asked about Beth, about Carl going to Toronto. Maybe he wanted to talk about that. No, if he'd wanted, he would have talked. But was there something wistful in his voice? Did he carry on the conversation too long, spin it out? Did she miss some cue? Or was it a normal Carl conversation, merely suffering in comparison with Everett? And what was it Everett had said, something about newspapers and the means of communication, or maybe the production of communication, leaning forward, candle-light?

The rain surged up outside, a crowd of murmuring voices, and Madeline slept.

"Fuck Matthew. Let's party," said Kelly, running up the red stairs. The air, the walls, the floor, shook with the bass beat, the dance beat.

"What did you say to the bouncer at the door?" said Madeline.

"I said we were going to trash the place. I said we were

going to burn it down. I said we were going to dance on the furniture."

"All right."

"He said Tuesday nights are always slow."

They dropped their jackets at the coat check. Kelly had on her shortest leather skirt, lace tights and a little lace top, black. Chains on her wrists and her hair spraying out like a roadside flower, like a weed, mountain aster or fleabane, that feathery magenta.

Beers, on top of a bottle of retsina and a few screwdrivers — the last of the vodka, the last of the orange juice — back in the kitchen.

"I sort of know that guy over there," said Kelly. "He's cute, isn't he?"

Kelly had to lean over and yell in Madeline's ear. Madeline smiled, shrugged, leaned back against the wall. All day long, in just her jeans and T-shirt and cowboy boots, she'd been getting looks and whistles and friendly jokes from gas jockeys and clerks at the 7-Eleven. Much more than usual. It was radiating off her, this thing, everyone could see it, they all wanted in.

And Madeline? Sunday was elation with exhaustion. But she woke up Monday morning wanting. Desire fierce as hunger. Lying in bed at dawn she put her hands to her throat, her belly, her hips. Like this he had touched her, here and here: the memory was absolutely tactile, the fact that it was only memory unbearable.

A day later nothing had diminished. Here in the dance club she leaned against the wall and smiled, and watched the crowd heave, and thought: if he were here, he'd touch me exactly like that, privately, on the small of my back. Or perhaps not at all, not in public. But we wouldn't be here. We'd be somewhere else, alone, naked. The thought was incredibly arousing. She deliberately blanked her face, afraid it was betraying her, mouth and eyes sagging into sexual stupor.

Kelly drained her beer. "Let's dance!" she said. The music and the strobe lights picked them up, triple time, carving space. The beat, the groove, went on and on; drunk inside it, Madeline rode rises and swoops, loops and reprises. It was like that, dancing. It could blank everything out, make only the moment matter. Everett would be another day. Meanwhile she let him go, she was loose in the music.

Kelly and Madeline came down the red stairs at closing time. No car; for reasons of drinking and of parking, they'd ridden the bus downtown. But the buses had stopped hours ago. The last taxi pulled away from the club.

"It's pretty much quit raining," said Kelly. "We can walk."

"To East Vancouver?" said Madeline. "Okay. It's a hike, though." The rain was hardly rain at all, a mizzling kind of mist condensing on hair and clothes. She was soaked through with sweat; the air hit her silent as a bath. They headed off down brick alleys, the sky scored with cables.

"Check the Smithrites," said Kelly, swinging herself up the side of a dumpster. "Shit. Nothing but paper. I love the sound of breaking glass."

The bottle smashed high on a blank wall. The sound was irrevocable: first shot, impossible act.

"Burn it down!" Kelly shouted. "Stop the city."

"Good arm," said Madeline.

"I pitched softball in grade eleven. You didn't know that, did you?"

A second bottle smashed. Kelly whooped. A police cruiser slid across the mouth of the alley, moved out of sight down the cross street.

"Cops," said Madeline.

"Whoops," said Kelly, and giggled. "Come and get us," she shouted. "We're dangerous!"

"Whoa," said Madeline. "Okay. We'll just keep it together while we cross the road. Okay?"

"Okay," said Kelly. "Watch me walk a straight line, occifer. I really could, you know."

The street was lit up, empty end to end. They crossed into the next alley. Madeline let out her breath as the shadows closed over them. And then the cruiser was at her elbow, materializing out of nowhere.

"Shit," said Kelly.

"Evening, ladies. Out late," said the face under the hat.

"Just walking home," said Madeline.

"A bit of noise back there," said the face. "Hear anything?"

"Oh, those guys," said Kelly. "Right? Those guys back there."

"The ones that were breaking windows," said Madeline.

"We cut down the alley to get away from them," said Kelly. "They were kind of scary."

"Did you see which way they went, ma'am?" said the face.

"That way," said Kelly.

The cruiser was already in reverse. "Thank you, ma'am," said the face as kaleidoscope lights exploded onto the walls. "You ladies get home safe now."

"Holy shit," said Kelly in the silence. "I need a smoke."

"Give me one too," said Madeline. Her hands over the match shook with bone-deep chill, and with fear, too. She wanted to sit down but the alley was wet and empty. In a minute they came out onto the next street.

An empty taxi turned the corner. Madeline hailed it.

They made tea in the kitchen, the rain starting up again.

"The cops couldn't have done anything to us," said Kelly.

"Drunk and disorderly, drunk in public."

"Having fun," said Kelly. "Being out at night and having fun."

"Living. Breathing. But they could, you know," said Madeline. "They can take you in and question you and say it was a mistake. It would be a *drag*."

"But they couldn't *do* anything," said Kelly. "Hey. There's still some retsina left."

The phone was ringing and the rain was pouring down and Madeline's head was pulsing pain in time to her heartbeat. Six, seven, eight, nine rings, and then silence. And then one, two, three, four. Suddenly she thought *Everett*, grabbed her blurry bathrobe and staggered down the tipping hall.

"Oh, hello, Tania," she said, knotting her robe against the damp. "Kelly? I'll see if she's in."

She pounded on Kelly's door, went in and shook her by the shoulder. Kelly groaned and rolled over. Clothes wall to wall, this room, and a sifting of dust on the mouldings, the bricked-up fireplace.

"Tania's on the phone. You're supposed to be at work. It's ten already."

"Oh fuck. Oh shit. Tell her I'm sick. Tell her I'll be in at noon."

Madeline went back to the phone.

"I think Kelly's coming down with the flu," she said. "She was out in the rain yesterday. Oh, I'm sorry. I can't either. I was just on my way out. I'm really really sorry. I'm working tomorrow, though, right?"

Madeline hung up and went to the fridge. No orange juice, no milk. She ran a glass of water, drank it down, filled the glass again and went back to bed.

Everett called Thursday evening.

"Hello!" said Madeline. "How you doing?"

"All right," he said.

"That doesn't sound so good," said Madeline.

"Work's being shit," he said.

"That's too bad," she said. "I really had a good time last weekend."

"Yeah," he said. "Me too."

"You completely positive about that?"

"Pretty sure. Did you want to get together this weekend?"

"I'd like that."

"I don't know if I should. I won't be much fun. It's been a pretty stressful week."

"Oh, you should," said Madeline. "We don't have to make you any more stressed. You can just sit around and relax."

"I probably shouldn't."

"You should."

"Okay," said Everett. "Come by — what? Saturday at sevenish?"

"Sure. That would be lovely."

"This place used to be a lot better," said Everett. "It looks like it's gone downhill. Suburbanites."

"Every bar is like that on Saturday night," said Madeline.

"This place used to have good bands."

"These guys seem okay." Madeline had in fact hardly noticed the band: cheerful noise, a mood.

"The drummer keeps losing the beat. Hear that?"

"Oh. Right, yes." *Don't worry* was what she wanted to say. *I don't need to be entertained. I'd be ecstatic just sitting out back in the alley with you.*

But maybe that wasn't it. Maybe she was meant to entertain Everett.

"Kelly and me got stopped by the cops the other night," she said. "Walking home from the dance club. I didn't know they could do that, just haul you over."

"They can do just about anything they want," said Everett. "Do you like that kind of music?"

"It's fun to get out and dance," said Madeline.

"It's always seemed extremely artificial to me."

"Yeah, well. Kelly needed to get out. She's really upset breaking up with Matthew."

"Matthew? He's that promoter, isn't he?"

"I didn't know that's what he does."

"I thought some of the guys from the paper would be here tonight. The sub-editors. They used to come here all the time."

"See, I had this idea for a series on alternative culture," said Everett. "Bands, artists, theatre groups. It could go in the weekend supplement."

"Sounds good," said Madeline. Black rain sluiced down the glass wall, the long sofa rode a pool of light on the pine floor. One, two a.m., later than that.

"The editors thought they couldn't get the advertising," said Everett. "They said it didn't have wide enough appeal."

"Shit," said Madeline. "So what happened?"

"They're running a five-part series on pet-care facilities. Pet cemeteries, boarding kennels, dog walkers, high-tech vets. The fashion columnist has to write something on poodle clipping next week. She's not happy."

"All the different styles of poodle clip," said Madeline. "There are different styles, actually."

"I wouldn't know," said Everett. "The editor has his head up his ass."

"Well, you never do read anything very interesting in that paper," said Madeline.

"It's a newspaper," said Everett. "It can't get too boring. It has to keep its readers. I just have to figure out how to pull some strings."

"Maybe when you've been there longer."

"It's just so exhausting," said Everett. "Sometimes I think they don't want any new ideas. Sometimes I think they do this on purpose, just to wear down anyone new so they give up."

The rain ticked against the glass. After a minute, Madeline leaned over and took him in her arms. It was like touching a stranger until he began to loosen under her hands. She wanted to give an embrace that said warmth, friendship, with an undercurrent of promise. But as she held him she saw that this was not in their vocabulary, not yet. He would not relax into her, kept that tense stiffness even after they began kissing.

It was too soon to begin kissing. Not too soon for Madeline to enjoy it, but too soon for the shape of the evening. She could feel on his skin the weight and pressure of what he had not yet said, of his sadness. And yet they were proceeding, step by step: hands under clothes, the fumbled buttons. Proceeding because that was what followed, proceeding without joy.

Afterwards, Everett slept, or seemed to. Madeline lay awake for a while, listening to the rain.

Madeline's tires slicked home through morning rain, grey businesslike rain, the day absolutely prosaic. Mid-morning, and as she rolled past Styx and Stoned she saw that the door was locked, the lights out behind the mauve dress. Was it Kelly or Tania who opened on Sundays? Back home Madeline parked and dashed up the front walk past sodden stalks of flowers, blighted blossoms, wet petals rotting and streaking the ground.

The house was chill and empty. Madeline changed into tights and a sweater, and brewed a pot of tea. The night and the morning after had left her exhausted, without elation. Not worried, precisely, but thoughtful. This sadness of Everett's had taken her by surprise. Sadness out of proportion to reality, she thought, to what he could and would accomplish, in fact had already done. She must somehow show him that, the fact that he was talented, brilliant, beautiful.

The front door banged loudly, and the door to Kelly's room slammed. Madeline could hear thumps and scufflings through the wall, and a giggle. But only one set of footsteps. She topped up her teacup. A minute later Kelly was in the kitchen doorway, leather and lace, with a blanket wrapped around her shoulders.

"Hi there," she said.

"Hello," said Madeline.

"Hello," said Kelly, and giggled. "Hi."

"Tea?" said Madeline.

"What are you drinking?" said Kelly. "Tea? No. Oh maybe I will. Shit."

Madeline put some cream in her own cup.

"Hello," said Kelly. "Shit. Do I look any different? Do I look okay?"

"I don't know," said Madeline. "You look kind of tired. I'm not sure the blanket matches your skirt."

"Oh shit," said Kelly. She started to giggle and doubled up. "I am so wasted. I am tripping so much. I've been up all night."

"I gathered," said Madeline. "What did you take?"

"Acid," said Kelly. "At least they said it was acid. Shit, like everything's still sort of you know kind of going up and down. Fuck I'm cold."

"I'll pour you some tea," said Madeline.

"This is so cool like," said Kelly. "You can see the little bits of fat in the cream going around in circles in the tea. This way and then that way. Look."

"Drink it," said Madeline. "You'll feel way better."

"I can't," said Kelly. "My stomach hurts. My face hurts too." She giggled.

"Were you supposed to go to work today?" said Madeline.

"Fuck work," said Kelly. "Yeah. I was. If you tap the cup they all start going the other way."

"I guess you aren't going in."

"That place is so boring," said Kelly. "You just sit on that stupid stool and smile at people. Besides it's a total rip-off. I feel so embarrassed when people come in."

"Really?"

"This is nice, putting my fingers in the tea. That really warms them up."

"You should go crash," said Madeline. "This is the boring part, coming down. Me, I'm going to take a nap."

She took her cup into the back pantry, Sue's room, and pulled the covers over her lap. She could hear Kelly bang cupboards in the kitchen, and then tromp into her own room.

In two weeks Madeline would have her own place, her books and records out of storage, space and peace. Sue's walls were an unfortunate faded yellow, the futon lay on bare floorboards, an old sheet — 1960s daisies, vaguely psychedelic — hung skewed across the curtain rod. Not by any means the worst place Madeline had ever stayed. But when she thought about Everett, she thought about space and light and ease, indistinguishable from the shine of his body as it moved across her skin.

Randy's wife saw the lizard jackets and that gave her an idea. She had an old deal kitchen table and a chest of drawers, irreparably layered in thick coats of boarding-house brown. Rather than strip down to dubious wood, could Madeline paint them? Mexican butterflies and smiling suns on the table, eighteenth-century nudes and cherubs for the drawers. Name the price, she said.

Madeline went to the library, photocopying and tracing art books, and across town to the expensive import shop that had inspired the butterflies. She bought some paints and went down to Randy's basement, sanding and priming and then marking in the outlines.

As she worked she thought about Everett. She was playing sentences, whole scenes, over in her head. He needed faith back, she thought; somehow she had to give him that. Not just convince him that she believed in him. That was not enough. Of course she did, that was a given. But she had to send him out ready to get what he wanted from his boss, from this world she did not really understand. The mystery to her was that he was not past fear, was not insulated from it by money, work, knowledge, the ordered and beautiful outlines of his life.

She played these scenes in her head, and after a while the work took over, the modelling of pale flesh. She thought how much she would rather be painting Everett lying back against green sheets, how after only two nights together she could trace him in the air with her hands, feel him all along her body.

On the second day she came upstairs for coffee and fresh air, and found Matthew at the kitchen table.

"Hey, yeah, Randy said you were doing some stuff for him," said Matthew.

"Painting," said Madeline, rummaging in the fridge for cream.

"I saw the jackets you did," said Matthew. "They're excellent. Randy and Dick really like them."

"Thanks." She was busy pouring her coffee.

"Randy thinks your work is cool."

"Thanks." Tell me something I don't know, Madeline thought, and then was surprised at her own bad mood. Well, paint fumes, even with the basement windows flung open, always left her thin-tempered. And this abrupt reversal, after barely speaking the first time they met — whatever this was about, whatever change of status it heralded in Matthew's little world, it was a bit obvious. She didn't know what it meant, but it was still obvious.

She opened the back door and stood on the porch taking deep breaths of rainwashed air. The coffee made a satisfying trail of heat down her throat. Matthew came and stood behind her.

"We should get you to do the album cover for Cryptic Neon," he said.

"They've got an album?"

"Any day now. They're brilliant."

"Don't young bands have to water down their sound to get a contract?" Madeline was still feeling contrary. "That's what some-one was saying to me."

"Not now. The major labels, they really want to sign that indie product. They want to cash in on the new sound."

"Well, if they get a deal of course I'd be glad to do the album cover. If you still wanted me to," said Madeline. Go away and let me get rid of this headache, she thought.

"It's a deal," said Matthew. "Here. Let's shake on it."

Everett telephoned that night.

"I've got to cover the leadership convention this weekend," he said. "So we can't get together."

"That's too bad," said Madeline. "I mean about the weekend. But doing the leadership convention is a big story, isn't it?"

"I guess. But everyone knows who's going to win. And he automatically becomes premier. That's what happens in a one-party province."

"Don't they have to call an election?"

"Yes. But not for a while."

"I didn't know that. That's really interesting. But look, this is a good chance. Maybe you can get a scoop or interview some politician."

"I hate these kind of shit stories. You never get past the bullshit and the PR."

"I can imagine. So anyhow, if we don't get together this weekend, when are you free?"

"I'm not sure. I'll get back to you."

"Okay. Look, you'll probably do some great story. Cheer up."

"Cheer up? I don't know why you say that. I'm not sad."

The cars slicked by on the street, rain ran down the glass past the violet snakes. The washed-out light was swallowed by dark walls, black clothes.

"These shoes have never been worn," said Tania. "They've been sitting in the back of some warehouse since 1963. Aren't they perfect?"

"Little spike heels," said Madeline. "They'll sell fast."

"They should," said Tania. "Have you seen much of Kelly this week?"

"Not really. I've been at Randy's most of the time."

"I didn't have a choice. I had to lay her off."

"Shit. Really?"

"Too much coming late, missing shifts. It's not that it's a difficult job. You know that. But I do need someone reliable."

"Was she upset?"

"I don't know. She didn't seem to be. I was a little worried."

Down in Randy's basement, Madeline had the chest of drawers on its side. One long voluptuous nude the length of the wood, and three cherubs. Maybe she needed to learn about the newspaper business. Certainly she needed to learn more about politics. Then she could give Everett good suggestions. She read the papers, after all. It wasn't like she didn't know anything.

Footsteps on the stairs.

"I brought you a cup of coffee," said Matthew.

"Oh, thanks," said Madeline. Her back spasmed as she straightened up. She sipped, and bit her lip to keep from saying *but I don't take sugar.* That would be too rude.

"These are excellent," said Matthew. "Really sensuous." He was squatting by the dresser. "You have a good eye."

"I traced them out of an art book," said Madeline.

"They're still great," said Matthew.

"You're over here a lot," said Madeline.

"Randy and I go way back," said Matthew. "I help him out with stuff."

"Someone was saying you were his promoter."

"Were they? That's cool. Not exactly his promoter. When they get big, yeah, for sure. But maybe I am, kind of. Yeah, maybe I am their promoter."

Kelly was eating scrambled eggs on toast for supper when Madeline got home. She'd driven all the way across town with the windows down, but a trace of headache still rattled behind her eyes.

"I got canned at work," said Kelly. "Surprise, surprise."

"Tania was worried about you."

"Tania should worry about herself when people find out what a rip-off she is. I'm going around, I'm going to tell everyone."

"You're pissed off."

"Not about getting the sack. Shit. I can find something way more interesting to do."

"She said you missed work."

"Shit, of course I missed work. Who goes in to work Sunday mornings? Tania doesn't. Catch her working Sundays."

"Well, she does own the place."

"Fuck yeah. And never lets you forget it, does she?"

"Can you collect unemployment insurance?"

"No problem. She put down *laid off*, not *fired*, on my separation slip. I'm laughing."

"That was nice of her."

"I guess," said Kelly.

Madeline parked on the dark sidestreet and got out of the car. Dripping water, hush of traffic in the distance.

"I don't hear a party," she said.

"Maybe hardly anyone's here yet," said Kelly. "I'll get the beer from the back. Matthew might come."

"Oh really? Have you talked to him since you broke up?"

"Uh-uh. Fuck if I care."

They walked around the side of the house to a mossed concrete stairwell. Kelly knocked; the door of the basement suite swung open to palpable smoke, red walls twenty years out of date.

"Hi guys," said Kelly. "Where should I put the beer? Is this all that's here yet, four people?"

"You guys make six," said a boy on the sofa. "Want a toke?"

Madeline shrugged off her leather jacket and sank into a beanbag chair. They were a long way from home, south and east almost to the suburbs; the drive had tired her, flicking wipers, the blurred road. It was past ten already; she could sense in her bones this would never materialize into a party. The boys on the sofa were younger than her, weedy under spiky hair, and she knew none of them. Besides, this was not her real life. A few years ago, yes, just possibly, but not any longer. She thought about Everett under the hard lights of the convention centre, then leaning over his computer terminal, Everett stripping naked and toppling between green sheets, waking at dawn and pulling her towards him, smooth and clean and insistent as rain.

"See, what I'm going to do is write TV shows," one of the boys on the sofa was saying to her.

"Really?" said Madeline.

"All you need is some connections," he said. "If you have the idea they buy it off you."

"Yeah?"

"What's important is the concept. It's like they hire someone to do the writing."

"So you have ideas," said Madeline, tilting her wrist imperceptibly to glance at her watch. Not even eleven. Kelly was in the kitchenette laughing her head off.

"That's what I'm working on."

"What kind of ideas?"

"Well, that's what I can't talk about. Obviously. Let's say it's like taking what's on now and changing it a bit. Then when you get well known you get a chance to do something creative. Right?"

"Right."

"We could call for pizza," said Kelly.

"Should we get two mediums or one large?" said the boy in the kitchenette. His hair was shaved above the ears, but long on top; bald skin peeked between the strands.

"We should see what everyone likes," said Kelly. "Who likes anchovies? I think they're gross."

"Anchovies are excellent, man," said the second boy on the sofa. He was hunched up rolling tiny meticulous joints.

"Anchovies make me puke," said Kelly. "If I have anchovies I'll puke all over your carpet. What about mushrooms? Madeline, do you like mushrooms?"

"I'm not hungry," said Madeline.

"I'm fucking famished. I've super got the munchies," said Kelly, and giggled. "Who wants pepperoni?"

Madeline leaned back and closed her eyes. None of this matters, I am not here, she thought.

"Fuck," said Madeline. "I should have told you not to lock the driver's door when you grabbed the beer." The rain was sluicing down steadily, well past midnight.

"Shit you look funny with your ass sticking out the back of the trunk," said Kelly. "You're not going to fit. Shit, I'm killing myself. Do you have to do this all the time? What about when you've got a skirt on?"

"That was a wash-out of a party," said Madeline. The engine sputtered, caught. The windshield was leaking; a large drop clung and fell from the roof as the car slid away from the curb. Madeline's knee throbbed, whacked on the emergency brake.

"Those guys are kind of nice," said Kelly. "I've known them for ages."

"Not worth the drive, though," said Madeline.

"We should go down to the beer parlour," said Kelly. "Or the tapas bar. It's still early."

"You can go. I'm going to crash out."

"Oh, I can't go *alone*. I don't know who's going to be there."

"Like Matthew."

"We could just peek in."

"I'm not up to it," said Madeline. "Actually, I saw him at Randy's this week."

"Oh really? You never said. Did he say anything about me? Did he look mad?"

"He doesn't really talk to me," said Madeline.

"Oh, he likes you. He thinks you're cool. He said so. You should have talked to him and said my name, seen how he'd react. Or I could come over when you're working. You could give me a call when he's there."

"I thought you broke up with him."

"Totally. We're totally through. But I just really need to know how he's taking it. I bet he's pissed off."

"Fuck," said Kelly. "I stood up too fast. I got really car-sick." She was standing in the middle of the front walk between the broken flowers.

"Come on. It's pissing down," said Madeline.

"Oh shit," said Kelly, and fell to her knees, retching into the garden. Madeline went up the front steps and stood under the porch roof, waiting.

She could phone Everett, or she could wait for him to call. She had phoned him several times already over the past few weeks, at work and at home, verifying times; phoning was not a big deal. This was not the 1950s. This was not the world of *Top Tips for Teens on the Dating Scene*, Madeline's rummage sale find: *A girl cheapens herself by telephoning a boy. A young lady is never pressing.*

Madeline could call or she could wait for Everett to phone. It didn't matter one way or the other. Really it didn't. But then why had she been sitting here, slouched on the sofa, staring for half an hour at the phone between her feet? Monday night, and the whole long wet weekend had left her empty. He might be tired. She would cheer him up. He might be just about to call her. He'd be delighted at the coincidence. There was no reason for this little spurt of fear.

She picked up the phone and dialled. The line was busy. She went into the kitchen, made a pot of tea and dialled again. Still busy. Half an hour later she got through.

"Hi!" she said. "You sound miles away. How's it going?"

"All right," said Everett. "Better."

"You were on the phone for ages just now."

"Someone from work."

"I saw your story on the front page. That's great."

"I lucked out with that leak about campaign fraud."

"Is the minister really going to resign now?"

"I doubt it."

"You sound tired. Are you?"

"Not particularly. Yeah, a bit."

"I had a pretty boring weekend. I went out with Kelly."

"Yeah?"

"This stupid party out in nowhere that never materialized. Then I locked myself out of my car again."

"Right."

"Are you coming down with a cold?"

"I don't think so. Look, I was in the middle of writing something. I left my computer on."

"Okay, I'll let you go. What's your schedule like? Can we do something sometime?"

"I might have to work all weekends now."

"We can do something during the week. I'm not fussed."

"We could."

"What days will you have off?"

"Look. I should have said this earlier. I don't think I've got time to keep this thing going, this thing with us. There's too much happening at work."

"Shit. I mean, what do you mean? I thought we were getting on well. Weren't you having a good time?"

"Yeah, of course. I had a good time those times you came over. I'm just not in a position to start up a relationship. I should have said this earlier."

"Well, I don't know if it's a *relationship*. But don't you want to get together again? When you have the time?"

"It's just not going to work, Madeline. Look, I got something coming through on call waiting. We'll talk some other time."

"Call me back tonight?"

"I got to get this thing written. Look, sorry, goodbye."

There was a dial tone and the floor dropping away beneath her like a runaway elevator. There was rain on the windows and her hands shaking, a burst of adrenalin like the moment after the car swerves out of control, not fear or anger yet, just a long shriek *no*. She hung up and dialled again, fast; the line was busy. Hung up and dialled again, five times in succession. Put down the phone with exaggerated care, went to the front window, looked out at the rain, went to the back door, opened it, took a big breath, started to shiver, closed it, poured another cup of tea, took a sip, dumped it down the sink.

The bare bulb lit the living room like a bad dream. She went into her bedroom and pulled the blankets up to her chin. There was a mistake, obviously. A misunderstanding. Had someone said something? Had he heard something? But what could he have possibly heard? Or did he think she didn't like him? Had she not been attentive enough, interested enough? Or was this fatigue, his depression?

It couldn't be left hanging. Obviously they had to talk, she had to explain herself. Prove herself. There must be some mistake. She scrambled out of bed and ran back to the phone.

Everett's voice on his answering machine was so calm, so matter-of-fact, that she knew nothing could be seriously wrong. At the same time, an abyss creaked open beneath her. The fear, the fear was starting.

"Um," she said. "Hi. Hello. Look, it's Madeline. About what you just said. I think maybe we should talk. If there's a problem or something. So you could give me a call or something. Bye."

She went into the kitchen, stacked some dirty dishes in the sink and ran the hot water. But the plates were dried hard, and she lacked the patience to scrape and scrub. She left them soaking, went into the living room and cranked up the stereo, went into Kelly's room and found a package of cigarettes, smoked three and phoned again.

"Hi, it's me," she said. "Call any time you get done. I'll be up late."

She smoked two more cigarettes, and was about to call again when she saw it was almost midnight. She called anyway, but hung up after the little beep.

Madeline awoke on the sofa shivering, her lungs like dust. Broad daylight. The emptiness took a moment to place. She picked up the phone, dialled Everett, got the answering machine and hung up. The pervasive light made her think with appalling clarity. If it were a mistake, he'd have called. If he were worried how I felt, he'd have called. He was sitting there knowing I was phoning, and he didn't pick up the phone. He was doing that all last night.

The stereo speakers were humming to themselves. Madeline got up and flicked the switch; the amp was hot. She lit a cigarette and went into the kitchen. The sink brimmed with dirty plates, fouled water. Balancing her cigarette on the counter, she reached cringing fingers into the cold murk, between the claws of forks and the teeth of knives, groping for the plug. It finally came free; the sink burped and gurgled. When she picked up her cigarette, it fell apart, soaked. She dropped it into the sink, found her jacket on a kitchen chair and headed out through slanting rain to the diner on the corner.

There was grey arborite, and flat eggs washed down with ketchup. Madeline ate because she was famished, but numbly, hot coffee in automatic gulps.

It was and yet it could not be. How could she want something so much, want it with every inch of her skin, and be denied it? How could he not see it and value it, her desire? It was not love, there hadn't been time for that loss of self. But love's first step, certainly. And how could he walk away when he was etched across her body? If she closed her eyes he was here, a shimmer of heat just out of reach, a knee not quite grazing hers under the bleared table.

It was a misunderstanding. But over what? Then it was not a misunderstanding. In that case she must reread every gesture, every word, every moment of slumped fatigue in a new way: directly personal. Could that possibly ever be the subtext to all those shimmering moments? And if it wasn't a misunderstanding, didn't he owe her an explanation? Wasn't he robbing her not only of himself, but of the truth?

If he wouldn't answer the phone, she'd force him to respond: knock on his door, walk into the newsroom, wait outside the warehouse in her car. He could not escape without closing things. Without giving her a chance to change his mind. Physically present, she could do that. She could do exactly that.

The waitress topped up Madeline's cup and slapped the bill on the arborite. Madeline slumped in the booth. No, she would not go after him. Something very close to pride was beginning to rise in her. She could clearly see the point at which she would begin to make an idiot out of herself, and worse: the point at which she would become a nuisance, a public hazard, pounding on locked doors in the middle of the night. She had never before felt so close to becoming the voice down the alley at two a.m. shouting, *open up and let me in, you bastard. I hate you. Don't leave me.*

So let go of the rage, then. That just prolonged the whole thing. But without rage she was left sliced open and raw to the wind.

So let go of the wanting, then. That was not so easy. There wasn't any way it would just evaporate.

Madeline got up, paid for her breakfast and walked out into the rain.

When she got home the answering machine was blinking at her. Her body flared as she hit playback. *Hello. This is Carl. I was calling about doing something this weekend. Are you busy this weekend? Anyhow, give me a call. Talk to you soon. Bye.*

He sounded pretty rained out too, Madeline thought. Maybe Beth was giving him a hard time long distance. Carl unhappy: that was a new thought. It didn't mesh with any previous picture of Carl, and she'd known him for years. Maybe the machine needed a new tape, maybe it was recording slow.

She went into the bathroom and stared into the mirror above the sink. Unmarked, this face, the same face as yesterday, this face that she'd always rather liked. And it wasn't enough, this face, couldn't get her what she needed.

Work at noon.

Saving face, another name for pride. Madeline set to work on hers: pale powder, one fashionable line across each eyelid, just above the lashes, dark lipstick blotted matte. She pulled on warm tights and a black dress fitted at the waist. It had to be flawless. A flawless mask.

It was raining, and it was Tuesday, and it was only the middle of the month, almost the middle of June already, nowhere near pay-day or welfare day. Still, for some reason every woman in town wanted a little vintage suit, a tight top with sequins, spike-heeled shoes that had never been worn. There was no reason Madeline could see for the flood of customers that afternoon. Maybe everyone was shopping to forget the rain. Styx and Stoned steamed with wet umbrellas, clouded windows, even the ten- and twenty-dollar bills clung like damp leaves as Madeline counted them into the cash register.

It kept her busy. It kept her mind on her performance, dark and elegant and gracious.

Kelly had come home and gone out again during the afternoon. Returning from work, Madeline deduced this from the pan on the stove, scarred with egg, and a coffee-cup on the arm of the sofa. Beached dishes still filled the sink; nothing had moved, including her dead cigarette. Acetone reek, banana peels and worse, from the garbage pail under the sink. That at least had to go, before the whole house stank.

Madeline pulled out the pail, and leaned to knot the bag. That's funny, she thought, I don't remember cooking rice.

Then she saw it wasn't rice at all. The little white grains were moving, grubbing their tiny bodies through the coffee grounds and crusts and furred lasagna. Madeline dropped the bag, and went and sat in the living room, shaking with disgust. She looked for Kelly's cigarettes, but they were gone. After a while she calmed down a little, found rubber gloves in the bathroom and carried the pail at arm's length out to the can in the alley.

Back in the kitchen, she looked in the fridge, looked in the sink, looked at the stove. The collapse was almost complete: this was a house that had stopped functioning. There was nothing to eat, nothing to eat it with, nowhere warm and cheerful to sit. Madeline had less than a week to go here, and she wasn't sure she could stand even that. It was the bare bulbs, and the stained floors, and the fact that for ever now this place would say disappointment and compromise, shameful waiting.

She went into the living room and phoned Everett. His answering machine came on. She hung up and went out to eat.

Carl called again that evening. Madeline lit a cigarette, her own pack now, curled herself on the sofa. A distraction was good. But she didn't have the energy. She really didn't.

"Have you heard from Beth?" she said. This was not a good time for a long chat. If Everett was going to call, it would be now. But on the other hand he could get a busy signal and keep trying. That wouldn't hurt him.

"Beth still wants me to come out to Toronto," said Carl. "It's pretty important to her."

"Are you thinking about it?" Dispersal, everyone moving on and out. Except her. She had come home.

"Well, let's put it this way. It's pretty important to her. It's pretty crucial."

"Has she given you an ultimatum?"

"No. She hasn't done that. Not an ultimatum. Beth wouldn't do that."

"I guess not." She'd play it a bit smoother altogether, wouldn't she, Madeline thought. I just bet she would.

"We're going to talk about it. She's coming out next week. She's got some time off."

"Shit. I mean, I guess you're pretty happy."

"It'll be good to talk about this face to face, for sure. What I was really calling about is, I'm house-sitting for my sister this weekend. She's on the North Shore. If you want to get out of town you could come over. I know you're really busy."

"I'm not doing anything. That would be so wonderful. This house is driving me up the wall."

"When do you move?"

"Monday. The movers are booked and my stuff's coming out of storage."

After Carl hung up, Madeline phoned Everett and got a busy signal. Walking home and then going out to eat in the little black dress had been a bad idea; she was chilled to the bone. Madeline scrubbed the tub thoroughly and took a hot bath. When she was finished, she called Everett and got his answering machine.

She didn't want music. She didn't want TV. She didn't want a book or a magazine or a drink. Madeline went to bed and pulled the covers over her head. Sleep would blot it out. If she slept for long enough, she'd wake up and it wouldn't hurt any more, it would all be gone.

But she couldn't sleep. She couldn't let go of the day, of the greyness and chill. And helter-skelter, against her will, the stories started to play themselves out. She would phone him, or meet him somewhere, or he'd phone her. And there'd be a reason, an excuse. Tears. There would be tears. He'd see her tears, he'd say he hadn't known, he'd been mistaken, he'd be touched. Her tears would melt him. He'd look at her with infinite tenderness and passion, intent as the first night he kissed her but without that reserve. And it would be all right.

This was not going to happen. At the same time, Madeline told herself, she was just planning for all eventualities. But this was not going to happen. Which left this little scenario as pornography. Or something worse: pornography of the emotions. At any rate, a melancholy intensely sexual. And she was wretched, she was finally and totally wretched, abandoned, she was sobbing into her pillow. She did not think, *I am ugly* or *nobody will ever love me;* she did not think she had lost her one true soulmate. She did not want to die. But all the same, for a while she lost her self, her picture of herself, her being in the world. There was no Madeline, only this misery; she no longer existed in any real way.

The front door slammed and Kelly yelled hello. Kelly and other voices. Madeline stopped in mid-sob; she would be asleep, dead to the world. She couldn't get up, not just because puffy eyes and sniffles raised stupid questions. She couldn't get up because she didn't exist, because she had nothing to say, because no one else existed either. Voices through water. She realized she needed the bathroom, and there was no Kleenex in her room. She wiped her nose on the sheet, ignored her bladder, willed sleep, sleep as an end to everything.

Madeline woke up the next day, worn thin, went into the kitchen and had black coffee; there was no milk in the fridge. In the living room, the boy with the half-shaved skull was rolled up in an afghan on the sofa, the room thick with smoke, stale beer and sleep.

Dressed, and the face, and work. Weary to the bones, but herself again. She ate on her way home from work, bought a carton of coffee cream, popped it in the fridge without looking at the sink and went to bed early. Everett didn't call; he was not going to call, he was gone. She fell asleep fast.

Madeline and Kelly climbed the double flight of stairs to the bar where the local bands played. Kelly flashed her membership card; Madeline signed the guest book.

"Oh shit he's here," said Kelly. "Oh shit there he is. We better get beers first."

They bought pint mugs, and Madeline followed Kelly to the end of the pub. Tonight Madeline was following. Nothing was going to bother her, though she did not really want to spend the night drinking with the boy with the half-shaved skull, or with Matthew. But she did not want to sit around that house all night, either. Kelly didn't seem to notice any change in her. But then Madeline was trying as hard as she could not to show any change. Still, Kelly ought to notice. If Kelly didn't notice, Madeline was going to try an experiment. Exactly how little volition could she put into the evening? How little could she get away with saying and doing?

"I was so wasted yesterday," said the boy with the skull, pushing back a chair for Kelly. "I had a fucking hangover."

There were four small tables in a row, vaguely pulled together, not quite making one long table; four clusters of people, a fluid grouping. Kelly, Madeline and this boy were at one end. At the next table were Matthew and Randy and some men Madeline didn't know. At the third table were some women: teased black hair, net gloves.

And at the fourth table, the one farthest away, was Everett. He was with two men in polo shirts. They looked like they had jobs, they looked like they could be reporters. And he was with a woman. It took Madeline a moment to place her. She had never seen her before, couldn't remember her name. But Madeline had seen her photo, the prominent jaw, chin-length hair, wide smile. It was a smudged black-and-white photo that made her look considerably younger, prettier, slimmer and calmer. It was taped up in the window of Styx and Stoned, heading a newspaper column about *scoring that perfect vintage pillbox hat to mix-and-match with mall bargains, a wearable look that's uniquely you*.

All of this, scouting out the tables, the hard shock to the solar plexus, recognition, all this took less than a blink.

"I was just useless yesterday," the boy was still saying.

"Sounds like you had a good time," Madeline said. "Too bad I missed it." She lit a cigarette and took a sip of beer. She was doing all right. She was doing good. She was holding it together.

Eventually Everett was going to see her. Or had he seen her when she came in? She couldn't tell a thing from his profile. She never had been able to tell a thing.

"I got to go to the can," Kelly said. "Shit. Come with me to the can."

"I don't need to piss," said Madeline.

"Come on! You've got to come," said Kelly, tugging at her arm.

They had to push past Matthew and skirt Everett. Neither man looked up, neither blinked an eye.

"Hey," said Randy. "How's it going, Madeline?"

"All right," she said. "I'll be back to finish off that table after next week, because I'm moving."

"No problem," said Randy. "It's looking good."

"Come on," said Kelly.

Madeline reapplied her lipstick, blotted it, fluffed her hair. Kelly hiked herself up on the counter.

"He's fucking pretending I'm not here," said Kelly. "Fuck, I'm just freaking. Look at my hands shake."

"Last time you saw him you broke up with him," said Madeline. "If you want to talk you should give him a call. Obviously he's going to think you don't want to talk to him."

"But I'm just freaking. He's being such an asshole."

"So forget him." Madeline's voice was sounding thin in the extreme to her own ears.

"I know, I know, I know."

"I don't have any advice," said Madeline. I really don't, she thought. And no patience, either. This adrenalin rush, it wasn't sex, it wasn't fear, and it wasn't pleasant, either. Emergency, waking to midnight's fire alarm, the moment before action.

They went back out and sat at the same table. Kelly and the shaved boy were talking magic mushrooms, and all Madeline had to do was look attentive. Look attentive and surreptitiously check out the table at the end. That fashion columnist, she was talking too much, laughing too much, waving her hands in the air. And Everett was swivelled round, he was looking at her intently, he was watching. But so were the other two men. There was a sudden lull, one of those hushes that slide through crowded rooms — *so this bulking great standard poodle decides to shake and my photographer is soaked in flea shampoo* — every man at the four tables, from the shaved boy down to Everett, looked up, leaned towards her, laughed — female hilarity, wit, Madeline stubbed out her cigarette and lit another one, the whole table was laughing, the noise of the bar surged up, now the fashion columnist was doing something with her hands, describing big puffs of fur on her muzzle and paws, she was sitting up begging for a bone, the men were killing themselves laughing, she had them good, she had them hooked.

"Mushrooms do nothing for me," said Madeline. "I just have never understood it."

"We should ask Matthew. Matthew would know," said the boy. He leaned over and tapped Matthew on the arm. Matthew was talking to Randy; he took a minute to respond. Wheeled round with his head ducked, didn't look at Kelly. Spoke dismissively, it seemed, went back to his conversation.

"Matthew doesn't know," said the boy. "But he'll tell us if he finds out."

It wasn't just boredom. It wasn't just the rush of anxiety. It was being stuck down here at the wrong end of the table, stuck down here right out of the action. Not that she could compete, not on the level of that braying, public laugh. Still, what she needed to do was work her way up somehow. Move up and talk to Randy. Work the crowd.

As if that would do any good.

"I'm going to go to that gallery opening. Those installation artists," said Kelly. "They're going to have free booze."

If I got up and got a beer, Madeline thought, I could come back and sit down in that empty chair behind Randy. Talk about furniture or something.

"Madeline. You going to come to that opening?" said Kelly.

"I'm not up for it," she said. "I'll just have another drink and go home."

"Randy," said Kelly. "You guys. There's this opening. Free booze."

Neither Randy nor Matthew looked up.

"Free booze," said the shaved boy. "That's pretty cool. Let's ask Matthew if he's going." He leaned over and tapped Matthew on the arm. "No, Matthew wants to stay here and catch the band."

"You guys. I'm leaving," said Kelly. "I'm leaving, you guys."

"Bye," said Madeline. She moved up into Kelly's empty chair; this put her beside Randy, across from Matthew, not quite in Everett's line of sight, not yet.

And what would this accomplish? What was the point? Well, he couldn't ignore her all night. At some point, after a few drinks, they'd come face to face. To what end? A display of her pure indifference? A friendly word? A tense little silence? She'd know when the moment came.

Most important, it had to be subtle. This was dangerous ground, very dangerous. She needed the upper hand, needed to slide inside his attention in a way that showed her absolute mastery of herself, her situation. She had to manoeuvre so he couldn't possibly snub her, so she couldn't possibly be left standing gaping in his wake.

The band came on. "Let's go watch," said Randy. The whole table stood up and pushed, rather diffusely, into the crowd up front by the stage. Madeline was standing with Randy and Matthew, trying to keep an eye on Everett behind them, near the bar.

It was too loud to talk, but Matthew kept leaning over, shouting things in her ear, the name of the drummer, their last gig, trivia. Distracting, but she wasn't listening; still, preferable to standing alone, to having Everett look up and see her alone. She tilted her head towards Matthew's lips, smiled as if hanging on every word; there was no need to reply.

Then the fashion columnist was on the dance floor. Not with Everett, with one of the men in polo shirts. Enormous relief. So that was it. That was all it was. She danced badly, self-consciously, and now Madeline could see what she was wearing: the skirt from a school uniform, dark pleats, ankle socks with frills, high-heeled red shoes. Possibly, on someone else, that outfit might look sophisticated, perverse. Just possibly. On the fashion columnist it was merely unfortunate: a frump, and trying too hard. And she danced badly. And Madeline had nothing to worry about. She turned around to find Everett, couldn't spot him in the crowd, started to push her way through, met Matthew coming back with a round of beer. Confusion over who was paying, she dug down in her jeans for her wallet, counted change, took her beer. The band was taking a break, the audience milling about. Madeline put her wallet back in her pocket, looked up, and there were Everett and the fashion columnist heading out the door. Hand in hand.

The rest of the evening snapped past, and then last call, lights up, voices too loud, faces strained and pale. They were downstairs, outside in the rain; a flurry of taxis, of undercurrents Madeline lacked the energy to puzzle out, little hesitations and pouts, net and dark nails tugging the door of a cab, and then they were walking to Matthew's, Matthew's the closest place.

They included Randy, at least, and one of the girls with gloves. But suddenly Madeline was walking down the wet sidewalk alone with Matthew. That was all there was, all this evening was providing.

The thought of an hour alone with Matthew paralysed her with boredom. She could not remember how one said good-night and flagged a cab, even that such an action was possible. No, it was more than boredom. It was aftershock, two knife-edge hours and another of flat hard noise, one pint too many. And after all, it was pleasant enough to keep walking bare-headed and soaked into nothing, into the night. Even with Matthew, who was telling some story that struck her as overinvolved and implausible.

They walked west past the office towers: cheerless angular plazas, concrete tubs of sodden petunias, the proud names of banks. Matthew led the way around back of an old apartment block, down a flight of stairs into the earth. Must, a gas leak, dirty sheets and the ceiling just that little bit too low, flailed mattress and sprung armchair where Madeline parked herself. Matthew put a kettle on the stove, flopped on the bed and started rolling joints.

After all, Madeline thought, if I'm here I have to be polite. I shouldn't have come if I'm going to sulk.

The marijuana helped. They passed the joint a few times. Madeline held it while the kettle squealed. Good grass, she thought, actually quite good grass. "Good grass," she said.

"It's all right, isn't it?" said Matthew. He came back with the teapot. He put it down on the floor and the whole room jumped and shifted. The clock stopped.

"It's all right," said Madeline. She leaned forward and handed him the joint. She watched herself lean forward and hand him the joint. She thought about watching herself lean forward and hand him the joint. She thought about how long that took, and how, after all, this was exactly what she needed. To get wasted. Exactly. To waste herself. She handed Matthew the joint and he handed her a cup of Earl Grey. This symmetry was pleasing.

Matthew was on his knees in front of the stereo. He had a record on the turntable, and he was lifting the needle and putting it down, here and there.

"This is where they do this old fifties song," he said. "This other song they were playing when that riot started." This is all for my benefit, Madeline thought, he's trying to be nice. Kneeling like that, Matthew looked looser, younger: a boy in his toybox. What was amazing was how each bit of music fell into place, how altogether they made a whole, how symbolically they managed to sum up — what? The evening? The past year? Her life?

The scent of the tea made her mouth flood. She sipped and her body warmed, fluttered. She closed her eyes for a while. When she opened them, Matthew was coming out of the bathroom.

She looked at him walking towards the mattress, watched

him flop down.

What hit her was desire like the sex in dreams, out of all proportion to the object. Having nothing to do with the object.

I'm incredibly stoned, she thought.

If I don't get up and leave right now, I'm going to be there, on that mattress, humping the shit out of him.

I don't even like him. I have no wish at all to sleep with Matthew.

The thought is impossible.

I'm too stoned to leave.

If I don't get up and leave right now.

If I sit in this chair. If I sit in this chair with my legs crossed all night, nothing will happen.

If I don't get up and leave.

The thought is disgusting.

If I don't let on.

Matthew leaned over and handed her another joint. Slow motion, the angle of her wrist, skin pale against the worn velvet chair. She looked at him as she inhaled. Eyes swollen, face slack. Shit, she thought. He's feeling it too. If I don't get up and leave. If I don't let on. She kept her face flat.

She gave him back the joint. He licked his thumb, crushed out the burning tip and kissed her. Hard. And of course she kissed him back. It was dream time, succubi and incubi and chimeras. It was the brain, the thinking, feeling Madeline short-circuited, it was the body on autopilot.

If I don't stop, if I keep my eyes shut, Madeline thought, then it won't go any further. If I keep kissing him I don't have to think about where this is going. If I just keep kissing him it won't go anywhere. There seemed a logical flaw to this argument, but she couldn't place it. She was getting enormous pleasure out of this kissing, modulation and variation. With her eyes closed, the world revealed itself as two mouths, the infinite shiftings between top and bottom lip, a flicker of tongue. This is absolutely disgusting, Madeline thought.

This went on for a while, tongue and lips and fingers. It went on for long enough that eventually the point of stopping slid out of sight like the last point of land. There was only ocean on all sides; there was only now. But since time had stopped long ago, since they were adrift, now didn't matter. The laws of land did not apply to those lost at sea. Everything was free, every act gratuitous. The pleasure this set free was incredible.

They stood up all at once and she toppled onto the mattress. Matthew was skinning out of T-shirt and jeans. There was nothing wrong with his body, not a thing. Heavier than Everett, not as muscled as Carl, a furze of light hair down chest and belly, hard penis thick rather than long, almost wedge-shaped. Shit, thought Madeline in a last minute of clarity, as she reached down and peeled off her panties.

Matthew felt heavy in her arms, not inert exactly but unwieldy, like driving a strange truck. She couldn't predict his moves, his abrupt changes of direction; clearly he would never dance across her body like Everett. His skin was harder, with a film of sweat. He was doing all the right things, the gestures towards nipples, nape, clit, but he was somewhere down inside himself. With Everett, wasn't it just his continual reticence that had said he was truly seeing her, judging her, truly present? Whereas Matthew was incredibly aroused, but it seemed to supersede her, to have nothing to do with her, with her real self. Matthew just wasn't there. And neither was she, then. As he rolled on top and began to thrust his way inside her, he kicked aside the bedding. She could smell the must, the damp. It took months for sheets to smell like that. *This is absolutely repulsive,* she thought one last time as she pushed herself against him in a spasm of disgust.

The orgasm wouldn't stop. It kept building and falling back, building up again, and then coming and coming. This too was possible only in dreams.

When it was over there was nothing to say. Matthew flicked off the lamp, and the window high in the wall shone out pale: dawn.

Madeline woke up a few hours later cold sober. As soon as she opened her eyes she knew where she was. Horror, sure, disgust, but something else, too. Titillation, what she'd feel if this were someone else's story. I can't believe I did that. She sat up in bed, looked at Matthew flung out across the mattress and wanted to giggle. A nasty giggle. But more than that, she wanted out. The sheets lay damp across her thighs, strangling her.

Madeline was fairly confident that if she disappeared now, before he woke, Matthew would barely remember. Certainly there would be no reprise, no little bouquet delivered at work, no solicitous phone calls. That suited her just fine. She wanted out of that room fast. And this too partook of the illogic of dreams, the pressing need to flee.

She gathered up her clothes and tiptoed into the bathroom. She could smell Matthew musky all over her body, but didn't risk waking him with a pounding shower. She dressed, wiped the gum of mascara from her cheeks, combed her hair and slipped out the door.

She walked quickly to the end of the alley before noticing the sun. There was wind off the ocean, white flying clouds against the blue, full morning pouring into the well of the city. After a while she saw a coffee shop, went in and ordered breakfast. She had, after all, not weathered the night so well: a headache, and raging thirst. Coffee, juice; in the washroom she lined her eyes and put on lipstick.

She did not want to go home and see Kelly. It was not guilt, exactly. She was just sick of everybody, sick of Kelly and Matthew, of Everett and the weedy boys.

This then could be a plan. She would not go home. She was already close to the park; she would go there, walk around the seawall, lie on the grass if the turf was dry. Popcorn for lunch, and she could feed the peacocks, pay to see the killer whale show, if time dragged. Or sleep on the beach.

At five o'clock she had to pick up Carl. Home in the afternoon, grab the car, throw her clothes in the back and stay on the North Shore all weekend. Monday she was moving. Monday she had her own place. Monday they would all be history.

Waves and spume on the beach, water brisk as winter, gulls twining, sailboats spinning. Madeline walked over barnacles across cormorant rocks. The sea spat in her face, crashed at her feet. She wished intently for full summer, late July. She wanted to be in that water, washed clean.

Instead, she stood leaden on the rocks. It was over, then, desire, it could only exist with an end in view, could only be thought of in relation to one body chosen above all others. And who could she want like that now? It was finished, she thought, finished for a good long while. There was only herself, here, paradoxically weightless and heavy as age, cut free from the world.

The wind off the harbour buffeted the little car across the span of the Second Narrows Bridge, lockstep in rush hour. Straight ahead, the mountains hung unnaturally close, each tree visible. Carl pointed out the freeway exit, towards the canyons. This was the flat middle of the suburbs, low ranch houses of thirty years back, cedar-shake roofs sunk in gardens given over to glossy tumbles of juniper and laurel, azalea and rhododendron. The cars in the driveways were neither new nor old, the sidewalks empty.

They drove past these houses to the edge of the subdivision, tipping downhill to a cul-de-sac where salmonberry and young alder leapt the concrete safety barriers, scraped windshield and hood as Madeline pulled over and parked.

"Take everything with you," said Madeline. "I can't lock the car."

She shouldered her pack and followed Carl down a flight of stairs set into the hillside. Concrete steps, cracked and tilted. Wild shrubbery, leather leaves, salal and Oregon grape, spat raindrops on their thighs. Windless here in the cleft of the mountain. The earth steamed, tangible heat and damp rising to meet their descent.

"My sister gets really cheap rent because nobody wants to climb these stairs every day," said Carl. The house at the bottom was identical to those passed on the drive, a little more worn, roof greener with moss. The kitchen opened onto a cedar deck level with tips of fir and hemlock in the canyon bottom. The silence was complete. Madeline could hear humming fridge, dripping tap, anxious mew of a cat outside the glass doors.

Dislocation sharp as crossing the border into a foreign country, exhaustion to the point of nerves, a second wind. Madeline's joints ached, but she knew she wouldn't sleep for hours. Picked up, shaken and set down again, pieces still fluttering into place. She went into the bathroom, took a scalding shower, dressed in clean clothes from the skin out and rinsed her underwear. The kitchen was savoury with simmering onions and garlic. Carl handed her a glass of wine and they went onto the deck. The sun slid behind a rim of mountain. From beneath their feet came the distant hush of river water, churning canyons, and a puff of chill air.

They ate dinner and took the bottle of wine into the living room, which contained two sofas angled into a corner, a stereo and a cheval glass.

"She keeps it empty to practise her dancing," said Carl.

"Right, she's a dancer," said Madeline. Stretched out on one sofa, speech took effort.

"She had a solo show," said Carl. "While you were away. It was pretty good. She used masks."

"It's nice to be here," Madeline said. "I couldn't stand it at Kelly's any longer."

"You were saying. Were you guys not getting along?"

"No, no. Just the mess. Dirty dishes and never any food."

"You could clean it up."

"I could clean it up. Yeah. But you know when it gets too much? The whole place gets depressing."

"You used to say things like this about Kelly before you went away."

"I did? I don't remember that."

"Oh yeah. She was living in this awful room full of spiders. You were really worried about her."

"I was? I said that?"

"That's why I was kind of surprised you moved in with her."

"What's worse now is this guy she's involved with," said Madeline. "Did I tell you?"

"I don't think so."

"Well. She's completely infatuated with him. They broke up and she talks about him all the time. She sees him in the bar and flips out. And he just ignores her."

"Sounds like a jerk."

"He's the sort of guy that she never knows what he's thinking or how he feels about her. As soon as her back is turned he hops into bed with anyone he can get. All the time they were going out, he was making up excuses why he couldn't see her."

"A bad sign."

"When they broke up," Madeline said, "I think he just phoned her up and said it was over. Or maybe they had a big fight. I'm not sure."

"She's just as well out of it."

"That's what I keep trying to tell her," Madeline said. "But she can't stop thinking about him."

The next day, after breakfast, Madeline followed Carl down the wooden steps at the back of the deck. No yard; a scrabble of underbrush fell quickly into forest, a narrow path, steep switchbacks under fir and cedar. Damp earth oozing water, sky invisible, trees chill as night.

"See those stumps?" said Carl. "You can see the mark of the axes. That's how big the trees were a hundred years ago."

"Amazing," said Madeline.

"Most of these trees are second growth," said Carl. "Some of them are older, they didn't get cut. You can tell by the bark. It's much thicker."

"It must have been amazing," said Madeline. She said that to please Carl, but she meant it, too. Or rather, she said it because she liked the sureness with which his boots bit the path, his open face, the way he seemed so clearly in the moment, unworried, free.

She didn't like his shirt, however: Madras plaid, tropical yellows and purple, stiffly starched.

"New shirt?" said Madeline.

"My mom sent it for my birthday," said Carl.

"Oh shit. Your birthday. It's around now, isn't it?"

"Last week."

"I totally forgot. I'm sorry."

"It's no big deal."

The path kept dropping towards the centre of the earth. Trees hung with moss, ferns overflowing the cleft of branches, saplings sprouting from the backs of logs and the crowns of stumps, the forest floor choked with growth and decay, too much, a tangle, a green wall. The roar of water grew louder. Madeline caught a glimpse of sunlight, a clearing, ahead and below. The path turned a corner and spilled them onto granite cliffs, huge rounded rock faces. Across the canyon the opposite bank caught the full morning. Thirty feet below, full flood green with silt raged between rock walls, spume dank as moss. For a moment the roar blocked her senses; she grabbed the trunk of a young tree on the lip of the cliff.

"You can go down that way and go swimming in the summer," Carl shouted. "After the water level falls a bit." He was squatting at the brink, elbows relaxed on knees, the bright shirt puffing around his waist. Madeline sat down with an arm around her tree, and lit a cigarette. Smoke on fresh air, an entirely different tang, sacrilege. The roar of the rapids blocked conversation. Besides, it was the easiest thing in the world to slide away from Carl, to slide into her own head.

This morning, then. Waking rested, disoriented, in Carl's sister's faintly damp guest room. The feeling of having crossed into a foreign country persisted. More specifically, of having fled peril and shame. This had not much to do with Matthew. Sleeping with Matthew was one of life's non-events: no weight, no reality. The shame was Everett. Her ability to trick herself, the gap between intensity of emotion and poverty of object. She had created all this out of almost nothing, wilfully, she now told herself, misreading everything. And even now she still wanted him, still thought here, at the edge of the precipice, in flashes about his body.

That would have to go, those thoughts.

Speaking of this, to Carl or to Kelly, would bring no relief, would merely make it harder to forget. And she was particularly loath to tell Carl. Why? He would certainly sympathize. But she did not want that. She did not want to risk creating that same odd gap, that distance, she felt whenever he mentioned Beth. Besides, she wanted her chance with Everett, her explanation. And if she couldn't have that, she didn't want to speak at all.

Maybe she would get it, after all. Maybe she would get it one of these days.

Carl stood, and Madeline followed him back up the path to the house.

Early afternoon, sun falling straight down onto the deck, straight down through the well of the trees and mountains. Madeline was stretched out in shorts on a lawn chair, Carl kneeling on the boards, driving nails. His shirt was off; muscles played across his back and chest. Madeline watched him from behind her sunglasses with abstract, aesthetic pleasure. *Nice body* wasn't something you could say to anyone you weren't sleeping with, she thought. Too bad. She wanted to say, to do, something nice, wanted to show she didn't take the weekend for granted. But without telling the story of the past month, there seemed no way to communicate her sense of rescue. She never wanted to leave this deck, never wanted the sun to set or the rain to fall, ever again.

"It's really nice here," she said, inadequately.

"It is, isn't it," said Carl. "I was thinking what you were saying about Kelly. I don't know. People get mixed up with people for the wrong reasons. Or they see something else in them than you do."

"Mm," said Madeline.

"I don't think you can tell her anything. I think that won't work. She has to see what he's like for herself."

"I think that's starting," said Madeline. "I think she realizes it's over."

"But I can see how it's hard for you. You have to decide how much of her you can stand. But it sounds like she needs a friend."

"I do like her," said Madeline. "When she's not going on about this guy, she's really fun. She's wild. She's not scared of anything, not scared of the cops."

"Sometimes what you like in somebody is also exactly what you don't like, too. And you've known her a long time, haven't you?"

"A really long time." *And we've been talking about her a really long time too.* "You don't seem to get involved with the wrong people," Madeline said. "You and Beth. That seems pretty solid."

"Me and Beth," said Carl. He sat back on his heels, picked up his shirt and wiped his chest. "Solid. Yeah. I guess we are pretty solid. I guess we are."

"So she's coming out next week."

"Yes. She's coming out next week."

"So are you going to go back east with her?"

"Well, when she graduates, that's where she'll probably work. She'll probably stay out there. That's probably what will happen. So she figures, and she really has a point, I either go out there now. Because why, she keeps saying, do this long-distance thing another two years. For what. So you can see she has a point."

"What do you think?"

"I can see she has a point. I can see that for sure."

"There's lots more going on back east," said Madeline. "The thing about this place, someone was saying to me and I kind of agree. It's really limited. It's like only failure is taken seriously. If you want to be really good at something, everybody tries to pull you down."

"I think every place is a bit like that," said Carl. "Actually I don't think people pull you down out here. Actually out here, what it is, more, is no one's paying any attention. Nobody cares what you do. You do something really good, and nobody pays attention. You do something really bad, nobody cares. That's what I think, anyhow."

"It's still kind of awful," said Madeline.

"I don't know. It means you can do anything you like. Only you have to do it for yourself. You can't be the sort of person who needs to have people watching. You have to be the sort of person who just does what they want to do. That's how I see it."

Supper, spaghetti with tomato sauce.

"Can I do anything?" said Madeline. "Can I chop something?"

"You can sit there and have your drink and talk to me," said Carl. "It's all under control."

On the beach or up the slope of the mountains, this time of year, afternoon lingered well into night. Here in the canyons the sun slid past the trees early, the earth breathed chill, there were frogs.

"If you're bored we could go downtown," said Carl.

"Oh, no."

"You're sure. It's Saturday night."

"No. I mean, unless you want to."

"I don't particularly. I was just seeing if you did."

"If you really want to go, we can."

"I don't. But I know you like going out."

"No. That would wreck it all. This is like being up in the bush in a cabin. It's like a holiday."

"It is, isn't it."

It was dark by now. Madeline and Carl had a sofa each, stretched out, the bottle of wine on the floor between them.

"This is the co-op radio station," said Carl. "I know the guy who does this show. What he does is go out and record ordinary sounds. All kinds of sounds. Then he mixes them together."

"Cool," said Madeline. "No, I mean it. I like it." Traffic, wind, voices and something sneaking up, creaking up, pendulum or gibbet, sliding away.

"He mixes them like music. One thing will come up, and

then another."

Madeline leaned over and topped up her glass.

"If you go back with Beth, when will you leave?" she said.

"I don't know," said Carl. "The boat's just about done. I could go this summer and get construction work. I could try to get into university for the fall."

"Shit," said Madeline. "That's fast. So you think you'll go."

"Well, we're going to talk about it," said Carl. "Beth's got a point. We can't really go on like this."

"I'll miss you," said Madeline.

"Yeah, well," said Carl. "See, here he brings in the first part of the piece again."

"It's kind of spooky. That ticking sounds like a giant clock."

"He's into clocks. He's into this whole idea of time. How you can speed it up or slow it down."

"You can. It just depends what you're doing."

"That's true," said Carl. "So you've been seeing that reporter fellow. Everett, right? So how's that going? Is that working out?"

"I wasn't talking to you about that, was I?" said Madeline. She didn't jump and spill her drink, didn't sputter a mouthful of red wine onto her T-shirt. But the room, under the grinds and squeals, the atonal industrial plaints of the radio, went still as ice.

"Weren't you?" said Carl. "It must have been Kelly. I guess I ran into her a while back."

"What did she say?"

"Not a whole lot."

"There's not really anything to say," said Madeline. "He wanted to see my photos of Berlin. We went out to dinner once. It was okay. We're not really on the same wavelength. I don't know him that well. We only met just before I went travelling."

She could hear her own voice, and her voice sounded entirely plausible. But she was starting to shake, frozen to the root.

"That's too bad. Kelly made it sound like it was happening with you two."

"Kelly exaggerates."

"Oh, well. He sounded like an interesting guy. I saw he's had those stories in the paper about campaign fraud."

"Oh really?"

"Didn't you see them? It looks like it might bring down the government. I just thought he'd be a really intelligent guy. Someone you'd find interesting."

"He's too wrapped up in his work. And I got the impression he's seeing someone anyhow."

"Oh, well," said Carl. "Too bad."

"No loss," said Madeline. She had her glass braced against her thighs to keep it from spilling. "Do you really swim in that canyon? It's hard to believe." A deep breath, and then another.

"The water level drops right down. It's perfectly safe. It's cold but it's nice. We should come up here in August."

"If you're still in town."

"True. If I'm still in town. You're right. If I'm still in town."

"I can't believe it's Sunday afternoon already," said Madeline. "I'm not ready for the city yet."

"I hope this isn't wrecking it for you, going grocery shopping at the mall," said Carl.

"Not at all."

"You were saying last night about wanting it to be like a cabin in the bush."

"This is like travelling. I've never been in here. We're not going to see anyone we know."

They were walking across the parking lot under a spotless sky. Right in the arms of the mountains, tucked up like a little logging town, Madeline thought. She was trying to place an odd feeling that had been creeping up on her all day. A kind of lassitude. Not hangover, not depression, nothing bad.

"I just realized what's wrong with me," she said suddenly. "I'm relaxed."

"Tomorrow morning you can drop me off at Mike's," Carl said. They were stretched on their sofas again, past midnight. "He always gives me a lift out to Delta." Jazz on the radio. "So we should get up early," Carl said. He didn't move.

"Okay," said Madeline. She eased herself deeper into the sofa cushions. Fatigue pulling her eyes. She opened them with effort. "How's the boat coming, anyhow?" she said.

"It's doing all right," said Carl. "The owner's pretty happy."

"Did you ever get that boat ride?"

"That one on my birthday? No, it was pouring all weekend."

"Too bad." The relentless tug of exhaustion. But keeping her awake was a feeling equally intense, one she often had travelling, the last night in town. She knew she would never sit here again with Carl, would likely never spend time with him again. Beth was coming, and then he would leave. They would be happy back east, where he'd grown up, where his family lived. Nothing to regret, on his behalf.

She didn't want to end the evening. It would be over soon enough, even this weekend dropped in her lap like a gift. They would get on with their separate lives. But she was not going to rush the ending, not going to topple into sleep a minute earlier than she had to. When Carl called it a night, she would too. But he seemed in no hurry.

"He might take us out again sometime," said Carl. "Now that the weather's changed. You should come."

"That would be nice," said Madeline. Last night she would have added: if you're still in town. Tonight was too close to the end to say that. We'll never go, though, she thought. Or he'll take Beth.

"We might actually get the yacht launched," said Carl. "That would be fun."

"Yes," said Madeline. A notion flickered across her mind, unbidden, asexual. You could sleep with someone just because you couldn't stand to say good-night, she thought. Too bad it doesn't work that way.

At seven Monday morning, Madeline dropped Carl off, and drove to her new house. The woman on the main floor came heavily to the door and handed over keys. The house was cut on the same pattern as Kelly's; Madeline climbed three flights to the attic. Shared bath and toilet on the second-floor landing. That kept the rent low.

Madeline's apartment ran the length of the house, narrowed by the tipped roof. The walls were pale blue, a shade lighter than the sky burning outside. The floors were old linoleum, but that couldn't be helped. Out the front window, over sink and stove, the view sailed north across warehouses and railway yards to the wall of mountains. Out the back, her fire escape opened into the top branches of an ancient bing cherry, glossy green fruit amid the leaves.

The movers were only an hour late: boxes and more boxes,

the bed and the bookshelves, sheets and towels, dishes and clothes. In their wake, silence. Madeline dropped onto the bare mattress, weightless with exhaustion. The windows were flung open, front to back. The breeze swept through, leaves rustled, shadows played across her face, she slept.

She woke late in the afternoon, went out for a hamburger, came home and started unpacking. The serious, concentrated business of investigating closet space, assembling bookcases, wedging tables into alcoves.

It felt almost as if the last month had happened on the other side of the ocean, far away now as the squat in Berlin, the hostel in Provence, as strangers on a train. She would live here, she would go to work, she wouldn't call Kelly, she wouldn't think of Everett; she would start clean, in a country where she was unknown.

A nice idea. But she would think of Everett, she would keep thinking of him for a long time; that was evident. And at Randy's she would see Matthew, and Kelly would no doubt drop by Styx and Stoned. Only Carl would be gone. Carl would be the only one who'd disappear.

Nevertheless, a weightless week. On Tuesday, Madeline went in to do a shift at Styx and Stoned.

"I've been advertising for a new cashier," said Tania. "Maybe two. Take a look at these application letters."

Loopy girlish signatures, brief résumés going back to grade ten jobs in doughnut shops.

"I'm going to have to travel a bit more this summer, go back east," said Tania. "Do some buying. I'd like you to take on a bit of managing. Come sit in on the interviews tomorrow. I want to be sure you get on with the new girls."

"I'm speechless," said Madeline. "I'm flattered. Of course."

"You know pretty much everything about the place already. And don't forget my solstice party this weekend. Cryptic Neon are playing."

Flawless days in the big blue bowl of the sky. Cutting down the back alley to the corner store, Madeline saw the roses. The houses in this neighbourhood were the same age as Kelly's, but shabbier, plainer, smaller: no gingerbread trim, no stained glass. But the roses. Every broken-back fence and sagging porch was lapped in roses gone wild. There were profuse little red blossoms springing up from the stumps of hybrid grafts. There were damp purple cabbages the size of saucers. There were climbers, improbable flame orange and shocking pink. There were buds fading yellow into pink, and others dead white as moths. Madeline crouched beside garbage cans, snapping blossoms from the undersides of fences, where they wouldn't be missed, where they could just possibly be mistaken for public property. No one noticed.

The vase perfumed her whole apartment. The roses drooped of their own weight, heavy with raindrops and tiny ants. After a few days, the petals dropped all at once, still in the shapes of living flowers.

On Thursday, stopped at a traffic light on her way home from work, Madeline saw Carl and Beth. They didn't see her, and she didn't honk, didn't wave. They were walking along the street, talking, neither happy nor angry: an entirely plausible couple. You couldn't call Beth's hair a bowl cut any more, Madeline thought, it was something more sophisticated, a sleek little bob. Really, she was actually quite pretty. A subtle kind of pretty, an old-fashioned face free of makeup, a face from a portrait gallery, a merchant's young wife of a hundred years past. They looked good together. Serious.

Madeline worked until closing time on Saturday afternoon. Then she locked the door, shut down the cash register and reached into the front window.

To get the mauve dress, she had to lift the torso from the plaster mannequin and carry her, an inanely grinning bride or dance partner, into the fitting room.

The dress still fit like a second skin, tight and sleek through the bodice so that each breath made Madeline intensely aware of her waist and breasts, her belly and hips. She looked gorgeous, ethereal. And then she knew she did not have the energy for this dress, not tonight. It would take too much effort living up to this dress, obeying or profaning it, either way. She let it fall, stepped out of the petals of the skirt and back into what she'd planned to wear. The black leotard and an Indian print skirt, pretty enough; it would fly out if she danced, and show no stains if she sat on the lawn.

Madeline slid the dress onto the mannequin, settled her in the window and headed out.

Tania's house was the oldest on the block, a jumble of sloping roofs and gables. It had been the original farmhouse before sub-division in the 1920s, and still held attached a sloping triple backyard full of ancient fruit trees. None of this was evident from the street. Madeline went through the front door swinging open, down a crooked hall, following voices, and stepped out onto a lawn gone long as hay. Tania came towards her in white muslin robes and handed her a glass of wine.

Guests were still arriving. Leather and lace, denim, colourful vests from Tibet and Guatemala, musicians and artists flung on the greensward. Bill, Tania's husband, had iron-grey hair in a short ponytail, and a haunch of something on a spit. Over the ruined orchard the sky was apricot, the terrible tender colour of lost summer evenings.

"Hey, shit, how you doing?" said Kelly. "How's your new place? Do you have a phone yet?"

"No I don't. It's great. I'm fine," said Madeline. "So. How's it going?" I have nothing to say to anyone, she thought.

"Excellent. Super excellent," said Kelly. "It's so cool."

"What's that?" said Madeline.

"Matthew and I have got it all worked out," said Kelly. "He's going to move into Sue's room until she comes back, and then we're going to get our own place."

"Excellent," said Madeline. "No, really. I mean it." Over Kelly's shoulder she saw Everett come through the back door onto the lawn, alone. He couldn't help but see her. He turned and went over to the barbecue, started talking to Bill.

Some other night will be my night for explanations, thought Madeline. She couldn't help that rush in the blood, though, the way her body leapt up in the first second before she had time to think. It was all still there. It wasn't going away any time soon.

Kelly kept talking and Madeline kept nodding, the jittery half-hour before a party jells, takes shape, made all the worse by the fact that whether she wanted it or not, she could feel Everett's trajectory across the garden hot as the sun's passage on her shoulderblades. Whether she wanted it or not. Pride and common sense said let it go. But that was not so easy. And maybe she didn't want to. Maybe the most painful desire was still more delicious than the limbo of wanting nothing.

Bill sliced roast lamb onto paper plates, the sun dropped another notch, Rod and Randy and Dick and the drummer wiped their hands, picked up their instruments and started to play. Not their usual music. Tonight it was old rock 'n' roll, *Maybelline why don't you be true* and *going to a party in the county jail.* Plates went flying, boots and jackets fell under the wisteria, the lawn was heaving, more people were pouring through the back door, things were really starting now.

Madeline went upstairs to the toilet. The tub was floating with ice and beer bottles. On the landing, she heard the boy with the half-shaved skull call hello from one of the bedrooms. The four of them were sprawled on a velvet bedspread from India, passing a joint. Madeline sat on the floor, took it as it went by, but shallow puffs. Whatever happens it certainly won't be him next, Madeline told herself. But the joint seemed to be having no noticeable effect. She left after a while, took a bottle of beer from the tub and went downstairs. Matthew was rummaging in the fridge and kept his head down as she passed. That suited her fine.

When she got out on the lawn she saw that no time had elapsed. The red sun still quivered between the office towers in the distance, the band was playing the same riff, the exact same line, *dancing to the border radio.* After that the evening became immensely easier. No time had elapsed, and for a while it seemed to be getting earlier, the sun rising, or perhaps the band was only repeating the same songs. At one point Madeline was chatting to Randy under a gnarled apple tree, but the band was still playing, the band never stopped, perhaps someone was filling in for him on bass but it was just as likely that he was both here and there, that if time could lose its grip, so could the stringencies of place.

Tania walked into the orchard carrying a lit taper, and points of light appeared in her wake; she had hung the trees earlier with tin cans containing candles. By the time she returned it was completely dark. The musicians were sweating, the crowd was dancing barefoot, Everett seemed to have disappeared.

"Hello," said Carl.

"Hello," said Madeline. This rush of gladness was entirely

different from the anxiety of Everett. It was its polar opposite, relief, completeness. "Where's Beth?"

"She's gone back to Toronto," said Carl. "I just saw her off at the airport."

"That was fast," said Madeline. "She wasn't here very long." By mutual accord they were walking away from the music, away from the dancers, down the quiet slope into the orchard.

"Well, things weren't going that well," said Carl. "We figured, why drag it out? She got a flight on stand-by."

"Shit," said Madeline. "I'm really sorry."

"It's all right, actually," said Carl. "We needed a change. It was either this or me go back east."

"So you're staying here."

"I like it here."

"So you guys actually broke up?"

"I think so. Pretty much. I mean, I'm sure one of us could always reconsider."

"Are you going to?"

"No. I don't think so, anyhow. I don't think I'm going to reconsider."

"That's too bad."

"I don't think either of us is too upset. It was kind of a relief. There's this little door in the tree."

"It's Bill," said Madeline. "He's an artist. This whole orchard is an installation."

"Inside he's got a piece of motherboard."

"Check this one out. He's got hood ornaments hanging like fruit."

"This tree is covered with reflectors."

"Bill is into used auto parts. You're going to stay?"

"Uh-huh. Oops, sorry, guys," said Carl. Madeline saw a tangle of white thighs rolling back out of sight into the night.

"Shit, they're going to freeze," she said, and laughed. "It's not that warm."

"I think we better watch where we step," said Carl.

"Tania's done well with these candles, though," said Madeline. "She's got one on every one of Bill's things."

"No dial tone," said Carl.

"Who would you phone if it worked?"

"I don't know," said Carl. "There isn't anyone I want to phone right now."

"That's too bad."

"Oh, I don't know. There's worse things."

"Do you want to go back up? We can watch the band from this hammock."

"That's an idea. I don't know if I'm in the mood for a crowd right now. Not exactly right now, anyhow."

"Kelly and Matthew are back together again," said Madeline. Hanging like this in net, she could feel the night air all over her body, like swimming. In a while it might be too cold. Right now she felt disembodied, floating, like the points of light and metal in the trees.

"That's great. That's really good for them," said Carl.

"Do you think so? It just seems like more of the same to me."

"They might work it out. Some people do."

"So they say," said Madeline.

"True. So they say."

There was a distant burst and report, a rattle like shellfire. The dancers faltered, they turned their backs on the band, they turned to face Madeline and Carl, but their eyes were tilted at the sky in the west, towards the office towers. There was another explosion. Madeline and Carl tipped their heads back and saw fireworks spreading above the trees. The band drew to a halt, laid down their guitars, wiped their faces, drank deeply. The sky broke open with red and yellow rain, petals and clouds and tracers. The dancers stood motionless and silent, gazing.

The band sat down on the grass, lost from view behind the crowd. But there was new drumming in the distance, syncopated and insistent. It was growing louder, it was approaching. Around the side of the house came a stilt-walker in patchwork tights, playing a flute. She was flanked by two tumblers doing cartwheels across the garden. The troupe that followed had drums around their necks, or tambourines, or they carried paper lanterns shaped like faces. They wore motley, and caps with bells, and their faces were painted; they snaked in a line through the crowd, drumming and dancing.

"It's the fools' parade," said Carl.

Over their heads the fireworks downtown reached their grand finale, the sky drenched in flame. The silence in the wake was like the end of a war. Up on the lawn the drummers were circling the dancers.

When Madeline and Carl had leaned back to watch the fire-works, they had tipped together in the hammock, shoulder to shoulder. In the silence that followed Madeline became aware of this contact, but didn't shift. First, there was no easy way to move in the hammock, short of climbing out and repositioning herself. This seemed unnecessary, excessive, even rude. Besides, it was comfortable, this contact, there was no denying that. She was too comfortable to move.

Up on the lawn the jugglers were flinging flaming torches above the heads of the crowd.

"Those are the fire dancers," said Carl. "We should go watch."

"I guess," said Madeline. Neither of them moved.

Carl leaned over and kissed her.

Some knowledges are there all along, some surprises only appear to be surprises for the briefest of moments, and then subside into having always been obvious.

Madeline kissed him back.

"I've been wanting to do that for a long time," he said.

"So have I," said Madeline. It seemed like a nice thing to say, and right at that moment she wanted it to be true.

PESADILLA BEACH

PESADILLA BEACH

"I baked two dozen this week but the kids inhaled them already," said Cammie. "I'll give you the last one and then Devlin and Caitlin will scream. You can't keep up with it around here."

"Well, thanks," said Amanda. She nibbled the oatmeal cookie and balanced her cup of peppermint tea on the arm of the futon sofa. Soft raw pine, the kind the buyer is meant to sand and stain to taste, only no one had got around to this, not for years and years, evidently: rings of coffee and a loopy childish ballpoint scribble, a darker splotch: grape juice? Blood?

"It's so cool you're temping at the college," said Cammie. "I couldn't believe it when you walked into the department."

"I was really lucky to get called in," said Amanda. "My UIC from that photo project ran out last month."

"It's really great you're still keeping up with your photography, too," said Cammie. "I remember hearing about your show last year. I didn't get to see it, though. You were doing something with older women, right?"

"It was through this drop-in centre," said Amanda. "Women that live in the rooming-houses down on Hastings Street. The idea was to teach them to photograph their own lives." Amanda had said this far too many times, over the three years it had taken to apply for the grant, run the project and navigate a small but satisfying amount of media attention. History, now. Her words bored her, the project bored her, and by extension Cammie, whose questions were old news, belated enthusiasm. But Amanda was sitting on Cammie's futon sofa, drinking Cammie's peppermint tea and eating her last oatmeal cookie; she was a guest, she would make an effort. "It was really quite interesting," Amanda added. "They came up with some amazing images."

"I can imagine," said Cammie.

"So Devlin must be really big by now," said Amanda, deliberately giving the conversation a nudge off course. "I remember when he was born." *Participants will develop a sense of self-esteem, empowerment and community through learning to document and analyse the conditions of oppression in their lives.* Amanda wrote that on the application form and, in the past tense, on the final report. Cribbed from an essay by a radical Brazilian educator. Amanda was aware that her boredom with the topic was something close to disgust, principally with herself. Her old women had taken photographs striking in content and composition, beginner's luck: pigeons and barbed wire, worn faces in winter black and white. The exhibition brought tears to the earnest eyes of the freelance reporter for the CBC; the women remained on welfare, gathering in the drop-in centre, dipping donated biscuits in instant coffee, flustering, quarrelling and complaining in the face of immovable fate.

None of this could be said to Cammie; Amanda barely understood it herself, this unease nudging like a stray cat at a door half ajar in her mind. "I don't think I've seen Devlin since he was tiny," she said.

"He's going on nine," said Cammie. "Can you believe it? And Caitlin's four. She's out with Jeff right now. They ought to be back soon."

"Time flies, doesn't it?" said Amanda. She had to push herself to follow the conversation, anchor herself in this room where the dull light of summer rain, barred by venetian blinds, sifted like dust over grey broadloom, off-white walls, beached drifts of newspapers and toys, bike pumps and camping gear. The carpet was worn in traffic patterns clear as cowpaths, sprinkled here and there with clusters of dark spots like scattered pebbles; even the cheerful futon cover, vaguely Navajo, seemed silted over.

"Time just flies," said Cammie cheerfully. "I've been in the ESL department for seven years this fall. I started out temping, like you. Now I'm clerical grade five. For what that's worth. The next step would be departmental assistant. But Marthe isn't about to quit. Besides, that job is way too much stress. I'll stick with being a secretary."

"Is Jeff working these days?" said Amanda. From where her deep lack of interest in this conversation? A fatal gap in lifestyle, a fatal lack in Cammie? Ten years ago, in her early twenties, Amanda had accepted such simple explanations. These days, she knew she brought her boredom with her. Amanda had sat in far more sordid rooms than this, listened to far more banal conversations, had revelled in searching out a zero degree of humanity under the ugliest circumstances. Not boredom today, then; rather, deeper sullen shiftings of refusal and resentment. Or anxiety.

"Oh, it was kind of a drag for Jeff," said Cammie. "You know the record shop where he was working part time for years. It went belly up a while back. So finally he got welfare to send him on this training project for computer technicians."

"He should be able to find work easily with that," said Amanda, politely.

"It's a super-hard program, though. They have to be in class every day at nine a.m. He's finding it pretty stressful. But I think he'll do all right. It goes a whole year. Speak of the devil," said Cammie. Down the hall, the front door jingled and rattled. A little girl came running into the living room. She was wearing pink corduroy overalls; her hair, blonde and silky, wisped down into her eyes.

"I went to the top of the jungle gym," she said. "I went to the top and I was a monkey. I was upside-down."

"You were upside-down," said Cammie. "Good for you. Caitlin, this is Amanda. You haven't seen her before."

"Hello," said Amanda.

"Hello," said Caitlin. "I was a monkey."

"So you were saying," said Amanda.

"Jeff," said Cammie. "Look who's here. You remember Amanda."

"For sure," said Jeff. He put a bag of groceries on the table in the kitchen nook. "We go back ages. When did I quit university? Twelve years ago?"

"It's amazing to be thinking in decades now, isn't it?" said Amanda. Jeff had not changed appreciably; he was still skinny, had kept the brushcut hair, the cheap high-top sneakers, in which she remembered him dancing on the sofa. Early on in the last decade. Everett and Dick's big eviction party in that old house down a long block of warehouses and body shops. A party where, she remembered, all tomorrows seemed equally possible and impossible. Shouting *no future* along with the mixed tape bringing on the most intoxicating premonition of freedom.

"A lot of water under the bridge, all right," said Jeff. "They had the free-range eggs at the food co-op but they only had hothouse tomatoes."

"I'll do that lentil thingy tomorrow night then," said Cammie, digging into the grocery bag. "Caitlin. There's no more cookies. Would you like a banana? Are you hungry?"

"I don't know," said Caitlin. "Okay."

"Come here and I'll cut it up for you," said Cammie.

"So you're starting at the college," said Jeff.

"Temping," said Amanda. "I don't know if I want to work full time. I want to keep doing photography."

"Good for you," said Jeff. "I haven't picked up a guitar since I started this computer course."

"They're working him so hard," said Cammie. "Here you go. Can you eat a whole banana?"

"It takes some getting used to," said Jeff. "I am not a morning person. Okay, you want to sit on my lap? Okay, put the plate here. Up you go."

"I got to chase Devlin down if we're going to get to Mom's for dinner at seven," said Cammie.

"He was heading off for 302 when I was coming in," said Jeff.

"I'll call Ann and have her send him over," said Cammie.

"Who is this, Caitlin?" said Jeff.

"It's Amanda," said Caitlin, and put a slice of banana in her mouth.

"We were introduced," said Amanda. She thought now that Jeff had changed. He seemed crisper, more focused. Perhaps he had just stopped smoking marijuana.

"Well, it's great catching up with you again," said Jeff. "Do you see anyone any more?"

"Not really," said Amanda. "I heard Cryptic Neon on the radio."

Cammie was hanging up the phone. "That's so amazing, they finally got a hit," she said.

"Their sound is totally changed," said Jeff. "They're doing

this new folk rock."

"I kind of like that song, actually," said Amanda.

"They've been around for so long," said Cammie. "Dick and those guys must be so excited. And Everett. We see his byline in the paper all the time."

"He did a story on my photo project last year," said Amanda.

"Caitlin," said Cammie. "Have you eaten your banana? Well, gobble gobble. Finish it up. We've got to get you into something nice for Grandma."

"I guess I should roll, then," said Amanda. She stood up and put her cup on the kitchen counter.

"Well, drop by whenever," said Jeff. "It was really good to see you."

"I know. I was so amazed when she walked into the office. I recognized her right away," said Cammie. "It was like, oh my God."

Amanda's boots went thump thump thump down the wooden stairs into the courtyard of the housing co-op. The pink stucco walls were sooted and stained by rain, the boxed flowerbeds, tall daisies, echinacea, sage and dill, beaten slantwise.

Her car was parked at the curb. Amanda sat in the driver's seat for several minutes watching the rain stream down the windshield. The whole afternoon, the whole week working with Cammie, had unsettled her.

Ten or twelve years ago, Amanda had had little to say to either of them. She had known Jeff longer, and better. This meant only that they knew more of the same people and turned up at the same parties, where Amanda drank heavily and talked fast and loud about things that seemed, then, urgent and important. With Jeff, more than most men, Amanda had had to slow down, backtrack, explain. This made her self-conscious and nervous. Did Jeff never sense her impatience back then, never feel snubbed?

Cammie had been peripheral; she had picked up with Jeff after several years trailing a man who had not wanted her, or not wanted to treat her well. Cammie, back then: a pale waxy blonde, a nice figure, pretty breasts, but always hunched over as if protecting her heart.

The rain blurred down the windshield, a dim screen on which Amanda willed two contradictory images to superimpose in time-lapse dissolve. Cammie of memory, long pale hair and bloodless face, thin arms, martyred silence in the corners of crowded kitch-ens while Matthew held forth at two a.m., thumb in his jutting cowboy buckle.

And Cammie in the present, the Cammie who had instantly claimed Amanda last Monday morning.

Amanda had not recognized Cammie, had smiled and smiled and nodded at this stocky woman a few years her senior. Short brown hair, a geometrical cut neither flattering nor daring. An unfortunate outfit, loose blouse tucked into matching loose shorts, a pretty print in oceanic blues, but badly cut, the bulky elastic waist. Amanda had stood smiling and nodding, quickly flipping through past offices, temporary typing pools, mailrooms.

When, after two minutes of overwhelming, multidirectional good will, Amanda had got it clear that this was *Cammie, Camel-lia, Cammie you remember? Back in that place on Victoria Drive?* she had been in response just as effusive, covering over the gap.

That first night, Amanda sat in the dark after supper, trying to place Cammie. This meant reconstructing her own life, the par-ties and demonstrations, the beer parlours and concerts and cof-fee bars, at which Cammie and Matthew and Jeff flickered at the edge of vision.

After a while, Amanda turned on the lamp and went hunting for her contact sheets, her old photographs. But during those years, she'd taken few personal photos. Whole rolls for the peace march, the student sit-in, an exposé on leaking roofs in the dorms, on chemical container cars shunted through a residential neigh-bourhood. Her friends were blurred faces in crowd shots, angry mouths below picket signs.

Amanda put away the photographs, and knelt by her CD collection. She had developed, latterly, a taste for blues vocalists and cabaret singers. Under these, though, an old cassette tape, scrawled label *dance party songs*. Local bands, early Cryptic Neon of course, and Stund, others she could no longer name.

They sounded unfamiliar. They could have been any garage bands of the era, from any city in North America. But after a few songs the beat began to carry her. More than that. Amanda began to remember how she had felt, certain nights, walking into dance halls or parties as if she owned the room. She began to remember the nonchalance, the beauty of being stripped down and ready for action, parties or protest marches equally exciting. Walking to the fridge to refill her wine glass, Stund hitting slow-building chords, Amanda knew, in her skin and tendons, exactly how it had once felt to be the eye of the storm, harbinger of the future.

The last song ended, the machine clicked itself off. The green eye of the amplifier hummed back at Amanda, who did not bother turning the tape. The silence left her hopped up, vaguely disturbed, deeply dissatisfied. Nothing could match the promise of that music. Nothing had. And after all, it was not an era. It was a few years at most, and it was, more than anything, connected to being very young, and to particular people, and it had not lasted; the bands had broken up, the people had moved away.

Now she realized that her attention had shifted. It was no longer the others who interested her. It no longer mattered what exactly had happened between Cammie and Matthew, or why, late one March night of sour rain and damped expectations, Matthew had leaned over and kissed Amanda, and Amanda had said *I really don't think so,* and flagged a cab and gone home alone, because her own melodramas were being played out elsewhere. It no longer mattered that Amanda had feared, for two days thirteen years ago, that Jeff desired her, and so she had rudely, unforgivably, snubbed him one afternoon in the student union pub. It no longer mattered whether Cammie had thrown a lamp or an ashtray or a glass of beer at Matthew, or Matthew's new girlfriend, or whether, as variously reported, she had threatened to kill him, herself or the other woman. It no longer mattered if Cammie got pregnant in her first month with Jeff, and blackmailed him into fatherhood, or whether they planned it, true love.

At the end of Monday evening, after forty-five minutes of hard-core thrash, half a bottle of wine and several dozen carefully indexed contact sheets, it was only Amanda who mattered, that faraway Amanda.

Who had she been? What had she lost, where had it all gone?

Today, Sunday afternoon, in the car in the rain outside Cammie's building, Amanda felt memory come surging up out of her bones. She had not known until this week that memory was tactile, that her body remembered everything, that she could feel the ghosts hovering at her elbow.

She put her key in the ignition and turned on the windshield wipers. The curtain of rain ripped open, baring the wet street.

Coming down the sidewalk by the park was a boy in a leather jacket, plaid shirt, striding along, head bent into the rain. A physical jolt so great Amanda almost hit the horn, almost waved. Because, in her present mood, he exactly resembled the boy with whom she had been in love during those years, a love that had cut her up and spat her out less publicly than Cammie's for Matthew, but no less thoroughly. It was all wound up with the way things had ended. It was wound up with things she had tried not to think about for years.

As the boy strode past the car, Amanda saw that he was very young, twenty-one, twenty-two, and beautiful. The other boy was of course no longer a boy; he'd be tilting towards forty by now, utterly changed; he had a job, she hadn't seen him in over a decade.

Surrounded by ghosts, Amanda let out the parking brake and drove home along wet streets in the long grey emptiness of Sunday afternoon.

The afternoon faded imperceptibly, silver to pewter to dusk; up above the cloud cover lingered the elongated northern day, summer's proud blaze.

Through the open window, clean wet air and the whispering rain falling dead straight, windless, on the flat platter leaves of the broadleaf maple. As the light dimmed, Amanda's book slid to her lap, the lens of the day snicked shut; following the cue of the sky, her white walls darkened to grey.

Hugh phoned at nine p.m., midnight in Toronto.

"The contract is going all right," he said. "I've met the professors for the fall. The courses look good." The line was so clear he sounded as if he were calling from down the block, as if he'd say, in a moment, *Why don't I drop by? Let's go grab some supper.* But he sounded tired, too, faded.

"How are you doing?" said Amanda. "How are you settling in?"

"All right," he said. "It's been hot. Humid. Thunderstorms last night. It never really cools down."

"So you're settling in."

"Yes. Sure. Things are falling into place."

"You sound a bit down," said Amanda.

"Do I? I guess the heat's pretty draining. How are you

getting on?"

"Oh, fine. I got that temp job at the college. And I ran into Cammie and Jeff. She works there."

"I don't think I know them."

"I guess you wouldn't. I guess I knew them before you. In school."

"Well, that's nice. That you know someone there."

"I guess."

"Isn't it? Are they nice? Was she friendly?"

"Yes. Really very friendly. I went to visit her today. It's just kind of weird, though. I don't know."

"Well, that's great you're meeting people," said Hugh. *Now that I've abandoned you,* was what he didn't say, aloud. "So you're getting on all right?" he added.

"Oh, yes," said Amanda. And that was, in fact, true. After all the discussions, the planning, the agreement to suspend the affair, to keep in touch, to wait and see, and after Hugh's packing, garage sale, subletting and second thoughts, after all this, driving home alone from the airport, Amanda had surprised herself by feeling, predominantly, relief.

She did not want to phrase it quite that way to Hugh.

"You're getting on all right," he said.

"Oh, yes. But you. You do sound a bit wiped."

"It's the weather here. I think things will work themselves out. I feel quite optimistic today."

"That's good then," said Amanda. After all, if he wasn't happy, if he was homesick or lonely or overwhelmed, it would do him no good to tell her. He could not, at this point, change his mind, bail out of the MA in urban studies, throw up the fellowship, evict his sub-lessee and come flying home.

Amanda suspected that, whatever the case, Hugh did not miss her, specifically. Their agreement was to not miss each other, and she knew how carefully he always fulfilled his promises.

"I'll write you a long letter then," said Hugh. "I'll send you those community development articles I was talking about."

When Amanda hung up the phone, the apartment was completely dark. Outside the rain murmured and shuffled.

Amanda had not been missing Hugh before he called. Even now she did not think it was Hugh, himself, whom she missed. The gap was more general. She wanted, right now, life and sunshine, colour and action, a hot meal and good company, attention. She wanted much more than Hugh, or she thought she did. For that reason she would not allow herself to say that she missed him. In his absence she wanted everything.

The agreement to not miss each other had been made primarily for her benefit, though Hugh had never quite said so. Neither had Amanda. But she was fairly certain he shared her fear that in his absence she would collapse, revert back to who she had been when they met, eight years earlier.

That had been at the end of a very bad time, at the end of the worst time ever, after everything was gone and ruined, the parties over, the dancehalls silent, the political committees defeated, the people who had been her friends scattered and lost. That was after her own heart was broken and scattered, and she no longer wanted to face the world. Hugh had met her at the end of the very bad time, and she had feared that, when he left, it would all come back.

But it hadn't. He had changed her, it seemed, because his love had been solid and reliable and intelligent, and his life determinedly private.

Still, when Hugh left, there was a gap in Amanda's life. There was Cammie. But Cammie opened straight into the past. When she thought about Cammie, the intervening decade collapsed and blew away.

For a long time, the bad years had blocked out consideration of the good ones, the way it all fell apart more significant than what came before. But the bad years no longer mattered so much, no longer seemed inevitable, though perhaps they were.

Now, though, for the first time, Amanda was seeing everything that had been lost, the intensity and exhilaration. Surely it must be possible to have some of that back. Surely it must be possible to have *friends.*

Outside, the night glittered and fell over empty boulevards and sodden lawns.

"Excuse me," said the boy. "Es mi problema." He was leaning over the hatchway between the hall and the office of the ESL department. Amanda was crouched at the base of the bookshelves. *Side by Side, Book One. Full Class Set,* she wrote on her clipboard, and stood up. Monday, mid-morning, the wide halls blank and beige, the hum of classrooms soporific as grade one.

"I have problema wit mi money," the boy said, spreading an envelope on the counter. His careful fingers suggested that the paper bureaucracy was a recent discovery.

"Let's see," said Amanda, squinting at the boxes and bars, the additions and subtractions, the codes and encryptions, of the stub of an unemployment insurance cheque. She turned over the slip, looking blankly at the symbol key on the back. "What's the problem?" she said.

"Iss problema," he said, smiling apologetically. "Iss poco mas." His voice had a soft lisp, a rural shyness. "Iss not big," he added. From down the hall, a chorus of twenty voices burst out in unison: *How are you today? I am fine. I am fine. Very very fine.* And again, louder: *I am fine. I am fine. Very very fine. How are* you?

"I don't understand," said Amanda. She dug deep, back into three weeks, six years ago, in Baja California. "No comprendo," she managed. Baja California. The whole trip marred, she had thought at the time, by a high faint whine of displeasure from Hugh, based in her failures at map reading, her jittery paranoia among Tijuana crowds. Her anxiety, perhaps, over pleasing *him.* Later, though, Hugh said she had imagined it all, he had never been angry. That was thousands of miles, thousands of tears, later. *No comprendo indeed,* she now thought, and pulled herself back into the present. "You must wait for Cammie," she said. "I am new here."

"Yess," said the boy, and smiled angelically. His face was expectant, open, painfully young. "Es problema wit mi money."

"You have to wait. For Cammie," said Amanda.

"Yess," said the boy, with beautiful incomprehension. "Es problema. You look."

"You have to wait. Cammie comes back. Five minutes." Amanda tapped her watch. *Mexican standoff,* she thought, except of course the boy was not Mexican, came rather from El Salvador or Guatemala or Honduras, out of the teeth of the civil wars. He was looking at her so hopefully that she couldn't turn away, go back to taking inventory. He nudged the cheque towards her; Amanda took it up, pretended to read. Over the top, she darted glances at him. His skin was cinnamon, a warm brown, smooth as a girl's, gazelle eyes, a certain Aztec sculpting to nose and cheekbones. Barely twenty, if that; eighteen was the minimum for the language courses, but students sometimes snuck in younger. Fifteen years between her and him, then, and Amanda was finding him, the longer she looked, stunningly beautiful. If the gap in years had been smaller, Amanda knew, if she were ten years younger, she would have seen him as raw, naive, an asexual child. As it was, it was just his untouched quality, and the little shock of recognition of possibility in the impossible, that stirred her. But impossible — yes. Amanda knew she had no intention, none at all, of rescuing a teenage refugee, knew she closed the door on wet cats, walked past fallen sparrows. Her flash of desire was perverse, secret, random, with no basis in the real.

Hugh's body had stood between Amanda and the world. That part of it, the sex, had never failed right up to the end. But minus him, her imagination was going to run wild; that was increasingly obvious.

"No comprendo," she said, making her voice, and her face, sad, apologetic, sympathetic.

"Si, si," said the boy, smiling luminously back at her.

Cammie came tapping back down the hall, and in through the office door, a Styrofoam coffee cup in one hand. "Rafael," she said. "You have your cheque. Let me see." The boy turned his beautiful eyes to Cammie, the thread snapped, Amanda stepped back to the bookshelves, began counting *Talk to Me! Conversation Skills for Beginners*.

"You have to tell them you go to school," said Cammie. Her voice had risen a notch, slower and clearer and louder; she sounded impatient to Amanda, though that was probably not the intent. "Tell UIC, I am in school. You get more money."

"Yess," said Rafael.

"Did you tell UIC?" said Cammie.

"Yess."

The door swung open again and one of the English teachers came in, carrying an armful of books. Late middle age, motherly or grandmotherly: iron-grey bob, long cotton skirt pulling across the stomach, crepe-soled shoes.

"Rafael," she said. "You have your cheque?"

"Si," said Rafael, and broke into a rapid stream of Spanish, too fast for Amanda to catch more than a word or two: *problema*, cheque.

The teacher held her ground in what seemed perfect Spanish,

idiomatic and fluent. The problem was evidently baroque, fraught. Amanda was watching Rafael. Now that he could make himself understood, his face held a focused intelligence, an intentness; there was nothing missing.

After a minute the teacher turned to Cammie. "I think we better call UIC ourselves on this one," she said. "Can we use your phone?"

"Of course," said Cammie. "Rafael. Come in." She opened the door, and he entered from the hall. The three of them disappeared into Cammie's office. *Working Together. Task-Based Fluency for Lower Intermediate. 15 copies, three damaged,* wrote Amanda. By now coffee break had spilled into the halls; there were teachers brushing past Amanda, lined up at the photocopiers, dropping binders and books on the worktables. The teacher with the iron-grey hair came out of Cammie's office.

"They're sorting it out," she said.

"You speak awfully good Spanish," said Amanda.

"It's a bit rusty," said the teacher. "We did spend five years in a village in Honduras in the seventies. Before it got nasty down there. We've been back to visit a few times. And I was down volunteering in Nicaragua a few years ago."

"That sounds really interesting," said Amanda, and meant it. She also wanted to cover her own embarrassment. She had seen this woman before, and thought *retired kindergarten teacher, hopelessly suburban*. Even now, she could not quite make the leap between her comfortable round face and her adventurous life.

"I had Rafael last semester," the teacher said. "The kid's been through a lot. A real survivor. Saw his family gunned down by the military, got out of the country, hitch-hiked up through Mexico, hid out in Los Angeles with a cousin, got up to Canada finally. Damn it, that was coffee break. I've got to get back to class."

"It's just incredible," said Cammie. "They change the entire ordering system and then they don't tell us, of course. So I'm calling down to see where the photocopy paper we needed yesterday has ended up, and I'm getting this bullshit about the new forms from central supply. Then Marthe is down on me like I should have known because she has to do quarterly attendance reports in triplicate and there's no paper. And I can't really *do* anything about that, can I?"

"No. I guess not," said Amanda. They were at a table in the staff lounge, eating the daily quiche special with Caesar salad. One glass wall of the lounge fronted the student cafeteria, packed elbow to elbow out there, worse, it seemed, than in Amanda's own university days. Or perhaps, she thought, it only looked worse out there from her new vantage-point of relative luxury.

"It's so great having you here instead of Gloria," said Cammie. "She's on sick leave. Her back went out. For the last month that's all we ever heard. Her back. Her allergies. This and that. All she ever does is complain. I can't stand that."

"Did you get Rafael sorted out?" said Amanda.

"Who?"

"That Salvadoran kid with the UI cheque."

"Oh right. Yeah. He forgot to check off one of his boxes. It's totally unfair, they expect us to deal with that stuff. We really need a translator around. It's just like that, complete stress end to end."

"Yeah," said Amanda. Through the glass wall she watched the students milling along the serving counters. English immersion, dark-eyed adults: Vietnamese, Latino, Arabic. The white kids in death metal T-shirts and shaggy bangs were doing high school completion; the ones with urban haircuts and black boots were in music or graphic design.

"It all seems kind of interesting," said Amanda.

"Well," said Cammie, "it would be a great job if it weren't for the students. Aren't I awful?"

"You could probably get quite a bit of mileage from a project like that," said Lane. His narrow face was impassive, but that didn't discourage Amanda. She knew he was never so noncommittal as when he scented a good idea or a workable scam, as if he feared, first and foremost, his own enthusiasm.

"I think so too," said Amanda, carefully matching his nonchalance.

"Everyone is interested in the anti-logging protests," said Lane. "Certainly we would have no trouble attracting attention to an exhibition here at the gallery. And David is planning to put his magazine columns into a book. He would need illustrations."

"It has possibilities," said Amanda. Lane's office was built into the back second storey of the gallery; they looked out a glass wall over an expanse of polished pine, high white walls, poster-sized scratchboard witches and demons, dogs and lizards, white lines on black intricate as engraving, eyes and teeth shining out of eternal night. Amanda wanted to giggle with delight, she wanted to laugh in triumph, just at getting here.

"It certainly has possibilities," said Lane. "The work you did in the Downtown Eastside, with those old women. The photos you took yourself. You'd obviously managed to build up a rapport. Get inside their lives."

"Thank you," said Amanda. She knew enough not to add what she felt, which was in this case shadowed, unclear, bound up with compromise and failure, but also with success: her growing ability to manipulate. To hold back and give people only what they wanted. As, in fact, she was doing with Lane right now. Or was manipulation only what the rest of the world called good manners? "I'm glad you liked the pictures," she added.

"They were very effective," said Lane, utterly deadpan, worn, weary. "I'd be very interested to see what you could do with the environmentalists. What I'll do is get you in touch with some of the people David interviewed. They're quite media-savvy. They were pleased with his articles. See what you can set up with them."

Lane walked her down the stairs and locked the front door behind her. Closing time, out on the wet long afternoon sidewalk. Down here, the rooming-houses and beer parlours were slowly being pushed back: swags of chains on iron stanchions curbed the brick cobbles, imitation antique streetlamps, recalling a past that never existed. Rain on plate glass, everything blurred and inconclusive.

Amanda walked down the street to her car. Even the parking lot was for sale, PREVIEW LUXURY ARTIST LOFTS FROM $200,000. On the curb sat an old woman shawled in garbage bags, a plastic tarp over her shopping cart. Amanda peered through the rain, didn't recognize her.

Inside the car, she bounced her fist off the steering wheel and finally giggled aloud. She could see it already, coaxing the picturesque from the mundane: keen young faces, tensed against police, and, later, camaraderie behind the barricade, firelit camp songs, fast film and long exposure. All that, yes. What she would not be able to admit to them, or even, really, to herself, though she suspected Lane already guessed, was the extent to which she might end by filtering all this through her own profound weariness, her sense that, win or lose, it was all the same. Except that it wasn't all the same; out there, in the mountains at the heart of the action, she might very well feel the urgency as sharply as anyone, the slaughter of trees older than the English language, raped and blasted hills, the sudden precious sanctuaries of ancient Sitka spruce, velvet-mossed.

Which did she most trust, emotional appeal or cold and knowing analysis? Amanda didn't know which way, in the end, she'd topple. But Lane, it occurred to her, did know, or thought he knew, which was almost the same thing. Amanda had her theories about the world, but Lane had his theories about Amanda. That in itself was flattering, that in itself made her wonder if she wanted him. Lane had at least ten years on Hugh, which meant he was pushing fifty, a number that shocked her more in the abstract than in reality. But his knowingness and reticence, while attractive, were too close to what had finally begun to weigh on her with Hugh. Always two steps ahead of her, Hugh. Or rather, when she got ahead of him, he didn't acknowledge it; one might even have said he sulked, if he hadn't had such good manners. She couldn't see apprenticing herself out like that again, arriving at love so open to change.

Against Lane and Hugh you could set the smile of someone like Rafael: absolute gratitude, thus pure acceptance. But that was even more impossible.

Amanda turned the ignition and crept out into the last choke of rush hour, crawling past the men lined up in the rain at the Salvation Army hostel, past the east end street hookers, glamorous leggy transvestites and real women dumpy and anonymous in jeans and sneakers, trawling for commuters in the flood tide of traffic.

On Thursday, Amanda brought jeans to work, and changed at five o'clock, in the staff washroom. Her old black motorcycle jacket, scarred leather, was in the trunk of the car. She folded her tailored skirt neatly into a shopping bag, laid the address Lane had given her on the passenger seat and drove south and east. Because unfamiliar, the streets seemed drearily anonymous in the rain: post-war stucco boxes, the equally utilitarian Vancouver Specials of the seventies, double carports and fig trees, and the occasional new house, built to the lot line in pink siding, calculated to contain the most extended family. These streets had been outside the city limits at the turn of the century; here and there, tall Edwardian gingerbread marked the sites of old farms. The house at which she stopped was most likely one of these, but it had been chopped and channelled, porches blocked in and windows boarded up, original architecture blurred.

The front door was answered, eventually, by a girl who seemed fantastically young, though she was probably twenty: a blunt, unmarked WASP face, sandy eyelashes, under matted dreadlocks dyed coal black, layers of sweaters and khaki against the cold summer.

"I'm looking for Jason," said Amanda.

"I don't think he's in," said the girl. She hung there in the doorway looking blankly at Amanda, seeming neither stoned nor deliberately rude, but merely unsure what to do next. In a moment, Amanda reconsidered. The girl was not unsure. She was completely unaware that she should do anything at all, that there were any social protocols involved here. Either that, or this was a particularly inscrutable hostility; Amanda's jeans and motorcycle jacket might not be enough.

"I'm a little early," Amanda said. "I was going to meet Jason here at six."

"He went out," said the girl, shifting her foot to block a puppy, vaguely malamute, that came padding down the hall. The girl leaned over, scooped up the puppy, looked with attention under his flopped ears.

"Maybe I can wait for him," said Amanda. She heard her own voice rising and slowing, Cammie with Rafael. "Maybe I can come in and sit down and wait."

The girl looked up as if she had forgotten Amanda's quite unnecessary presence. She shrugged. "If you want," she said, and turned back into the house. Amanda stepped inside, and followed her down the hall to the kitchen. Patchouli, a heavy fug, undercut with dog urine and cigarette smoke; the buckled plaster papered over with concert posters, the high ceilings, all intensely familiar from long ago.

"See, he's still scratching," said the girl. "He's still got that stuff there." She was talking to a boy, equally young, who was sitting at the kitchen table. He took the puppy onto his lap, and checked his ears with serious concentration. "Earmites," he said. "They're really bugging him."

"I should get some more of that stuff they told us and put it on," said the girl. Her voice struck Amanda as quintessentially adolescent: adult in timbre but shot through with childish hesitations and rushes.

"I came to see Jason," said Amanda.

"He went out," said the girl to the boy.

"Jase," said the boy. He looked at Amanda. "About the photos. He should be back soon. Sit down or something. Hey you. You're a tough little guy. Hey."

Amanda sat on a wooden chair. The girl left the room. The puppy grabbed the cuff of the boy's plaid felt shirt jacket, tiny teeth and tiny growls.

"Yeah. Sic 'em." The boy jiggled his arm, but not enough to dislodge the jaws. "His mom's a real Alaska husky. He's going to be huge."

Ride it out, Amanda told herself. *Go with the flow.* Jason would either appear or not. "He's got those real husky blue eyes," she said, conversationally.

"He's going to be a great dog," said the boy. "Hey you. Yeah."

It occurred to Amanda that perhaps she was not expected to say anything; certainly she did not feel, after a day at work, quite up to milking conversation from this child. Though he was not that young; he had a skimpy goatee. However, even that advertised youth, rather than otherwise. His beard, after all, had not begun to creep down his throat, up his cheekbones, out his ears. All in all, he struck Amanda as skimped, unfinished, in familiar and depressing ways, lacking Rafael's promise of luminous and unpredictable gratitude.

Amanda settled into her chair, and looked around at the kitchen: dim ceilings, spacious, but cluttered with spice bottles and jars of rice, with stacks of newspapers and boxes of cans for recycling, the fridge swirled in pink and black spray paint. The disorder gave the room an air of danger and revolt which Amanda herself had once cherished, but today found depressing; it no longer spoke to her of defiance, but merely of an inability to cope.

The back door opened and another boy stepped in out of the rain. *A different type altogether,* thought Amanda: clean jeans and an old suit jacket, a head of curls, pink cheeks.

"Hello." He leaned across the corner of the table and shook her hand. "I'm Jason. You must be Amanda. I'm really sorry. I'm a bit late."

"No problem," said Amanda. "Actually, I was early. I haven't been waiting long." With a click, everything solidified, came into focus. Her relief showed her, in hindsight, how anxious she had been.

"Cody," said Jason. "This is Amanda. She's going to come out to the island to do those photos for David."

"Yeah, right." Cody smiled at her, warm and open, with the ease of absolute unconcern. "Yeah, she's been waiting for you."

"Let's go sit in the living room," said Jason. The sofa there was sagged and split, the front porch swallowed the afternoon. Jason switched on a lamp. Amanda sat lightly, almost afraid to breathe. She had come here expecting to negotiate her project, prepared for suspicion and reluctance: who, after all, would want the flat eye of the camera snapping after them through private nights and dubiously legal days? She was fully aware that Jason had just spoken as if it were decided. Perhaps, then, the whole project was less fraught than she had expected. The protests took place, after all, in the public sphere. She was not, now, wheedling access to the cramped privacy of old hotel rooms painted hopeful pink, to the regrets and shames of old age at the brink of the world. So it was going to be easier, then. The task now was not to jeopardize Jason's surprising acceptance.

"I've been following the logging protests fairly closely," she said, which was not true. "This one, though. This particular valley. It's just really starting to become an issue, right?" It was never a mistake to ask a question, to let the other person carry the weight of the conversation.

"It's an amazing piece of old-growth forest," said Jason. "An entire ecosystem. The lumber company plans to start clearcutting next month. There's a whole community of activists living down on the beach, getting ready."

"Do you live there?"

"No, well. I'm actually staff with the Environment Federation. I do a lot of co-ordinating so I'm in town over there. Or in

Victoria. Cody lives on the beach. That's why I thought I'd meet you over here. He can fill you in."

"So he's with the federation too."

"No. The guys down there are on their own. I mean, of course we're behind them one hundred per cent. But this way, they can do what they want and then we can deal with our own funders."

"Clever," said Amanda. "So they can do things like spiking trees and you don't get flack for it."

"Nobody's spiking trees any more," said Jason. "It was really bad PR with the woodworkers' union. It's too dangerous for the millworkers. And that logging truck that got torched last month. I actually think the lumber company did that themselves to have something to blame us for. The federation only supports nonviolent protest."

"Oh, of course," said Amanda blandly. Nevertheless, she liked Jason, or rather, she knew how he would react, she knew fairly well the extent to which they would co-operate. "I can probably get out in a couple of weeks. My job will be over then."

"Excellent," said Jason.

"Did you get another work placement for after Gloria gets back?" said Cammie.

"Actually, I'm taking a week off," said Amanda. They were inching their way up the coffee-break line. Amanda filled a china mug. Too late, the scorched whiff warned her the coffee was unpleasantly flavoured with almond extract. Amaretto Surprise.

"Are you? I wish I could. This place is really getting to me," said Cammie. "I'm going to be really bad. I'm going to have a brownie. Screw the diet."

"Actually, I'm going over to the west coast of Vancouver Island. I'm going to check out the logging protests for this photo series. Lane wants me to. You know, Lane at the gallery."

"Oh, Lane? Is that what he's doing now? Oh, you're so lucky. That sounds like so much fun. I wish I could go with you. I really need a vacation."

"You certainly made a hit with the guys," said Lane. "David says Jason is incredibly enthusiastic about the whole idea."

"Jason seems to be really on the ball," said Amanda. "He knows all about the different trouble spots. Very well organized."

She was not lying, but she was certainly trying to imagine what Jason would, ideally, want said about himself. This suggested not quite that she didn't trust Lane, but that she expected him to talk. He had told her quite a bit about Jason, before the meeting; she could only assume the information flowed both ways. That was not bad, if you knew in advance. Amanda had gotten in trouble, in the past, though not with Lane, by misinterpreting gossip as particular, personal intimacy, a promise of loyalty, a bond. Now she was warier.

"Jason's on his way up, all right," said Lane judiciously. "A very skilled young man. He also works for the provincial New Democrat Party. In the riding for the opposition critic for Forestry and Resources."

"I think he'll be very helpful out there," said Amanda carefully. "I don't think the protesters on the ground are terribly well organized." She meant Cody.

"I wouldn't think so either," said Lane. "But of course that's what you'll find out." He almost smiled a rueful, weary smile. "Certainly, you've made a conquest with Jason."

"He genuinely seems like a nice kid," said Amanda. *Kid*, not *guy*, or *fellow* or even *young man*. She did not consciously plan to step back and denigrate him, even so very slightly as this, but the moment she spoke she saw it was not a mistake. Lane would not repeat this, not to Jason. More important, it reasserted that, in the end, she was on Lane's side, that if she was exactly halfway in age between Jason and Lane, she nonetheless sided with adulthood, with the subtle, the compromised and the wary.

"Oh, he is," said Lane. "Definitely a nice kid." The good will in the office above the gallery, in the pale light, was almost palpable.

Amanda took the early ferry, and spent an hour and a half on the windy deck, watching the green water and the greener Gulf Islands slip past. The clouds were breaking, scudding sun; at Nanaimo, she inched off the parking deck and drove into a land of dark second-growth fir, steeply sloped. By afternoon she was over the tall hump of the Island Range, and off the tarmac, the car bucking like a greenbroke colt on rutted logging roads.

Along the Island Highway, a respectable fringe of forest shaded the traveller. Now, well into the back country, Amanda was passing whole mountainsides covered in planted trees, some man-high, others nursery stubs lost in a wasteland of deadfall and fireweed. In the distance, fresh clearcuts, hillsides stripped bare, waste timber left as it fell, the soil washed and channelled, the logging roads clearly visible in raw switchbacks.

As she neared the west coast, the light began to shift and clarify, the sky whiten, reflecting the glow of the sea. Following Jason's map, Amanda parked in a final cul-de-sac against a wall of fir and cedar. There were a few cars here, an old van, an ancient Volvo wagon. As promised, a red bandanna hung on a branch at the trailhead down to Pesadilla Cove. The name marked, she knew, almost the northernmost reach of the Spanish fleet sailing up from Old Mexico in the eighteenth century.

She climbed stiffly out of the car into a silence beyond the reach of motors. The trees sighed far above in sea gusts that did not reach her; in the distance, a hush of surf.

Amanda locked her car, and shouldered her backpack. The trail descended steeply, in places rank with standing mud, in others skidding deliriously down bare rock face. The trees were big and old, not the biggest or the oldest, but good first growth, furrowed bark, rainforest moss, hanging ferns.

The trail levelled out at the base of the slope, with a glare of white light ahead. Here the shore pine was beaten back into slanted thickets, and the trail led between dense tangles of green bush. The sound of surf filled her head while the path went on, crossed a reedy brook and then deposited her suddenly at tideline, a tangle of driftwood, of huge beached cedar logs, stripped and polished by the sea. She began to hop and clamber. From atop the logs, she had a view of the whole long sweep of silver sand, the curve of a shallow bay banked at each end by rock faces, breakers rolling and smashing in the cold sun. Down the cove, the thin trail of camp smoke, a few bright dots of tents up against the forest. A beached kayak, a black dog running. The wind hit her full in the face, fresh with the open ocean.

It was all a lot bigger, all less obvious, all much farther away from the city than she had expected, no cozy campsite at the end of the trail. Amanda hopped across the logs to the water's edge and began to trudge up the hard-packed sand to the distant scattering of tents.

Cody was squatting by his fire, tenderly feeding small bleached sticks of driftwood. Amanda had pitched her own pup tent near his, on the beach grass of a small glade blocked from the sea wind by a wall of bush. This end of the shore, she saw, was drier, underlaid by the same shelves of granite that sheered up behind, forming the southernmost wall of the cove.

It was warm out of the wind. In T-shirt and jeans, Amanda sat on the grass behind Cody, feeling oddly dislocated, picked up and shaken and set down: the dawn rush to the ferry terminal, the two-sailing wait at Horseshoe Bay, then the long drive alone across the mountains, clenched shoulders on washouts. And now here, where there was altogether too much sky, sea, sand and wind, too much of everything except people. Cody might not prove enough help; this thought made her anxious.

"So where is everybody?" she said, conversationally.

Cody snapped a stick across his knee and edged it into the flame's transparent tongue. "Around," he said, after a minute. "They'll be back later." Satisfied with the fire, he stood up and went over to a pile of pots and boxes under a tarp lean-to. He measured lentils, water from a ten-gallon jug, sliced an onion against his palm.

"You pack in water?" said Amanda.

"Yeah. We have to," said Cody. He was squatting by the fire again, peering into the pot.

The malamute puppy came paddling through the grass, stopped and started snuffling at Amanda's boots. She ruffled his fur. He didn't pay any attention, merely began gnawing, without much effect, at her bootlace.

Overhead, the wind soughed through branches; out behind the wall of bushes, the Pacific heaved and broke, incessant, monotonous.

Go with the flow, Amanda told herself. This anxiety had to do with getting started. She wanted to be doing something, if not actually taking pictures yet, then introducing herself, sliding into people's confidence, their lives. She now saw that she had expected, if not a welcome, at least recognition. Something akin to walking into the drop-in centre and meeting, around the chipped kitchen table, all her old women having coffee. She had expected to step over the tideline into a tight little community, cleverly negotiating suspicion, resentment and enthusiasm too. She had not expected to step into diffuseness, everyone hidden or gone.

Wait, she told herself. She took deep breaths, yoga style, let the sun warm her bones. Meanwhile she would watch Cody: army pants low on the hips, rubber thongs, an old T-shirt. She thought that his torso seemed too long for his legs, which perhaps contributed to her impression of his youth as incompleteness, rather than glowing promise. Jason had glowing promise, but then Jason did not live on a beach. But still, Cody moved with economy, even grace. For him, she saw, pots would boil, but not boil over, guy lines would stay taut, the thin finger of smoke would continue to point straight up into the blanched blue afternoon. No scorched fingers, smoke-scoured eyes, no miserable midnight flapping of rain-soaked nylon.

Lying back on the grass, Amanda finally let the sun seep through her, melt her, gave herself over to the afternoon.

When Amanda awoke, the sun was tilting into the north-west, towards a rising bank of cloud. Her face was dry, her head light. After a while, Cody came back from the direction of the beach and dished out lentil stew for both of them. Plate on lap, facing Cody, still dazed from sun and sleep, Amanda found it easier to strike up conversation.

"The weather's been good," she said.

"All right," said Cody. "Last month it was pissing down."

"What about those clouds?" Amanda said.

Cody squinted consideringly; he thought. "They might blow over," he said. "It's hard to say."

"This is a good camping spot," she said. This was how it was done, then: keep it practical and obvious. "I guess you can't drink from that stream down by the trail."

"No. It comes down out of swamps. We get our water at the river. Or in town."

After they ate, Amanda offered to wash the dishes. Outside the glade, the sea wind hit her full in the face as she hopped across the beach logs. The tide was high; she leaned at the water's edge, scrubbing forks and bowls in wet sand. Rinsing them, however, was difficult. The breakers crashed and ran shallow up the sand, swirling around her boots, then fled back. Skittering to avoid wet feet, she tilted the dishes into the surge, feeling extremely incompetent.

Plates rinsed, Amanda moved out of the reach of water, and

squatted on her heels. Sand, sea and sky were fading grey; behind her rose the dark forest. She had offered to do the dishes in
order to leave the glade, to sit alone and watch the colourless
sunset fade down behind the clouds. But as she sat there, the
growing feeling was terror. Nightmare terror, as she'd never felt
in waking life, not terror of anything real, not of bears or sharks,
tidal waves or prowlers, not the jitters that struck her that first day
in Mexico. This was of another order altogether. The size of the
sky exposed her, cracked her shell, left her raw and open on the
sand. Amanda stood up and ran through the dusk to the tideline,
the wall of bushes, Cody.

After dark, there was a bonfire farther along the beach, in
between the logs. Amanda followed Cody, watching the dark
figures hulking against red light change, as she stepped inside
the circle, to separate and ordinary faces: mildly friendly, mildly
interested, but no introductions. Amanda considered announcing
herself to the group, but lacked the courage, and sat quietly on a
log beside Cody. She did not know who, here, was aware of her
project, and who was not, or who approved and who didn't. But
her reticence was based in something stronger, or deeper. She
sensed, around the campfire, a mood that had always defeated
her. Looking at the young faces — Cody's age or slightly older —
she was reminded of nights ten, twelve years ago, walking into
the old house where Dick and Everett were living. No one said
hello, no one was ever introduced. Back then, you either knew
everyone, or you pretended you did. Even at the time, she knew
the group cultivated exclusivity precisely by making outsiders
feel uncomfortable. The boy she had been in love with, even he
had done it, certain nights in bars, on street corners, in cafés,
chatting intently to musicians, artists, various contacts and scam-
masters, while she sat staring at his shoulders, the soft nape of his
neck, razor-cut.

Meanwhile, here on the beach, the conversation was looping
around the fire. Despite Jason's briefings, Amanda felt culpably
ignorant; she kept quiet and listened. There were earthmovers
and logging trucks massing on a ridge behind the river. There
was a Supreme Court ruling in two weeks. There was a land-use
report. The Supreme Court ruling would be next week. It might
not come down for a month. What had happened to the injunction? What had happened to Bob, on trial for public mischief

after that blockade last fall? The land-use report was useless. The Supreme Court was in the hands of the lumber industry. The opposition critic on Forestry and Resources had mentioned Bob in the legislature. No way. It was on the CBC. Shit man.

There was beer, though not much, and marijuana, quite a lot more. Amanda cradled a cold bottle between her knees and puffed as the joints went by. The man on her left, she saw now, was considerably older than the average, older than her, too: long fair hair thinning at the brow, eyes seamed, teeth chipped.

"You been down here long?" Amanda said.

"I been down here a long time," he said. "Off and on since the seventies."

"Oh really?" said Amanda. "Living on the beach?"

"On the beach, up in the bush, all along here."

"It certainly is beautiful here. Peaceful," said Amanda.

"You feel that, eh? You feel that energy coming off the land? It's sacred land out here. Holy land. You feel that?"

"I guess," said Amanda. She was registering the first tickle of unease, a personal distant early warning signal based as much on his tense face in the firelight as on his words, which struck her as suggesting a particularly uninteresting cosmology.

"You feel the land. It's waiting," he said. "It's watching."

"I guess," said Amanda. Out beyond the circle of light, invisible waves sucked and whispered at the sand. She remembered her moment of terror at sunset. "I know what you mean," she added, reluctantly. She did not want to be in this conversation, but she wanted to be talking; she needed to start somewhere, and the beer and the joints were softening her.

"Of course you feel it," he said. "See, I could tell when I saw you. You're one of the people who see."

"Um," said Amanda.

"See. The land is waiting. It's not going to take any more destruction. It's going to rise up. There's going to be earthquakes and tidal waves. There's going to be landslides and fires."

"And spiked trees," said Amanda.

"That's all part of it," he said. "We're all part of it. We're earth's warriors out here. And everything's going to change." He was leaning towards her, almost trembling.

"Yeah," said Amanda.

"See, I could tell you feel it too. I can tell what you're

thinking. You have a beautiful soul. You know that? No one's ever told you that before. Right? Right?"

"Um," said Amanda. "Well, no." He had inched closer to her on the log. Amanda crossed her legs away from him.

"See, but you're one of the warriors," he said. "You're part of the whole thing. You just have to relax. Go with the flow."

He was not quite touching her, not yet, but that was clearly imminent. Amanda swung round to Cody with her brightest smile, her perkiest voice.

"Cody," she said. "We were just wondering if you'd heard when the loggers are moving in."

Cody was leaning over, talking to the boy on his other side. They looked up, not, as far as she could see, at all reluctantly, though at the moment she could not afford to consider that.

"Well, maybe tomorrow. Maybe not," said Cody.

"Maybe in a few days," said the other boy. "The federation will let us know when they think it's happening."

"So it's just up the hill," said Amanda. She could feel the man behind her on the log, feel his hand or knee hovering, nearly brushing her thigh.

"Yeah. The last turnoff before you get to the trailhead," said Cody.

"I don't think we've met," said Amanda.

"Dylan," said the boy.

"Amanda," said Cody. "He's from Victoria."

"Oh really? That's interesting." Amanda slid casually off the log, and squatted in the sand facing Cody and Dylan. She could feel the air humming behind her: thwarted intensity.

"Not really," said Dylan. "It's all bureaucrats and tourists. Hanging flower baskets."

"Tea at the Empress Hotel."

"You got it," said Dylan.

Amanda glanced over her shoulder. The log behind her was empty.

Past midnight, Amanda followed the small circle of Cody's flashlight back over the driftwood and into the glade.

"You were talking to Chance for a long time," Cody said.

"*Chance?*" said Amanda.

"He's a cool guy," said Cody. "He's been down here for ever. He really thinks about things a lot."

"Really?" said Amanda.

"He's interesting. He's a really spiritual guy. He's kind of a holy man. A hermit."

"Oh really?" said Amanda. They had reached the campsite. By the light of the last embers, she poured a scant quarter-cup of water, brushed her teeth, spat into the bushes.

"You should get him to tell you all that stuff," said Cody. "He understands things."

"I should," said Amanda. This was the most Cody had said to her, to date, and the most enthusiastic he'd been, the most emphatic and positive. She did not want to cut him off, insult his friend, argue; she liked that openness in his voice. Besides, she was not quite sure how to phrase her disagreement, not sure even from what it stemmed.

Ten minutes later, the source of her unease came to her, but by then she was already curled up in the cold slippery nylon of her sleeping bag, stripped to T-shirt. The night outside was profoundly, impossibly dark, saturated with the murmuring of wind and sea. It struck her now that the dark locked them down as surely as any jailer. You would not want to climb that trail in the dark, could in fact barely find the mouth in back of the tortured shore pine. Let alone drive three hours of logging roads out to the freeway.

This was not, however, the source of her unease. She was thinking about Chance. Amanda had met, in her travels, holy men, and women: Buddhist monks, Catholic nuns, various lay people who took seriously the disciplines of meditation and contemplation. What they had in common, if they were on anything resembling a true path, was an aura of peace, of a central still spot at the heart of their lives. A knack of slowing time, of letting time expand and breathe. Chance had none of that. Chance was wired and pushy, and he made her nervous. This was nothing she could tell Cody; if he didn't see it himself, he'd never understand. Chance was not in the least bit holy. Chance, she decided, sliding into sleep, forgetting at the moment the thought slipped across her mind, Chance was more like the other thing. Not holy. The opposite.

Full-blown morning, the wind dying down under firm blue sky, low tide, the beach stretched to half a mile of hard rippled grey, tide pools in granite outcroppings. Amanda and Cody walked towards the distant water, carrying breakfast cups and bowls. Amanda was still unsure how far she could presume on Cody's company, his attention, but she had ceased worrying. She would wait and see. The ocean, the air, the wind: some weight had blown away overnight. Everything, she thought, would work out. Meanwhile, on this long wet beach, she had the dream sensation of walking and arriving nowhere, amid wheeling gulls.

The tidal pools cupped tiny worlds of limpets and urchins, of anemones hesitating, drawing inwards, under Amanda's shadow as she squatted, peered, poked tentatively with a spoon.

At the water's edge, Cody skinned out of his T-shirt, rolled it up dry on his thongs beside the dishes and walked knee-deep into the ocean. He was wearing another pair of army pants, chopped at the knee; Amanda had on spandex bike shorts. She unlaced her boots and followed him, leaving the puppy sniffing and worrying at the edge of the foam.

The water was biting cold. In a moment, her calves were numb. And the ocean moved, surged — ankle-deep, with the sand running away below her feet, a moment later flooding ice to her thighs, choking her breath. Cody, ahead of her, whooped and fell head-first into a swell. Amanda backed out and sat, in wet shorts, on the wet sand. Her legs were red with cold, the hot sun baked her shoulders. Cody did not stay in the water long. A minute later he was wading towards her, grinning, shaking hair out of his eyes. His darkened shorts hung heavily below the points of his hip bones: a furze of light brown hair to his belly, the bare chest. He did not have a particularly good body, by any of the current terms of aftershave and underwear ads, or the gay pornography that inspired them. The proportions were off, Amanda thought; muscled up, beefed out, he'd look clumsy, while as it was, he was too loosely jointed, too slight, concave. But all the same. How was it possible to have a waist and belly without a hint of excess, how was it possible to be so unmarked by time? She saw, all at once, what she had not known herself at his age, what Cody could not possibly know either, what he would be unable to see: that youth, just youth itself, was intoxicatingly beautiful. There was nothing you could set beside that, nothing that compared. This despite the fact that she herself had lost little, in comparison for instance with Cammie. Here on the beach her legs were firm enough. But they didn't glow.

"Water's great," said Cody. He seemed extremely naked as he leaned down, his bare arm nearly brushing hers, to pick up his thongs, his T-shirt, his bowl.

"Freezing," said Amanda.

"You'll get used to it," he said.

Half an hour later, barefoot tiptoe through the wide tidewrack of bull kelp and bark chips, onto the powdery sand above, guitar chords from between the beach logs. Familiar enough: someone was playing Cryptic Neon, their new song, the one that was on the radio. Cody and Amanda walked up the spine of a scoured log, looked down on Dylan, his hair falling across his cheek, the wet black Labrador flat on his side in the sun. *Baby, it's the world calling, No wrong number this time,* sang Dylan. *It's the world calling, Collect she ain't got no dime.* He didn't look up.

"He's good," said Amanda. The sun scorched down, her shorts dried dusty to her skin. Down the beach, running figures, the bright flash of a Frisbee, gulls.

"Yeah," said Cody. He picked up the puppy, and skidded off the log; Amanda followed him up the beach. "My mom used to go out with their drummer," he said. "Cryptic Neon."

"Roger?" said Amanda.

"No, the guy before that. He quit a long time back."

"Well, that's kind of interesting," said Amanda, politely. It did not strike her as interesting so much as oddly unsettling, opening the gap she had been, all morning, ignoring.

"Yeah, it was, sort of." They were toiling along the soft sand above tideline, feet sinking and slipping, hints of sharp shells, of pointed sticks, under powder. "It was after he left things got kind of bad for her," said Cody.

"Yeah? Like how?" said Amanda. Automatically, she was matching the rhythm of his speech, slowing and spreading her words, while mentally she held her breath: confession coming, or if not that, then at least information more private and personal than she had any right to hear. More personal, more private, at least, than she had any intention of giving, on her part.

"Well, that was when she really started drinking," said Cody. "That was when it kind of got out of hand. That was when I took off, got out of there. Five years back. But she's getting it together now. She's doing all right. She's going to these meetings."

"Well, that's good," said Amanda. "Where's your dad?"

"He's lived out on the Gulf Islands for ever. He's wild. He's sort of this old hippie biker. He's got an oyster farm."

"An oyster farm."

"He used to be growing dope out there. But I think he's pretty much stopped. The scene out there was getting kind of weird."

"It must have been kind of neat, though, having a cool mother," said Amanda, blandly lying on several levels. She did not think it sounded pleasant, and she did not think she would admire his mother; she was reading dismaying abysses of mismanagement, irresponsibility, collapse, into the bare outlines of Cody's story. But mild approval, acceptance, kept stories coming; shock and outrage shut them down.

"It was all right," said Cody. "It was harder for my little brother. He was too young to get out. He's not doing so well right now."

"What did you do when you took off? Go live with your dad?"

"Just around. With friends. It's kind of heavy at my dad's, guns and Rottweilers and things. He's freaked about getting ripped off."

"And now you live down here."

"Yeah. I want to get set up in Vancouver again. I want to go get my high school at the community college."

"I know someone who's working there."

"Yeah? They're kind of real snots there. They can be really tight-assed when you go in to ask them things. I don't mean your friend."

"She's probably like that too," said Amanda, cheerful betrayal. The hot sun was straight overhead, glaring down on a world entirely new, stretched level to the horizon. Yesterday, arriving, the sense was dislocation. Today, it was a sharper flood of the surreal, specifically personal. Cody could have been, very likely was, some small blond child, Devlin's age, hair to his shoulders and torn jeans, running tag through the crowd at a rock concert in the park, sound check blowing away on the breeze. Ducking past Cammie wanly waiting for Matthew. Cammie, who, through Matthew, was closer than Amanda to that crowd, who could probably name Cody's mother. Blink an eye, and Cammie's the curt school secretary, gatekeeper of application forms. Yet if you teleported Cody back in time he'd fit right in, though not, Amanda reflected, quite into her own crowd. But close enough. Only if he looked at Cammie today he'd never see her. Whereas Amanda was still Amanda. Which suggested Cammie still thought she was Cammie. It made no sense, this question of time.

"The office staff there are kind of stressed out," Amanda added, an oblique apology.

"Yeah?" said Cody, neutrally, not deliberately rude, just uninterested: the inner lives of those in power, of grown-ups, were of no concern to him. Amanda saw this, recognized it; she was getting, moment by moment, the sharpest sense yet of having stepped backwards into time.

At the campsite Cody stacked the dishes, then sat in the sun whittling at the straps of his knapsack. Amanda unpacked her camera, its clean black bulk, the glint of the lens untouchable as eyeballs, all this technology vulnerable and fragile in a world of salt spray and sandy wind, woodsmoke and grit. Out in the sunlight, she moved slowly around Cody. Focus and shoot. The tent, the fire, the sleeping puppy, the line of Cody's cheek, the light on his skin, the impeccable slope of his back, visible vertebrae. Through the lens she looked him up and down. The tide hushed in the distance, the day slowed to a point and stopped. These were not the photos she had come to take, but they were a start, they held all the long hot drowse of the summer day.

Point and shoot. The bushes rustled, snapped, the black Labrador came trotting into the clearing, the puppy bounded awake, there was sniffing and circling and a moment later Dylan, carrying his guitar case.

"We just got word," he said. "The loggers are moving in today or tomorrow. We're heading up the ridge right away."

The day slowed to a point and then split open. Cody was on his feet, jackknife in pocket, knapsack forgotten. "You talked to Jase? He knows it's on?" he said.

"Chelsea and Suri were in town. They were at the fed office. We're going up tonight."

Breaking camp did not take long. Cody had his tent down, his backpack filled, in time to help Amanda shake out her sleeping bag, roll and reroll her tent. Within an hour they were toiling up the wet trail, not speaking, pacing their breath. As they climbed into green shadows, the roar of the surf fell away into afternoon hush, broken only by the skid of boots on rock, the slurp of mud. Amanda felt the heave and push of her thighs against the slope, the backwards tug of her pack, badly loaded. But she was buoyed up by gusts of adrenalin, rushes through her stomach and chest, anticipation undercut with notches of fear. Time seemed simultaneously speeded up and slowed down. She noticed tiny details — spindly white mushrooms, the scuffed toes of her boots, the clench and release of Cody's calves leading the way up the hill.

When they reached the clearing, however, the pace slowed. There were more parked cars, half a dozen, all, like Amanda's own, mud-caked to the windows. Dylan was there, and Chelsea and Suri: deep tans, long hair, layers of old T-shirts, and braided bits of Guatemalan string at their wrists. Chance was sitting in the open hatch of the van, smoking. By daylight he looked faded, harmless. He nodded at Amanda; she gave him a bright, impersonal smile, but didn't walk over to talk to him.

They were waiting for Greg to come up from the beach. They were waiting for Nick and Sue to come back from town. They would go before dark, if not sooner. The federation had word from Victoria. The logging company acted in secrecy. There would be police, there would be private security guards, they would break heads, this would be the showdown, it would set the tone for the summer. The summer was going to be hot. It was going to be wild. Dylan went down the trail to the beach. Cody threw a stick for the black Lab. Suri and Chelsea were braiding each other's hair. Amanda leaned back in the sun. Chance seemed to have disappeared. Dylan took a long time coming back. Nick and Sue never did arrive. Greg came up from the beach after Dylan. They could wait for Nick and Sue. Nick and Sue would know where they were. They would guess.

The sun was sinking behind the trees by the time Amanda pulled out of the clearing, with Cody and the puppy in the passenger seat, Dylan and Greg and the Labrador in the back. Woodsmoke and patchouli, and wet dog. It felt much longer than twenty-four hours since she had reached the beach. It felt like weeks; the engine grated in her ears, the forest jolted past alarmingly quickly.

The turnoff was ten minutes away, a dirt track bending uphill through raw and recent clearcut. At the junction with the main logging road sat a tin trailer, locked and shuttered. Amanda rolled cautiously over ruts and stones, the undercarriage catching, now and then, with a jolting grind. The mountain stretched away a thousand feet above and below, a low tangle of deadfall and waste timber, splintered stumps, washed in waves of purple fireweed.

"There's the other guys. We should stop here," said Dylan.

"Are we far enough up? Should we be up farther?" said Greg.

"We should be closer to the turnoff," said Dylan.

Suri and Chelsea were sitting on the hood of the Volvo. Amanda braked. The disputed valley was half a mile farther, a ridge of trees visible against the sky.

Dylan leaned out the window; Greg and Cody peered over his shoulder. The road got way worse farther up. The loggers would have to come up this road. Unless they came in the back. They couldn't; the other side of the valley was too steep. So they should all park here. They should park farther down. They should put up a blockade right at the junction. They should wait for Nick and Sue.

Amanda cut the motor and got out, leaning against the driver's door. The voices fell away into silence underscored by the hum of insects. The sun poured straight down on the shattered slope, the gutted soil.

In the end, she pulled a tight three-point turn, bumped back down to a hundred feet above the junction and parked on the verge, the car alarmingly tipped. The Volvo stopped behind. Amanda and Cody, Greg and Dylan heaved their packs from the trunk and stood looking for a campsite. There was the road, raw and rutted, washed down to rock and reddish sand. There was the clearcut, a tangle of shifting and rotting branches. Finally, they pitched camp on the verge, kicking stones out of the ground, unpleasantly close to the hot hoods and exhaust pipes of the cars.

Amanda felt wound up, unsettled, unconnected. The level of improvisation was making her deeply uneasy. Or, rather, she wanted a form, a shape, for her rush of adrenalin, her presentiments of courage. She wanted action, she was ready for it, completely. But the evening sun kept burning into the empty swath of road. Cody had dropped away, back into himself. Tent pitched, he was squatting on a rock a few yards up into the deadfall,

puppy between his knees, staring down at the junction, the abandoned trailer, the stretch of main road visible for a quarter-mile
until it rolled over a hillock and fell from sight.

Dylan and Bob had walked down towards the trailer. Amanda
followed them.

"I guess the loggers won't be coming in tonight," she said,
conversationally.

"It's late," said Dylan.

"They're tricky," said Greg. "They're fucking scum. They could
come any time."

"Shit," said Dylan. "You hear that? That's an engine."

"Fuck," said Greg. They waited, straining at the edge of sound.
Farther up the hill, Chelsea or Suri laughed, a car door slammed.
The hum in the distance began to solidify. "That's a truck. Shit,"
said Greg.

"We should tell the others," said Dylan.

"This is it, man," said Greg. "It's fucking going to happen."

Amanda glanced up the slope towards the tents. Cody was
gone from his rock. Thin trails of smoke from behind the cars,
the puppy yelping. Defences down, the supper hour, domesticity, village life. While out here, at the brink, they listened to the
rumble of the approaching enemy.

"Fucking assholes," said Greg, squinting at the bare road, the
concealing hillock.

"We got to go up and tell the others," said Amanda.

"Yeah," said Dylan. Neither of them moved. In the immense
silence of the ruined mountain the engine was steadily growing
louder. Set faces in the slant light, battle fever. Exactly. Whatever
was coming over that hill, thought Amanda, whatever phalanx of
private security guards, RCMP, logging trucks and bulldozers, it
was better than waiting. Whatever was coming over the hill was
the whole point. Everything made sudden, lucid sense: the scope
of their sacrifice, the dedication in which she was also now involved, here at the edge of the continent. The last stand. All this
was gloriously visible. It was epic. Amanda saw herself feeling
this, she saw Greg and Dylan feeling this, she wondered too if
they saw themselves feeling it, or if they registered their rush of
elation at a level more innocent, less divided, purer than hers.
I've got to get my camera, she thought. At that moment a little
brown compact car, an old Honda or Toyota, bumped over the

top of the hillock.

"Oh shit," said Dylan, and started laughing. "It's Nick and Sue."

"Finally," said Greg.

At twilight the boys were hauling logs and branches out of the clearcut, stacking them across the mouth of the junction just above the trailer. They set up a campfire just behind it, red light on the barricade, on a dozen faces.

"There'll be more people coming up tomorrow," said Greg. "There'll be federation people coming up from town." Dylan had his guitar; he was playing Cryptic Neon. *She don't say maybe,* sang Dylan, *she say someday.* Suri and Greg, Nick and Sue sang along. *It's the world calling, baby.* Amanda sat beside Cody, but Cody wasn't talking. That seemed all right, though; it seemed part of the step, the shift, they had taken into the public. Tonight, from now on, was all on the record, from now on it was the group. It would make no sense, tonight, to talk about mothers and fathers, to talk privately. All that was clearly on hold, superfluous to what was coming.

Dylan put down his guitar.

"We have to think about what's going down tomorrow," said Greg. "Everyone has to think about how far they want to go. You have to think about whether you want to get arrested. It's okay if you don't want to. But you have to work that decision through."

"We should do some workshops on civil disobedience tomorrow," said Nick. "What to do when they come after you."

"We have to really have our strategy together," said Greg.

"Oh, totally," said Suri. "That's totally important."

Everything was clear now, everything made sense, Amanda thought. Words no longer mattered except as they marked complicity, bound the group. What made sense was that they were here at the brink of action, that very soon they'd be acting. History and events were going to take hold. There wasn't any way that they couldn't win, even in the temporary defeat of arrests and injunctions. All of that just pulled public opinion more to their side. Amanda had never felt so alive, or not for years.

Dylan was singing again, old protest songs, folk songs. Amanda, who couldn't carry a tune, sat back and watched the faces in the firelight; they seemed tonight, to her, extraordinarily beautiful, and brave, and fragile.

Chance was on the other side of the fire, back in the shadows; Amanda had purposely put as much distance between them as possible. Now she saw that Chelsea was sitting between his knees, and that he was rubbing her shoulders. Even at this distance, it struck her as a performance both affected and ominous, his serious, uplifted face and Chelsea's bent head, her braids falling past her cheeks. Affected, ominous and disgusting, Amanda thought, quite aware she was imputing to him inflated powers, and aims far murkier than what he was probably after, simple seduction. If Chelsea had the bad taste or the lack of judgement for that, it wouldn't do her any particular harm. And it was manifestly none of Amanda's business.

"Jase is here," said Cody. Raw wide morning, and Amanda squatting on the verge within the smell of cold engines, toasting a slice of whole-wheat bread over a narrow fire. She picked up her tin mug of tea — soot-smeared, a few flecks of wood ash floating — and followed him down the rutted track. She was already aware that one of the things they were going to miss here was water, in any form; her nails were rimmed in black.

Down at the cutoff by the trailer sat a jeep, or a jeepette, a tidy little all-terrain vehicle. Jason was standing in front of it, squinting up the hill; Everett was stepping out of the passenger's side.

"I know that guy," said Amanda. "He's a reporter."

"Oh yeah?" said Cody. "Jase. What's up, man?"

"Hey," said Jason. "How you doing?"

"Hello," said Everett. "Lane said you were up here."

"Yeah, well," said Amanda. "It's actually pretty interesting."

"I bet," said Everett. "You're going to see some action here all right. This is the next big hot spot."

"Do you know when they're moving in here?"

"Soon. I should think. The legislature is extending the sitting over this. Ray's supposed to be making a speech today."

"Ray?"

"The opposition critic on Forestry and the Environment."

"Oh, right," said Amanda. Dylan and Greg, Suri and Chance had come down the hill by now, and were chatting with Cody and Jason. Amanda and Everett were standing a little to one side, a little apart.

"You've been doing some pretty interesting stuff," said Everett. "You seem to get yourself right into the action."

"Yeah, well," said Amanda, modestly. She was watching Everett, watching Everett watch her, watching his gaze trickle over the cluster around Jason. Amanda had last seen him a year and a half ago, at the end of the women's photo project. Before that, not for a decade, more or less, at the end of some party or concert that had not panned out, a night when all the limitations of life had become drearily clear, a night that had ended with Everett and his friends, leather and crewcuts, slumped on back stairs in the rain, radiating contempt and boredom. A night in which it had seemed clear to Amanda that she counted as part of the problem, and not the solution.

When Everett had turned up to write about the photo project, Amanda had been struck not so much by his having aged as by his having flushed and thickened. But today, under full morning light, he looked as thin as ever in his hiking-store khakis, thin and worn; his hair was receding.

"You have a lot of flexibility, working like this," said Everett. Keyed as she was to the old Everett, Amanda could nevertheless locate in his voice, in his face, nothing but approval and interest. "You aren't tied down to someone else's deadlines."

"That's true." Amanda was responding to the unmistakable note of envy in his voice. For Everett to envy anything she did made Amanda, for a moment, almost dizzy. She hadn't, until this minute, thought of her presence here as productive enough to be called *working*. But obviously it must be significant, and significantly close to chances at visible success. Coming down the hill five minutes earlier, Amanda had felt primarily sooted and silted, crumpled and smeared. Now the dirt was something else. Mark of authenticity, of her commitment to experience. Behind the lines, behind the scenes. Backstage, where Everett always yearned to be, frequently was. If he envied her, it meant that she was closer to the source than she had thought.

"I'll introduce you to these guys," Amanda said, generosity mixing so seamlessly with pride, pure showing off, that it didn't even occur to her to wonder where one began and the other ended.

"I'd like that," said Everett. The circle opened as they stepped towards Jason and Cody. Introductions all around; Jason took care of that.

"Stuff's really going to be coming down here," said Dylan. "It's really going to be hot."

"Yes," said Everett. "Have you heard when they're coming in?"

Cody had stepped back from the group, and was playing with the puppy, tug-of-war with a broken branch. Chance had come up at Everett's elbow, sidled up, thought Amanda; he was watching Dylan and nodding.

"We're ready for anything," said Dylan.

"There'll be some more people coming up from the federation this morning," said Jason.

"We've got to take back the earth," said Chance.

"We should have twenty, fifty people up here by lunchtime," said Jason.

"Excellent," said Dylan.

"Earth is the mother," said Chance. "We've been destroying her. Raping her. This is the last stand."

"The federation has been getting an enormous amount of support in Vancouver," said Jason. "Excellent media coverage."

"I've been down here on the beach for twenty years," said Chance. "I've been watching this going on."

"Oh really?" said Everett. "You live down here?"

"The land is going to rise up," said Chance. "We have to pay with our bodies. We have to pay with our souls."

"Chance," said Jason. "I wanted to ask you something. I wanted to ask you about building a lean-to. I've got some tools in the truck I wanted to give you." Jason did not quite take Chance by the elbow; it was more discreet than that. Chance broke off mid-sentence; his face swung, hesitating, registering perplexity.

"He seems kind of an interesting character," said Everett, watching Jason guide Chance up the road towards the barricade.

"He's kind of a cool guy," said Dylan. "Sort of a shaman."

"Yeah," said Amanda. A white van came jolting over the hillock and parked a hundred feet down the main road. Two large cameramen dropped from the cab and came trudging up the road, lenses alert, panning over the clearcut, the locked trailer, the brush pile barricading the side road, the knot of people chatting by the jeep. Amanda and Everett stepped back; Jason, without Chance, stepped forward to meet the reporter, a small man with a careful haircut.

Later, high noon, windless, the sun straight overhead erasing every shadow. No shade from the brambles and deadfall, no shade under the barricade. Inside the cars, heat like an oven; the gallon jug Amanda hauled from her back seat was bathwater hot. The cameramen and the van had disappeared; Amanda and Everett, Jason and Dylan, Cody, Suri and Chelsea sat on the dusty ground by the jeep drinking Coke from an iced cooler. The day was devolving, for Amanda, into the torpor of delayed connections in unfamiliar departure lounges: that mix of a jittery need for action deadened by rising lethargy, anxiety undercut by the growing conviction that no movement would ever again be possible. She held the chilled can against her temple, willing away the threat of a heat headache.

She had taken photos of the tents, the meagre campfires, the parked cars, the barricade; through the viewfinder, even this last looked merely a rubbish heap, a slash pile undifferentiated from the broken hills that filled her vision. Waiting for action, everything was diminished; she could not, somehow, capture the fizz of anticipation in black and white.

"Ray should be making his speech right about now," said Jason.

"I wonder how it's going to go down," said Everett. "I wonder how it's going to come across on TV."

"Ray's good with the media," said Jason. "Ray comes across really sincere."

"He got some excellent coverage when he was talking about Bob's case," said Everett. "Joel was telling me how they researched that. Amanda. You know Joel."

"It doesn't ring a bell," said Amanda.

"He was living in that house down on Pender with me and Dick. Back in the early eighties."

"Maybe," said Amanda.

"He's Ray's assistant."

"Joel's a really great guy," said Jason.

"Dick's done all right," said Everett.

"Hasn't he," said Amanda. "I hear him every time I turn on the radio."

"Of course their sound has changed a lot," said Everett.

"That's true. They used to have a lot harder a sound," said

Amanda. Something had shifted fundamentally, all right. "Back from when Cryptic Neon started," she added. Everett pulling her into the conversation. Treating her like an equal, like someone who'd been there, back at the beginning.

"Of course it isn't really the same band," said Everett. "It's only Dick and Rod left. The others are all younger guys now."

"Oh really?" said Amanda.

"And they've been out in Toronto for a couple of years now. That's actually where they're based."

"Oh yeah?" said Amanda. As trivia, this did not particularly interest her. She was listening instead to the undertone, which she thought had shifted again. "There are a lot more record labels and distributors out there," she hazarded.

"They're going on tour with Roadhog in the fall," said Everett.

"Oh really?" said Amanda, brightly. She had never heard of Roadhog.

"Roadhog are replacing their bassist. They're getting the guy from Wallow," said Everett.

"Wallow are really hot," said Jason. "I saw them in Seattle last summer."

"They might be breaking up," said Everett. "They lost their record deal."

"That's too bad," said Amanda. Yes, she thought. The rules were shifting, or maybe she had misread them at the start of the conversation. Everett was neither drawing her in nor drawing her out. It was another game altogether. As long as she seemed to understand what he was saying, his comments would grow more arcane; sooner or later she would have to concede defeat. This had nothing to do with finding common ground. "That's really awful about Wallow," Amanda said. She had never heard of Wallow, either.

"It's been coming for years," said Everett. "Their lead singer is a junkie."

Amanda was suddenly deeply weary of the conversation. The heat came down like a fist clenching. "I didn't know that," she said, letting go of her bluff.

"That's why the Penitents broke up," said Everett.

"I never saw them," said Amanda.

"They were excellent live."

"I don't think I ever heard them," said Amanda. Three blanks in a row, and Everett would have to concede victory.

"I have the first Penitents album," said Jason. "They were hot."

"They've only got the two albums," said Everett. "That and a bootleg tape you can get in the States."

"Oh really?" said Jason.

Mid-afternoon, and a small parched wind puffing fitfully out of the clear sky. Jason and Everett had driven back into town with Dylan. Amanda stretched her fly sheet from bumper to deadfall, making a low-pitched orange shade. Cody had faded out; she had not given him much thought all day. Now he suddenly appeared, squatting outside in the sun.

"I'm walking up to the valley. Maybe you want to come."

"Can we?" said Amanda. "Aren't we supposed to wait?"

"The loggers aren't coming today. Not this late. You should see it. If you want to."

"Oh, yes. Yes, I do." She had not, until now, given the valley itself any thought; the junction, the road filled her view. Still, of course it made sense to see the valley. But, following Cody up the track, Amanda felt deeply uneasy. She did not trust in the least his reading of the situation. Greg and Dylan, whom she now saw as far more central, knowing far more, were perfectly ready to believe in things happening, yesterday, at sunset. And when things happened, she needed all of them on film; she needed to be there, at the barricade.

Walking up the hill Amanda was also aware of another tug, the tug of property. There sat her car and her tent and her sleeping bag, and her good Gore-Tex rain jacket, and here was coming no one knew what in the shape of earthmovers and tow trucks, bonfires and hurling bottles. And she was walking away.

The land rose steadily, sweat soaked her back, the heat pounded now in her skull, little hammers of heat. They walked without talking. Ten more minutes took them to the point at which she had found the parked Volvo the previous night. Just beyond, a winter creek had washed out the road. From high above them, a wide chute of round stones plunged across the track and down the hill. The debris of a log bridge, snapped and twisted, lay half buried under sand and gravel. Cody stepped out nonchalantly, hopping from rock to rock; the wash was nearly dry, a thin stream pooling underfoot. Amanda followed. The heat headache, the vertical tilt of the land; after three steps she was seized by vertigo. The wash slid a thousand feet down the mountain, bare of branch, root, handhold, a long fast plummet to death. Twenty feet at most to cross, rock to rock, and she couldn't do it, couldn't move, forward or back. Panic, and shame too, but while the panic could imagine all the shame to come, could step outside itself to see her crouching there on a boulder unable to move, the shame couldn't budge her.

Cody reached the other side of the wash, and glanced back.

"I'm stuck," said Amanda. He was looking back at her so blankly that she was deeply embarrassed. "I can't do this," she said.

Cody came hopping back over the rocks. "It is kind of freaky here," he said, balancing easily, glancing at the chasm. "Hold onto my hand."

"It's not going to do any good," said Amanda, but in fact it did. Gripping, she slowly stood up and then followed him, boulder to boulder, across the wash.

They were much higher by now; looking back, Amanda saw the road stretching out past the hillock, entirely white and empty under the sun, and the dulled glint of parked cars. A minute later she was on the ridge, and the camp was out of sight. There was more breeze up here, coming off the blue glint of the ocean a few miles away.

The clearcut ended abruptly at a dark line of trees. Cody plunged into the shadows, following a narrow path; Amanda followed. The trail dropped steeply and the temperature plummeted, a chill breath seeping up from damp earth. As they descended, the trees became bigger, the vegetation thicker: swaths and veils of moss drooping from branches, furred trunks, clumps of vivid fern, a tangle of deadfall and nurse logs. At the bottom of the trail stood a spruce twelve feet across at the base, huge roots thrown out as buttresses, the bark ridged and cracked. Amanda squinted upwards; the tip was lost in the motes and branches of the forest canopy.

"Shit," she said. She had of course seen photographs, filtered rays through green distance, camera titled skyward, and the federation poster, on the wall of both Cammie's and Cody's kitchens: half a dozen figures linking arms around a massive bole, dwarfed to elves in red and yellow Gore-Tex. Amanda had been ready for big trees, had been ready as well for the little lilt of awe and wonder that she vaguely thought constituted a spiritual, or proto-spiritual, experience. What she hadn't been ready for was the *presence* of the tree, its indisputable materiality. It stood on its feet like some impossibly large animal that only grew more impossibly large as she approached: a purebred Percheron hitched, perhaps, to a brewer's dray in a Canada Day parade, or an unexpected elephant looming up in some cramped zoo. The massive tree was massively disturbing, visually; it altered all known proportions.

"Yeah," said Cody. They went along the trail, the hot white glare of a riverbed shimmering to one side. Not all the trees were giant; most were merely large and old. But at one bend in the path, four trees lined up in receding perspective, each bigger than the last, the illusion of a forest from before recorded time.

"All of Vancouver was like this," said Cody. "You can still see the big stumps on the north shore."

"And they levelled it all in a hundred years. This is all that's left." Amanda could taste the clichés on her tongue as she spoke, the residue of pamphlet and editorial, but here, staring down these trees, the words seemed newly original. Or rather, there did not seem anything else to say.

"Pretty much all," said Cody. "There's a couple of other places people are blockading too. We can get down to the river here."

The water was low, running clean brown pools between white rocks. They hopped boulders to the sandbar, where the sun still streamed down from the afternoon sky, and the top leaves of the cottonwoods flickered green to silver in lost currents of air. To both sides, the water burbled and murmured, a complex layering of sound, hypnotic. Cody leaned over and drank, then splashed his head. Amanda washed her hands and her face, gingerly; the water was glacier-cold. Sitting back on the dry gravel, she was overcome by lassitude. Too many people, too much movement, too much waiting. But Cody had brought her here; she owed him an effort.

"So you want to go back and do your high school completion," she said.

"Yeah." Cody was flicking pebbles into shallow rapids. "Dylan was saying his cousin's an electrician. He makes really good money. He's working all the time."

"I think electricians do pretty well," said Amanda.

"But you need all this math and science. It's really hard to get in."

"If you got your high school you'd do fine. You just go to the technical institute." Amanda's own tilt, and the tilt of the people whose lives she knew, was towards academia, not trade school, and towards the social sciences and art, not technology. "It can't be that hard to get in. You could even go and do environmental studies or something at the university."

"Yeah, I could." Cody's neutrality suggested that he could but he couldn't imagine it. "It all just takes so long. All that time in school. Listening to teachers."

"You're really young, though," said Amanda. "You got lots of time. Besides, it's not like sitting in high school. It's actually fun. You're learning things."

"Yeah? Greg's friend is opening a café on Commercial Drive. He's going to serve vegan food. No animal products, no dairy."

"I heard they've got a diploma in sustainable forestry. That might be kind of interesting to do. Since you're into the environment."

"You need something like Greg's friend where you're running your own thing," said Cody. "Then you have time for your own life."

"I guess." The idea of small business, entrepreneurship, bored her, called up the kinds of tasks she was successfully avoiding now: behind the counter of the coffee bar, gift shop, bookstore, making earrings or hair-clips or muffins. People like Hugh, on the other hand, sold their skills to organizations far more interesting and multidimensional than any they could launch themselves. Cody as electrician, and for that matter Jeff as computer technician, seemed an almost perverse limiting of possibility. And Cammie as secretary? Well, with women it did not seem to matter so much; women had more freedom to be merely practical. And besides, Cammie had the children and Jeff to support.

"I think there's going to be tons of work in environmental issues," she said. "They're just waking up to the problem. I have this friend in urban studies right now. He's saying he really wishes he had a good background in science. He could shift into recycling and waste management. So if you started now you could be really well placed."

"Yeah. I guess," said Cody.

"You really should," said Amanda.

The walk back to camp took them up through the chill forest, and landed them with a physical shock — the heat, the wide hard light — on the devastated rim of the clearcut. You could hardly credit, thought Amanda, that two or three years ago this smashed battlefield, this Somme of trees, had been co-extensive with the woods from which she had just stepped. Yet everywhere were the stumps to prove it.

From the hill above the washout, they looked down on the camp. Nothing had changed, nothing had happened. They had been gone an hour.

The next day and a half passed in a hot daze of pure boredom, intensified by anxiety, by waiting. Here in the midst of mountains, ten minutes' drive from the beach, twenty to a wood lake, five to the eaves of the forest, they nonetheless were camping on the hot, hard shoulder of a dirt road.

On the afternoon of the next day, the cameramen returned without the reporter. Someone, Dylan or Greg, set fire to the barricade; it burned pale in the sunlight for the evening news. On the afternoon of the third day, Dylan came back from town and said the federation had word the logging company was holding off until the land-use report came down. Ray made a speech in the legislature, and a sound bite hit the national news.

Amanda leaned against the hood of her car and listened to Dylan and Greg, to Nick and Sue and Suri. There was no point staying up here if what the federation said was true. If the land-use report was coming down next month. What if it was coming down next week? There were tensions and inertias Amanda sensed but had neither the knowledge nor the energy to decipher: a bluffness to Nick's statements, a hint of a whine to Sue's replies, undercurrents that suggested it would take a wearyingly long time to reach consensus. There was no point going back to the beach if it meant moving back up here in five days. There was no point staying here. Did the federation have accurate information?

In the end, they were back on the beach before sunset, a paradise of comfort now, of convenience and wash-water, of space and tranquillity.

"What should I be doing?" said Amanda. She was sitting on a massive beach log, a fibrous old cedar bleached silky grey. A clean hard breeze whipped off the blue sea.

"Hard to say," said Nick.

"Get it, boy. Get it," said Dylan. The black Labrador retriever galloped down the sand.

"I could stick around. Or I could go back to town and come back when it looks like things are heating up," said Amanda.

"It's good being down here," said Nick. "Getting into the feel of the place. You have to be down here a long time for that."

"Yeah," said Amanda. They had been back at the beach for two days. Too much fresh air, perhaps, or the anxiety of waiting; something, at any rate, was beginning to irritate her. Were they all immensely relaxed, laid back, chilled out, cooled down, to a point where decision became an unbearably assertive act? Or were they all, herself included, wired and tense, this flat nonchalance merely a subtler kind of aggression? Nick was looking out to sea with a blank half-smile, his gaze on the middle distance; he wasn't going to be any help.

"Can you make any kind of realistic guess when they're going to be moving in?" said Amanda.

"Hard to say," said Nick. "Jason will let us know if he hears anything."

"It's good down here," said Dylan. "There's a real sense of community. A lot of ideas getting shared."

"Yeah," said Amanda. Perhaps, after all, this irritation was only her own reaction, her own symptom of being irremediably torn between city and wilderness. It seemed for ever she had been away, but it was less than a week. Certainly she could feel the attraction of staying here, letting time unspool along the beach, spumes and tangles of time knotted and wasted like the bull whips of bull kelp withering above the tideline. If you stayed out here, certain things would prove dispensable, all right. Tension, if you ignored Nick's tight, bland smile. The grit and toxins of the city. Ambition, perhaps, and all those jittery social considerations. Also your job, your apartment and your bank account. If she left tomorrow, she could call in and claim the contract — holiday replacement, data input — she'd been offered for next week.

"It's really special out here. We're building something important," said Dylan.

"Oh, for sure," said Amanda. It was her lack, no doubt, this desire for movement and adventure. Which, after all, she'd come out here seeking. But what would it mean to live within the sound of the surf long enough that all memories of the other world dropped away? It would not, perhaps, take so long, the skull emptied of traffic, sirens, jackhammers, Muzak. And who would she become, this Amanda washed clean? She thought vaguely that someday she should try it, someday when she'd planned ahead, saved money, had no pressing business, no ties. Only she would come out alone, she'd come out with no tasks, nothing to irritate her. Someday, though; not today, not this month or this year.

"You're going," said Cody. "That's too bad." He really did look disappointed. This surprised Amanda, and deepened her unease or regret or guilt.

"Yeah, well," she said. "I'll come back when stuff is happening. I guess I've got to work next week."

"I might be in town sometime," said Cody. "Depending."

"For sure give me a call," said Amanda. "I'll show you how the photos came out."

She was sitting on her heels in the glade, making no effort yet to strike camp and pack. The hush of wind in the wall of shore pine, and the surge of the breakers, the puppy rustling through the beach grass. The journey ahead seemed endless, the glade a pocket of pure rest and sanctuary.

"I really should thank you for helping me set up," said Amanda. "For cooking all those dinners. For this beautiful campsite." Her words, as they fell, seemed stilted, though she was sincere. Perhaps their falsity was based in the fact that, ten years ago, she would have taken Cody's help in the spirit it was offered: completely for granted. That was just what you did for anyone who was on your side. Just as, back then, even at parties, you never sought out the hostess and thanked her for a lovely evening at four a.m. when she was giggling on acid or vomiting in the back yard.

"That's okay," said Cody. He looked embarrassed; he clearly hadn't expected thanks.

"I guess I should start packing," said Amanda. "I guess I should get going." She didn't stir.

Cody shouldered Amanda's pack and walked with her up the trail to the parked cars. Piece by piece, she felt the beauty of the beach drop away from her.

"For sure call me up when you come into Vancouver. Maybe I'll be back here before then," said Amanda, unlocking the driver's door.

"Yeah. I will," said Cody.

The drive back was long and tiring, past the bare junction where the barricade was a smudge of charcoal on the dirt beside the tin trailer, then down all the rutted, empty logging roads. When Amanda's tires hit the humming blacktop three hours later, she felt as if she were flying, floating, newborn.

In the white washroom aboard the ferry, Amanda looked in the mirror for the first time in nearly a week. Under fluorescent strip lighting, against sterile walls, wedged between the comfortable bulk and freshly laundered T-shirts and shorts of summer travellers, she loomed up not nearly so outrageous and exotic as she had imagined, as she had felt walking up from the car deck full of sights seen and risks taken. She did not look at all like Chelsea and Suri, who were very young and very pretty, and on whom tangled braids and torn T-shirts were piquant revolt. She looked much more like the women beside her in the mirror, the suburbanites and American tourists caught up in the mix of anticipation and anxiety attendant on choreographing family excursions. *Ashley. Come here and wash your hands.* Amanda resembled the women beside her in the mirror, if only they hadn't bathed in a week. Her face was tanned but it was dried out, parched, too; up close in the mirror she saw the pores were embedded with black soot. Her hair, dirty, was scraped back into a flat braid, dowdy as an old photo of a Depression-era farm wife squinting off across the dustbowl. There was sand in her scalp, sand in her boots, sand in the pockets of her jeans. And she smelt of woodsmoke, her hair and her arms, her jeans and her boots, saturated with it.

Hugh phoned that night, while Amanda was rubbing her face with oatmeal paste, and readjusting to the novelty of walls, floor and ceiling.

"So how you doing?" she said. It took an effort to remember their last conversation, an effort to remember him at all.

"All right," said Hugh. "Not bad."

"What are you up to?"

"Meetings all day. All a bit exhausting. What about you?"

"I've been over on Vancouver Island for a week," said Amanda.

"Oh really? That sounds nice. A holiday." Hugh's voice was washed thin, weary. It had sounded that way the last time they had talked. Amanda remembered, now.

"Actually, I've been taking pictures. At the anti-logging protests." The roads and mountains, the sea and the sky, looped through her mind. Not a week, then. Weeks and weeks, a summer, a lifetime.

"Oh really? Oh, good for you. Tell me about it."

"It's for Lane, at the gallery. He said if I got some good shots we could do an exhibit."

"Lane," said Hugh.

"You remember Lane," said Amanda.

"Yes. Of course. Lane."

"Is that a problem?"

"I don't know if it's a *problem*."

"Well, it sounds like you have some concerns around it," said Amanda. Hugh, worn out, dropping vague hints she was supposed to catch, too scrupulous or too exhausted to come out with what he meant. To mute or dissemble her irritation, Amanda spoke with exaggerated care. "It sounds like you have some issues with Lane."

"I don't know that I do," said Hugh. "I'm not sure I should be saying this at all. I've heard things about Lane. How he operates."

"Like what?" said Amanda.

"That's it," said Hugh. "I can't really remember. I don't think I'd really trust him, if I were you."

"Oh. I don't *trust* him," said Amanda. "But what could he do? If he wants the pictures, he wants them. I guess he could not want them, in the end. That wouldn't be the end of the world."

"As long as you have your eyes open," said Hugh. "I don't actually know anything."

"You've been away a whole week. It doesn't seem that long. It seems like two days," said Cammie. "Did you have a good time?"

"Oh yes," said Amanda. "It's beautiful out there."

"I don't know when we're going to have time to get away,"

said Cammie.

The students surged beyond the glass wall. Inside the staff lounge, the voices peaked with coffee and the hilarity of lunchtime release. So much movement, so much noise. After three days back in town, Amanda was still painfully aware of the artificiality of urban textures. Canned air, canned music, under her feet cheap carpet and then concrete, and below that not earth but a floor of classrooms, then two levels of staff parking lots. Under that, presumably, somewhere, soil sunless and sterile, beyond the reach of worm or root. While up here on the surface, despite the high perfect summer day blazing away outside, she was sitting in sealed rooms that had the stale tang of airplanes.

"I hung out with the protesters. I took some photos," said Amanda. Out on the beach, the pull had been citywards, finally. But here in the staff lounge, after three and a half hours back at work, she already missed, in her skin and bones, the sea breeze, the clean blast of sun.

"That sounds fun," said Cammie. "I'm really envious. So you're down in data entry now? How are they there?"

"It seems okay," said Amanda. "Kind of slow. I guess they'll find more for me to do."

"Slow," said Cammie. "We should be so lucky. Gloria's back. That's fine, that's all right. But all this stuff has piled up. All this stuff we didn't know about. Marthe is on a rampage. I shouldn't even have taken lunch."

"Is Gloria still complaining?" Amanda finished her canned soup, and speared a canned bean with her fork.

"That woman," said Cammie. "That woman is going to drive me up the wall. She really is."

The screen of the computer held a virtual copy of the registration forms that were stacked at her elbow. This was the triplicate copy, and the printed information — variously clear, helpful block letters, loopy girlish print, and the painful ponderous efforts of those new to the Roman alphabet — was blunted and dulled to pale blue through two layers of carbonless carbon paper. In some places, that paper had obviously slid under effort. Numbers were cancelled by the slash bars delimiting day/month/year. Postal codes disappeared under *please print firmly*. After a few minutes, Amanda saw that the form, on paper, did not quite replicate the form on the computer screen: the layout was slightly different. This made everything that much slower.

Three-thirty in the windowless room in the basement. A grip or twist starting up in her right shoulder, after hours at the keyboard. Dreary addresses under her fingertips, third-storey walkups south and east, near the house where she had met Cody and Jason. Basement suites with low numbers close to Main Street, dividing line between shabby east and glamorous west. Under her fingers, a city, a universe, of hopeless apartments, damp carpets, wide hot desolate streets.

Whereas, out on the beach, you'd walk into that clear hard wind, into nothing.

Smudges of grey trembled, blurred, straightened and congealed into dim negative on the white foot of the enlarger. Cody wading out of the ocean, carrying the puppy, dark against a darker sky. Amanda lowered the lens, making him larger, filling the frame, focused again. Then she switched off the enlarger and, redly lit by the safe light, fumbled with the folded lips, the black envelope, of the box of paper. Paper in place, the enlarger on and off, then the three trays of chemicals, the vinegar reek of the stop bath. Finally the cold running water of the bathroom sink, and the pegged line above the tub, cleared tonight of laundered stockings and panties. Curling slightly, dripping softly, moments of the past week hung before her. Amanda double-checked the box of paper, and turned on the bathroom light.

Dark, and quiet, and late. Amanda had worked past midnight; her back ached. Once she'd started, it hadn't been possible to stop, hadn't been possible to halt the slow appearance of pieces of preserved time. Of course they weren't synonymous with reality. Amanda, on discovering photography, had wanted above all to fix the exact tone of light and shade, colour and expression, and had been foiled, disappointed. Now she saw how the photograph lied, lied beautifully. Or rather, how the photograph became itself an artifact, artificial and contingent as a pencil sketch.

In these preserved moments, no doubt about it, Cody looked good. Loose and wild and nonchalant. As if he just that moment had walked up out of the ocean.

Amanda went into the living room and sank down on the sofa in the dark. Out the front window, downhill over warehouses, the arc lights, blots and blurs, of the gantries and wharfs. They were working late down there, too: plaints and squeals, shunting trains and banging containers, and under that the low late-night mutter of the city, the city's endless mumble.

"You're so lucky you have the time to do photography and stuff," said Cammie. "I have no time for myself. No time at all."

"I guess I'm not as busy. I don't have kids," said Amanda, drowsing on the park bench in the heat and haze of Saturday afternoon. This past week of data input, coming up into the endless evening sun mole-dazed at five-thirty, Amanda had felt the heavy tug of wasted time, slaughtered hours. Data input was certainly not *time for myself.* But neither was photography. Photography required *time for photography,* a different concept. The camera created its own imperative. Thus, subterranean, that familiar itch of irritation with Cammie, the suspicion they were talking at cross purposes, which Amanda registered only as boredom. None of this was clear to her today, facing the shallow sedgy lake, the somnolent mallards. What was most clear was the bone-deep tediousness of the past week. Compared to this, the longest day squatting behind the barricades now seemed an unbroken span of pure freedom.

"You're so lucky," said Cammie. "I just come home drained. I couldn't even think about doing anything creative after work. And even now we're getting subsidized rent, we're still broke by the end of the month. I don't know where it *goes.*"

"Maybe Jeff will get a job after he finishes this course," said Amanda.

"He might," said Cammie. "If he manages to finish. They're running him ragged. He has to study every night. It's too bad the record store went belly up. He really took it hard."

"There seems to be lots of work in computers," said Amanda. "He could even go back to university." Down in the sand, Caitlin knelt earnestly with spade and toy tractor, and wide-brimmed pink hat.

"Yeah. He could," said Cammie. "He's talked about it. But it takes so long. Another couple of years at least."

"Do you know my friend Hugh?" said Amanda. "He's out east doing a Master's in urban studies right now."

"Oh really?" said Cammie. "I used to like doing creative stuff.

I remember making up these T-shirts with block prints once. They came out cool. And I made these masks."

"Oh really?" said Amanda. That would be a Cammie she had never seen back then, not the waif hunched in the kitchen at the tail end of parties. "Do you still make things now?"

"God no," said Cammie. "I barely have time to catch my breath. It's really awful. I liked doing creative things. I know I am a creative person, actually. I just don't have any time for myself. You're so lucky."

"I guess," said Amanda. That morning she had spread her prints on the kitchen table, shuffling them with a critical eye. They were good, some of them, very good, especially the ones of Cody. They had what she had hoped to capture: the minutiae of life back of the scenes, pointing up, though she couldn't afford to examine this too closely, exactly what was most inconvenient, poverty-stricken, non-urban, exotic, about the camps. One black pot on a small fire, the lone tent against clearcut, Suri and Chelsea with complex rags, beautiful cheekbones, ruined hair, laughing in morning light, cuddling dirty cups against the sea. Pictures, then, posed like an anthropologist, pictures to mark for the viewer both the tremendous gap, and the ease with which it could be imaginatively, empathetically jumped.

The act of snicking the shutter made that moment, that one two-hundred-fiftieth of a second, significant. It made all of them, Cody and Chelsea and Suri, Dylan and Greg and Nick and Sue, the dogs and Chance, into icons. But at the same time these photos were still irrelevant. They were the flip side of the tapestry, but the real side, the side that made all this matter, would be the photos of action. Of protest and police, of violence or its hovering threat. And that, of course, she hadn't yet captured. But she would. As soon as Jason called long distance from the fishing village where he was quartered, as soon as he said they were heading back to the junction, she'd hop in her own car, be there half a day later.

"I guess I'm lucky to have some flexibility," said Amanda.

"You're so lucky to have something to do that really expresses yourself," said Cammie.

Caitlin came trotting up to the bench. "I want my bucket," she said.

"Your bucket," said Cammie. "I don't know if we brought

your bucket, honey. Here. Is your sun-hat on? We don't want you frying. She's got my skin, I just burn like a lobster. Let's put some more lotion on you, sweetie. I can't believe we used to just run around all day in the sun when we were kids. I guess we're all going to die of skin cancer. Do you want a juice?"

"Okay," said Caitlin, tilting her chin forward helpfully.

"Put the bunny through the hole," said Cammie. "We can almost tie bows now, can't we."

"I tied my shoes," said Caitlin.

"You did, too," said Cammie. "Mostly we stick with Velcro. Put your straw in here. Don't spill it. You'll get all sticky."

"I dug a hole for the apartments," said Caitlin.

"*Did* you," said Cammie. "We didn't bring your bucket, honey. Your bucket is on the balcony. Remember you were watering the flowerboxes this morning? It doesn't end. It's one thing after another. Wipe your chin. You're sticky."

"I like this one," said Amanda.

Cody was sitting at her kitchen table, window wide to a tugging summer breeze. His hair lifted and fell against his neck, salt-faded at the tips. The edges of the photographs rose and trembled like breathing, then dropped flat. Cody looked, shuffled, his face clear and blank.

"I like this," he said. The malamute puppy, sitting at attention on a beach log, eight by ten: every hair, every whisker, in perfect focus.

"Take it," said Amanda. "No, really. I just run off more. It's easy."

Cody, in faded beach khaki, leaning across her kitchen table. Ikea beech, a modest enough choice, when she had deeply desired a particular gate-legged oak, 1940s utility, too expensive, in the back room of a Main Street antique shop. Only, against Cody, the room, the whole apartment, revealed itself as something other than the roughly renovated second floor of a house already condemned by the proximity of the waterfront, of railway yards and light industry. Against Cody, the apartment revealed itself as a spacious opening of white walls and varnished hardwood, of cleanliness and ease. Amanda wondered what he made of it, whether he noticed.

"This is looking up at that big tree in the river bottom," said

Amanda.

"Oh yeah?" said Cody. He seemed interested enough, he seemed relaxed.

Amanda wasn't. She was on the edge of her chair, holding her breath, tentative as if she had coaxed, within her walls, some forest creature, imperfectly tamed.

A stronger gust of wind tossed through the window; the photographs lifted clear of the table, stirred like dead leaves. Amanda threw her arm across them, laughing. Perhaps a little too loudly.

The walls of the café belonging to Greg's friend were sponged the colour of sunflowers; the crockery was mismatched Salvation Army. Amanda shook soy sauce into her soup, which was thick with beans and vegetables but bland. Facing Cody across a table like this was surprisingly unsettling. When she had met him, less than a month ago, that rainy afternoon out on East Thirty-fifth Avenue, she had not in the end cared if they made no conversation, had greeted Jason with relief. But opening the door to Cody this afternoon, Amanda had been surprised at the warmth of her response. Warmth and concern, and curiosity too. And now nerves, in an unfamiliar variety. It was not the anxiety that she remembered feeling around Everett and his friends, so many years ago: anxiety over her ability to fit in and carry it off. None of that concerned her with Cody. The gap was so clearly in the other direction that she was ready to be uncomplicatedly charmed by any pockets of specialized knowledge he might display: camping tips, perhaps, or new bands, or the intricacies of the logging protests. Ready to be charmed as she'd be with someone else's precocious child.

But Amanda would never be feeling this nervousness with a child. She was watching Cody's face, closed and thoughtful in these novel surroundings. Her anxiety was only partly over the slowness of conversation, a difficult slowness for Amanda, though perhaps not for Cody. The anxiety was more over the new flash of curiosity, a curiosity that had developed since Amanda had left the beach, that had bloomed along with the grey shadings, the dim underwater faces, taking shape all this week at the bottom of her developing tray. Those faces loomed up from the fog bank or snow flurry of white paper, and froze in time. Cody, again and again, pinned and mounted. And unreadable.

And no less unreadable, Amanda now saw, here across from her in this skimped restaurant. What the week on the beach and the stack of photographs told her was that he was, for her, something different. Within familiar bounds, of course. But what familiar, what different? A month ago she had not been interested. Now she was; now she had intimations of pockets of courage and hardship, of patience and endurance, of knowledge, of his essential value and importance, which she was sure Cody didn't recognize in himself. But she didn't know where to begin her investigation.

"The waitresses here work for their meals," said Cody. "That way they don't lose anything off their welfare cheque."

"That's clever," said Amanda. "Aren't they afraid of getting caught, though?"

"They haven't yet," said Cody.

Another pool of silence. Cody didn't seem concerned by it; he didn't, at least, try to break it. So perhaps, thought Amanda, this was *companionable silence*, not a state she cultivated. They didn't know enough people in common to exchange gossipy small talk. The weather had been glorious for days. She couldn't bring herself to praise the food. They had ascertained earlier that the loggers were still nowhere near the river-bottom spruce; that was exhausted as a topic of conversation. So let it be silence, then.

Dylan came in through the glass door, the black Labrador retriever pushing past him.

"Hey man," said Cody. "How you doing?"

"All right," said Dylan. "I talked to Steve."

"Yeah? What's happening?"

"It's on. We can get it together tomorrow."

"Excellent. What did Mark say?"

"Ben is going to talk to Mark and get back to Chelsea."

"All right."

Amanda sat back and watched Cody's face open with interest and intelligence. She wanted to make it open like that; she wanted whatever it was that lay underneath.

"Windigo. Windy. Here boy. Come here," said Dylan. The black dog was in fine high spirits, across the café and under tables, snuffling feet. He came trotting back past Dylan, panting and grinning. "Sit, Windy. Sit, boy," said Dylan. "Good dog." The

Labrador looped away again, down past the waitress, who leaned over and patted him. "Sit," said Dylan.

"Get Chelsea to call me when Ben talks to her," said Cody.

After eating they went and sat in the park down the street. Someone was going to turn up, or wasn't, or might. The day was taking on the same rhythm as life on the beach, that slow unfurling. Greg and Chelsea turned up after a while. Amanda wanted them gone, all of them, with their laughter and allusions and interjections. She wanted Cody alone. Alone, given enough time, she'd get him talking.

They lay under the shade of dark firs, on grass browned by drought and by a smothering sift of pine needles. Out in the burning sunlight on the lawn sat another group, cross-legged and intent, playing hand drums: bongos, African tam-tams, various stretches of hide and wood. The beat rose and fell, hypnotic and drilling, rousing and soothing, on and on into the summer afternoon.

Amanda took leave of Cody at eleven p.m., dropping him and Greg in front of an old house on a busy street.

"Too bad I've got to work tomorrow," she said.

"Those guys should be in. I don't see a light," said Greg.

"See you around," said Cody.

They hopped out of the car and went up the front walk between overgrown cedars. Amanda rolled away from the curb, headed north. She had not, for over a decade, spent an evening this formless. Her life no longer supplied swelling and dividing groups of people, no longer provided chance encounters in parks and cafés, ceaseless movement and company that was either charming or deeply exhausting. Clearly, however, Cody could not be separated from his friends, or not easily.

In front of the darkened house, while Cody was peering out the window, in the gap before he skidded off the front seat, Amanda had had a sudden urge to lean over and hug him, in the safe and neuter style of her feminist friends. She didn't; the moment passed too quickly.

Driving away past locked and glaring shop fronts, she felt the physicality of that impulse solidify, become less neuter. Of course, that way lay impossibilities. Cody was no more eligible a target for these stray perverse urges than Rafael. This flicker meant nothing, Amanda told herself; let it go and it would fade, of its own accord.

"So things went well," said Lane.

"Yes," said Amanda. "I think they did."

"But there weren't any confrontations. The loggers and police didn't show up."

"No. We did move up from the beach to the blockade site. For a few days. It seemed to be a false warning."

"Yes," said Lane.

"You heard?" said Amanda.

"It may have had something to do with Ray's speech. It was useful to be able to send the camera crews up there for some colour. Maybe. I don't actually know this."

"I don't think the protesters know. Or they didn't say."

"I'm sure Jason wouldn't tell them. Again, this is all just supposition."

"I won't mention it to them."

"They'll figure it out, eventually," said Lane.

"I doubt it."

"Maybe not, then. But the photos turned out all right."

"They did," said Amanda. "As far as I've got. They'll make more sense when I get some action shots."

"When are you going back up?"

"Whenever," said Amanda. "As soon as I hear they're moving in. Jason is going to call me."

"He's still on-side with this. With the photos."

"Absolutely."

Amanda put down the phone. The long summer evening slanted against the mountains across the harbour, haze on blue above the bulk of the wheat pool. Endless, this light, these afternoons, beneath which walked Cody, somewhere in the city; he wouldn't leave town again until he'd cashed his welfare cheque. The perversity of the tickle, the urge to touch, that had hit her in the car. Boredom, that's all, Amanda told herself. Nothing else standing between her body and the world. But, once admitted, the mind refused to let go. Thinking, after all, could do no harm. However, the more she thought — on these brilliant empty evenings, or rolling her shoulders against cramp at the computer terminal in the windowless basement of the college — the more plausible it became. Not plausible in any practical sense. She could not imagine Cody in her life, her real life, without immense reorganizations, without explanations and arrangements and difficulty. On the other hand, of what precisely did her real life consist? Was it only Hugh who had provided a façade of adulthood and complexity, of little restaurants and intelligent conversation? Still, Cody did not seem, exactly, possible at this level, the level of social life; Amanda skimmed past practicalities as she shifted him in her mind.

Where Cody became plausible was in some entirely separate fantasy, luminously remote from her friends, and from his. Seduction scenarios that unrolled in social isolation: windswept beach, fogged river valley, or the equally desolate wilderness of the blank skidding city streets at two a.m. All of this highly unlikely, of course, and yet also so mundane, seeded with such realistic details, that it couldn't help but seem inevitable.

Tonight, slumped in the shadows of her apartment, watching the light fall to the north, Amanda was aware she was talking herself into a pointless infatuation. She was talking herself into it, which meant, in theory, that she ought to be able to quit: to talk herself out of it. But she didn't want to. So she wouldn't.

"Oh, God." Cammie took a bite of quiche, and sighed again. "I am just thrashed."

"Marthe on your back?" said Amanda.

"No," said Cammie. "Actually, she's on holiday this week. It's more Jeff."

"Oh really? I thought you guys were getting on so well." Amanda hadn't, in fact, thought anything of the kind; she hadn't given much thought to Cammie and Jeff, in the present, solved and finished. "You guys seemed fine when I was over there."

The corners of Cammie's mouth went down in an expressive moue; she settled into her chair, chrome and orange tweed, the same vintage as the college itself: cheerful expansionism, early 1970s, somewhat the worse for wear, for years of austerity. The college was probably the same age as Cody, Amanda thought idly. But he wasn't the worse for the wear. On the other hand, would he be in ten years? In twenty?

"So is Jeff being a jerk?" Amanda said, with one-quarter of her attention.

"Is Jeff being a jerk," said Cammie. "Not really. Yes, he is. He is actually being a jerk."

"Oh really? How?"

"I don't know. He gets doing this silent number where he won't talk to me. You know?"

"I can imagine."

"He gets all wrapped up in stuff that's going down. Then he sits at the breakfast table with this newspaper in front of his face."

"You said he was having a hard time at school."

"But he should be talking to me about it. Not this *grunting*. I mean I ask him what's wrong and he says nothing. You know?"

"I can imagine." Cody, thought Amanda, would be silent too. But it would be silence of a different order. She could imagine all too well Jeff's uninteresting withdrawals and sulks and absences. Cody's silence was focused, important. Inside it she might even learn to relax.

"I say to him, look, if you're upset, if you're mad, I have to know."

"Does it work? Does he talk?"

"Yes. No. Sometimes. He says nothing's wrong. Then he clams up again. He knows it's important to communicate. But he keeps fading out. Even when I'm practically yelling at him."

"Maybe he just has different ways of dealing with stress."

"But you can't bottle it all up like that and not talk about it. It's *sick*. It drives me up the wall."

"I can imagine," said Amanda. With Cody none of this would happen. Just to the extent that he was impossible and implausible, all this dreary tug and pull of the couple would be eliminated. Of course nothing was going to happen with Cody. But as a concept, he saved her from all this, from even the faintest idea of domesticity. Cammie knew where she was going to be, who she was going to be, for the next twenty years, for ever, thought Amanda. Whereas she herself was wide open to possibility and adventure and even, in a mild way, transgression. Cody was the proof.

"I know Jeff's school is really hard. But he has to talk about it," said Cammie.

"For sure." Amanda was far from bored. Other people's confessions and complaints were endlessly revealing, at least the first few times you heard them. More important, to just the extent that

Cammie revealed herself as hopelessly limited, Amanda was revealed as the opposite. "So what does Jeff do, exactly? When he's
being like this?" Amanda wanted to know, she genuinely did;
that came across in her voice, as she intended.

"It's like he doesn't want to be here," said Cammie. "Lights
on, nobody home. I'll be talking to him and then I'll stop and he
won't say anything. I feel like an idiot."

"Yes." Minute by minute, Cody, or the idea of Cody, was
becoming more and more precious. Whatever problems a young
boy could throw at her, Amanda was fairly sure she was more
than equal to them. And they'd have nothing, nothing at all, in
common with Cammie and Jeff.

Out beyond the glass wall, the students were milling. The
boys in black T-shirts, the girls in cut-offs, were in the high school
completion program. Where, in fact, Cody was planning to be,
this coming fall. Another implausibility, sitting over staff quiche,
watching him disappear in the crowd. Of course, Amanda had no
intention of working here in the fall. There was a permanent
opening coming up in data entry in September, clerical grade
two down in the windowless basement. The personnel department had already suggested she apply. But surely something else
would turn up, in the interim. There might be money to collaborate on David's book. She could not quite see a winter inside the
grid of the computer.

"I guess you should talk to Jeff," said Amanda. "Discuss how
you communicate." The easiest platitudes, from the easiest sort of
pop psychology, from the easiest sort of magazine. *When Your
Man Won't Talk: Five Sure-Fire Ways to Save Your Marriage.* "Men
don't deal with things the same way as women."

"Oh, I know," said Cammie. "That's what I'm finding so *frustrating.*"

"I blew this one up as well," said Amanda. "He's got this piece of
driftwood in his teeth. And here he is curled up asleep."

Black-and-white prints, matte finish, eight by ten. Amanda
and Cody were sitting on the back steps of the old house on
Thirty-fifth Avenue, the porch tilting down to a scuffed and
shrunken yard: garage renovated into rental cottage, three old
cars, homeless now, taking half the lawn. Beyond the broken
picket fence, dented garbage cans and dirt alley sat the faded

backs of other houses, paved yards, recumbent tricycles, children shrieking past, shooting water with orange plastic Uzis, lost in the growing hysteria of the hour before bedtime.

"They're nice. They're really good," said Cody. He looked pleased. The puppy in the flesh came padding out the kitchen door and snuffled inconclusively at Amanda's ankles. She lifted her beer bottle out of reach of his damp nose.

"You got your cheque sorted out. You're going back up," said Amanda.

"Tomorrow. If Greg has the car working."

Amanda sipped her beer. Outdoors, it tasted sour, full, rich, taking her all the way back to high-school parties, hiding out on the rocks down by the boat launch. At the end of the lane the evening faded slowly into an apricot glow, north-north-west. Amanda had not expected the house to be empty, had not expected to find Cody entirely alone. That seemed a tremendous opportunity, but for what she wasn't sure.

"I went over to see my mom," Cody added. "She called me up."

"Oh really?" said Amanda. "How's she doing?"

"All right. I don't know. She's kind of freaking right now."

"How so?"

"She's not getting along with the people downstairs. They're kind of the managers and they're getting uptight. They're going on about her leaving her garbage bags on the porch. That kind of shit."

"Sounds like a drag," said Amanda.

"My mom doesn't take shit from anyone. She comes in the other night and they've stuck this note on her door about something. So she starts knocking on their door and they come out and start yelling at her. And she goes she's going to beat the fuck out of them. So now she's freaking she's going to get evicted."

"So she's still drinking."

"A lot less. Sometimes."

"I don't know there's a whole lot you can do," said Amanda, carefully.

"She's doing a lot better," said Cody. "But she won't let anyone mess her around. She's wild. People can't handle that."

"It must be kind of hard for you," said Amanda, probing.

"It's okay," said Cody. "I know how to handle her. You just

got to stay calm when she gets like that. She's really nice when she's in a good mood. My brother's too much like her. He yells back and then she slams him. Not so much any more."

"Still," said Amanda.

"When my brother was a baby and we were still living over in Kits by the beach, that was nice. We could walk down barefoot and go swimming all day. Now it's all condos over there. It's really expensive."

"Yeah."

"I really like being down by the water. What I really want to do is go away and get a cabin somewhere. Live on the beach."

"Hard to make a living. Hold down a job," said Amanda. She had herself been thinking something similar, not that long ago. Now, though, a week in the city and she felt its claims and pulls as strongly as ever. At the same time, listening to Cody, she saw water, sun, space. The surf at Pesadilla Cove blended, for a minute, with a half-memory of some adolescent excursion beachwards, Kitsilano, downhill past old wooden houses, past young mothers in patchwork skirts and waist-length hair carrying blond naked toddlers. The close of an endless summer, just before the wrecking crew arrived. A vacant, because impossible, nostalgia. "You can't really have a cabin and *work*," she said, more emphatically.

"You could still get welfare," said Cody. "That would be enough."

"I guess," said Amanda. "It's not that much, though." From where this contrariness? Her general plan, improvised as the evening revealed itself, was to ease out, from Cody, confession and trust. This little rush of irritation was counter-productive.

"It's okay money," said Cody. He didn't seem to register her resistance or brusqueness.

Amanda, mentally, took a deep breath. "What would work out is if you had some job you could do that paid well when you needed money," she said.

"For sure. I might go tree-planting with Dylan next spring."

"That would be all right," Amanda said. Tree-planting was not what she had in mind: impossible exile, chain-gang labour of superhuman effort. "You can't do that for ever," she said.

"I know guys in their forties still doing it," said Cody.

"I guess," said Amanda. "That's still pretty young."

"I guess," said Cody. "Hey you. Let go. Sic 'em. Yeah. You're tough. Tough little guy. Yeah you are."

By eleven p.m., the last flush had faded above the mountains in the north-west. The house was still empty when Amanda drained her second beer and walked with Cody to the front door. Here she lingered, finding it difficult to leave. Habit, perhaps, after a week of curling into her sleeping bag ten feet from his side. The house loomed dark and quiet, newly desirable in its disorder, in the ways that disorder struck memory, resonated. Herself, Cody's age, descending similar front steps, in the same fug of patchouli and dog, into lost nights that seemed, now, impossibly rich and promising, impossibly free.

"I'll be going over tomorrow, I guess," said Cody.

"Jason will call me when the blockade goes up again," said Amanda. She hovered a moment longer on the porch. Cody was standing two steps above her; there was no dignified way to reach up and hug him. And now, at this moment, she was not quite sure she wanted to. Despite nostalgia, Cody seemed again impossibly himself, locked in and unknowable, and painfully young. It did not seem credible she had ever been that young, herself, that lost and unmarked.

Maybe, thought Amanda, as she eased her car away from the curb, she was misreading Cody's silences. Perhaps they were based in sexual unease, perhaps he was responding to her without understanding that it was her own interest to which he was drawn. In that case, of course he'd be awkward with her, thinking it impossible or forbidden. This was a line of logic that quickly led to infinite regress: her awkwardness responding to his awkwardness, responding to hers.

On the steps under the porch light, Amanda had, at the end, not made a move. But by the time she'd turned onto Kingsway and was rolling north into the city, she saw exactly how it could have gone. Possibility without urgency.

She drove home along empty streets, spangled not with neon but with backlit plastic signs marked out in block letters, in red and yellow, black and white, above shop fronts and parking lots.

"It must be late in Toronto," said Amanda.

"I guess," said Hugh. "I wasn't sleeping. I thought I'd try calling you again. See if you were in yet."

"That was nice," said Amanda. It was, too. She'd arrived home from Cody's house awake and alert, ready for conversation. Her first reaction, picking up the phone, was a rush of warmth. That was as it should be. But her second reaction was a foreboding of exhaustion. Or at least of all the points in her life at which Hugh was now, possibly, irrelevant. None of this bore examining. "It's really great to hear from you," Amanda said, with emphasis.

"So how's it going?" said Hugh. "Did you hear anything more about that permanent job at the college?"

"They said I'd have a good chance," said Amanda.

"It pays okay, you said. It's in the union."

"Yes. I don't know. It's just so *boring.*"

"You could take it and then switch to something else. Move up. Or do it for a while and save some money."

"I could." Amanda had in fact said exactly these same things to Hugh, typing her résumé in the spring. He was merely echoing her own words, and that was proof, it seemed, of his irrelevancy. Now that he'd abandoned her, he no longer had the right to know what she wanted. "I need time free to do photography," she added. "This office work is incredibly draining."

"I guess that's true," said Hugh. "You shouldn't get tied down to anything you hate."

"Don't worry," said Amanda. "I'm not about to." This came out altogether fiercer than she'd intended. "Sometimes I think the thing to do would be to just leave the city," she added. "Go and live in a cabin. Have all that time to do what you really want to do."

"I know the feeling," said Hugh. "Except what would you live on? I guess if someone won the lottery."

"There's welfare," said Amanda. "No one needs all that much money." She was dimly aware that she was picking a fight, or trying to. Aware, too, that by some oblique process, best left unexamined, she was attacking Hugh with what had most bothered her about Cody. If it bothered her, then it should bother Hugh.

"I've certainly thought about it, too," said Hugh. "A cabin in the bush looks more and more attractive, from out here."

If her stance, borrowed from Cody, didn't bother Hugh at all, that made Hugh clearly irrelevant, meant he could not, in the end, differentiate between the right and the wrong way to live, or between her real views of life and this perverse impersonation.

On the other hand, as she spoke the cabin took life, mossy and substantial, blotting out the beige office and the dull plock of computer keys. As Amanda spoke, she half convinced herself. But Hugh doomed himself by agreeing.

"I can't see you in a cabin," said Amanda. "You'd go crazy with boredom in three hours."

"You're probably right," said Hugh. "Though I could probably keep busy. But right now I do seem tied to the city for a while."

"So how's it going out there?" said Amanda. She was not particularly interested in anything Hugh could say, right now, strained through two thousand miles of cable. Change the subject.

"It's not bad," said Hugh. "It's kind of lonely. I do miss you."

"You miss me?" said Amanda. Her surprise was only partly pleasurable. "Really?"

"Of course I do," said Hugh. "You sound kind of shocked."

Monday afternoon, stop and start through rush-hour bottlenecks and paving crews, the gagging fumes of fresh asphalt, heat shimmering like cellophane above the dull glint of stalled cars. Going six o'clock by the time Amanda pulled up on the verge outside her house. Inside, the air was pooled and stale, the dust smell of old walls, the vinegar tang of photographic stop bath spilled in the sink. Amanda flung open the back door to the fire escape, the front window to the mountains, and peeled off her tailored skirt. Taffeta lining clung wet to her thighs, creased from the drive home. She reached up the back of her T-shirt, unsnapped her bra, tugged the shoulder straps down over her hands, snaked it off and tossed the shed skin, lycra and lace, over the back of the sofa. Clothes hurt, on a day like this. In the windowless basement, work had slowed that afternoon to a standstill. Some blockage or log-jam farther up the paper stream had halted the flow of triplicate registration sheets. For three excruciating hours Amanda had sat bored beyond belief behind the terminal. Finally asked to carry a memo across campus, she'd dawdled down the concrete stairways, past the boxes of petunias under blazing sun. Time crawled; all the clocks on campus halted in their tracks.

Now, home, finally home, Amanda poured herself a glass of juice and flopped on the sofa. Unpleasantly slick, that old brocade on bare thighs. Damp skin on upholstery: sweating and staining. The back of her T-shirt was soaked through from the hot seat of the car. A shower, then, but she lacked the energy, reached for the remote control instead.

The careful haircut was familiar, but not immediately placeable; it was the sweep of broken hills, the hot dead dust, that hit Amanda. The story he was reporting did not make much sense. Clips behind the barricade, rebuilt, a kind of directionless edginess, stand-off. Greg and Dylan, Nick and Chelsea. Suri. How the lens of the camera, the eye of the national news, bracketed them, made them glow. The angles were hand-held, the edits brusque and odd. The heart of the story took place in ten jumbled seconds. The camera wheeled round to some kind of scuffle, protesters foot to foot with private security guards and several impassive, embarrassed Mounties. There were shouts, taunts, and then some boundary was broken, some invisible line transgressed. The clip rolled again, slow-motion, inconclusive. The voice-over, deeply thrilled, restraining excitement, said something about possible criminal charges, about assaulting a police officer, about the court subpoenaing the tape, about the television station retaining lawyers, about the Press Council's reaction, a talking head from the Civil Liberties Association.

Amanda in her underwear sitting bolt upright now, on the edge of the sofa. No message from Jason on her answering machine; she'd already checked. No answer now when she dialled his number in the fishing village, long distance. No answer at the federation office downtown.

"We're here to stay," Nick had said into the teeth of the camera. "We're here for the duration."

Decision, or indecision, took an hour at most, the long, stale pointless summer evening glowing on outside, Amanda pacing from kitchen to living room, ten steps, letting the television news rattle on past highway accidents and housing starts, escaped children and missing criminals. At seven o'clock she called in sick to the answering service at the college personnel office, pulled on jeans and boots, rolled up her tent, locked the doors and windows and drove through the bloom of golden light to the ferry terminal.

The sense of freedom flooded her the moment her tires hit the smooth hum of the highway, the moment her speedometer edged up past fifty, sixty, seventy. Eighty kilometres an hour, eighty-two, eighty-three, hovering past the speed limit. Movement and decision. As she crested the span of the Lion's Gate Bridge, the whole hot and compromised city dropped away behind her like shed clothing, like the irrelevant constraints of waistbands and underwire. The pop radio station played, by some miracle of synchronicity, three good songs in a row. *Down by the railroad track, don't look back.* You could do exactly what you wanted, as Cryptic Neon had. You could do exactly what you wanted, when you wanted, and it would pay off, pay off big. Cody knew this but Cammie never had. In this wild flight into the sunset, past the mountains of West Vancouver hung with the cubes of modern mansions, Amanda thought she had never felt this happy or this complete, this free, caught in such gorgeous balance between the purely personal and the historical, the grand significant gesture.

Her pace slowed considerably on board the ferry, constrained to the slow green swell as the Gulf Islands inched past. By the time Amanda's ferry docked on Vancouver Island, the sun was touching the spine of the Coast Mountains. She reached the end of the pavement well past midnight, solidly dark. Half a mile on the white washboard road under an immensity of shattered stars seemed foolhardy enough. The excitement had worn into fatigue, the ache and clench of back and neck. She pulled to the side of the road, and slept in the hatchback, the cooling engine ticking and pinging under her. Outside, abyss of night.

Amanda woke at grey dawn in a grove of broadleaf maple, mossed and flooded with morning warblers. Dew everywhere, on the wide leaves, on the dust, trembling freshness. She ate trail mix, blended nuts and raisins, and drank water, ravenous. While she was spitting toothpaste into the roadside weeds, a green Forest Service pick-up truck belted past and disappeared around a corner. Amanda rolled up her sleeping bag, got behind the wheel and arrived at the junction before ten a.m.

She parked below the barricade and the tin hut, and walked up the side road. The smoking ruins of the bonfire, scattered beer bottles, and the camp sleeping. There were more cars and more tents than before, straggling uphill along the ruined road. But it was all, for a moment, strangely insubstantial. Caught off guard. Chelsea's Volvo, Chance's van, other cars. No tidy jeepette, no Jason.

Greg ducked out of a tent and straightened up, rubbing his eyes. "Hey," he said. "Shit was happening yesterday all right." His voice was excited, satisfied.

"I saw on TV," said Amanda.

"How did that go?" said Greg. "Did we get good coverage? Did we make the national news?"

"It was the top story," said Amanda. "There was some kind of fight with the cops, right?"

"Fight," said Greg. "Sort of. Not exactly. They were provoking. They really were. Pushing."

Dylan came crawling out of his own tent.

"Hey," said Greg. "We made the national news. Top story."

"Excellent," said Dylan.

"What's happening today?" said Amanda.

"The cops are coming back," said Greg. "It's going to blow. For sure."

This, however, did not happen. The day unrolled under a white sun that scorched the dew, parched the roads. The long leaves of the fireweed hung limp among the deadfall, the baked body of her car stung Amanda's fingers. The cloud of dust lifting, just before noon, over the rise of the main road resolved, as they rushed towards the barricade, into Jason's little jeep. Under the tentative shade of a stretched tarp, they drank iced water and listened to his news. The television station was refusing, on principle, to hand over the tape of the scuffle until demanded by the court. There was nothing on the tape that could be incriminating. No one had done anything wrong. Still, if the court got hold of it. The court could frame them up, easy. The real question was whether there weren't more tapes, ones they hadn't shown on TV. Tapes that the cops wanted to seize before the defence saw them, that might in fact prove police brutality. Dylan had a bruise on his shin. But they hadn't arrested anyone at the site, had been scared to, in front of the cameras. It was great. It was fucking great. They knew when they were outnumbered. Fucking try anything again. That blockade wasn't ever coming down. And it was all on the national news. Excellent.

Amanda stood and listened, feeling in her bones and her skin the rightness of being back here, heart of the action. The beige office and humming computers were another lifetime, utterly unreal. Time could spool away down there, underground, a lifetime could unwind in pure and perfect boredom. Out here all that shattered, the lie that jobs and clothes and rent mattered at all. How could the city have held her, even momentarily? In the heat she stood quietly, at ease, awaiting the coming battle.

Cody had appeared. He was standing perceptibly closer to her, sitting beside her: some new level of intimacy, growing in ways Amanda hadn't quite charted.

The day passed like that, buoyed by the memory of yesterday, the anticipation of what was to come. Amanda took out her camera, snapped a few shots, but there was little point in this. Back home lay all possible angles and permutations of campfire and tent, of dogs and Cody. There was nothing to do now but wait for action. Not, however, bored. Wired up like this, Amanda couldn't be bored. Her ears were cocked for the murmur of traffic in the distance, tensing at the low drone of a seaplane. And there were more people, strangers, to meet and chat with, trade news and rumours. It was not quite a party atmosphere, not quite that expectation of release and enjoyment. The mood was, perhaps, something closer to carnival, or the anticipation of carnival. They had stepped out and overturned the law, would do so again, and soon. Resistance had proven the easiest thing in the world, the most natural. It was so easy, the police had turned back so quickly, in retrospect no one could believe this hadn't been tried years ago. None of this was said aloud, but it was in the air: success.

The campfire unrolled, rich in camaraderie. Leaving and returning, Amanda saw, lent her the feeling of homecoming, a jump she hadn't anticipated.

She had pitched her tent near Cody's. They walked up the hill past midnight, a bright gibbous moon hanging in the west above the rim of the mountain. Sidelit, the ruts on the road threw stark shadows; the stars were dimmed. As the glow of the camp, the voices and laughter, receded, Amanda became increasingly aware that they were alone together, alone in the night. Aware, too, that this prefigured exactly one of the scenarios she had carved out on her long flight west the previous evening. Cody alone, on a moonlit mountain.

"Greg overheated on the Island Highway," Cody was saying. "There's this giant fucking hole in his radiator."

"Oh really? Oh shit," said Amanda. Nothing was going to happen. Out here moonlight was common as streetlamps. The gap between them was mundane, prosaic.

"We had to stop every ten miles and pour in more water."

"Oh really?" said Amanda. Her ideas were entertainment for a long drive, a boring job. What, after all, would she want with this child?

"There was all this *steam,*" said Cody. His enthusiasm betrayed him, all right, thought Amanda. At the same time, she was touched. Anyone else, Hugh for instance, she couldn't imagine cheerfully travelling stop and start like that. Burst radiators, Automobile Association towtrucks, the fretful squandering of paid holiday time, tears. Her tears. She would have lasted fifteen minutes, maximum, in Greg's car.

"It looked like it was going to blow up," Cody added.

"So did he get it fixed?" said Amanda. They had nearly reached the tents; they were walking more and more slowly.

"Nick gave him this stuff after that you pour in and it seals it up for a while. There's a guy in the village can fix it free."

"That's lucky," said Amanda. Down the road, the campfire flickered red. A burst of laughter, and the chords of a guitar. Everything Amanda had idly planned evaporated in the presence of Cody, live. He was impossibly young, impossibly distant; they had not yet reached anything near intimacy. He knew nothing about her, never would, while she could run circles around him whenever she tried. Acting would invert all the rules of seemliness, of logic and order.

"He thought he had it fixed before he left," said Cody.

"Oh really?" said Amanda.

"This stuff you pour in is kind of cool," said Cody. "It swells up and plugs the leak."

From down below, a flourish of guitar chords, almost Spanish, laughter, the clink of bottles, beercase rattling. The slam of a car door, more laughter. The enormity of the whole endeavour hit Amanda, the audacity of what they were doing. Flouting government and police, courts and multinational logging companies: the world turned upside-down. From the moment you said no, none of the rules applied. From now on, everything was wide open.

Buoyed by a thrilling sense of her own capacity for transgression, Amanda leaned over and kissed Cody.

He kissed her back, which Amanda had been certain enough would happen; he was far too young to have doubts or to make conditions. Ardent lips, holding nothing back, and yet, as she put her hands on his shoulder blades, his T-shirt worn dusty soft, he felt strangely insubstantial. It was all pleasant enough, salt skin and an odour of woodsmoke and crushed leaves, but Amanda was hardly relaxing into him. A parody, almost, of passion, tilting her belly against him, lips now on his very smooth throat, just below the ear, indrawn breath, his and hers. A parody not because she wasn't finding him delightful to taste and to touch, but because she couldn't shake an essential self-consciousness. Amanda sitting back, up in the clearcut on a charred stump, perhaps, watching Amanda down here on the road allowance seduce, seduce. The softness of the small of his back, her fingers sliding under the band of his army pants. Tactile pleasure on the edge of becoming desire, but not quite, not quite. Partly blocked, Amanda half realized, her mind looping ahead, by the question of what would need, soon, to be said. If he was in fact far too young to make complications and conditions, to resist adventure, how would they proceed? What was it like, what had it been like, back before she had learned to discuss things? Back before sex had required the elaborate foreplay of needs and expectations, past traumas and current responsibilities, above all explanation?

Amanda was thinking furiously, obsessively, but not that clearly, aware mostly that she was waiting for Cody to pull back and *say* something, explain the exact limits of his availability. But as the minutes went on, his clean young tongue flickering, filling her mouth, his erection hard against her thigh, her own fingers sliding under his waistband, between wet head and tight belly, his little gasps, she saw that nothing was going to be said. In one way that was a relief, prefiguring the casualness with which, years into an affair, you tilted and toppled into bed. But in another way it was oddly disconcerting, losing the whole realm in which she'd painfully learned to perform, the give and take of communication.

Perhaps, then, it was up to her to speak. There wasn't, however, here on this moonlit mountain, anything she wanted to say, any conditions she could remember wanting to make.

They moved into Cody's tent, and fell on the unfamiliar chill of his sleeping bag. The odd sense of dislocation persisted. Para-doxically, though, despite the lingering sense that she was ob-serving her own every movement, Amanda was extremely con-scious of bodies, of the physicality of it all. The extreme thinness of nylon walls, the looming mountain, footsteps crunching past in the dark, and the strangeness of peeling off her jeans and boots in this unfamiliar tent, rolling naked against this unknown body.

Cody was slim and ardent, and extremely aroused. Aroused, thought Amanda dimly, in a particularly straightforward way. Which was not to say that he lacked talent or experience; he knew the places to search for on her body, knew what would procure pleasure. Or what would have brought pleasure, if she hadn't been so persistently aware of the oddness of two bodies coming together like this, without words.

She slept.

Waking at daybreak in Cody's tent, Amanda felt dislocation, exultation and trepidation, the strangeness of a new country. Warmth, of course, that languor. But right after, immediately and perhaps primarily, a private little shock at her own audacity. For a moment she tried to imagine, but could not, what might lie ahead. In the languor, then, a suspension of action, even of be-lief. Cody slept on, breathing lightly, curled up away from her, the puppy at his feet. The tangle of sleeping bag and blankets they had improvised was less than satisfactory; slippery nylon gummed Amanda's shoulder, rough wool scratched her thigh, the thick zipper passed at an angle under her body, deeply im-printing flesh. She could smell herself, sweat and the stale fish of old sex, and woodsmoke; she smelled like Cody, which was not in itself unpleasant, but her whole body craved, like thirst or hunger, a hot shower. A hot shower alone, ten minutes of soli-tude to get her bearings, plan her next step, and then a fragrant cup of coffee at the polished kitchen table, while Cody slept on. So that by the time he woke and came stumbling into the kitchen, charmingly rumpled and sleepy, naked or in just his army pants, or perhaps her second-best bathrobe, she'd know exactly what to say, what to do.

There would be none of that distance here in the tent. The wilderness might stretch above and below, out to the infinity of the Pacific, all around nothing but blank forest, but at the moment all that space was pointless superfluity. If she wanted tea or coffee, she'd have to dress her soiled body in last night's clothes, panties and jeans at the foot of the sleeping bag, by the flap of the tent, bone-deep dew-chill of damp cotton. Then she'd have to crawl out to the bleak glare of the road allowance, build up the fire, boil water. Say good-morning to everyone else, watch their studied nonreaction as she emerged from Cody's tent and re-entered it with two tin cups twenty minutes later. It didn't bear thinking about; the idea exhausted her.

Instead, Amanda rolled over to face his back, and let her hand rest lightly on his waist, the skin dry, smooth, delicious. A moment later Cody, wide awake already, rolled over to face her. Nose to nose. His face serious and unreadable. A stranger's face. Amanda squelched the fleeting thought that if his face was unknowable it was because, at some fundamental level, it didn't interest her. At some fundamental level, she couldn't be bothered with the archaeology, the dissection, because what that face contained was old news, things she had learned and passed beyond. Although that didn't mean that she understood him, not yet.

"Well," said Amanda.

Cody didn't speak.

"It's all right," she said. "Isn't it? You're into this?"

"I'm into this," he said. "Yeah." That blankness, Amanda now saw, might be pure acceptance, might be relaxation, ease. Or it might not; she couldn't judge, not up close like this.

"I enjoyed that," she said. "I mean last night." Cody reached out and brushed a strand of hair off her face. "We need to think what we want to do with it," Amanda added. "I mean, what do you want out of it? How are we going to arrange this?"

"I don't know. Play it as it goes," said Cody. "You know."

"Yes," said Amanda, although she didn't know. "I guess."

And after all, there was a great deal she liked about him: the shine of his skin, the spareness of his waist, the certain knowledge that it would take nothing at all to arouse him, that he was here and waiting, that he was, for now, entirely in her hands. Had rolled over towards her hugely erect and was merely waiting, patiently, politely, for what the morning might offer. Adventure coming so easily, so young, that he felt no need to insist.

Such an apparent offer of uncomplicated pleasure that, despite the gathering feeling of unreality, despite too her unpleasantly furred teeth and tongue, Amanda rolled towards Cody, hugging him with her whole body, and kissed him.

Forty-five minutes later, tea on a rock in the broad flat sunshine, the dislocation resolved itself at least partly into exhaustion, physical and emotional: lack of sleep, restless sleep, a wobbly weakness to the thighs, but also a saturation. As if she had used up her capacity for words. Amanda had washed, in the partial privacy between the tent and the deadfall, rough cloth and cold water under which her flesh had momentarily seemed to congeal and gain strength. But now she was melting again, sweating already under mid-morning sun.

Cody didn't register visible change. He moved quietly around the fire, brewing and stirring, impaling slices of multigrain bread.

Dylan crawled out of his tent in boxy green swim trunks and rubber thongs, stood blinking and tossing back his hair. Longer legs than Cody, thinner all over, but, nearly naked like this, the same shimmer of extreme youth. And, Amanda saw, with surprise at herself rather than Dylan, the same beauty. She had not looked at Dylan before, had scarcely given him any thought. Now she saw that Cody wasn't going to stand between her and anything. His body wasn't going to block out any view of the world. Rather, it might be having, so far, the opposite effect, bringing the world into sharper and sharper focus.

"Nick's gone down to the village," said Dylan. "Get some groceries. They're going to hear about the land-use report today. Maybe."

"We need some more bread," said Cody. "I should put in for some rice, too."

"He's getting that," said Dylan.

"What happens with the report?" said Amanda. Dylan didn't appear to be registering any change at all between her and Cody. Either none was visible, or he didn't care, took such things entirely in stride. Might, she thought a moment later, have assumed Amanda and Cody were lovers all along. Closed or open secret, either way, consciousness of the past night flooded her now as delicious complication, the new subtle complexity of her life here.

"The report," said Dylan. "Well, it could say go ahead and log. That's kind of what we're expecting, right? Or it could ban logging, make a wilderness preserve. Then the lumber companies would probably go to court and appeal. But actually none of it is law until the legislature passes it. Then the companies can still sue for compensation. Or they can say fuck it and see if they get fined."

"Right," said Amanda.

"If it says go ahead, shit comes down right away," said Dylan. "They're going to march right in. If it says stop, then there'll be a bit of a breather."

"You figure it's going to say go ahead," said Amanda. She had heard all this before, or variations, around the campfire last night. But she wanted to keep Dylan hanging there, so naked and sweetly oblivious in the hot white morning, a possibility newly revealed, though she'd never act on it.

"Sounds like it," said Dylan.

"Nick should get those other guys to come down from town," said Cody.

"I think he's going to," said Dylan.

Cradling her tin cup, Amanda relaxed into the sunshine, into the ease of incomprehension.

Afternoon, the long hot drowse. The past night with Cody did not seem to have altered his day, his behaviour or routine. He had sat around the tent, sat by Amanda, most of the morning. Now he faded out, was not in sight up on the rocks of the clearcut or down by the barricade. Amanda had given little thought to his movements since the first few days on the beach, while she had been sliding into his routine. Cody appeared and he disappeared; until now, not a problem. This afternoon, however, Amanda had a foretaste of unease. Earlier, she had wanted solitude, waking in the rumpled blankets, and even, in flashes, while sitting on the rock at breakfast. Now, however, she felt lost, uprooted, unprotected. Soon she would want him again; that was already evident. At the moment she didn't, but this saturation or satiation left her dazed, left her oddly bored and restless. Self-conscious, too, as if the night were written on her face.

Forcing movement, Amanda crawled into her own tent, took out her camera and changed to a telephoto lens. If the logging trucks and the police did arrive tomorrow, she might well get her best shots a little away from the action; she would walk the road today, and plan some vantage-points.

The long lens pulled at her neck as Amanda scuffed down

the dirt track; she held the camera clear of brambles as she climbed a few feet onto a log in the clearcut, and focused experimentally on the tin hut. Then she hopped back to the road, walking downhill under the raging sun.

At the bottom, near the barricade and the charred sticks of the last bonfire, Amanda turned to see Suri, Chelsea and the black Labrador ambling towards her in the heat haze. She had not sought out the girls before; they had seemed peripheral, caught up in their own friendship, less tuned than the boys to the realities of politics and strategy. Nonetheless, watching them approach, she felt a rush of warmth. She had accepted, until now, her status as watcher and recorder, as outsider. But perhaps that was shifting.

"Wait," she said happily. "I should get a picture of you guys like that."

"No," said Suri. Chelsea dropped back behind her.

"You guys look really great, though," said Amanda, raising her camera.

"No," said Suri. "That's what we've got to talk to you about." Her voice was newly tense; her sentences rose tightly, like questions.

"Fine," said Amanda. "No problem." She lowered her camera.

"No, I think it is a problem?" said Suri. "I think it's a really big problem? Because nobody asked us about this."

"No, it's okay," said Amanda. "I'm not going to take your picture. No sweat."

"It's totally bigger than that," said Suri. "It's not just this one time. It's this whole thing with the camera. Taking pictures everywhere. I mean like no one said you could."

"I talked about it with Jason," said Amanda, truthfully. "I talked about it with Cody and Dylan and Greg," she added. This was not, strictly speaking, true, but they had raised no complaints. "I talked about it the first night when I arrived at the beach." This was not at all true, though it was what Amanda knew she should have done.

"But it wasn't brought to the whole collective," said Suri. "We never discussed it as a group. We never said you could."

"It's no problem," said Amanda carefully. "I won't take any more photos of you if you don't want me to. Just say no."

"It's totally a bigger issue than that," said Suri. "It's about whether we want anyone from outside in here photographing us."

"I feel totally violated if someone takes my picture without asking," said Chelsea. "It's like someone's attacked me."

"It is, kind of," said Amanda, pleasantly. "I know how you feel." This was the discussion, more or less, she had expected to initiate, manipulate, and win weeks ago, when she first met Jason and Cody. Taken off guard, Amanda was aware that she could only be on the defensive, but that it was disastrous to react defensively. Refuse to engage, refuse to rise to the bait, to argue. "I certainly don't want to make people uncomfortable."

"It's that, but it's way more," said Suri. "I've been talking to people. It's like what's happening with the television station. There's this film that the cops are after so they can decide to lay charges."

"Maybe," said Amanda. "They have to go to court."

"They can subpoena anything they want," said Suri.

"I don't see how it relates."

"It's totally the same thing," said Suri. "That's what I'm trying to say. When the cops see you taking photos they'll seize your negatives. Then they'll use them in court."

"I won't hand them over," said Amanda.

"You don't have a choice," said Suri.

"I could burn them if it came to that," said Amanda. "Or bury them in the back yard."

"Then they get you for contempt of court," said Suri. "You go to jail."

"So what is it I'm hearing you say?" said Amanda.

"Like the whole collective has to reach consensus on this," said Suri. "You can't just walk around taking pictures of all kinds of stuff."

"But ultimately it's going to help enormously," said Amanda. "If we do this gallery exhibition. You're going to get enormous support."

"It's not worth the risk," said Suri.

"I just feel completely unsafe if someone's pointing a camera at me," said Chelsea. "It's like you're really attacking me."

"But I've come up specially to do this," said Amanda. "I've taken time off work. It's all been agreed with the gallery." She recognized as she spoke that these were weak, useless, even dangerous arguments: not credentials, but markers of outsider status, her commitment to the larger world.

"But nobody talked about it with us," said Suri.

"I was up last week and no one said anything."

"That's because we didn't know what you were doing," said Suri.

"I thought it was all worked out," said Amanda.

"It wasn't."

"Obviously there has been a misunderstanding," said Amanda.

"Obviously," said Chelsea.

"You're right," said Amanda. "I really hear where you're coming from. This is something the collective really should discuss." Mirror Suri's language back at her: pre-emptive solutions. "When can we have a meeting and vote?"

"We don't vote," said Suri. "We go by consensus. Everyone has to agree, and anyone can veto a decision."

"Oh really?" said Amanda. Vistas of immense time and effort were opening before her, visions of boredom and anger, too. "Well, we certainly need a meeting. When can that happen?" she said as cheerfully as she could.

"Whenever. I don't know, exactly," said Suri. "We usually have them on Saturday. We could have an emergency meeting. But some of the core collective are in Victoria right now."

"The loggers might come in before we discuss this," said Amanda.

"Totally," said Suri. "Absolutely."

"So what should I do then?"

"We've just been telling you," said Suri. "There's totally a problem here."

"You want me not to take photos," said Amanda.

"That's sort of what's at issue," said Suri.

"Maybe we'll have a meeting first," said Amanda.

Walking back up the hill, Amanda saw Chance. He was squatting by the side of the road, immobile in the heat. He watched her pass.

Completely exhausted, Amanda crawled into her own tent and fell on the sleeping bag. The heat surrounded her like a fist clenching. The anger she was choking back, breathing out, letting settle, was as much at herself as at anyone. She had foreseen this, at the very beginning. Could she say Jason had betrayed her?

Yes, no, maybe. She had known better, she had known what to do, and she hadn't done it.

There were various strategies. Argue brilliantly and convince the collective, whenever it finally convened. Or busily gather support here and there among the campers. Campaign.

These responses occurred to her first. As she sank into the heat of the day, it also struck Amanda that if the collective had never formally permitted her photography, it had also never formally banned it. Of course, Suri and Chelsea could make it uncomfortable enough for her. But if the police arrived tomorrow, who would stop her, in the heat of the moment, from snapping away?

And what about the possibility of subpoena and incrimination? Surely, thought Amanda, she could outwit that if the time came. Of course she would never burn her negatives. But surely they could disappear, or she could be a test case, with the lawyer from the Civil Liberties Association. Immense publicity, that would bring. Immense.

Under heat and exhaustion, logic began to break and shimmer, geometric non sequiturs, until, with a rush, Amanda tumbled into sleep.

Amanda woke in the changed light of late afternoon, thick with sleep, unrefreshed. She lay heavily on her sleeping bag, soaked in heat, wet with it, the tilting sun elongating fronds of fireweed across the roof of her tent. Last night, this morning, this afternoon, seemed an age away, everything altered and difficult. If she sat up, pushed her hair off her face, crawled out to the flat evening light of the road, she would meet Cody. Suri. Chance. Chelsea. She would have to talk, exert herself. Meanwhile, through the nylon walls, a mere scarf or curtain between Amanda and the world, came voices near and distant, laughter, car doors opening and closing, a dog barking, more laughter downhill. Life was proceeding out there, while here she lay, pinned to the ground by fatigue and by a glimmer of disgust.

Sitting up in the stale tent took an effort of will. But the air on the road was surprisingly cool, in comparison: a fitful breeze, the easing tension of sunset. Surprisingly colourless, pale, restful, compared to the hot flood of orange light through nylon. Cody was sitting by the fire, stirring dinner in a blackened pot. He looked up and smiled, he moved over to give her room on the rock beside him.

"I slept for ever," said Amanda. "I guess I was tired."

"I didn't want to wake you up," said Cody.

In her current mood, simultaneously numbed and tentative, his statement struck Amanda as touching: he had looked for her, had made a decision not to wake her. All evidence of, perhaps, more interest and consideration than she had been attributing to him, lying minutes ago in the haze of heat.

"Did you take off this afternoon?" she said.

"Dylan wanted to pick up some gear he stashed on the beach. We thought we'd just be a few minutes. It ended up taking all day."

"Did you go swimming?"

"Yeah. It was great. You should have come."

"I didn't know you guys were going."

"It was kind of last minute."

The flickering breeze, in itself like swimming, clouds curdling above the rim of the mountain. The heat was dropping away from Amanda, leaving her weightless, silver.

"When does the collective meet?" she said.

"The collective?" said Cody. "I don't know. Whenever. Bob's been away a long time. If he comes up here he breaks bail."

"This was something Suri was saying," said Amanda. She had not yet made up her mind whether to fight publicly for some kind of permission, the honourable route, or merely to pretend that afternoon's conversation had never happened.

"Suri's into organizing meetings and stuff," said Cody. "She's really political."

"Yeah," said Amanda.

"She's really sharp with that kind of stuff."

"She was saying something about me taking photos," said Amanda. "She didn't like it."

"Oh yeah? She probably wouldn't."

"Why so?"

"I don't know," said Cody. "You know."

"I guess," said Amanda. "She said the collective should be voting on it."

"The collective? I guess it could. I don't know when it's going to meet."

"Sounds like the loggers will be here before the collective meets," said Amanda.

"You think so?" said Cody.

"Wasn't Dylan saying?"

"That was before. That report got released today. So they're holding off."

"The land-use report came down?" said Amanda. "What did it say? Are they making a park?"

"No. They're going to do another study. So the logging company has to wait for that. So they're going to start hearings or something next month."

"So they're not going to log until that's over?"

"Nick talked to Jase and it's sort of all up in the air."

News which, later, around the campfire, ate up the evening. Amanda approached nervously, expecting challenge from Suri or the spreading sphere of her influence. But nobody mentioned photography, subpoenas, assault charges. The land-use report, the upcoming protest in Victoria, changes and shifts and delays and half-victories, took up the evening. Sitting back beside Cody, Amanda watched Suri for the first time. Was it only Amanda's anxiety, or was the girl really front and centre now, holding forth, did she really wield much more power, socially, politically, than Amanda had assumed? Or was it merely some reverberation of the afternoon's argument, leaving both of them hyper-attuned, Suri to further assertion or aggression, Amanda to reticence?

Whatever it was, Amanda was beginning to find everything weighing on her, the looping speculations, her own unease. Escape would be the opposite: the private, the personal. And it was that, escape more than desire, that led her fingers, teasing, teasing, to play under the hem of Cody's T-shirt. Fingers up his backbone, out of sight, playing the little knobs of his vertebrae, while he chatted across the fire with Dylan. Of course, if she wanted solitude, Amanda had only to stand up, say good-night, walk up the road to her tent. Cody would follow later, perhaps. But she didn't want solitude. She didn't want company, the group, and she didn't particularly want sex, either. She didn't want anything or she wanted to be lifted out, remade, redeemed. Fingers now slipping lower, sliding, experimenting. Until Cody's hand slid down to her own thigh, until they stood up and backed into the shadows, and walked up the hill together.

In the morning, flat grey light, cloud cover, colours quenched, and a chill steady breeze, the threat of rain. If Greg drove into the village and left the car with the mechanic, Amanda and Cody could follow and pick him up, drive him back to camp. They could find Jason, they could get some news, they could buy some food. Another gust of wind, fine spit of drizzle.

"Great idea," said Amanda.

An hour west on logging roads and another hour on tarmac, a two-lane highway along the rim of the ocean, pale light welling up behind the shore pines. Then, early afternoon, the road sloping fast to a small harbour, dark water under rounded mountains, low clouds, frame houses, gently rocking spires of fishing boats, empty streets.

Greg was waiting out of the rain, on the front porch of a small house. Behind, in a lighted garage, sat his old Datsun station wagon with the hood flung open.

"Jase is up at this other guy's house," he said. "The kayak guy. Tim."

The rain was coming down steadily now, slanting out of the west, driving against the windshield. Amanda followed directions out of town, and up the slope overlooking the ocean. Tim's house was suburban ranch, cedar-planked, new. Out front sat a trailer loaded with kayaks bottoms up, red and yellow fibreglass hulls slick with rain against the dim forest. Inside, a wall of glass doors opened onto a wooden deck, and a sheer drop to black rock and spume, dull distant surge and roar. The horizon was invisible, grey water blending into grey sky, the heaving Pacific leached today of colour and life.

Tim turned out to run a business doing tours and rentals, whale watching and canoe camping into the national park. Hugh's age maybe, but with a sunburned blond beard, leather face, keyed up and friendly. He was sitting with Jason at the dining-room table. Amanda dropped her day pack in the corner, and pulled up a chair. Tim got up to make her espresso coffee in a hissing little electric steamer that sat on the countertop.

"There's a leak in the water line," said Greg.

"Kirb'll get it done," said Jason. "Kirb's an excellent mechanic."

"You got Kirb working on it," said Tim, from the kitchen. "Right on. He'll do it."

"Or it could be a problem with the coolant," said Greg. "That's what Kirb was saying."

A gust of rain hit the glass doors. Amanda felt, or perhaps merely imagined, the ghost of a draft knifing past the weather-stripping, a chill.

"It could be the coolant," said Tim. "For sure. Or the rad." He set cup and saucer in front of Amanda. "It's Nicaraguan dark roast," he said. "From this co-operative down there."

"Thanks," said Amanda. Fatigue and dislocation, but coming more strongly than ever, fatigue outlining colours, tracing shapes vividly. She warmed her fingers on the hot cup, still feeling in her bones the jolt and rattle of the morning's drive. She did not want to stand up. She did not want to go back outside, squinting into the cold needles of the rain.

"It might be the rad," said Greg. "For sure."

Cody came back from the bathroom and went out on the deck. When he slid the doors back, a gust of rainfresh air swooped like a trapped bird around the dining room. He closed the doors behind himself, and stood hanging over the rail, engrossed in something or nothing below.

"I bet it's the rad," said Jason. "If it isn't the coolant it's the rad."

Amanda sat with her back to Cody, her back to the grey ocean, and drank her coffee, sip by bitter sip.

Two hours later Everett arrived. By then they were already drinking beer. The rain had set in chill and solid, mist smudging the tips of the hemlocks on the cliff above the house. Everett's jacket was dripping, his hair soaked to his scalp.

"I'll build up the fire," said Tim, sliding open the glass screen of the fireplace. "I'll turn on the fan."

"How does that work?" said Greg.

"It goes by convection," said Tim. "It heats the whole house."

"How long does a cord of wood last?" said Greg.

"You're back up here," said Amanda to Everett. "Have a beer."

"I will, thanks. In a minute." Everett had hung his jacket by the door. Now he was sitting on the hearth, rubbing his hands and tousling his hair. "We're doing a feature on alternatives to the resource industry. Tourism. Bed and breakfasts. Hotels."

"Kayak rentals," said Amanda.

"Exactly," said Everett. "You knew Tim before in Vancouver,

didn't you?"

"No," said Amanda.

"Ecotourism is really going to take off," said Jason. "It's a sustainable industry."

"We had to turn groups away this summer," said Tim. "We're booked right up."

"The federation is pushing for a government grant for re-training in the service industry," said Jason.

"Though I can see why the loggers would get upset," said Amanda. "You go from a union job in the mill to waiting tables for minimum wage."

"For sure people are going to have to be flexible," said Jason.

"Our tour guides do all right," said Tim. "They work on a bonus commission system. We tried at the beginning to get local people. But it didn't work out. Now we hire a lot of university students in the summer."

"That's excellent," said Jason. "Job creation."

"You look pretty wet," said Amanda.

"Soaked," said Everett. "It's going to be coming down for the next week at least."

"You find it works better than an airtight stove," said Greg.

"Absolutely," said Tim.

"It looks like the logging company is holding off until the hearings," said Amanda. "It looks like we'll go down to Victoria for the protest at the legislature this weekend."

"Not great weather to be camping on the blockade," said Everett.

"No. Not really."

An hour later they had opened the second case of beer.

"See," Greg was saying, "what the logging company is doing is playing this waiting game. They figure we're going to get bored. They figure they can wait us out."

"Exactly," said Jason. "They figure we'll pack up and go home."

"We have to up the ante," said Greg. "We have to really make our point."

"How are you going to do that?" said Everett.

"The federation is totally behind nonviolent civil disobedience," said Jason.

"For sure. That too," said Greg. "But there's going to be direct action. There's going to be violence. You can feel it. People are getting really pissed off at being dicked around. There's this total level of frustration building. It's a powder keg out there."

"That's true," said Amanda. "I've been at the camp all week and there's definitely a different mood than before." She would not have reached Greg's conclusions on her own, true. But as he spoke and she replied, the size and truth of his statement loomed up before her as tangible as a tree or a mountain, and as undeniable. The headiness of facing the truth, the real and dangerous truth. She was finishing her third beer.

"The federation can't support violence," said Jason.

"This is stuff that would be spontaneous," said Greg. "It's not like it's anything anyone is planning. It's more like a mood. An uprising. Everyone getting prepared for when it starts going down."

"And you'll be there with your camera," said Everett. "On the scene." The tenor of their conversation seemed to have shifted once again, back towards Amanda's first perception, two or three weeks earlier, of his unexpected envy and admiration. Of the end of their last conversation, the undercurrents of irritation and competition so long ago in the hot sun beside Jason's truck, she had now only the faintest memory. Envy and admiration, then, and something else, some warmth.

"Oh, absolutely," said Amanda. "That's going really well." Watching him watch her was almost as if she stepped back and watched herself watching herself; this she dimly perceived. He was a witness, he had known her for ever, he knew how far she'd come. So that impressing him was merely a more circuitous route towards impressing herself, acknowledging her own value. The logic of this came immediately as inspiration; it was not worked through. Amanda drained her beer and reached for her fourth bottle, flicked the lid.

A moment later she found herself saying, "The photos are going really well. But now that it's all set up I'm getting this weird kind of flak from some of the people at the camp."

"Oh really?" said Everett.

"Who from?" said Greg.

"It's not such a big deal," said Amanda. Mistily she remembered that she had not yet decided how to proceed, had more than half decided anyhow to ignore the issue. "It probably wasn't a big deal."

"Who was giving you flak?" said Jason. "That's such a drag."

"It's no big deal," Amanda said. "It was just Suri and Chelsea. They were saying it hadn't been approved by the collective."

"It was approved, wasn't it?" said Jason. "It went to the collective."

"I don't know," said Greg. "The collective hasn't met in ages. What are the photos for, anyhow?"

"We were going to do this exhibit at this little gallery in Gastown. Then maybe for this book. That guy David that did the interviews last year."

"David's great," said Jason.

"Sounds all right," said Greg. "What was Suri saying to you?"

"Nothing, really," said Amanda. "It wasn't such a big deal." By now she badly wanted to bail out of the conversation. Sober she would have been able to prevaricate, perhaps, been able to steer and jump to safety. Sober, of course, she would never have headed anywhere near the topic. At the moment she perceived that safety existed, some calm backwater of platitudes and distraction. But she could not imagine how to reach it, could not imagine how to proceed in any direction but dead ahead, over the rapids. She braced herself. "It was just this idea Suri had," Amanda added. "She was worried if I took shots of action, the cops could get them and use them in court. I said she was being silly, but. You know."

"Like at the television station," said Everett. "That's going to court, actually."

"Of course it's totally different," said Amanda. "I told her all that. But she was still going on that it had to go to the collective."

"It probably should," said Greg. "Suri's really up on all that stuff."

"But we don't really have time," said Amanda. "The collective. If it never meets. If it's not really functioning." She collected her wits enough to backtrack. "I mean, I totally agree that it ought to go the collective if that's what people want. I totally think that's important."

"I never thought about that and the cops seizing photos," said Jason.

"I would never give them to them," said Amanda. "I'd burn them first. We could go to court. Test case."

"I can see where it would be a problem," said Jason.

"Only it's not going to happen," said Amanda.

Tim came in from the kitchen carrying a wire basket full of steamed prawns. "We get these right off this guy's boat," he said. "They're fresh today."

"This is amazing," said Amanda. "This is wonderful." She served herself, and started peeling. Up close the prawns were dramatically, even disturbingly anatomically complete. Black blind cooked eyes, antennae like some super cockroach, curled little insect legs that disintegrated under her fingers as she tugged and snapped. The pink tails did not break cleanly from the inedible torso; her plate was soon stained with dark traces of intestine and bowel. "Delicious," she said. Little faces on her plate, complete with little mouths. What did prawns eat: plankton? Algae? This meal, delicacy that it was, did not bear too much scrutiny. The only possible approach was to be unabashedly ogreish.

Cody had drifted back to the table. Vegan, he was making a meal of brown bread and salad. He had been quiet on the drive from camp, and silent since Everett arrived. Now he sat hunched up at the far end of the dining-room table, looking uncomfortable and extremely young, a child silenced at a dinner party. Bolting his food. Not repulsively; he was making no audible noise, neither chewing open-mouthed nor hunching over his plate. But he was eating fast, efficiently, the way he ate over the campfire: stoke the body and get on with the task at hand. Young and uncomfortable and a long way away, down the wrong end of the binoculars. Amanda did not know how to reach him, and did not at the moment care.

No. That was not true. She knew exactly how to reach him, she knew exactly how you went about making a friend, a lover, feel at ease. You drew him into the conversation, you went and sat beside him, you asked him questions, asked him how he was feeling. You went into the kitchen and searched for some more substantial dinner than bread and lettuce, some tasty alternative protein source. Amanda knew all the things she could do, should do, watching Cody down there at the end of the table, head bowed. She knew these things, and she chose not to do them. Or rather, as she put it to herself, the situation chose for her. Because, topping up her wineglass, she saw how long it had been since she'd had a chance to really sparkle in company. She had never sparkled around the campfire, certainly, neither young nor audacious enough. But tonight, undivided attention seemed hers for the asking.

This conviction had been growing while she talked about Suri, when, despite discomfort and risk, Amanda had registered with pleasure that the eyes of everyone in the room were on her. And, in fact, in order to repair that breach of discretion, she needed more attention. Needed to charm and delight them into truly trusting her. If she sulked away into a corner with Cody, she was losing a valuable opportunity. Behind this lay the realization, hazier because less admissible, that she was charming and delightful just to the extent that she seemed attached to no one. And really, was she attached to Cody? Did the two nights she had spent in his tent constitute a relationship, an affair, anything with public weight or status? If she went and sat beside Cody, jollied him out of his slump, the group would dissolve, the men would turn to each other, she'd no longer be the focus. Tim would start talking about storm-cladding, Greg about his car, Jason about government grants; no one would look at her again.

This knowledge flashed past as she peeled a prawn, as she sipped her wine, as she watched herself wax richly witty. Cody could, Cody should, take care of himself.

After supper there was Everett's bottle of good Scotch whisky, on ice in front of the fireplace. Quite a bit later there was general commotion and bustle as Tim dragged blankets and sleeping bags into the living room, Amanda standing a bit stupidly by, aware that her nose and chin were numb. Eventually she lay in the dark beside, but not touching, Cody. When she closed her eyes the floor dipped away like the island ferry in a stiff chop. Her mouth flooded with saliva; she swallowed, felt the warning bite of stomach acid rising in her throat and bolted for the bathroom. With the door locked, trying to mute her gags and retches, horribly ashamed, Amanda vomited whisky and wine and beer, prawns and bread and salad. Little legs and antennae, little eyes, in the soup of the toilet bowl. Her head kept spinning against the cold pink porcelain, her stomach clenching empty on itself, her throat seared and burning. Finally she washed out her mouth and stumbled back into the dim living room, the reddish glow from the patented fireplace, burning logs, and the dark logs of Cody and Greg sleeping, or pretending to.

Amanda woke late the next morning, in a living room full of the cold grey glare of rain and ocean. The other bags and blankets were gone; the house seemed vacant. She sat up and the room spun; she stood and it tilted alarmingly. In the kitchen she found a drip pot of coffee on the back burner and drank it: scorched. Headache, stomach ache, bleak misery, the evening's pleasure evaporating as evanescent as mist, and as unrecallable. She had not been that drunk, she had not been sick, for years, for a decade. Whatever it had meant back then, whatever transgression or adventure or risk it had once represented, now, in the cold grey light of her thirty-third year, it was only sordid and deeply embarrassing.

After a while Greg and Cody came in, looking fresh and rested, healthy and rain-spangled. Amanda drove back downhill to the garage, dropped off Greg and drove with Cody the two hours back to camp. The rain had lightened but was still falling steadily; under the bridges on the logging road, newly swollen creeks raged dull brown. At camp there were fewer tents; some people had returned to the beach, others to town. Rivulets and creeklets ran down the rutted track, down the stripped slopes of the clearcut, where the fireweed was pounded slantwise by the rain.

Amanda's tent was sagged and sodden, water pooling in the creases, her sleeping bag damp at the edges where it lay against the nylon wall. Cody rigged up a tarpaulin and brought out a tiny gas cookstove. Amanda huddled in this inadequate shelter. Her headache was receding but she felt unutterably weary; her skin and muscles ached and she lacked all volition, all possibility of movement and action. Cody, on the other hand, was coming alive again, moving with ease between the stove and the tent, unbothered by the rain, by the big hood of his rubber coat, by the red chill of his fingers.

"Tim must be really making money," he said. "He sure has a huge house."

"It was all right," said Amanda. Tim's house was newer, cleaner, larger and better furnished than any place she had rented herself, as an adult. But it was smaller than the house she had grown up in, less substantial also than the one she dimly imagined awaited her future, once the pieces of her life fell into place.

"He owns it," said Cody. "It's actually his own house."

"Land's pretty cheap out here," said Amanda.

"He started that whole business himself. Now he's got five

guys working for him. And he owns all those kayaks out front. Good boats."

"I guess he's doing okay," said Amanda. Tim did not particularly interest her. At the moment nothing particularly interested her, sitting hunched up immersed in bodily misery. Today, under the sodden blanket of clouds, the fate of being tied to a fishing village at the edge of the continent for the sake of an ordinary house and an ordinary income seemed a wilfully perverse exile. "I guess he likes it out here," she added. Of course she had thought, in flashes, about a cabin in the bush. But that constituted limited and focused escape, rejuvenation, a species of retreat. The village did not promise dramatic solitude; Tim's business appeared rather to require the opposite, a gregariousness she found, now, exhausting even to imagine. And he couldn't get away. He had no choice, no future, no possibility of returning to the city. "He's kind of stuck out here," she said now. "Isn't he."

"I guess," said Cody. "I didn't really think of it like that."

There was no campfire that night. Amanda crawled early into Cody's tent, which was pitched on higher ground than her own, and somewhat drier. Inside the penetrating chill of the nylon sleeping bag she curled up shivering in all her clothes, in her damp wool socks. She had missed the chance of showering at Tim's house, and had not undressed for thirty-six hours; her T-shirt was gummed to her back, her sweater smelled of smoke and beer and wet sheep.

A disgust, an exhaustion, with the body and all its possibilities. And yet, when Cody came in quite a bit later, Amanda was all over him immediately. Not desire, exactly, but some equally exigent demand for comfort, for contact, for the warmth of human skin. If he was surprised, he didn't say so; he kissed her back. The part of herself that was sitting back watching was aware of the element of performance, aware and applauding. It was good, this imitation of desire, it was skilled and talented. She was pushing things, keeping one step ahead, pressing him down on the air mattress, skinning out of her own jeans, unzipping his army pants, shoving up his sweater, then his T-shirt, to bare his smooth young chest. And really, here in the light of the candle-lantern, his body was astoundingly beautiful, the shine of it emerging from the dimness of khaki drab and rough blankets. Astoundingly beautiful just when she couldn't really desire it, substituting this ravishment bordering on hysteria.

She knelt above Cody, straddling his body. He was naked from collarbone to mid-thigh, his clothes pushed up and pulled down, revealing only what was strictly necessary. The flat blossoms of his nipples hardened, ripened, into berries under her tongue. He was gasping, melting, giving way, arching up towards her, his face turned sideways, lost in the blankets. She leaned lower and traced with her tongue the line of furze down his belly, circling over the very soft skin below his tan line. Teasing now, playing, drawing things out, precisely aware of where he lay erect and wet and waiting against his belly, precisely aware and just skimming, missing. He tilted his hips towards her, his breath a short hiss of pain. Amanda pulled back for a moment, fingers idle at the top of his thighs, and looked down at him. Face turned and lost, limbs tangled invisible under heavy clothes and blankets, and the bared stretch of torso, pale in candlelight, replicating the pose of some ruined statue. The self, the soul, escaping into ecstasy. As she could not, it seemed, not tonight. For a moment Amanda hung there above him, hovering between admiration and a wisp of jealous rage at the ease with which he could give himself away. Mixed, however, with pride: pride at her own performance, evoking this passion.

The body like the torso of a broken statue, save for one detail, the erection huge and swollen red, the pulsing vein, another order of being unrelated to the pale skin on which it rested. As if it had been merely tossed against his body and lay where it fell. A rubber toy, a joke novelty, or no, thought Amanda. Something from the ocean, unfolding in the crevices of a tide pool. She leaned down and put him in her mouth: salt and sex, the exact flavour of the sea. His gasps were of assent, relief. After a moment she slid back up his chest, and lay nose to nose on top of him. He reached for her, fumbling as if surfacing from sleep, reciprocating, trying to touch her. Amanda ignored that, pushing his hands away from her thighs as she tilted him upwards and slid him inside her. She was not yet wet or relaxed enough, and she forced herself down on top of him, feeling him enter at an odd and slightly uncomfortable angle. He did not resist, or insist on her pleasure; he came quickly, extravagantly, gasps and moans and his body convulsing against hers.

After that they lay side by side, companionably. Cody was

soon asleep. Amanda, despite fatigue, lay awake. Not foiled desire, not that frustration, though now that it was over, finished, she could feel muted stirrings of excitement, numbed and distant. She was fairly certain that if she let Cody sleep for an hour, she could wake him ready and willing to concentrate on her. But she did not want that, would not do that. What did she want? Warmth and attention, companionship and understanding, some rounded and complete token of success, of recognition? Amanda could put no name to the lack, knew only that the antidote existed nowhere on this blasted and ruined mountainside, nowhere on this rainswept island.

She lay inert the next morning, playing dead after waking to Cody stirring beside her, pulling up his pants crouched away from the touch of wet tent. After that she slept heavily and late, struggling back into her own clothes a little before noon.

The road outside the tent was a brown churn of mud, running with water, but the clouds were paler, the rain diminished to a fine drizzle. There were fewer tents and cars, and the barricade was pulled to one side, tossed back into the slash heap on the slope. Bleak and anonymous, a back road anywhere, under the thick white sky.

Cody was standing with Greg and Dylan down by the junction, beside the tin trailer. It tilted perceptibly on its foundations; weeds and young alder sprouted around the blocks. The doors and windows were nailed shut.

"We could always go in there and dry off," said Dylan.

"Could," said Greg. "Locked up pretty tight."

"Hello," said Cody. "We're thinking of heading back down to the beach tonight. Then we can hit the demo in Victoria tomorrow."

"Sounds good," said Amanda.

Packing wet tent in damp knapsack was difficult and unpleasant. Amanda had left her car at the foot of the hill the night before, below the barricade. She did not want to try driving up now, hazarding mud and ruts. Indeed, a little way down, at this very moment, Dylan and Greg were rocking Chance's van from behind, revving engine and spinning tires, shouting commands. If she could drive up to her campsite, Amanda would thrust everything into the hatchback, unpacked, unsorted. As it was, she needed to pack for the walk downhill. In the end she balanced her knapsack on a boulder out of the mud, and fought with the wet shroud of the collapsed tent, dirt and water on her hands and face.

An hour later, as she crossed the brook and stepped up on the silver hulk of a beach log, the surge and white light of the ocean hit her like a dream of space and peace. With Greg and Dylan, she followed Cody down to his glade behind the shore pines, and pitched camp.

Alone, Amanda went back out of the glade, and down the beach. No one was visible, no tents or dogs or distant figures, just a few trails of thin smoke from inland behind the bushes, pale against the rise of fir and hemlock. In front of her, the tide was receding over the hard rippled flats, grey water on grey sand, out to a grey horizon. As she walked she let her mind fall empty as the day. At the north end of the cove, as far as possible from the campers, she climbed partway up a granite cliff, giant barnacles smashing underfoot, colonies of huge blue mussels, dankly bearded, and the surprising purple splay of oversized starfish glued to the wet undersides of cliffs. Above the waterline she settled into a grassy nest beneath twisted red arbutus. Out of the wind it was warmer. Leaning back against the cliff, she drifted near or into sleep, letting time slide.

She woke to a flurry of rain against her face, blowing off the ocean; the sky was darker. Down on the beach again, the wind buffeted her; in the distance, the low tide smashed in plumes and geysers. By the time she reached the glade, the thighs of her jeans were soaked to the skin. The wind penetrated even here, behind the shore pines, flapping the wet tents on their guy lines. The fire was out.

"It's going to blow all night," said Dylan. "There's a gale warning for Juan de Fuca Strait."

"We've got to get an early start anyways for the rally," said Greg.

"We're going to get soaked down here," said Dylan.

"We're going to fucking blow out to sea," said Greg. "It's going to be a fucking hurricane out there."

"Makes sense just to go up and sleep in the cars tonight," said Cody.

For the second time that day, Amanda wrestled with her wet and muddy tent, numb fingers tugging pegs, wrapping the stiff guy lines. The day was beginning to take on, for her, some of the dimensions of a forced march. And beneath that foot-soldier's blank obedience? She did not want to huddle on the beach through a gale, supperless, without coffee. She did not want, either, to tramp back up that steep path. She wanted to be lifted out of all this, lifted into sunshine or a hot shower. It did not occur to her that she could leave, now, that she had always been free to leave, that two hours would get her to a beachfront motel. She had to see things through to the end, to at least the rally in Victoria tomorrow, which she'd leave early to catch the ferry back to the mainland.

At the top of the cliff, by the parking lot and the trailhead, they strung a plastic tarp from the open back of Chance's van to a convenient young fir. Under this Cody built a small fire, set out his tiny stove and brewed a cookpot full of tea. The rain fell heavy and straight, pinging off the roof of the van, running off the tilt of the tarp. But the forest broke most of the wind, which sighed and creaked far above in the hemlocks.

As dark fell, Dylan and Greg, Suri and Chelsea, Amanda and Cody crowded into the back of Chance's van, sitting up against the side walls wrapped in sleeping bags and blankets. Down the centre of the van lay the Labrador retriever, his fur clumped with rain and mud, his heavy tail thwacking happily against their feet. Amanda did not want to be here, in Chance's van. However, there seemed no choice, at least until she left, with or without Cody, to sleep in the hatchback of her own car. Chance, at least, was paying no attention to her; likewise Suri or Chelsea.

"We got to do honour to Mother Earth," said Chance. "We got to fight for her with our bodies and our spirits. We've destroyed her. She's in pain, she's suffering."

Amanda glanced at Cody, wanting intensely a moment of shared skepticism, a raised eyebrow, an imperceptible twitch of the lip. But Cody's face was blank and serious.

"No one else is going to save her," said Chance. "We're the caretakers. We're the only ones who see."

"Absolutely," said Suri.

"When I think about what we're doing," said Chelsea. "The toxins. The sludge. It's like we're putting it into our own bodies when we put it into the ocean. It's like we're polluting ourselves."

"We have to totally re-evaluate all our priorities," said Suri.

"As a society. We have to organize around that. Tear everything down and start over. That's the only way we'll survive."

"See, we are part of her body," said Chance. "She gave birth to us. We owe her our lives. When we hurt her, we're hurting ourselves."

"We really are," said Chelsea.

"We need to come back out here," said Suri. "This is where we can really build community. Living off the land. This is where it will start."

"I'm not ever going back to live in the city," said Chelsea. "It's so totally false there. I feel like everyone's spitting on me. There's this total aggression."

Amanda leaned back against the wall of the van, in the shadows cast by the candle-lantern and by the fire burning outside. She read the mood tonight as elegiac, farewell to place and cause, but it was a parting warmth from which she felt entirely excluded. She could not, after all, pull out her camera and snap the gorgeous low-light photos that composed themselves around her: Chelsea's ardent face half lit, Dutch Renaissance tones, bright flesh emerging from shadows. As recording eye, Amanda sensed, she could have reduced the group to a study in youthful enthusiasm, the grace of the form outweighing the content. Reduced from active observer to passive participant, though, she felt sullenly alone. Wilful naivety all around, it seemed to her, on top of an inability to organize the simplest things in life. The futility of the past weeks came roaring at her like a creek in full flood, like surf, and knocked the ground from under her. Everything soiled and spoiled, failed and foul, the wrong place and time, her eternal inability to find the real shining centre of the world. To find anything worth doing, or worth doing well.

Amanda was the first to leave, ducking through the wet to her car, pulling open the door to flatten the back seats, crawl inside and curl in her sleeping bag. Rain close above her, drilling the roof of the car, patting the ground, trickling from bumper and bough, multilayered sound. When Cody crept in beside her, she woke from first sleep but, as that morning, lay still, keeping her breath level.

Shunting trains, the crash of containers on the waterfront, a single loud slam. Or so it seemed, waking Amanda from a tediously detailed dream, some strange and leafy city where she sat at a bar-café endlessly waiting for a cup of fresh coffee, and screaming in rage at the waitresses. When she had first moved to East Vancouver those waterfront explosions had jolted her awake in terror: propane tanks, spontaneous combustion at the wheat pool, evacuation and disaster. Fortunately she was used to them now, she knew they meant nothing. Confidently Amanda opened her eyes and saw first dawn, a hint of growing light, through the glass of the hatchback above her. All misted pale between the grid lines of the defroster. For a moment she was profoundly disoriented. The rain had stopped; it was profoundly still outside. Then, in the distance, she heard a raucous cawing of crows rising, disturbed, wheeling and complaining. After another moment she realized she was alone in the car. She leaned over, opened the door and peered out at the parking lot. The cars sat motionless, the windows steamed over, blind. Chance's van was gone. The dawn air hit her raw and biting, impossibly cold for summer. She slammed the door and huddled back down in her sleeping bag.

When she woke again, it seemed completely light, or as light as it would get, under cloud cover and hemlock. Cody had the passenger door flung open; she could hear voices outside, motors running.

"It's time to get going," he said. "If we want to hit the rally by noon."

Amanda reached for jeans and sweater, thrust her feet into her wet and muddy boots and stumbled out into the clearing. Cody handed her a cup of tea. Chance's van was parked and idling, the Labrador was sniffing in a concentrated way along the edge of the forest, Chelsea and Suri were in the front seat of the Volvo.

They pulled out in convoy onto the logging road, Amanda driving Cody and Dylan and the dogs. Ten minutes took them to the junction, to the ruins of the barricade.

The trailer was still smoking, broken open and twisted like a tin can, its spilled guts the charred ends of office chairs and papers.

"Boom boom," said Dylan.

"*Boom*," said Cody.

Dylan laughed.

"Holy shit," said Amanda.

"They can't exactly ignore that," said Dylan.

"It was abandoned anyhow," said Cody.

"You mean you guys," said Amanda, sharply aware that there was some protocol here which she would probably miss, some attitude she had to strike between being already and always supremely in the know, and being interested in the details. She did not think she would ever find the protocol. She felt deeply weary.

"Shit happens," said Dylan.

"It does," said Cody.

"It goes boom," said Dylan.

Cody laughed.

On waking, she had read Cody's mood, the mood of the camp, as anxious, businesslike, focused on arriving on time at the protest in Victoria. Now she saw how they were buoyed by great restrained glee. But it was not contagious. The bombed trailer impressed Amanda; she wished, as they jolted past, she had the courage to stop the car, to snap the wreck still smoking and steaming from every angle. More: she yearned to have captured the moment of impact, the tongue of flame or puff of smoke, the blurred movement. At the same time she wanted out of there, she wanted the boys out of there now, immediately, before anyone noticed the damage; she wanted them set down safely in the anonymity of the city. To stop and photograph the trailer would take the courage to defy Dylan and Cody, and Suri and Chelsea as well, who were following hard on her tail, the bouncing Volvo in her rearview mirror. To stop would also mean reckoning with her own fear, which evolved, as the slippery logging road uncoiled up and down hill, hour after hour, into a heartstopping conviction that around the next corner lay a police blockade, discreet arrest, disaster. And as she drove, she realized exactly what it would have meant to return home with a photo of the trailer twisted and smoking, clearly snapped hours or days in advance of the television crews.

Deep fear, then, gut-deep fear, while the boys sat suffused with joy. But the fear did not cancel her curiosity, or rather her curiosity was amplified by pride, pride foiled and thwarted. She had, in the end, not gotten backstage, or not to the real backstage, not to the heart of the action. If you were there, you knew how it went; if you weren't, you couldn't ask. She had learned that long ago, she had learned that with Everett and his friends, and the boy with whom she had been in love. And it still held true. All the years with Hugh slid away, play-acting, it now seemed, at trust and caring and adulthood. Who had she been back then, back at the start? This was who she had been, standing on the outside, looking in, yearning and craven.

They hit the smooth surface of the freeway without seeing another vehicle, and Amanda began to relax; it was impossible, now, to prove they had come from the direction of the beach, the junction, the trailer. Scattered frame houses and house trailers in the ragged forest, bush reclaiming failed farms carved out early in the century by settlers misled by the lushness of the vegetation. A mill yard, bright wet stacks of orange and yellow boards, the cone of the hogfuel burner drooping a low stream of smoke into the heavy air. "Boom," said Dylan happily. "That'd show them."

Late breakfast or early lunch in a diner advertising salmon-fishing charters. As they climbed out of the cars, Amanda saw all over again how clearly they were marked, here in this rainy little logging town. She walked into the restaurant keyed for confrontation. But the place was empty of customers, and the waitress served them without comment.

They rolled through the suburbs of Victoria shortly before noon, and down to the city centre and harbour promenade, the great grey gothic revival hulk of the provincial legislature. Sunday tourists with umbrellas, cab horses flop-eared in the drizzle, frilled skirts of hanging fuchsias in hanging baskets and, up on the wide steps, planted banners unfurled and the measured tones of amplified speech, of oration. The crowd was gathering, thickening, below. Campers like her companions, bush seasoned, with dreadlocks and sooted fingernails. Urban punks with multicoloured hair and high-laced boots, rings in noses and ears, eyebrows and lips. What Amanda thought of as variously environmentalists or hikers or old political activists, with scrubbed faces and expensive Gore-Tex jackets, neatly trimmed beards.

The protest unrolled more or less as she had imagined, no different from dozens of others she had attended and photographed. The wind caught snatches of words, pulled them past her, out to sea. *Will not stand for this devastation. Demand a moratorium. Last old-growth temperate rainforest in the north-*

west. She was free enough to take photos, as she did, for a while. But minus the heart of the action, the heart she had missed, they were pointless, no different from anything that would make the front page of tomorrow's newspaper. The punks with their black flag drooping in the rain. Bearded dad, toddler bundled up in her waterproof stroller, clutching a stuffed plush killer whale. Tourists, who had packed only white Bermuda shorts, shivering, puzzled and dubious, at the very back of the crowd.

Amanda left after an hour and a half, drove to the ferry terminal at Schwartz Bay and waited another hour and a half in a slow queue of traffic, finally easing up the wet hollow ramp into the parking deck. On the mainland, the freeway cut through sodden pasture and fields of light industry, arced over the lumber mills along the dull wide Fraser, and into the city past miles of low wooden houses, green lawns, wide streets, the scramble of stoplights and hissing traffic, too much confusion.

Her apartment was chill and musty; a week's laundry lay in a pile on the bedroom floor. Amanda took a hot bath and made an unsatisfactory meal of canned sardines, a bruised apple, peanut butter on soda crackers, capers and green olives. While she was lying on her bed trying to think of a good excuse with which to phone the personnel office at the college, she fell asleep.

"Everett said he was at a party with you on the island," said Lane.

"Oh really?" said Amanda. "Did he?" Very casual.

"He was telling me what happened to the photos. How the protesters didn't exactly go for the idea." Lane's voice over the telephone was level, too level, the kind of flatness that could hide amusement. Or worse.

"That wasn't really an issue," said Amanda, dead level back at him. "It was only one of the girls there, really."

"But it sounds like it didn't come off, at any rate."

"I got some good pictures, actually," Amanda said. "But no, not the ones of real action. Not the ones we kind of wanted at the core of the exhibit."

"That's too bad," said Lane, neutrally.

"Now it seems like it's on hold, permanently. What with the hearings and all. You know." Amanda was talking too much, explaining too much; she knew that. But Lane's mild silence on the other end of the line was deafening. "It was really incredibly chaotic out there. Quite frustrating."

"It sounds it," said Lane. "Looks like we picked the wrong spot all right. I don't know if you've seen the papers. About ten miles away they were chaining themselves to trees two days ago. Different bunch, I think. Great media coverage."

We picked? thought Amanda spitefully, childishly. You sent me there. Aloud she said, "Win some, lose some."

"I guess," said Lane.

"They really were incredibly disorganized," she said, a bit more emphatically. Outside her living-room window, late summer held full sway, intense heat with a weary edge.

"So it sounded from what Everett told me."

"Oh really? What did he say, then?" She should not be asking, she knew that before she spoke; she knew enough at any rate to keep her voice level, betray no need. At least she thought she had.

"Oh, nothing much. Very much what you said." Lane wasn't giving anything away. "You must drop in if you're down in Gastown. We can go for coffee or something." This was not an invitation, as far as Amanda could tell; it was dismissal. His voice was so distant she knew she'd never again climb the stairs to the back office looking out over the polished floor of the gallery.

"For sure," she said.

After she hung up the phone, she walked up to Hastings Street for milk and eggs at the convenience store. In the vacant lot across from her house, the tall grass had headed out to long-haired seeds; the leaves on the cottonwood hung limp. Still green, but not growing, the long hot deceptive stretch before autumn. The warehouses tilted towards her in the slant sun, bare and silent after hours.

The next morning she phoned the personnel department. To her amazement, they seemed to believe her when she explained, with vivid detail, how she'd called in sick with food poisoning, how the doctor at the clinic had panicked, admitted her to the hospital with suspected strep virus of the bowels and put her on intravenous drip. As far as Amanda knew, strep virus of the bowels did not exist. However, she managed to be detailed about the vomiting, and outraged about the intrusive nature of high-tech health care. Hospitalized without her telephone book, Amanda elaborated, when she staggered out three days later she had lost her house key and ended up staying with a friend out in Surrey; her landlord returned from his cabin Sunday night to let her in. The receptionist was sympathetic; her cousin had the exact same thing happen. Amanda hung up the phone exhausted with the performance, and fairly certain that she had not been believed, that it would all catch up with her sooner rather than later. Later that afternoon the supervisor called her and said the data processing job was hers for the asking, full-time permanent, in mid-September, if she came back to work the next day.

Hugh phoned that night.

"Classes start in two weeks," he said. "I'm getting kind of hyped about all that."

"That's nice," said Amanda.

"It is," he said.

"No, I was agreeing with you," said Amanda.

"I know you were. And it is nice. I've been buying textbooks. There's one about how cities get divided into these zones of state control. You'd love it."

"I'm sure," said Amanda. "I got offered that job in data processing."

"Excellent," said Hugh. "Are you going to take it?"

"I don't know," said Amanda. "I mean, really I'm a photographer. Aren't I?"

"Are you?"

"What do you mean, am I?"

"I mean that's what you like doing. But it's not how you earn your living."

"I did the photo project. That paid good."

"But really even there it was more of an organizing job," said Hugh. "Teaching. Social work."

"So? What are you trying to say?"

"I'm not trying to say anything," said Hugh. "Just that you aren't making a living from photos."

"I could. Sure I could."

"But do you want to?"

"What do you mean, do I want to?" said Amanda. "Of course I do."

"But it isn't real immediate. I mean, you were just saying

how the gallery project didn't take off. It's not like your super-committed to just your photography. It's not like that's all you do, all you want to do."

"Sure it is," said Amanda.

"But it isn't how you're living right now."

"You have *no right* to tell me how I'm living," said Amanda. "You have absolutely *no right* to sit on your *ass* on the other side of the country and make *pronouncements* about what I do or don't do. You have no right to say *anything at all* now that you've left."

"Sorry," said Hugh.

"Sorry isn't okay," said Amanda. "You just have no right to say anything to me about *anything*."

"This is a nice little café," said Cammie. "It's new. I like how they've sponged the walls this golden brown colour. They have a play area for kids at the back."

"People let their dogs run around loose inside," said Amanda. "I've been here before."

"You go play, honey," said Cammie. "You go look at the dollies back there. And the trucks."

Amanda glanced casually around as she entered. The place was nearly empty this heat-scorched afternoon, and she saw no one she recognized. Except the waitress: Cody's dreadlocked room-mate, slouching towards them with chipped blue nailpolish and smudged tattoos.

"Chocolate zucchini cake," said Cammie. "And some Tiger Spice tea."

"Same but coffee," said Amanda. The girl gave no sign of recognizing her, and perhaps she truly did not.

"I don't know," said Cammie. "Jeff is going completely weird on me. I don't know what's going on."

"You could ask," said Amanda.

"I try. Like I said, I try. Honey. Don't go under the tables. Stay and play nice back there. You know I used to be totally different than this. Way more easygoing. When I was young."

"Yeah," said Amanda. "I see that in myself, too." This seemed like a reasonable thing to say, though she did not particularly feel it was true. She was watching the waitress, who was slumped against the counter, staring out the door at the hot sidewalk. At her feet lay the young malamute, no longer a winsome puppy. Rather, a half-grown wolf.

"I still think about that a lot," said Cammie. "I still think about Matthew all the time."

"You do?" It was the first time his name had been mentioned between them in a decade.

"I heard he's doing okay. I wonder what he'd be like now."

"Totally different," said Amanda. "I got the impression things didn't end that well between you two."

"God, no," said Cammie. "He was an absolute jerk about it. He really put me through the wringer. And I totally stood for it. I get so mad when I think about it. Honey, that's the lady's cup. Don't touch the lady's cup."

"So why do you think about him, then?"

"Well, it's so unresolved. I never really told him what I felt about it all. I want to show him I survived it all. I don't know. I want him to see that I've done all right. I'm holding down a job. I've got Jeff and the kids."

"It wouldn't really do any good, would it?"

"Sure it would. It would make me feel good. It would make me feel terrific, actually."

"I guess," said Amanda. "I can kind of see that. Remember the guy I was going out with then? Mike?" She had not said his name either for almost a decade. Framing it now seemed risk, effort; the name hung in the air quivering, portentous, the knife edge of confession, of collapse.

"Mike?" said Cammie. "Oh yeah. You know, someone told me Matthew comes through town still fairly regularly. I kind of wonder what would happen if we ran into each other."

After heavy slabs of cake, they collected Caitlin from the play area and helped her stack the picture books and alphabet blocks nice for the next little girl. They were heading out the wide-open door, Cammie leaning for a free local newspaper from a wire rack by the entrance, when Cody walked in.

"Hello," said Amanda.

He looked very young in the full sunlight, on the familiar street, shockingly young.

"How you doing?" he said after a minute.

"All right," said Amanda. "I'll give you a call."

"Sure," he said, after a perceptible pause.

"We can have lunch," said Amanda. "Or something."

"Right," said Cody. He was looking over her shoulder at the dreadlocked girl.

"Who was that?" said Cammie, out on the sidewalk. "No, honey, I can't carry you. You're too big."

"One of the protesters. You know. From the photos I was doing."

"Oh, right," said Cammie. "They're making them younger and younger, aren't they?"

"Seems so," said Amanda. "I got some good pictures of him, though. Some great poses." She could feel the dangerous pull to say too much, to hint and play coy.

"That sounded like so much fun," said Cammie. "What you were doing up there. When is the exhibit?"

"I don't know if it's going to come off now," said Amanda. "Lane's kind of backing out. You know Lane. You always have to watch your back."

"That's too bad," said Cammie. "At least you had the experience. Honey, that's dirty. Don't touch. That's been in someone's *mouth.*"

When she met Cody coming through the door of the café, Amanda had no intention, none at all, of phoning him. But the urge built through a succession of long golden summer evenings alone, counting off the days now until autumn, watching the beautiful light sink across the mountains above the gantries and the wheat pool. The waste of such endless, precious evenings.

She phoned three times before someone answered the phone, at ten p.m. Music in the background, voices, life. Cody eventually came to the phone.

"Hello," she said. "It's Amanda."

"What's up?" he said. "How are the photos going?"

"All right," she said. "How are you?"

"Okay," he said. "Just got registered for the college. Hold on, I'll be there in a minute. I'm on the telephone. No one. Not Bob. Sorry about that. Hanging out. You know."

"Yeah," said Amanda. He sounded definite, alert, friendly; he sounded smarter and happier than she had remembered. Really, they had not had such a bad time together.

"So what are you calling about?" he said, pleasantly enough.

"Wait up, Greg. I'll be there right away. Sorry. It's these guys."

"Sure," said Amanda. "I won't keep you. I wasn't calling you about anything in particular. I just thought we could get together. Or something."

For a long moment Amanda heard nothing but the distant rattle of music and laughter.

"I don't think so," said Cody. "I'm kind of busy."

"It doesn't have to be all day or anything," said Amanda. "I mean, we could talk." She said this automatically, hearing the absurdity as she spoke: they had, after all, never talked yet, as she understood talking.

"I don't think so," said Cody.

"Just coffee or something," she said, aware that in another moment she would be perilously close to begging, perilously close to losing her dignity.

"No," said Cody.

"Look, are you mad about something?" she said. "Should we talk?"

"I'm not mad," said Cody neutrally. "It's just not a good idea."

"How come?"

"Look," he said. "I got to go now."

"Bye," said Amanda.

Driving home from work, stop and start towards the waterfront, traffic report and weather, hot and sunny, and the news. *An estimated hundred thousand dollars' damage caused by the bombing of a logging company branch office in a valley currently the subject of land-use hearings at the provincial governmental level.* The radio voice fast, excited. *The Environment Federation expressed its dismay today. Police on the island working to determine the cause and the date of the explosion, and investigating reports that a logging company employee may have died in the blast.*

"Bull*shit*," said Amanda out loud to the radio.

On the television news, not Jason but presumably one of his superiors, *we sincerely regret and do not condone violence.* Shocked reaction of loggers, grizzled baseball caps against virile green mountains. The Office of the Attorney General was *eagerly awaiting a coroner's report involving clothing found at the scene.* After all this, the twisted trailer, no longer smoking and steaming, was somewhat of an anticlimax. The story spiralled, over the next few days, upward alongside the land-use hearings; on the penultimate day of hearings, the vice-president of the logging company spoke in two-inch headlines with Everett's byline, *voluntarily withdrawing from the disputed area in order to minimize risk to life and limb from further gratuitous acts of violence.* On the six o'clock news that night, loggers' wives with small-town haircuts held children to their bellies and spoke over their heads about *what am I going to feed my children if they save all the trees, are trees more important than children, that's what I want to ask these so-called environmentalists, what about the family.* The women set their lips, righteous, indomitable; the children stared up at the camera, unblinking, serious.

Amanda followed all this in a fury of disbelief and scorn, unable however to miss a newspaper or a broadcast. In the basement of the college, typing data, she set her teeth to avoid answering the coffee-break chat about *going too far and alienating support, I used to recycle everything but now I don't think I'll bother. If that's what it's all about.*

The news was finally released that the trailer had been abandoned since logging ended on the slope the previous year, that it contained no computer or telecommunications equipment and that the tractor cap found in the wreckage was bloodless. This information came buried at the end of Everett's Sunday supplement feature on bed-and-breakfast destinations in the rainforest, complete with a posed shot of Tim, wetsuit and paddle. The news never made it, as far as Amanda could see, to television or radio.

Harvest Vegetable Quiche, the egg floating on a spoonful of frozen mixed corn and peas. Amanda opted instead for a Custom Deli Sandwich, and sat chewing her way through a thick wedge of brown bread and dry alfalfa sprouts.

"I've got until Friday to say whether I want the job in data processing," she said.

"Oh really?" said Cammie. "That would be super-great if you got on permanent here."

"I guess," said Amanda. "I need to really make time for my photography if I'm going to take it seriously. I really have to figure out how to do that."

Through the glass wall of the staff lounge, she saw the students milling by the cash registers.

"There's Rafael," she said.

"Who?" said Cammie. "Oh, that guy. He should be finished by now. I don't know how he keeps getting his benefits extended."

Behind Rafael stood Cody, carrying a heavy textbook under his arm and talking to another boy, shagged hair and black T-shirt.

"Isn't that that guy you were talking to?" said Cammie. "In the café?"

Amanda jumped, not physically but internally. She had not thought Cammie was paying any attention, to anything. That she had powers of observation and recollection was profoundly disturbing; it altered everything.

"Oh, I don't know," Amanda said. "It could be."

"I'm sure it is," said Cammie. "He seemed really nice. He seemed to like you. He kind of blushed when you talked to him."

"He did?" said Amanda. "I don't remember."

"His ears went pink. It was kind of cute."

"It's not the same guy."

"I'm sure it is. Maybe he's going to school here."

"I'm sure it's not the same guy," said Amanda firmly. As she spoke, Cody turned with his sandwich into the crowd; he did not look up. If he had, he probably would not have seen her anyways, beyond the glare of the glass wall.

AEI-290